1

WINTER CREPT BACK INTO SPRINGTIME TO REMIND THE city that it would come again. The large windows rattled as a strong wind drove sheets of rain against the ancient police headquarters building. It was chilly inside but the old radiators remained silent. The furnace had been turned down in anticipation of summer. The few men inside wore sweaters or raincoats to ward off the early morning cold. In the dying hours of their shift their minds were occupied with completing the unending river of paperwork and the promise of a warm breakfast.

"Call for you, Lieutenant." The desk man had to raise his voice over the all-night radio station they kept on to insure they remained awake. "Line eight."

"This is Russo," he said into the receiver.

"Y'all might not remember me—my name's Annie Robinson and I lives across from the Winklers. You know, that Dr. Winkler y'all want for killing his wife, that woman he was livin' with down by Pike Street?"

"I remember you, Mrs. Robinson." He remembered her well. He could picture her thin black face with its delicately wrinkled skin and her wide eyes, so alive and alert despite her years. He had left his card with her when they had been investigating the Winkler killing.

"Now I don't wants to get nobody into no trouble, you understand what I mean." Her voice was low, almost a whisper. "But you asked me to call if I should see anything goin' on 'cross the street, you remember?"

"I remember."

"That Winkler ain't much. I know he's a doctor and all, but he still ain't much. His wife wasn't so bad. Had her nose in the air a little, is all. But that Winkler, he ain't no more than trash. You understand what I'm telling ya?"

"Yes."

"Now you won't tell nobody I called you, will you? I wants to help the law and all that, but I don't want to get myself in no trouble either, you understand what I mean?"

"Don't worry, Mrs. Robinson. Anything you tell me will be strictly between the two of us."

She amused him, but he choked off a chuckle. "That's a solemn promise," he assured her.

"I trust you," she said after a short pause. "I been watching out the window a while ago. You know us old folks, we don't need much sleep. I been up for a while just killin' time, watching the rain mostly. Anyway, this old car pulls up in front of the Winklers' and Dr. Winkler gets out and runs up into his house, then the car pulls away."

"Is he still inside?"

"Suppose so. I been watching and he ain't come out the front and the old car ain't come back neither, so I guess he still in the place."

"Thanks, Mrs. Robinson. We appreciate your information."

"Is there goin' to be shooting?"

"There might be," he answered. "Maybe it might be

Also by William J. Coughlin

THE
STALKING
MAN

WILLIAM J.
COUGHLIN

St. Martin's Paperbacks

THE STALKING MAN

Copyright © 1979 by William J. Coughlin.
Excerpt from *The Judgment* copyright © 1997 by Ruth Coughlin.

ISBN: 0-312-96487-0

Printed in the United States of America

Delacorte edition published 1979
St. Martin's Paperbacks edition/January 1998

St. Martin's Paperbacks are published by St. Martin's Press, 175 Fifth Avenue, New York, NY 10010.

10 9 8 7 6 5 4 3 2 1

a good idea if you stayed down in your basement for a while."

She chuckled. "I'm over seventy. No reason why I should be down in that cold old basement and miss all the excitement. I'll be peeking out the window to see what happens."

"If anything starts, you get behind something."

"Don't you worry about Annie Robinson, I didn't get this old for nothin'."

Lieutenant Anthony Russo hung up and dialed the precinct in which the Winkler home was located. He explained very carefully to the precinct watch-commander exactly what he wanted done. He had the watch-commander repeat his orders so there would be no mistake.

"Come on, Rosinski," he said to his partner, "we have to pick up Dr. Winkler. He's sneaked back home."

"Shouldn't we get a search warrant?" Rosinski had listened to the telephone conversation with Mrs. Robinson. "If you protect that woman we have no excuse to go breaking in over there. We'll need a warrant to protect ourselves."

"I don't think so," the older officer replied. "Come on, I don't want him to get away."

The rain was diminishing but the streets remained wet and slick and Rosinski drove as fast as he deemed safe for the conditions despite Russo's urgings that he speed up.

As he had directed, three scout cars waited at the intersection Russo had indicated. He hopped out of the still moving car and had a few fast words with the uniformed policemen. Detective Joseph Rosinski waited in their unmarked car. He half listened to the intermittent calls on the police radio. The rest of his mind was filled with a growing apprehension. He wondered about older men, like Russo, who seemed to take danger in stride, without apparent concern for their lives or well-being. Rosinski had been delighted with his assignment to the homicide bureau; it meant less personal danger. He had done his time as a scout car officer and as a precinct detective. He was glad to be off the street, away from the sudden confrontations and the anxiety of the unknown. Now, suddenly, he was back. He took his revolver from its belt holster and made sure it was loaded.

Russo returned to the car and climbed in, his raincoat glistening from the mist that continued to fall. The darkness of the night was turning into a dirty gray dawn. "Drive down Riopelle Street to Saginaw," Russo commanded, "hang a right and then take a left into the alley between Pike and Holcomb."

"Right." Rosinski slammed the car into gear and pressed down on the accelerator.

"Goose it," Russo said, despite the increasing speed. "I'm in a hurry."

Following Russo's instructions Rosinski found the route and then turned into the narrow passageway of the alley.

"Hold it right here," Russo said.

"But the Winkler place is down about the middle of the block," Rosinski protested as he brought the car to a stop.

"I know it. Just hold your horses." Russo looked at his watch. There was sufficient daylight now that he could see it. He waited a moment and then opened his door. "I'm going down the alley a short ways. Keep the motor running and your eye on me. You may have to move fast."

"Hey, Lieutenant—" Rosinski's protest was cut off as Russo climbed out of the car and was gone. He watched the older man walk slowly and casually down the empty alley, staying close to the decaying garages as he moved, using them as a shield between himself and the Winkler house.

Rosinski rolled down the car window so he could hear if Russo called.

The cold wet mist chilled his cheek. Rosinski was startled to hear the "whoop" of patrol car sirens. They sounded very loud and he knew they were in front of the Winkler house on Pike Street, sounding their sirens. He watched Russo draw his long-barreled revolver. Suddenly the older officer became tense and alert, his casualness gone.

A running figure burst into the alley, a flapping coat held in his hand. He skidded on the wet pavement as he turned toward the waiting officer.

"Hold it!" Russo's sharp words floated back to his partner.

The middle-aged black man hesitated, his head turning as if debating his chances of trying his luck in the other direction.

"I'd hate to shoot you, Doctor," Russo said, almost kindly. "Put your hands in the air."

He hesitated for only a moment. Then he dropped the coat and both hands jerked toward the sky in the traditional sign of surrender.

Rosinski grinned as he watched his partner. He was a marvel, this veteran detective. He had planned the whole thing, a scheme to flush the man from cover, like a hunter working a dog across an autumn field. Rosinski wondered if he would ever develop the kind of instincts Russo possessed. He hoped so.

*   *   *

He was glad he had surrendered to the urges. Attempting to control himself had been exhausting and restricting, producing anxiety and fatigue from the never-ending battle. He had abandoned the contest and now he was relaxed and free. It was an exhilarating freedom.

As before, he had gone forth to select a suitable victim.

A train rumbled past. Its vibrations rattled the glasses on the bar; the noise of its giant engines blended in with the noise from the blaring jukebox. The train passed and the music from the jukebox reasserted its mastery. The singer's nasal voice rode above the sliding notes of steel guitars, telling of a workman's poverty and family devotion. It was Nashville music, thick with nostalgia for a happy past that existed only in the songwriter's mind.

The victim was five foot four.

The bartender served him and then retreated to the far end of the bar where he leaned his protruding belly against the support of the beer case, and studied a crossword puzzle book. The bartender was oblivious to the music, to the customers, and even to the train noise outside. Like an oriental mystic he had attained perfect meditation.

There were only a few people in the bar. An alcoholic couple sat silently together at the other end of the bar. There was no conversation between them. They sipped their drinks with their eyes fixed on the smoke rising from their cigarettes, as if it might eventually spell out some secret message.

She was watching him, he could sense it.

Two old men were locked in contest at the battered shuffleboard table. One grinned in victory, exposing a single yellow tooth. The other swore, gulped down his beer, and prepared to even the score.

It was like a thousand other workmen's bars nestled in the shadow of railway yards. They all looked alike: dingy, their wood and fabric discolored by the dust and grime of the yards, and their tables and wooden floors worn down by a million passing workers, leaving an everlasting aroma of stale beer and sweat.

He signaled the bartender for another whiskey. He paid with a twenty-dollar bill, leaving the change in a stack of small bills sitting before him as bait.

It was almost midnight but he felt no fatigue. It was as if he were once again hunting with his father, waiting in the early morning mist, waiting for the sleek shape of a deer to drift in from the mist, waiting to kill, all tiredness lost in excited anticipation. Those were the only times of the year he was allowed to spend with his father—those short hunting seasons. During those few magic days he was permitted entry into the rites of manhood. He experienced the pungent smell of whiskey and the racy chatter of cards and gambling, and when he was fifteen, the whores of Hurley, Wisconsin. Those hunting trips had been like dreams. They had been like magic carpets and for a short while he was away from his high-strung mother and her emotional demands. For a short while he had been a man.

· In the mirror behind the bar he could see her approaching. She was pretty in a tough way. Young, but her cold eyes seemed to cast a pall of crafty age over her features. He waited.

There was no sound of any trains now and the record had changed. The old saloon was filled with the pleasant contest between a banjo and mandolin picking out an old bluegrass melody, a good beat, soft and harmonious.

At the time, he had considered it a personal insult that his father had picked such an untimely season to die. The trees had begun to change, autumn had begun and the deer season would soon open. His mother was working, so they had sent his cousin to tell him the news. His young cousin, embarrassed and knowing that more was required, was not capable of compassionate tact, so the words had just spilled out, so cold and unreal. His father had told him he had an easy desk job, yet somehow a part of his heart muscle had torn away and he had died at his desk, instantly and without warning. He had never quite forgiven his father, although he realized the man had had no choice in the matter. Still, it was the ultimate rejection and abandonment; he was destined to remain trapped with his screaming mother, perhaps forever.

He pretended he didn't see her come up and sit on the stool next to him. He fixed his eyes on the battered television set above the mirror, but he knew she was there and his pulse quickened.

His father had taught him how to hunt big game. The animal's keen sense of smell and hearing constituted delicate alarm systems and warned of the approach of the hunter. It was best to find a place where they were known to come and then lie in wait for them there. Let them come to you, that was the trick. Patience, a successful hunter needed patience. His father had taught him to wait until the animal was close, to wait until there was little chance of missing.

Her cheap perfume seemed to envelop him. He was at once both repelled and excited by the strong scent.

"You're new around here." Her voice sounded slightly strained as if she were trying to project a tone and quality more splendid than her ordinary speech.

He looked over at her without replying. It was a good tactic; they were always a bit unsure if the man made no response. She was even younger than she had looked in the mirror; she wore heavy makeup to cover her youthfulness. Her large young breasts strained against the cheap material of her thin blouse.

"You with the railroad?" she asked.

He shook his head. "I'm working on a construction job." He had selected the worn coveralls and the white plastic hard hat as his hunting costume.

"Live around here?"

He grinned at her. "No, I'm from out of town. I come from St. Paul."

"You're a long way from home," she said.

"Yeah."

They sat quietly. She pulled a cigarette from her small purse and waited a moment to see if he would light it for her. When he made no effort to move she lit it herself.

"We don't see too many construction people around here," she said. "Used to see them all the time, when the railroad was buildin' things, but that's a long time ago.''

He nodded in mute agreement.

Patience, his father had instructed. He felt agitated, it was hard controlling himself. He wanted to start, to hurry and make the arrangements. She was as good as his now, but still he had to force himself to remain calm and play out the game.

''How long have you been away from home?''

He looked at her and grinned again. ''Too damn long.''

Her eyes narrowed slightly as she studied him. ''Lookin' for a little action?''

''I've thought about it.''

''I'll give you a good time.''

He appraised her slowly. ''I don't have any doubt about that, honey.'' He smiled. ''But I don't know if I can afford you.''

''Fifty bucks for a regular party,'' she said, ''and seventy-five for something you'll never forget.'' She flashed her best professional smile.

He shook his head sadly. ''Don't get me wrong, honey. I can see that you'd be worth every penny, but I have to send most of my money back to my family in St. Paul, so I ain't exactly rolling in the stuff. How about a little fun for twenty-five? I can afford that.''

She paused only for effect. ''Well, for a guy who's as cute as you, I'll make an exception. Twenty-five, but you have to pay for the room.''

''Hey, what room? I've got a camper-trailer parked down at the yards. I live in the thing. I've got a little stove and it's pretty cozy. It should do all right unless you want to go somewhere else.''

"Hell, trailer or room, it makes no difference to me."
She took him by the hand. "Let's go, lover."

He gulped down the last of the whiskey as he allowed
her to pull him away from the bar.

*　　*　　*

*His father had trained him to be a good shot, but in
the excitement of his first hunt he had only wounded the
animal. He had been surprised that he experienced a
shivering thrill at the animal's high-pitched scream. He
found he enjoyed watching the agony of a dying animal.
When his father died, he thought he would never have
that kind of opportunity again.*

*The other patrons of the bar paid scant notice as
they left. It was good, they would have little to remember
about him. He gripped the girl around her fleshy waist
and led her down the street toward the dark and deserted
railroad yards.*

His pulse raced with anticipation.

*　　*　　*

The cross-country journey of the refrigerated railroad car
had originated in Boston. There its yawning cavern had
been packed full of boxes of frozen fish—the product of
coastal fisheries—destined for transport to the waiting
midwestern markets. From Boston the car had sped to
Cleveland where more than a third of its cargo was un-
loaded. Toledo was the next stop, and again a third of

the cargo was transferred into waiting refrigerated trucks. Kansas City was the last stop.

In Kansas City, the car, together with other refrigerated cars, was shunted off to a siding to wait until the schedule called for the unloading to begin. One of the yard workers noticed a broken seal and called the railroad security police. There had been a nationwide wave of railroad theft and it was expected that all or part of the fish would be gone.

Although it was unlikely that any thief would endure the car's frigid interior, nevertheless several railroad policemen assembled just to make sure. One of the officers pulled the hand latch and pushed the sliding door open. A cloud of misty freezing air blossomed from the door. The officer took out his pistol and searched the inside with a flashlight. Finding nothing, he hopped up into the car, his breath fogging in the arctic-like air. He walked to the back of the car and inspected the boxes with the beam of his flashlight.

She had been stuffed behind the last row of boxes. Frozen solid, a light frost covered her face and arms; and although the frost helped to disguise the damage, the officer knew at once she had been beaten to death.

The Kansas City Medical Examiner later substantiated the officer's on-the-spot appraisal. The body was that of a female, approximately twenty to twenty-five years of age; five feet four inches tall; 135 pounds. Her skull had been fractured in two places, her nose smashed and her lower jawbone nearly wrenched from its joints. One arm had been broken and most of her ribs had been fractured. The examiner said there was evidence that whoever killed the girl had continued to beat her long after she was dead. He described this action as ''frenzy.''

After the corpse had thawed, fingerprints were taken

and transmitted to the FBI in Washington. The dead girl
was identified as Mildred S. Evans. She was twenty-two
years old, had been arrested eight times for prostitution
and convicted twice. She had been born in Gary, Indiana,
but all her arrests had been in Toledo, Ohio.

The Toledo police were notified, but they could add
very little to why the girl was killed. She was a known
prostitute and reported to be a loner who usually worked
in the vicinity of the Toledo railroad yards. She had no
pimp and lived in a small apartment by herself.

Mildred S. Evans's mother in Gary was notified. She
shed tears for her dead daughter but told police she had
expected her daughter to come to such an end. The girl,
she said, had fallen in with a bad crowd in high school,
had become uncontrollable and had left home.

Mildred's mother refused to pay for the funeral and the
battered remains were buried in a pauper's grave.

No one thought of Mildred S. Evans again, at least not
for a while.

* * *

He never wore a watch. It was a prejudice instilled in
him as a boy by his German father. His stern father was
of the opinion that watches were made for lazy people,
clock watchers he called them. His father often lectured
that a good man was not dominated by time; he dominated it; therefore he did not need a watch. However,
there was a small wall clock in the office law library, and
as he stretched he noticed that it was midnight. It surprised him that time had flown so quickly, and for the
first time he realized he was tired.

The Winkler trial had gone fast, at least in comparison
to other murder cases he had tried. The proofs—which

consisted almost exclusively of opposing psychiatric witnesses—had been quickly put in and now all that remained were the closing arguments and the judge's charge to the jury. It would be close. He had built the defense of insanity very carefully. But the prosecutor had also done a skillful job. Dr. Winkler had killed his wife, dismembered her, and sent the various parts to her relatives. He had admitted it. It was bizarre behavior, but otherwise Winkler seemed to be quite sane. It would be touch-and-go and much would depend on the instructions the judge gave to the jury.

Thomas Knapp reviewed his handwritten notes. They constituted his proposed jury instructions and if accepted by the judge would play an important part in Winkler's defense. He had carefully briefed each section, citing important legal precedents, building a history of the defense of insanity from the famous M'Naghten case decided in the English House of Lords in 1843 to People v. Teague. The latter was a case he himself had tried which had established the present state rule on insanity, namely that it was a substantial disorder of thought or mood which significantly impaired judgment, behavior, and the capacity to recognize reality. The infamous Edward Teague, the "Stalking Man," had been found guilty by reason of insanity based on that definition, and now Knapp hoped the same would hold true for Dr. Winkler.

Knapp had thought of the Teague case more than once during the past few days. The officer in charge of the Winkler case—Lieutenant Anthony Russo—had also been the policeman who had hunted down and caught Edward Teague. Knapp had sensed the policeman's hostility as the Winkler case progressed. Probably Russo had never forgiven him for the Teague outcome.

His knack for total concentration had been a lifelong asset; but now that he was through with his work, his mind was released from its task, and he was once again back in the world, the real world, a place he often found distasteful. The empty law office echoed to the sound of his movement. He left his notes on Martha Flowers's desk. She was more than his right hand, she was a jewel and he often called her that. Like himself, she was a craftsman who was interested in turning out the best possible product, and her work reflected it. He knew she would come in early and have his notes typed perfectly and ready for submission to the trial judge.

The night guard took him down to the elevator and unlocked the main building door for him.

It was chilly and there was a feel of rain in the night air. He was apprehensive as he walked along, the only pedestrian on the street.

During the day the city was bursting with busy people. Its giant auto plants throbbed with life; its streets were clogged with rivers of flowing cars and trucks, most of them produced in the city. Four million people made the place go; they made it clang and thump with mind, muscle, and sweat. But that was during the day.

At night, life continued in the suburbs. But the central city—the downtown area—was a dangerous place, empty and forbidding.

The sight of a slowly cruising scout car reassured him.

There were only a few cars in the yawning cavern of the underground parking garage. Climbing into his Cadillac, he felt secure as he flipped on the door locks. He guided the car up the circular ramp and waved to a nodding night watchman as he pulled out of the garage and into the street. Only a few cars moved on the surface

streets. As he entered the entrance ramp to the expressway he settled down for the drive home. He flipped on
the FM radio and found some soft music. Traffic was
light and he enjoyed the drive; it would take him twenty
minutes to arrive home.

His mind kept returning to the Winkler case. He re-
played the testimony of each witness mentally, reviewing
everything like a chess master reviewing his game moves.
Having carefully built a delicate web of evidence to il-
lustrate Winkler's madness, he would argue it in the
morning and give it his best. Again, he recalled his father's often repeated rule: if something is worth doing, it
is worth doing well. "A typical Kraut," he said to himself aloud.

He exited the expressway and drove through the business section of Chippewa Hills, the richest suburb in the
area. Downtown Chippewa Hills at midnight looked just
as expensive as it did at any other time of the day. It was
clean and trim, its shops glittering with diamonds and the
trappings of wealth.

He drove for another mile and then turned through the
giant stone pillars that proclaimed the entrance to "Idaho
Springs—an exclusive place to live," according to the
small and tasteful sign hung between the pillars. The
word "exclusive" really meant "expensive," but it
sounded better. He drove along the winding road past the
large houses that served as symbols of status and money.
If one could afford to live in Idaho Springs, one had it
made by any definition.

The garage door opened automatically in response to
the electronic device he held in his hand. After he parked
his car next to his wife's sports car, the garage door silently closed behind him.

The kitchen was dark, a condition that annoyed him. She did it purposely, knowing he would have to grope for the wall switch. He found and flipped on the silent mercury switch and walked to the refrigerator. He had forgotten to eat dinner, and now hunger reminded him of that neglect. A plate of cold chicken was covered with clear plastic wrap. He removed the chicken and a half-gallon of milk and placed them on the kitchen table.

Even before she spoke he sensed she was there. He could feel the anger.

"Where the hell have you been?" Her voice was low and the words were spoken from between clenched teeth.

He didn't reply immediately, knowing that delay infuriated her. "I was at the office," he said as he bit into a chicken leg. He noticed that it was a bit underdone.

"I have been calling your office since nine o'clock."

"I turn off the bell when I'm working late, you know that." Her cheeks were coloring as he spoke and he could smell the alcohol on her breath. She was especially nasty when she had been drinking. The chicken seemed to turn to cardboard in his mouth.

"It might interest you to know . . ." She paused in midsentence. "Then again, I suppose you wouldn't really be interested anyway. After all, he's only your son."

"What happened to Tim?"

"Really interested, or is this just some sort of act?"

He carefully put the chicken down. "Where is Tim?"

She snorted. "Oh, he's all right now. I had to take him to St. Joseph's emergency room, as if that mattered to you."

"It matters," he said, as evenly as possible. "What happened?"

"He had a pencil in his mouth and he was running.

He fell and the pencil jammed into the roof of his mouth.''

''Bad?''

She shook her head. ''Luckily, no. They put in one stitch. He bled quite a bit.'' Her voice softened for a moment, then her eyes flashed again. ''I have been calling ever since it happened. Now I demand to know the truth—where the hell were you?''

There was no point in even trying to eat. He folded the plastic over the chicken but poured himself a half glass of milk.

Her face was strained with anger. Only thirty-five, she was still a beautiful woman with raven hair and striking features, although the early puffiness around her dark eyes was a promise of what drinking would eventually do to her carefully tended face. She was a small woman and would have had a weight problem except for tennis and swimming, activities that kept her trim.

''Where *were* you?'' The words were a harsh whisper but the promise of a scream rose within her.

He gulped down the milk. ''I told you. I was at the office. I have to make the final argument in the Winkler case tomorrow morning. I was working on that.'' He looked down at her, feeling sudden pity for the anguish she had suffered. ''I'm sorry you were upset. When something like that happens, call the building. They have a night guard. He'll come up and give me the message.''

''Or call you at your girl friend's place.''

''I was working.''

''Bullshit!'' She spat the words at him. ''What the hell do you take me for, a fool?''

There could be no reasoning with her, not in her present mood. She was eager for combat, eager to loose the demons. And he could feel a dark anger rising within himself, but he ignored it. It would do no good to talk now. It could only end in another raging fight, and he could not bear the thought of expending his energy on such a useless activity.

"I have to be up early for court, Helen. You're all set for a good old knock-down battle, but I can't oblige you. I'm tired now and I have to get some sleep."

"I'll bet you're tired," she snarled. "A good one tonight, someone who spurred you on? I'll just bet you're exhausted."

He shrugged and walked past her.

In her rage she kicked at him, landing a painful blow on the back of his calf. He ignored her and continued climbing the stairs toward their bedroom.

"I don't want you in the same room with me," she screamed at him from below. "Park your ass in the spare room. For all I know you have VD coming out your damn ears!"

He nodded, grateful for the prospect of being away from her. The alcohol always brought this out. When they were first married it had amused him, her proclivity for vulgar language after a few drinks. He thought it was cute then. It was no longer cute.

He looked in on his son. The boy's youthful form was hunched up on top of a mound of blankets and his breathing had a peculiar nasal sound. He supposed Tim was breathing with his injured mouth closed. The boy stirred for a moment and then lay still again.

Ellen also slept soundly. Like her younger brother, she had grown used to the rages staged by her mother. Perhaps they saw their mother in a different light than he did. He hoped so. Children sometimes were far more understanding than adults.

* * *

The spare room offered little comfort. He could hear his wife bustling about and cursing in their bedroom. It was an irritation, just loud enough to be annoying. He recognized it as a challenge, but she would get no fight from him tonight. He lay awake, staring at the ceiling.

There had to be more to life than this, he thought, knowing that he was indulging in self-pity. Yet it seemed so unfair. He believed in no god, so there was no avenging or punishing deity exacting some penalty or penance from him. It was inadequate, but his work was the only thing he had, his sole reason for living, his only defense against his troubled world. It was well after three o'clock before Thomas Knapp drifted off into a disturbed sleep.

* * *

Lieutenant Anthony Russo sat in his darkened car for a moment. He had already made up his mind that he would go in, but the pause was in the nature of a gesture to himself, a silent protest against his own folly. It was the culmination of a halfhearted conquest; he had not really intended that this woman should take him seriously.

She was a strikingly pretty woman, probably in her early thirties. Russo had been attracted to her from the moment he had first seen her. But then, so had the rest of the police department. For a while her presence in the identification bureau had been the talk of the headquarters building, where pretty women were rare. Her soft auburn hair and twinkling eyes had acted as a magnet, but she had made it clear that she wanted nothing to do with policemen after hours. Still, some of the younger officers persisted in their efforts.

Russo had worked his way up to an easy acquaintance by the end of the winter. He was good at it, practiced; two former wives and a string of girl friends attested to his way with women. If he had been a race horse he would have been classed as a fast starter who faded at the finish. His relationships were never very permanent. He really liked her and that bothered him. He wanted no serious emotional entanglements, not any more. A quiet evening, maybe dinner and a movie, and then to bed: that had become his *modus operandi* with the women of his acquaintance. Nothing serious, just pleasant, no ties, no real emotional involvement. For the most part, his female companions resembled him. Like him, they usually had a history of broken marriages, and, like him, they were wary of being hurt. They too were interested only in a few moments of mind-dulling relaxation, like adult children playing house.

She was different. To continue was unfair to her, he knew that. Still, unfair or not, he opened the car door and walked to her apartment entrance.

He caught a glimpse of himself in the polished full-length glass in the apartment house vestibule. A touch over six feet, he owed his muscular build and classic Roman nose to genetic gifts from his Italian father. His Irish mother was responsible for the light blue eyes and the boyish mouth, soft features in an otherwise hard face. His jet black hair and dark complexion were also marks of his Italian heritage. He felt he was a mismatch of two different physical types, yet women told him he was good-looking. Russo had to admit, even to himself, that he aged well; he looked much younger than his forty-seven years.

He felt foolish, embarrassed by his age and his intentions. He wondered if he had read her wrong, if she was only interested in him because of his reputation, as though he were an interesting specimen she wanted to study close up. He had seen the others try: the young men, lean and handsome, using all their charms on her, like a million searchlights trying to penetrate the mist that protected her. But she had laughed them off.

Slowly, with his practiced ease, Russo had begun to work on her. He courted her in the style of a runner who was jogging just to keep in shape and who really did not intend to race. At first they laughed at little things, stories he would tell her; then they had longer conversations, sometimes on serious subjects. He began to take her out for coffee: a small thing, just a break in the working day. He remembered her concern after he had been hit during an arrest struggle. His jaw had swelled up but without much pain. She had reached across the coffee-shop table and her fingertips had gently touched his bruised skin. He could still remember the touch.

He was wryly amused at his own anxiety on the way up in the elevator. He felt like a schoolboy calling on his first date. He was hardly that and the reaction made him feel even more foolish. He decided he would see her, take her to dinner, then drop her off. No more, just that. Reassured at the thought, he mentally excused himself from any entanglement. She would be pleasant to be with, just a longer coffee date, that was all, he thought, and armed with that concept he softly knocked on her apartment door.

The door opened quickly. She had been waiting.

Without meaning to, he gasped at the sight of her.

Her lithe figure was held in a skin-tight black sheath dress which accentuated every soft curve of her body. Her hair had been styled like an auburn sunburst framing her soft oval face, emphasizing her beauty. Her full lips parted in a slow, satisfied smile as her dark eyes sparkled with pleasure at his reaction.

"Like me?" She spun slowly for his inspection.

"Yes." He just managed to force the word out.

Her smile widened in amazement. "Are you planning on coming in?"

He tried to return the smile as he stepped into her apartment. "You look lovely."

"Thank you," she said, taking his coat. "Sit down and make yourself comfortable, Tony. Can I get you a drink?"

Her apartment was nice, one of the older types with rooms built wide and high, designed for comfort. She had furnished it in a solid comfortable style, too, no collection of feminine bric-a-brac.

He noticed both the spicy aroma and that her small dining table had been set for two.

"Hey," he called, "I thought I was taking you out to dinner?"

She came out of the kitchen with two frosted martini glasses in her hands. "I know," she smiled, handing him a drink, "but I don't have much chance to show off my cooking abilities. I thought tonight it might be nice if we had dinner here." She sat opposite him, exposing a slender black-stockinged leg. "Of course, if you mind, I can freeze the dinner and live off it for a week."

"I don't mind, although I was looking forward to

showing you off. I don't get much of a chance to squire beautiful young women around.''

''That's not what I hear.'' Her eyes seemed to laugh as she looked over the rim of her glass.

He felt embarrassed. ''The police department invented gossip, Marie. You can't believe even half of what you hear down there.'' He took a gulp of the drink. It was strong. ''What's for dinner?'' He hoped to change the subject.

''Veal scallopini.''

''Lots of tomato sauce?''

She nodded.

''You know how to please an Italian.''

''Do I?''

Again she seemed amused, and he felt uncomfortable. ''Yeah, load us up with spicy sauce and lots of pasta and you have a happy ethnic. Anyway, that's the secret of most Italian restaurants—that, and the bread sticks.''

''Speaking of sauce . . .'' She got up quickly and hurried into the kitchen.

The meal was good, very good. He managed to restrain himself and ate delicately. At one of his relatives', he would have rolled up his sleeves and dug in, but here, with her, he curbed his natural instincts and observed polite table manners.

He helped her clear away the table, and in the refrigerator he discovered a large pitcher of martinis.

Russo felt warm and full, and the martinis had produced a nice euphoria.

Marie switched on a stereo set that rested among potted plants in a multilevel wall rack. Soft music, sweet and melodious, added to the charm of the moment. She sat next to him on the sofa.

"Music okay?" she asked.

"Fine. Everything's just fine, Marie—the food, the wine, the martinis. There's no place in town that could match this. It's perfect."

"You're sure?"

He was acutely conscious that her shoulder and leg were lightly touching his own. "You can bet on it."

"Have you known many women, Tony? I mean, really?" Her large eyes looked up at him. He couldn't detect any taunting this time.

"I've been married twice, I told you that. I'm an old man, Marie, I've been around a bit." He quickly added, "Of course nothing like those damn department stories. God, you'd think I had my own public relations man, the way those things get around."

"You said you're an old man, but forty-seven isn't old."

"How did you know that, my exact age, I mean?"

She smiled slowly. "Remember, I work in the identification and records department. I looked you up."

"Why?"

"I was interested."

"Well, how did I score? Am I older or younger than you thought before you checked the file?"

Her eyes never left him. "As a matter of fact, older, not that it matters."

He laughed. "Oh, it can matter. In a couple of years I'll retire to some guard job, lose my hair, and grow fat."

"What will happen to all those ladies?"

"What ladies?"

"The ones who rely on Tony Russo for their love life. If you're right and only half of what I hear is true, that leaves quite a few lonely women, if you give that up with your job.''

"Hey, that's a lot of bull. Christ, who have you been talking to?"

"Something wrong with me, Tony?"

"No, why?"

"I just wondered. Here I am, dressed in my sexiest outfit, perfumed and, I hope, alluring. I've just wined and dined the ranking lover in the police department, and nothing is happening. So something must be wrong with me. You haven't even made the slightest advance."

Russo felt himself flush. "Look, kid . . ."

"Don't call me kid."

"Okay. I'm very attracted to you. God, what man wouldn't be? But there's at least a fifteen-year difference in our ages. I don't want to get serious with anyone, Marie, I've struck out too many times. I really like you, and I respect you. You're a nice young woman, you don't need to get mixed up with any broken cop."

"Kiss me, Tony," she said softly.

"Marie, it's just that—"

She reached up and pulled his head down, pressing her velvet lips against his. Her hands gripped him with surprising strength.

Whatever reservations he had burst like a rotten dam, and all the desire for her that he had always known was there spilled out.

Without even being aware of it, he moaned her name again and again as he eased her down, his mouth tasting hers, his blood pounding within him.

2

So that no passing police car might get curious he had raised his car's hood. He was parked at an angle so that he could still see, but if a scout car came by he could explain that he had engine trouble and was waiting for a tow truck from the garage. There would be no other reasonable explanation for a lone man sitting in his car in that part of the city at that time of night, at least no innocent explanation.

He kept his eyes glued on the club's entranceway. The outside lights had been extinguished and several waiters and band members had departed, but not the girl, at least not yet.

His cigarette's glow provided the only illumination in the car. The streetlight's reflection was shut off by overhanging branches and he waited alone, hidden in the dark, his eyes fixed ahead.

He could remember the excitement of waiting before, as a boy, his back against a tree, his rifle across his motionless legs. Waiting and hoping.

He fingered the tire iron on the seat beside him. The feel of the cool hard metal soothed the tension.

It had been a long drive to Akron and he was tired. He had told his employer he had pressing family business and he had told his wife it was a business trip. Both were accommodating. The Akron street was still wet from earlier rain, and the street lights were like rows of lonesome soldiers, their light doubled in the nocturnal reflections of the damp pavement.

He could still remember that feeling when he had been stationed at the tree as a boy, the memory was acute. In the bushes he could hear the soft noise of a moving animal; the sound came nearer and he raised his rifle, ready. Come on, for God's sake, come on—he could remember the gripping but pleasurable anxiety, and his quickening feelings now matched that earlier youthful tension.

It had been a lousy night for action. Of course, Tuesday night was a bad night anywhere in the world, and Akron was certainly not a sophisticated city. Even if you counted the rubber plant and the other industries, Akron was still a place for farmers. Of course, farmers liked their fun too, he knew that, but not usually on a Tuesday night.

He had roamed and searched the dingy downtown area, but he could find no girl. But at the Palace Club he had sat at the bar and watched the woman undulate above him, her fleshy abdomen bumping and grinding in an imitation of sex. He had offered her money but she had refused. She pretended that she was not a whore, but he knew better. No decent woman would expose herself and do those things.

His tension turned to panic as he wondered for the first time if there was a back exit from the club. The long drive would have been for nothing. All the careful preparation would be utterly wasted. Suddenly the panic vanished.

She walked out into the street.

He watched. Even at a distance he could recognize her. There was something sensual about her, he knew it was her. His car window was rolled down, and he could faintly hear her call good night to some man who shut the door after her. Alone, she walked hurriedly down the street.

A good hunter, his father had told him, knows instinctively when to act. Patience and instinct were the trademarks of a hunter. The quarry was all that mattered. Now, as if in obedience to his father, all thoughts except for the girl fled from his mind. He forgot any possibility of being caught, all he cared about was the hunt.

He quickly slipped out of the car and quietly closed the hood. Never losing sight of her, he eased himself behind the wheel and started the engine. Putting the car into gear, he pulled away from the curb and rolled forward in slow, deliberate pursuit. She was alone. Even the street was empty.

She had parked a distance from the club. The owner wanted to keep all the available parking spaces vacant for the customers, so the band, waiters, cooks and performers were ordered to park away from their place of employment.

She had left her car on Sander Street, on the other side of the small park. It was not Akron's best area at night, but it was not the worst. Since February she had been parking there and nothing had happened. She crossed the empty street, noticing but not worried about the darkened car slowly moving down the street. Probably looking for an address, she thought. The park was empty as it always was at that time of night, and she still felt a slight shiver of apprehension, despite the number of nights she had walked across it without incident. She hurried along, listening to the sound of her own heels striking the pavement.

Suddenly she was conscious of another sound: the thumping of running feet. She turned to look. She tried to get away but he was on top of her too quickly to allow escape. She was shoved roughly into the dark bushes, a kick jolting into her throat before she could cry out. It must be some kind of joke, she thought, before pain turned her world red.

*   *   *

The Akron doctor had come out with the detective. It was the medical examiner's curiosity that had brought the two men to the small park. Several children whirled away on a self-propelled merry-go-round. Others laughed and shouted as they played on the city-provided swings.

"Is this where you found her?" the doctor asked, looking at a clump of bushes.

"Right behind here." The detective led the way. "You can see that the blood soaked into the concrete of the walkway. It looks like she put up one hell of a fight."

"There was no fight," the doctor said, squatting down to examine the concrete. "All this blood came from her. Whoever did it literally kicked her to death. If she had fallen from a ten-story building she couldn't have had so many fractures." He stood up.

"We're checking her boyfriends," the detective said.

"Maybe one of them got a little jealous or something. You know how these dancers are, they got so many romances going they have to keep a scorecard." The policeman stopped, noticing the doctor's frown. "You don't think it was a boyfriend, Doc?"

The doctor shook his head. "No, at least not judging from the viciousness of the attack. I think we have a crazy on our hands." He looked at the policeman. "Of course, that's only an educated guess, but I think you boys had better stay on your toes for a while. There have been no other killings like this, but I would still take a few precautions."

"Like what?"

"That's your end of the business. What was her name again?"

"Marilyn Rogers."

"I think Marilyn Rogers was killed by a madman. Probably someone who hates women, at least judging from the ferocity of the attack. I'd be inclined to put a few extra men on the street for a while."

The detective shook his head. "That's impossible, half of the department is pulling double duty now." He sighed. "Well, maybe we'll get lucky."

"Lucky?"

"Maybe your 'crazy' was just passing through town."

* * *

"I don't like funeral homes," Rosinski said, still carrying on his earlier protest.

"Who does?" replied Russo, watching the city slip by as the unmarked police car sped along.

"He was your friend, not mine."

Lieutenant Russo turned and looked at his younger partner. "He was a cop, a brother officer, that's a bond, even if you didn't know him."

"Hell, he was retired. If I was retired too, maybe then I could see some connection, but not now."

Russo ignored him. He thought again about Marie Coyle, as he had almost constantly since their night together. The episode was becoming more like a dream than reality. His mind was emblazoned with images of Marie and though it was pleasurable, he was disturbed by his feelings about her. He had vowed that he would never again lower his defenses, but it was happening and he was powerless to stop it.

Russo returned to studying the neighborhood as they moved through it. Once a prosperous area, it now had a neglected look. A few of the stores were vacant. Russo knew the city. He knew every street and alley of the auto-producing giant; he knew the city as a doctor knows the arteries, veins, and tissues of the body. But, just as a doctor knows the early signs of cancer, Russo knew that the symptoms were there and that this neighborhood would soon turn sour and die, like so many others.

"The funeral home is on Wentworth Street," Russo said.

"I know. They buried an uncle of mine out of there, two or three years ago." Rosinski turned at the next intersection. "How come you want to go over now? I'd have thought you would have turned out for the services tomorrow or maybe paid a visit tonight. Last night was family night and tonight is when they expect the friends. That's how they usually run those things."

The older policeman stared out the window for a moment before replying. "To tell you the truth, Rosinski, I'm trying to avoid the widow."

"Huh?"

"I doubt if any of the family will be around now. It's too early in the day. I can pop in, sign the book, take a last look at Charley, and be on my way. That's the best way, I think."

"That's sort of odd, ain't it?" Rosinski was curious, but he didn't want to appear as if he were prying into the other man's affairs; still, he couldn't let the matter drop. "I mean, he was your partner for years. I'd think that you would like to have a word with his old lady."

Russo shook his head. "She hates my guts."

"Oh?" Rosinski waited for Russo to continue but he didn't. Rosinski tried to make the next word sound as nonintrusive as possible. "Why?"

Russo shifted around and glanced over at the younger officer. "We were young detectives, Charley and me. Both of us were full of hell in those days. Christ, he was a wild man, at least where women were concerned, anyway. We did a lot of chasing together." He paused as if lost in thought and then continued, "I had been married and divorced. To tell you the truth, Rosinski, most of the chasing around was Charley's idea, but his wife always thought I was the one leading him astray. She hated me. Finally, toward the end, things got so bad she forced old Charley to transfer to the holdup bureau, you know, to get him away from my bad influence." Russo's voice became a bit softer. "Oh, we'd still see each other now and then, you know how it is. But I suppose all that chasing caught up with Charley. He was only on the holdup squad for a couple of months when the old ticker started acting up. He had a heart attack and they gave him an early disability retirement. That was last year. I went over to the hospital while he was recovering from the heart attack.'' Russo chuckled softly. ''His skin was gray, ash gray, and he looked like he was going to die right there and then, but damned if he wasn't making a play for a big rawboned blonde nurse.''

''Maybe that's what killed him.''

Russo shook his head. ''Nope. I don't know if he got anywhere with that nurse, but he keeled over taking out the garbage.''

''The only way for a devoted family man to go.''

''Oh, don't get me wrong, Charley always took good care of his family. But women were like an obsession to him. He couldn't help himself. I took him hunting up in Canada at a place where they fly you in. We were part of a doctor's party, about six of us. Jesus, it was in the middle of nowhere, and I mean nowhere. On the second day Charley came into camp with two of the ugliest Indian women you ever saw. I don't know where they came from, or how he found them, but for the rest of the trip he was fooling around with those two like they were movie stars. Charley didn't do too much hunting, needless to say.''

''Sounds like my kind of man,'' Rosinski replied. ''I'll take a nice soft woman over a moose any day.''

''If you'd seen these Indian women, you would have taken the moose.'' Russo laughed softly at the memory. ''One of them had a goiter and it looked like she had two heads. The other one had no teeth and was partially bald. Got the picture?''

Rosinski whistled.

''They were probably the only women around for two hundred miles. Somehow he latched onto them and the three of them had a big time while the rest of us went tramping through the woods. Charley liked all women. He preferred it if they were pretty, but if they weren't he never let that prejudice him.''

''You never told me much about him.''

''He was a good cop. He had a natural flair for it. We made some pretty big busts, him and me. Funny, I was thinking about him during the Winkler trial.''

''How come?''

''Dr. Winkler has the same lawyer—Thomas Knapp— that the Stalking Man had. Same defense too, insanity. It brought back a few memories of old Charley. God, how he hated that Knapp.''

''Why?''

''Edward Teague was called the Stalking Man because of the way he went after his victims, all female. He was a woman-hater and a killer but he was smart and clever. He killed a lot of women and tortured a lot more. It bothered Charley that Teague would be enjoying the relatively easy world of a hospital. He felt Teague belonged in prison.''

''Knapp got him off?''

''Not guilty by reason of insanity, that was the jury's verdict. That Knapp is a good lawyer, but the law is all screwed up on the question of insanity, at least I think it is.''

Rosinski grinned. ''You're just sore because Knapp got Winkler off too.''

''Maybe,'' Russo said. ''Pisses me off sometimes. We break our asses to bring in a psychotic monster and because the courts and the legislature can't get together, the bastard either goes free or sits around some ward goosing the nurses.''

"Sour grapes," Rosinski grinned. "I think you don't exactly love Knapp either."

"I'm not crazy about him, but if it wasn't him it would be some other lawyer. Look, if a man is really crazy he is not responsible for what he does. Everyone agrees with that. But the Teagues are something else. They damn well know what they're doing, and they do it very well indeed. Some doctor gets on the stand and says they have a compulsion, and a jury excuses their past sins."

"What about Winkler?"

"There's a good case in point. The old doctor gets ticked off at his wife, kills her, and then cuts her up and sends the parts to her relatives. Surprise! Now the jury says he was insane. Why? Because he cut her up and mailed her. Hell, other than that, he was acting like any other murderer who knocks off his wife. The fact that he cut her up afterwards and mailed her apparently convinced the jury that the poor man didn't know what he was doing. Hell, he knew *exactly* what he was doing. He was pissed off at those relatives too. He was getting back at them, nothing insane about that."

"Maybe if we did our job a little better."

"*Better!*" Russo cut him off. "I'm a detective. Jesus! We proved every fact that existed, no more, no less. Christ, I can't climb inside a man's head. We did our job. Society blew theirs."

"What about Teague?"

"Well, that was different. Teague may be mad. No matter how you look at it, he is as dangerous as a cobra. Actually, probably a lot more dangerous. At least he's off the streets, that's something. But Charley took that case personally. We both did a lot of work on it." Russo shook his head. "You know, Charley was a fine detective. He probably could have ended up as an inspector if he'd have stayed out of beds for a while."

"Now I'm sorry I didn't get a chance to know him."

Russo looked at him. "Why? Because he was a good cop or because he was a womanizer?"

A grin spread over Rosinski's heavy Slavic face. "Because he was a womanizer. Hell, Lieutenant, good cops are a dime a dozen."

Russo snorted. "Christ, maybe it's all done by computer. They keep sending me the same types for partners. Maybe the machine is stuck."

"Here we are," Rosinski said, pulling the car into the deserted parking lot of the funeral home. "How about I wait out here until you come out?"

Russo shook his head as he opened the door. "No. I want you to see how my partners end up."

*   *   *

Knapp had holed up in the attorneys' room to escape the horde of newsmen and television cameras out in the hall. The attorney's room was a small oasis, just off the courtroom, exclusively for lawyers, where they could review their pleadings, grab a quick smoke, or just relax for a moment before going to work before the judge.

The window of the attorneys' room looked down on the court parking lot, and Knapp watched as a green state station wagon drove in and parked. Dr. Winkler was escorted from the vehicle by three huge attendants. From a distance Winkler looked like a small boy sandwiched between large adults. Knapp knew that the attendants were probably specially selected, chosen from the largest men they had at the State Center for Forensic Psychiatry. That was the new name for the Hospital for the Criminally Insane, but only the name had been changed; the institution remained a grim, walled, redbrick complex straight out of the last century.

He had visited clients there and each time had left with a crushing sense of depression. The inmates looked like a group of performers about to act out a mad play with appropriate discordant background music. Personally, he felt if given the choice, he would choose prison. At least in prison you could find people to talk to. They might be twisted, but not crazy.

Hearing a commotion outside, Knapp opened the door and looked out. He recognized the man trying to push his way past the television cameras. "Over here, Dr. Rose," he called.

Dr. Rose squirmed past the crowd to join Knapp in the attorneys' room. "Quite a group out there," the doctor said. "They must expect fireworks today."

"They'll get them, too. How have you been, Doctor?"

"Just fine, Mr. Knapp. Somewhat depressed and tired," he smiled frostily, "but still able to cope."

"Well, that's something, I suppose."

"And you, Mr. Knapp, how have you been?"

"Depressed and overworked, same as you." Knapp laughed. "It's been a long time, Doctor, I haven't seen you since I defended the Stalking Man."

Rose's features stiffened. "You mean Edward Teague?"

Knapp nodded. "Yes, of course. Does that tag 'Stalking Man' still bother you?"

Rose lit a cigarette. "Edward was a sick man and I suppose he could have been the Stalking Man. But I am now convinced that he is completely innocent of all those charges. Even in the depths of his illness I do not believe he was truly capable of those assaults.''

''And murders,'' Knapp added.

''Especially not the murders, Mr. Knapp.''

''The police had him cold, Doctor. I'm surprised you feel this way.''

The doctor irritably blew out a stream of cigarette smoke before replying. ''I know your reputation, Mr. Knapp, but I must differ with you. As I recall the evidence, it was all circumstantial. There were no eye witnesses and even the few survivors could not positively identify Edward. As I said, he was a sick man at that time, but I don't think he was the police's Stalking Man, or anything like that.''

''You'll have to admit the murders stopped as soon as Teague was picked up.''

The doctor's thin face twisted into a cynical smile. ''That's legal proof?''

''Well, it isn't exactly admissible, but you have to admit there is some persuasion in it.''

Dr. Rose studied the cigarette as he rolled it in his long fingers. ''I can prove that supposition wrong.''

''How?''

''Edward Teague has been out of the hospital and on his own for almost one year.''

''You have to be kidding. There isn't a judge in this country who would let Teague go free.''

''I'm surprised at you, Mr. Knapp. You're a lawyer, surely you know we have the legal right to release patients on probationary leave. It is not only our right, but our duty to help them adjust to the outside world. How long the leave is and what the conditions would be is completely up to us, as it should be, since we are the only ones who can truly know the mental state of the patient.''

"Good lord, Doctor, Teague killed eight women and battered the living hell out of a half-dozen more.''

"But you don't know that, Mr. Knapp,'' the doctor protested. "Edward Teague was ill when all that happened. He was an easy target for the police—a convenient 'nut' to tie up their case. I don't believe Edward was ever homicidal.''

"I produced a half-dozen psychiatrists at the trial who testified he was mentally ill and extremely dangerous. These doctors were distinguished men in your own field, surely their opinions must mean something to you.''

Dr. Rose sneered. "They sat down with a sick young man for maybe a half hour. They talked to him. They had nothing more than that upon which to base their opinions. Besides, they obviously believed he had committed those murders. With a premise like that, they could form no other opinion under the circumstances.''

Knapp felt a rising anger at Rose's arrogance, but he refrained from continuing the discussion.

"Are you appearing in the Winkler hearing?'' he asked the doctor.

"That was my purpose in coming down here today.''

Knapp frowned. "I received no notice that you would appear for the prosecutor.''

The doctor chuckled without humor. "Mr. Knapp, I plan to testify on behalf of Dr. Winkler. That is, of course, if you agree to call me as a witness.''

"Have you examined him?''

"This morning. I spent several hours with him. He is depressed, but not seriously so. He has a small personality problem, but he has coped rather successfully with it throughout his life. He worked his way through college

and medical school. There have been no previous anti-
social incidents, nor has he brushed with the law before.
His judgment is intact, his abstract thinking is normal,
and his intelligence is above normal. In fact, he requested
that I testify this morning. He thought the testimony of
the head of the state's Center for Forensic Psychiatry
would add some weight to his side of the case.''

"You realize, Doctor, that a criminal court jury has
found him not guilty of murder by reason of insanity and
that this hearing is to determine if he is, in fact, insane.
It is before a different court. If he is adjudged sane here,
he goes scot-free.''

"I am well aware of that, Mr. Knapp." A smug grin
played across Rose's sharp features. "You're not sug-
gesting that I change my opinion, are you?''

Knapp shook his head. "No." He turned and looked
out the window. ''Before we get in there, let me ask you
a question that's bound to come up.''

"Go ahead.''

"How do you explain your opinion in the light of the
facts? Dr. Winkler injected his wife with an overdose of
morphine, cut up her body, and then mailed the pieces of
her corpse to her relatives. Are these the actions of a sane
man?''

Without a moment's hesitation the doctor replied,
''Winkler has a passive-aggressive personality. It is a personality defect although, as I said, it has caused him little
difficulty in life. However, the constant discord with his
wife finally provoked an anger that he could not handle
because of his defective personality. He killed her out of
sheer hatred—not an unknown emotion even among the
sane, you will have to admit that. Then, because he held
her relatives responsible for the split between his wife

and himself, he mailed the parts to them, quite symbolic, really, and in keeping with his exploding emotions. Not everyone who kills is automatically insane, you know.'' Rose smiled. ''Dr. Winkler does have a personality flaw, but he is quite sane within the definition of the law.''

Knapp nodded. Winkler was as good as on the street with the prestige of Dr. Rose's position and testimony behind him. It would be a remarkable courtroom win, but he felt no sense of elation. He realized he resented the small, strutting psychiatrist and questioned his diagnosis, even if it did hold the key that would release Winkler.

''Will you testify this way on the stand?'' Knapp asked.

''Of course.''

''Tell me, what is the essential difference between the Stalking Man and Dr. Winkler? I'm asking out of personal curiosity, it has nothing to do with the hearing.''

''If anything is wrong with Dr. Winkler, it is related to his basic personality flaw. In other words, there is no disease present, just a different way of handling problems from that which we ordinarily consider normal. Edward Teague, whom you persist in calling the Stalking Man, was seriously ill when I first saw him. I diagnosed his problem as simple paranoid schizophrenia. Like your friends, Dr. Winkler. Edward too has a highly developed intelligence, but he suffered from a disease which left him with diminished insights and impaired judgment. At the time of arrest he was confused. He was not really sure of his identity or what he had done. This is why he confessed to those killings. When one suffers from schizophrenia one is highly suggestible. I'm sure that if the police had told Edward that he had shot President Lincoln, he would have agreed. He was quite ill.''

"When did he get better?"

"Almost immediately. We now have an arsenal of drugs to use to fight mental disease. Chlorpromazine hydrochloride has proved very useful in the treatment of schizophrenia. I employed a combination of drug therapy and counseling with Edward. The results were almost miraculous. I came to be very fond of Edward. His response to the treatment was excellent and he now leads an absolutely normal life."

"And he's been out almost a year?"

"Without the slightest trouble. At first he was understandably frightened that people would recognize him because of all that dreadful publicity. But he lives in a different area and no one has connected him with his past. As I said, Edward is an intelligent man. He holds a good job and provides very nicely for his family."

"*Family?*"

The doctor's wide smile underlined his personal sense of triumph. "He married one of my other patients; a young lady who had a tendency to hysteria but who is also recovered. She has a son by a previous marriage. As a matter of fact, I was best man at their marriage. They are a very nice little family and doing very well."

"Did you notify the court or the police of Teague's release?"

"Of course not. I don't live in an ivory tower, Knapp. If the authorities got wind of it they would have turned the whole thing into a public circus. They would have come after that young man like the Salem witch-hunters. He is quite safe from all that."

"Suppose you're wrong?"

"What do you mean?"

"Just suppose that Edward Teague was guilty of all

those murders. And, if he is so intelligent, suppose he put one over on you, that he is shamming the acts and responses of a sane person. Now, if that were true, what would happen?''

''He would kill again, using the same pattern, if he actually was the Stalking Man.''

''Isn't that a big risk to take?''

Dr. Rose's small face twisted into a smirk. ''Have you seen any more killings? That's what you said was so persuasive a minute ago. No, Edward Teague was never the Stalking Man. He is healthy, happy, and far away from people like you.''

''You speak as though I were his enemy.''

Rose smiled in his habitual, superior way. ''Edward had several delusions when he first came to us. He equated you with some kind of god. I suppose it was because of your efforts in his behalf. He was afraid you would turn on him and destroy him. It took a while to make him see you were merely a lawyer doing a job, nothing more. Also, he was afraid of that policeman, Russo. Again, he saw the policeman as some avenging god. He was quite sick then, of course, and in time I think he saw both of you in your true perspectives.'' Rose's tone was derogatory. Apparently he didn't think much of the lawyer or the policeman.

''Where is Teague now?''

A crafty look played across Rose's features. ''I'm the only person who knows that and I intend that it shall remain that way. That young man deserves a chance. He is carried on our books as being on extended leave. Should he become ill again we can always take him back. I keep a close check, never fear. But for his protection I have all his records under lock and key.''

Knapp studied the doctor for a moment. "You seem to have taken on quite a responsibility. It could be a risk."

"It is my function to act in the best interests of my patients. Edward is my patient and I intend to protect his mental health."

A court officer stuck his head into the room. "The judge is ready, Mr. Knapp."

"Be right there." Knapp held the door open to allow Dr. Rose to precede him. As he followed the doctor toward the courtroom he literally bumped into Lieutenant Russo, who was snuffing out a cigarette.

"Sorry," Knapp said.

Russo turned and recognized the lawyer. "Well, how do you feel about all this?"

"What do you mean?"

The policeman's eyes were hard. "You're going to set this Winkler free to walk among all of us. Doesn't that bother you, just a little, Counselor?"

Ordinarily Knapp would have ignored him, but he stopped and looked at the policeman. They were about the same age, both in their late forties. Knapp was taller and had steel-gray hair, but Russo resembled him in build although he was more muscular. They were very much alike. Suddenly Knapp felt he had to justify himself to the detective.

"I'm a lawyer," he said evenly. "I work with whatever evidence or witnesses I have. I don't manufacture anything, you know that. If Winkler goes free today it's because the witnesses and evidence show he should go free under the law of this state. I am doing my job."

Russo's face did not change expression. "I'm sure the late Mrs. Winkler would be very impressed with the majesty of the law.'' The policeman turned and walked into the courtroom.

Knapp paused before following him. He was deeply troubled. He had told Russo the truth. It was his job to defend people like Winkler with every lawful means, just as it had been his job to defend Edward Teague. But now this explanation somehow seemed hollow, and he began to feel something very much like a sense of guilt. He made an effort to forget his feelings and to concentrate on the task ahead as he pushed through the doors into the already crowded courtroom.

*   *   *

He eased up on his speed as the state road joined the federal highway leading into town. It was flat land, flat farming land that seemed constantly to repeat itself— planted field, white house, planted field, white house— until the landscape seemed to run together in his mind. Although he had driven only a few hours, the boredom of the flat land made the time seem like forever.

He thought again, ruefully, of the black girl in Louisville. He had been cheated. He had come up behind her and pushed her down the iron stairs. Somehow she had broken her neck in the fall. There had been no terror, no thrill. She had died and cheated him. He had smashed out his anger and frustration against her dead body, but he had found no satisfaction in it. It would be different this time, he promised himself.

He drove past the sign welcoming him to Kokomo, Indiana. Moving with traffic he was soon on a one-way street passing auto dealers, feed stores, and supermarkets. His tires bumped easily over diagonal railroad tracks as he slowed and made a right-hand turn. It was Sunday and everything was closed. No one was on the well-kept streets. The residences in the town were old but very neat and well maintained. He noticed an old woman pruning her rose bushes as her husband sat on the porch reading a newspaper. It was too peaceful. He began to feel panic. It had to be here.

*   *   *

The men at the hunting camp had laughed at him. They drank, played cards, and hunted. He hunted too. But that year game was scarce, and none of them had had even a shot at a deer. He cried in frustration and they had laughed. Even his father. They didn't understand and he couldn't tell them. He had to kill or surrender his purpose for living. They continued to laugh at him until he shot the big buck.

He stopped at an ice cream stand and stretched his legs. He took a place in the line behind a chubby little girl who was buying cones for her family waiting in one of the parked cars. He idly noticed the rash of acne covering the girl's neck and back. Too many sweets, he thought. He did not approve of too many sweets for children. Having ordered a small cone, he then licked it quickly to prevent the already melting ice cream from running into his hand. It was unseasonably warm for an April day.

It was almost mid-afternoon, and he had to start back to Chicago soon so that no one would wonder where he was. It was important that no one question where he went and what he did. It was very important.

He flipped the remains of the cone into a trash can and climbed back into his car. He remained parked for a moment, surveying the people in the other cars. The autos were filled with families mostly, out for a treat. A couple of teenagers drove up; the girl's loud giggling rose above the blasting music of their car radio. She skipped out of the car, her young breasts bouncing as she trotted playfully before her boyfriend. The two of them held hands as they waited in line. Reed-thin, the boy wore faded jeans and an old sweat shirt. As they waited he pressed his groin against the girl's rounded buttocks. The sight both aroused and embarrassed him. He turned the key in the ignition and pulled away from the curb.

Not yet having a plan of action he turned randomly at the next blinking light. It was U.S. 31, a two-lane highway leading to Muncie, Indiana. He was alone on the road and so he floored the gas pedal, just to enjoy the release of the feeling of speed. He was doing over eighty miles an hour when he saw her.

She was standing in the shade of an overhanging tree as he roared past, her thumb pointed skyward in the traditional sign of the hitchhiker. He was going so fast he almost missed seeing her.

The tires screamed as he braked. He had to pump the brake pedal to avoid rolling the car. Finally, he skidded to a stop. Jamming the car into reverse, he watched out the rearview mirror as he threaded his way back. As he approached he could see her plainly in the mirror. Young, not quite twenty, she stood next to a well-worn backpack. She wore tight hiphugger jeans that revealed the firm flesh at her hips. Her faded cotton plaid blouse had been tied up in a bow between her breasts, exposing a soft but trim stomach. She took a last deep drag on her cigarette, throwing it away as the car backed toward her.

He had found out about it first from his cousin Hilda. Hilda was a few years older than he and she had come

*to stay with them for two weeks during the summer. He
had found himself strangely excited by the sight of her.
She was tall and ungainly, an unattractive teenager, but
she had allowed him to see her undressed. He sensed that
she knew he peeked at her. They had gotten together in
the basement. It had started out as a game of tag but
ended up as a wrestling match on the floor. She was
almost as strong as he was. He smelled her, a hot, sweaty
smell, and he felt her flesh, hot and moist. She reached
down between his legs and he hit her. She screamed. She
sounded just like a wounded deer. Suddenly he was out
of his mind with pleasure. She struggled, and the more
he hit her the more she screamed. His mother had come
running down and pulled him off. She sent Hilda home
on the next bus, but he could not forget her pain-filled
face or the screaming. He had his first sexual ejaculation
that night as he writhed, hearing the screams and seeing
once again the terror.*

"Hop in," he said, pushing open the passenger door.

"I'm going to Fort Benjamin Harrison," she said, with
no emotion. "Are you going near there?" She chewed
gum as she spoke, her narrowed eyes appraising both the
driver and the car.

"I'm going right past there." He spoke slowly so that
he would not betray his excitement.

She slid into the seat next to him. She wore open san-
dals and he noticed that her feet and toes were dirty. She
reached around and slipped her backpack into the back
seat. He saw the fullness of her thighs as the denim
stretched against her legs.

She offered him a cigarette as he pulled back on the
highway. He declined. Without asking permission she

reached across and pushed in the dashboard lighter, her hand coming close to his leg.

"Where you coming from?" he asked.

"Ann Arbor."

"Are you a student at the University of Michigan?"

She shook her head, inhaling deeply on the cigarette. "No, I know a boy there. I stayed there for a while, now I'm going to see another boy down at Fort Harrison."

"Is he in the army?"

She nodded. "Yeah. He's due to get out in a few months. I met him in Florida last year. I called to make sure he was still there."

"Is that all you do? Just travel around?"

"Can you think of something better?"

"How do you live?"

She expelled a stream of smoke, her eyes staring ahead at the highway. "How do you live?"

"In other words, it isn't any of my business."

"Something like that."

He smiled at her. "That's fair enough."

They drove in silence, listening to the low music playing on the car radio.

"Are you hungry?" he asked.

"I'm always hungry." She said it without any inflection, just a flat statement of fact.

"There's a pretty good restaurant back in Kokomo, can I buy you dinner?"

"Okay, if you want to."

He slowed down and then made a turn at the next crossroad. He wet his lips in anticipation. He remembered seeing the place. It would be perfect.

"I saw your Illinois plates," she said. "Where do you come from?"

"Chicago. I was a salesman."

"Was?"

"I'm through with all that. I'm going to buy a farm."

"Sounds lousy."

"Farming?"

"Christ, it's just an unending round of work." She again looked at the highway. "What do you expect in return for the dinner?"

"Nothing."

"Bullshit. You figure maybe I'll lay you or something."

"Look . . ."

She smiled a cold smile. "Don't get yourself in a lather, man. If it's a good dinner, I just might throw in a blow job."

He saw the place coming up. It was far removed from its neighboring farms. A FOR SALE sign was set up in front of the vacant frame house. The driveway was empty and the barn door was open. It was deserted.

He pulled into the driveway.

"What the hell is this?" she snapped.

"I'm thinking of buying this place," he said. "Want to look around?"

"In other words, you're all hot to trot right now, right?"

"I just wanted to show you around the place."

"Shit." She climbed out of the car, flipping her cigarette onto the lawn. "Well, where do you want it, the house or the barn?"

"Come on, I'll show you the barn."

"What's the matter, did you have a boyhood fantasy about being laid in the hay or something?" There was no humor in the remark. "Okay, let's see your goddamned barn."

He liked the barn, it reminded him of that basement when he was a boy, it was dark and damp. He breathed deeply to control his excitement. In the dark shadows she looked like the remembered image of his cousin. She unknotted her shirt and slipped it off. She wore no bra.

*   *   *

He advanced toward her. He hoped no one would hear the screams.

*   *   *

The woman's hand shook as she held the telephone.

"That's right, this is Maude Hennipin over on the Trunk Road," she said. "Mr. Finley, the real estate man, is the one who asked me to call the sheriff's department." She nodded in response to a question. "Yes, that's right, Mr. Finley. He was checking the Van Tiem property, the farm that's up for sale, and he said he found a body in the barn." Again she nodded as she listened. "That's what he said. He said the body was nailed to the barn wall." She paused again. "I'm sorry, Mr. Finley can't come to the telephone right now," she said. "He's in my bathroom being sick."

*   *   *

Because the girl—or what was left of her—had been purposely nailed to the inside wall of the old barn, the story was put on the national wire by the Kokomo newspaper.

It received nationwide coverage—not big coverage, but widespread.

Thomas Knapp read the small piece on page eight of his newspaper. It was just a short synopsis of the hideous facts. It reported that the dead girl—a runaway—had been beaten savagely long after she was dead. Her body had been nailed in the barn in a mock crucifixion. Knapp immediately thought of his former client, Edward Teague.

* * *

Tony Russo also read the story of the Kokomo killing. Murder was his line of work and variations always interested him. He had learned long ago that of all the animals on earth, man was the most vicious and inventive when it came to destruction. He had always wondered if there was some definite relationship between imagination and evil, although he had known artful killers who possessed only a subnormal intelligence and had the imagination of a grape. Still, sometimes it seemed that inventive evil went hand in hand with an inspired but warped mind.

"Some weirdo killed a girl in Kokomo and nailed her to a barn," he remarked to his partner, Joe Rosinski. "I think we should send a teletype to the Kokomo people and get a full report."

"Why? We haven't had anybody nailed to a barn around here. Hell, we don't even have any barns. What's the connection?"

"Just a hunch, I guess. I suppose every time I see something like this I think about my old friend, Edward Teague."

"The Stalking Man?"

"The one and only. Meanest son-of-a-bitch I've ever known. I really didn't understand the meaning of the word *psychopath* until I met him."

"A real looney, huh?"

"A complicated one. He hated women, or hated his mother, and took it out on all other women. According to the doctors, anyway. He was completely insane but his intellect was never limited by his madness. He was as smart as a fox even though he was absolutely crazy. He was damn hard to catch."

"That was your big bust, right?"

"Yeah. Someone started killing women for no obvious reason. Teague wasn't so good at it at first—a half-dozen women escaped with only a beating. They were damned lucky.

"The newspapers tagged him as 'The Stalking Man' because of the way he would follow the women he had marked for killing. Some of the survivors will hear footsteps for the rest of their lives. In fact, that's how I nailed him—on the 'stalking' bit."

Rosinski listened; Russo seldom talked about himself.

"I thought the killer might be a hunter, by the way he went after his victims. I checked up north and found a killing right in hunting country that matched his methods and style exactly. Although the survivors never quite agreed, I knew what he looked like in a general way. He was young, tall, blonde, with pimples—and he wore glasses.

"Since I figured a killer would probably be a loner and not the kind to stay with the others at hunting camps, I just drove north where the killing happened and made the rounds of motel operators. The hunting season and the northern killing coincided. I asked whether any of them had seen a young man of that description during the season. Sure enough, an old Swede up there remembered a guy, staying by himself for only a few days. The girl up there had been killed during those few days. Teague had registered under his own name and had even given his correct license number. He really thought he could never be caught.''

"Easy from then on, right?''

"Not really. None of the survivors could make a positive identification, and he wasn't saying anything. I finally sat down and started needling him, saying he didn't have the nerve or the brains to kill all those women. He was screwy of course, and that really got under his skin. He started yelling that he had killed them and began to pour out details even before I could give him his constitutional rights.''

"I remember the headlines when he was charged,'' Rosinski said. "It was really a sensation.''

"Yeah.'' Russo smiled at the memory. "I even made *Time* magazine with that one. The big shots around here suddenly turned real cool, they thought I was after their jobs. But they relaxed when Teague was carted off to the nuthouse and the publicity died down.''

"You got a citation out of it.''

"That, and a few dimes, will get you a cup of coffee any place in town.''

"Looks good on the record, though.''

"Big deal. In a couple of years I'll retire and end up as a bank guard or a company security man. No one will remember Edward Teague except me.''

"I suppose.''

Russo glanced at his watch.

"Got a big date or something?'' Rosinski asked.

"You've been looking at your watch every few minutes for the last hour."

"I do have an appointment," Russo said dryly.

His young partner laughed. "It ain't with your dentist, I can tell you that. Why don't you take off early? I'll cover. There's nothing much going down today anyway."

Russo couldn't tell his partner that his appointment was with Marie Coyle, the beauty who worked in the identification bureau. He was tempted to tell because he knew Rosinski would be greatly impressed. Russo still felt foolish about their age difference, and he knew that if word got around that he was dating her, Marie's reputation would come crashing down to the rather low level he himself enjoyed. That would never do. He could see there were going to be problems in maintaining this relationship, although the mere thought of her quickened his pulse.

"I'll wait until the shift is done," he said evenly, aware that Marie didn't get off till then, anyway. "Thanks."

"She really must be something, Lieutenant. I never have seen you so preoccupied before."

Russo smiled. "You're mistaking preoccupation for early senility. You will have to know the difference if you expect to make good at promotion time. A good word from a senile senior officer can do you a lot of good. It's like a union, you know."

Rosinski's broad Polish face cracked into a wide grin. "She must be something to get you all worked up. And, by the way, I know senility when I see it. The chief of detectives is senile."

"Well, maybe you do know the difference at that. Old

Tom is senile and if he gets any worse they may make
him commissioner." Russo glanced again at his watch
and then stood up. "I may duck out a few minutes early
at that. Send that teletype to Kokomo before you leave;
I'm really interested in what they have down there."

Rosinski nodded as Russo left the office.

Russo hurried to the elevator and down to the street
where he retrieved his private car from the senior officers'
parking lot. He pulled out into the street in front of police
headquarters. Police had begun to stream out of the building as the day shift ended.

The sight of her sent a thrill through him. Skipping
down the steps, she strode proudly out of the main entrance. Her whole bearing seemed to advertise joy. As he
pulled to the curb, she recognized him and ran to the car.

She opened the door and slid in next to him. "Well,
hello."

"Hi."

Suddenly, and without warning, she threw her arms
around him and her warm mouth sought his eagerly and
aggressively. He held his foot on the brake and half
pulled away.

"Well," she said in surprise, "if you don't like that
sort of thing . . ."

"Hey, it was great, but there are people going by."

"Afraid?"

"No, but . . ."

She came at him again, her dark eyes laughing. He
surrendered and returned the kiss. They parted and he
became aware of the two young uniformed officers staring at them. He put the car into gear and sped away.

"You're quite the retiring violet, aren't you?" There
was laughter in her voice.

"And you, Miss Coyle, are what we in police work call an exhibitionist. We find people like you working in topless places, or if male, flashing at old ladies in buses. I am a police officer and I know all about these things."

"I didn't know you were a cop," she laughed, "or I never would have climbed into the car."

"Oh yes, I am an officer of the law. And another interesting thing about exhibitionists—female type—they are well known to be frigid."

She slid in close to him and ran her hand over his inner thigh. "I'm distressed to hear that, Officer, because I had planned quite an evening for the two of us, but now that I know I am a frigid woman, I know I really wouldn't enjoy it at all. You had better drop me off at the first topless place we pass, I might as well accept my fate."

"Fortunately, Miss Coyle, in addition to being what you term a 'cop' I am also an unlicensed psychologist specializing in liberating frigid women. I think I have the evening free to devote to a group therapy session."

"Group?"

"You and me."

"Okay, in that case, I am yours, Doctor."

"You won't be sorry." He turned into the left-turn lane and headed toward her apartment.

For the moment, all thoughts of Edward Teague had vanished.

3

As HE APPROACHED THE CITY EDWARD TEAGUE TURNED off Interstate 65 and came in via Meridian. He expected to see NO VACANCY signs and he was not disappointed. Every hotel and motel, no matter how old or decrepit, was filled. It was not the big race week, that was a month away, but it was almost as busy; now was the week of qualifying-time trials at Indianapolis. Crews assembled from all over America to combine their skill and luck at putting together a huge but delicate racing machine that could fly down the oval brick track and qualify for the country's biggest race, the Indianapolis 500. And not just the crews came.

* * *

Americans had long engaged in a violent love affair with the automobile. Indeed, they sacrificed thousands to it each year: victims laid out upon concrete and asphalt altars. Americans loved their cars, they loved speed, and they loved the Memorial Day race at Indianapolis. And so they came, not for the race, but just to sit in the stands and watch lone race cars roar around the track, fighting time. To many it would have been the most boring event on earth, but to the true fans—the real car nuts—it was heaven, and they came by the thousands and filled the hotels, motels, and boarding houses of Indianapolis.

As the giant shark is followed by pilot fish, so the assembly of giant crowds on land attracts human "pilot fish" who swim along in the dark shadow of the throng. Criminals of all kinds, pickpockets, con men, hustlers, and gamblers, eager to part the faithful fans from their money.

And the girls.

All kinds of girls, mostly young, but also a substantial number of veterans. Some had come with their pimps, some had come alone. Some had made reservations at hotels, others had brought house trailers or motor homes. Money! Its delicious smell lured them to the wild time in old Indianapolis.

* * *

The Police Department of the City of Indianapolis had been the subject of great upheavals and graft investigations. Many of the younger officers had the vivid picture of the arrest and disgrace of other policemen in their memories and so had abstained from temptation. Some of the older, more experienced men pretended reform, but had only become more cautious in their illegal and lucrative sidelines.

It was an older motel, not fancy, and beginning to run down. The neighborhood was declining, and the owner was no longer putting money into repair or maintenance; letting it go, like a dying relative.

Sergeant Drum and Patrolman Harvin sat in their unmarked car. They were middle-aged men, still muscular but beginning to run to fat. They had been partners for years and had even come to resemble each other, like a long-married couple. Race month was their Christmas season. It had always been so, and although they had to make some adjustments within the new department, they managed to keep their earnings up to their former level. They were vice squad men.

They sat quietly in their car, parked directly across from the entrance to the old motel. Like patient fishermen they waited silently, relaxed but watching for some action.

Once in a while Drum might talk briefly. Harvin would grunt replies. They were comfortable with each other and no additional conversation was needed.

A new Ford, one of the so-called luxury-economy models, pulled up into the parking apron in front of the motel office. A white man in his thirties got out, looked around for a moment, and then hurried into the office.

"See the girl?" Drum asked.

"Uh huh," Harvin replied. "A dinge."

"Looks like we have caught some sin about to happen, partner."

"Seems likely."

In a moment the man emerged from the motel office and jumped back into the Ford. He drove through the archway into the motel's interior, a parking court surrounded by rows of motel doors.

They could no longer see the car.

Drum looked at his watch. "Right about now he'll just be opening the motel door," he said.

Harvin merely nodded.

Still intent on his watch Drum reported his guess at the progress made by the couple. He sounded like a baseball play-by-play sportscaster as he announced the imagined progress taking place in the motel room. "He has to have his pants off by now," Drum said. "Let's go."

The officers pulled into the motel parking lot. Drum walked into the office. "Hi, Charley," he greeted the clerk.

"Oh Jesus, Drum, not again."

"Fighting crime, Charley, always fighting crime."

"No rough stuff this time."

"Not likely. Let me have the key, eh?"

The desk clerk handed over the key.

"If everything goes well, Charley, there'll be a buck or two in this for you."

The desk clerk shook his head. "No thanks, Drum."

The sergeant's eyes narrowed.

"Look," the desk clerk protested, "I ain't going to say a word. What you guys do is your own business. Hell, you're cops. I just don't want to be part of it."

"Suit yourself," Drum said, stepping out the door and nodding to his partner.

The two officers walked along the narrow concrete walkway until they came to the doorway of Unit 15. Harvin reached into his coat and extracted his .38. Very softly, but quickly, Drum inserted the key into the lock and slammed the door open. Harvin rushed into the room, followed by Drum.

The black girl was naked and she cursed at them as they entered. The white man was just coming out of the bathroom clad only in his shorts and socks.

"Police," Drum said, snapping out the leather case and exhibiting his badge.

The blood drained from the face of the half-naked man. He started to speak, but no words came.

"Well, well," Drum said, his face solemn, "it seems we've stumbled onto a little sin in our fair city." He looked at the man, his eyes narrowing. "You're under arrest."

Before the man could say anything, Drum strode to the dresser and felt through the empty trousers, finding the wallet in one of the rear pockets. He, flipped it open. "Well, Mr. Charles E. Hughes, of Louisville, Kentucky," he said, "I suppose this is the lovely Mrs. Hughes." He grinned at the naked black girl.

"No," the man stammered. "No, I was, it was . . ." His face seemed to sag at the hopelessness of his situation.

Drum and Harvin were well practiced in their art. They frightened the man until he was ready to say anything or do anything. They informed him that they would arrest him on a morals charge and notify his family and employer. Then the subject of money came up.

The black prostitute was allowed to dress and leave. Then the white man paid Drum the "fine." They left him to contemplate the error of his ways—an error that left him two hundred dollars poorer.

It was turning out to be a fine night.

Their next stop was outside the old Claymore Hotel on Sixth Street. Many of the girls brought their tricks there, it had always been a good prospect in the past. Although not as rewarding as some of the newer motels, it was much surer.

The officers decided to grab a bite of dinner first, just a quick sandwich and a beer. The night was young and they couldn't afford to waste too much time eating. That could wait for a slower season of the year when there would be plenty of time for leisurely meals.

They positioned themselves and watched a thin black prostitute lead an elderly man in rundown clothing through the entrance of the Claymore Hotel.

"What do you think?" Drum asked his partner.

"Not promising," Harvin replied. "He's probably been saving up all month to get laid. Doesn't look like any real money to me."

"Yeah. Not worth our time."

"Yeah."

They waited, once again lapsing into easy silence in the quiet comfort of the darkened car.

A new Chevrolet moved slowly down the street until it stopped and then backed into an empty parking space.

"Out-of-state license," Drum said.

"Illinois," Harvin replied.

"You got good eyes."

Harvin just grunted.

They watched a tall, good-looking man emerge from the driver's side. A small and plump woman slipped out of the passenger side of the car.

"Well, look who we got here," Drum said.

Harvin smiled. "Little Mary. I thought she went down to Covington to work."

"She did. She works for Sweet Henry. You remember, he moved all his girls down there because the action was getting too slow around here."

"Must be back for the races."

Drum nodded. "Everybody's gotta make a living."

The tall man took the small prostitute's arm and escorted her up the few stairs to the hotel entrance.

"Mutt and Jeff," Drum said. "Christ, she's just a hair under five feet tall and that clown looks to be six feet two—maybe six three."

Harvin chuckled. "Let's let 'em get going. I'd like to see them in the sack. You know, sort of a novelty act."

"Yeah, me too. Of course, she could always just blow him. Height don't make no difference then."

"Wouldn't be going to all the trouble of getting a hotel room if that was the case. You know Little Mary, she would have taken care of him in some alley."

"Yeah, I guess that's right."

Drum looked at his watch. "We'll have to allow a little extra time. Those damn elevators in the Claymore don't work."

"I hope the desk clerk has sense enough to put him in a room on the ground floor. I don't feel like walking my ass off tonight."

"Yeah."

They waited. After a few minutes Drum once again began his imaginary play-by-play. He kept up a quiet commentary as he watched the minutes tick by.

"Even if she's giving him a trip around the world," Drum said, "he must be pronging her by now. Let's go."

They left the car and walked across the street to the hotel.

Drum walked up to the desk clerk, who was reading a magazine and didn't see him coming.

"Hello, Harrison," Drum said softly, causing the elderly man to jump from his battered chair.

"Jesus, Drum, you scared me."

"Give me the pass key," Drum said. "What room did that big guy go into?"

"Big guy?"

Drum frowned. "The one who was with Little Mary."

"Oh him." The clerk smiled, exhibiting a mouthful of rotting yellow teeth. "I didn't get a good look at him. He was hiding back of the phone booth over there by the stairs. A lot of them do that. Christ, you'd think they was on *Candid Camera* or something. I give the key to Mary. I guess she took him up. I wasn't watching.''

''What room?''

''204,'' he said.

Drum scowled. ''Why didn't you park them in a ground floor room?''

The clerk shook his head. ''Jesus, Drum, this is the first of May. Damn near every room we got is filled with honest-to-God customers. I keep a few rooms vacant for the girls, though. You can't ignore your regular clients, you know.''

''Seen Sweet Henry?''

''Naw. I think he's still down to Covington. He probably sent Mary up to work here for the time trials. She knows the territory and nobody's gonna fool around with one of Sweet Henry's girls, even if he ain't around. He can always come up and pay you a visit, if you know what I mean.''

Drum nodded and took the pass key. ''There'll be a couple of bucks in this for you, if everything goes okay.''

''I can use the money,'' the old man said, going back to his magazine.

The two hefty policemen slowly climbed the wide staircase to the second floor.

*   *   *

It had never occurred to him that blood would have a distinctive odor all its own, a peculiarly delicate yet exciting smell. His father had dressed the deer, and he had kneeled down to inspect the large puddle of blood that had collected in the earth's depression. Ever since that first experience, he had always liked that smell.

*   *   *

He held her in the empty bathtub. Her eyes were wide with pain and fear, silently imploring him to stop. The blood made her skin slippery and he had to hold with great force in order to prevent her from squirming away. He was panting from his efforts, that and the excitement of the smell of blood and the sight of her.

He heard the key in the door. It was an old hotel and the locks were worn and noisy. It was as if he were dreaming it, that the sound of the key was the beginning of a nightmare. They were coming after him, they would catch him and once again they would stop him and put him away.

He tried to slam the bathroom door but Drum was quick and knocked it open. He stared up into the shocked eyes of the policeman.

"Holy God!" Drum stopped in the doorway.

Don't be afraid, his father had instructed him. Rely on your basic instincts to get you out of trouble. Be careful, he had told him, but if in danger, rely on your instincts.

He brought the long knife up, concealing its blade under the cover of his bare left arm. The tip sliced past the detective's tie, slipping past the side of the sternum bone and through the heavy flesh, sliding like an obscene silver snake into the chambers of Drum's heart. Drum was jolted back, his assailant following him supplying the killing force.

"Hey, cut that out," Harvin shouted, not seeing the knife, nor the shocked and dying eyes of his partner. He reached into his hip pocket and pulled out his soft leather blackjack.

He disliked violence. Harvin suffered from bursitis in his right shoulder and it hurt to exercise the joint; nevertheless, he moved forward quickly and raised the sap.

The falling body of his partner crashed into his hips, throwing him off balance, and the sap landed harmlessly on the assailant's naked shoulder. Harvin was about to draw his pistol when he experienced a flaming hot sensation in his groin. He tried to take a deep breath but could not. He was stabbed, he knew that. He desperately tried to unholster his gun and defend himself, but he was powerless to move as he felt the jolting and paralyzing blows of the blade repeatedly slamming into his midsection.

Jesus, Harvin thought to himself. I wonder what they'll think when they find the money on us. It was his last thought on earth.

His father's advice had not failed him. He had relied on his instincts and his instincts had not failed him. He felt triumphant.

His chest was heaving from the exertion. It had happened so fast and it had been almost silent. The dying girl was trying to scream in the bathroom. She emitted a bubbling gurgle, the only sound she could produce through her severed vocal cords. He moved to her, and though he was tempted to persist in taking his pleasure, he knew he was in danger so he quickly finished the job.

He lifted her body from the tub and then washed the blood down with hot water. He climbed into the tub and turned on the shower, washing the blood from his own naked body. He stepped out of the shower and toweled himself off as he gingerly stepped past the blood and bodies. He dressed quickly, taking time to make sure he left no trace of himself or his fingerprints in the room. Slipping out the door, he made sure it locked behind him and then he hurried down the hallway to the dingy EXIT sign over the stairway. He was on the street in less than a minute.

It was early evening and Indianapolis was filled with a symphony of normal city noise. The traffic was light. He climbed into his Chevrolet, snapped on the lights and motor, and pulled away from the curb. He felt triumphant, exhilarated.

And it had been an unusual experience for him. He had never killed a male before.

* * *

Knapp had neglected to listen carefully to the question and he knew that could prove to be an embarrassing mistake. The night law-school students were much more serious than their daytime counterparts, and their minds seemed to be honed to a sharper edge. Having to work and fulfill the demands of graduate school at the same time was a burden that only the best seemed able to weather. He had to be careful with them; they were quite capable of painting him into an intellectual corner.

It was a large class, over eighty freshmen with a handful of worried repeaters, and each seemed eager to demonstrate his ability. He taught the night school's criminal law course, a two-semester ordeal that was required for graduation. Tonight's topic was the defense of insanity. They had reviewed the cases, past and present, covering the subject. He felt at ease; no one knew the abstracts of the modern rules better than himself—he used them often in defense of his clients. To Knapp the defense of insanity was no theoretical formula, but a real tool, sometimes the only protection against a harsh and unfair application of the law itself.

Mr. Tobias had asked the question. Tobias was a graduate engineer, precise in thought, who sometimes found the often imprecise application of the law baffling.

"I'm sorry, Mr. Tobias. Would you be kind enough to restate the question?"

Tobias seemed all eyes and hair. He wore his hair long and affected a large walruslike mustache. "What do you do, as a defense lawyer, if you think your client is faking insanity?"

They had just covered the Supreme Court decision in People v. Teague, the case he himself had tried. He wondered if a personal barb might be hidden in the question.

"First of all, if you contemplate using the defense of insanity, you have your man examined by qualified doctors. Now, if for some reason, you feel that their opinions might not be valid, than you can have him examined by another doctor or set of doctors. Remember, you are the lawyer, not the jury. You must rely on the opinions of the professionals you employ for that purpose. You expect your clients to rely on you as a professional; therefore, you must rely on your experts. If he is faking, that really is a medical judgment. I'm not a psychiatrist and I haven't had the benefit of their training and experience; therefore, I let them tell me if he is sick or not. If they say he is sick, that's my position. Then it's up to the jury to make the final decision."

Tobias frowned. "But suppose you really know in your

heart that the man has fooled the doctors?''

"Mr. Tobias, are you interested in the defense of insanity or in debating legal ethics? I try to be ethical, but that is a subject taught by another man here.''

Tobias shook his head. "I don't know about ethics, but this definition of a substantial disorder of thought or mood''—he was quoting the rule—"significantly impairing judgment . . .'' He stopped. "Hell, that could apply to just about anybody at some time in their life. I mean, it's vague. One doctor could see it one way and another guy a different way. Shouldn't a rule be something standard, that sets up limitations of some kind . . .'' He was interrupted by the class bell.

Knapp smiled. Tobias wanted an engineer's rule, something that could be fed into a computer and from which an answer could be obtained, a positive, detailed, and explicit answer. None of the students moved, although technically the bell freed them.

"Look, the law is a little like the shifting sands of the desert in some respects. In some areas it is changing all the time. I'll admit that it can be vexing sometimes, but believe me it is never boring. You may have a case sometime in the future, Mr. Tobias, which may completely change the rule set up by the court in the Teague case.'' He paused. He didn't want to get into a debate that could go on all night. "The next shifting sand dune that we will study is the defense of intoxication. The next five cases will cover that topic; please read and brief them before the next class. Thank you, gentlemen.'' He stood up and the class accepted this as his signal that he was through for the night.

Many nights he stayed on to talk to his students, to help them, or just to enjoy their company and the challenge of their minds. Tonight was different. He took up his books, thrust them into his briefcase, and hurriedly left the school.

Teague had been on his mind since he read of the killing in Kokomo. It seemed to haunt him tonight. The dry legal language contained in the court's decision had brought back to him the ghost of Edward Teague. In his mind he once again saw the charming, nice-looking man who was madness personified. Now, according to Dr. Rose, Teague once again roamed the streets, a free man. The fact that he, Thomas Knapp, had been an instrument in the process that released Teague bothered him deeply, but he didn't know what he could do about it. The knowledge had come to him in a way in which he could still be charged with Teague's legal affairs. Ethically, could he tell the police? Did he owe a duty to Teague, who the doctor said was completely recovered, or did he owe a duty to society, to alert someone that the Stalking Man was free?

Tobias's question had touched a nerve, although the young student had no way of knowing that his inquiry had been in the mind of his teacher for several days.

He was tired but he didn't want to go home. Home meant either battle or some other emotionally draining confrontation. Soon Helen would give up and go to bed. Until then he had to find a way to kill some time.

Drinking was dangerous. He had seen too many good lawyers use alcohol as a tranquilizer or pressure valve, interposed as a buffer against the onslaught of their profession and the demands of their lives. Eventually it ruined them. So sitting around a bar was out.

The class ended at nine o'clock. Helen would still be up. He decided he could kill an hour or two at the office.

The brief on the Mease case still needed a few finishing touches. He left the campus and returned downtown.

The night guard took him up to the firm's floor.

The lights were still on, and he was surprised to hear the rapid rattle of an electric typewriter as he opened the door.

He loudly called "Hello," to avoid frightening whoever was working late.

"Hi," came floating back. He recognized Martha Flowers's voice.

He walked down the hall and found her seated at her desk. She looked tired, but her smile was bright and she seemed glad to see him.

"What keeps you down here tonight, Martha?"

"A bit of catching up," she said easily. "We were getting behind in some of our mail, expense accounts, a few small things like that."

"How's it coming?"

"I'm almost through."

"Is your husband picking you up?"

"No."

"Then you drove?"

"No, I took the bus. I really hadn't planned on working late when I came down this morning."

"Well, finish up and I'll drive you home."

"You don't have to do that, Mr. Knapp. The buses run quite often at night. I'll be just fine."

He paused for a moment, studying her. She was a handsome woman, not yet forty. She had a pretty face although her beauty was minimized because she tended to look severe. She hid her full figure behind well-tailored but unrevealing dresses and pants suits. She looked the very model of a pleasant, competent career woman.

"I'd like to drive you home, Martha. Downtown at night is no place for a lovely lady like you." He silently debated with himself whether to reveal his own needs. "Also," he said it slowly, "I feel the need of company tonight. Have you ever felt that way?"

"Yes." She spoke the word softly, her eyes avoiding his. "If it isn't too much trouble, I'd be pleased if you could drive me home."

"Do you realize how formal we sound with each other?"

"This is a business office. We should be formal."

He laughed. "Martha, how long have you been my secretary?"

"Two years."

"Well, I think after two years of daily contact we can loosen up a bit with each other without the world coming to an end." He waited for a response, but none came. "That is, of course, if you want to."

She continued to avoid his eyes.

"Look, can I buy you a drink on the way home?" Knapp asked.

She looked up at him, and her large eyes appeared to be almost tearful. "That sounds nice," she said quietly.

"Good! Let's call it a night."

He waited while she put away some papers and neatly covered her typewriter with a plastic cover.

He felt strangely exhilarated while they made small talk waiting for the elevator. Martha Flowers—he had never thought of her in a personal way, at least not as a woman. She was a valued business associate, a piece of efficient machinery who turned out a perfect work product while exhibiting a smiling face. Now he was acutely aware that she was indeed a woman—a very attractive and desirable woman. And he suddenly realized he really knew nothing about her.

The elevator delivered them to ground level and he escorted her to the garage and to his car.

"You know, Martha, I don't even know where you live."

"The Riverside Apartments, out on East Martin."

"I know the place." He swung the Cadillac out of the garage and sped along the empty streets.

He looked over at her. "There's a small place near there, called Charley's Wharf. Have you ever been there?"

"Once."

"Shall we stop there for our drink?"

"That would be fine."

As he drove along, his eyes adjusted to the dim light in the interior of the car and he noted that Martha had great legs. He felt guilty that he'd even noticed, she was too much a lady for that sort of thing.

"How's your son?" she asked.

He remembered telling her about the pencil incident. "Just fine. The doctor said he'll have no trouble. Of course, it is just one thing after another. That's the problem with having children."

"I can imagine."

"You and your husband have no children, as I recall."

"No. He never wanted to have children."

"And you?" He instantly regretted the question; it was none of his business.

"I would have preferred to have had a family," she said, looking out the window, away from him.

"I didn't mean to pry, Martha."

"I know you didn't." She turned and looked at him,

her face troubled. "There's something you might as well know, Mr. Knapp. I've been meaning to tell you, but the right time just never presented itself."

He waited.

"My husband is divorcing me." She spoke softly, as if confessing a shameful sin.

"Oh, Martha, I am so sorry."

"You needn't be. We should have done it years ago. We've lived as strangers for several years now. Very civilized and all that, but no affection or love on either side. I understand he's got a girl friend and that's the reason for bringing the action. I won't oppose it."

"Do you still live together?" Again he regretted the impertinence of the question. "I'm sorry, it's none of my business."

"He moved out last week. That's why I was at the office. I just couldn't bear the thought of going home to that empty apartment. That may sound silly, but I'm used to having someone with me and I'm having a hard time adjusting to the new situation." There was a tremor in her last few words.

He looked over at her. She was on the verge of crying. It was the first time he had seen her exhibit any emotion. He had just supposed she'd been born cheerful, and it never occurred to him that she too might be shouldering a ton of troubles.

"How about family—isn't there anyone around who can give you some moral support?"

She pulled a cigarette from her purse. It was the first time she'd smoked in his presence. Her smooth face was reflected in the flame of her lighter. The cigarette seemed to relax her. "I have a sister. She lives in California. That's the extent of my family. I have a few friends—

lady friends—but I haven't found much comfort there. Lots of sympathy, but little comfort.''

''I suppose.''

She looked at him. ''You've got a few troubles of your own at home.''

He nodded. ''You're my private secretary, you know the whole situation, or most of it.''

''Would you be terribly shocked if I proposed a—well—a change in plans?'' she asked.

''I promise not to be shocked by whatever you say.''

''I would like that drink with you, Mr. Knapp, but I would like to invite you to my apartment for it. I think it might help me if I just didn't have to face that place alone.''

''Sure, Martha. No problem.'' He was pleased that she asked, and surprised at his own rising excitement.

They arrived at the giant apartment complex. Her apartment was large—one of the so-called luxury units overlooking the river. Although tastefully decorated, the place was coldly impersonal, as if to reflect an icy compromise between two isolated people.

''Six rooms with a river view, just like the name of that play,'' she said.

''It's nice.''

''I'll fix the drinks.'' She seemed more sure of herself in her home surroundings. ''What would you like?''

''Scotch and soda, if you have it.''

''That's easy.'' Her laugh was relaxed. ''I thought you might want something more difficult. I'm not much of a bartender, I'm afraid.''

''I'll help you,'' he said, following her into the kitchen.

Like her work area at the office, the kitchen was efficiently organized, with plenty of work space cleverly arranged around the appliances. A swing-out cupboard revealed a well-stocked bar.

"My husband entertains . . . entertained a lot," she corrected herself. "You know how salesmen are." Martha quickly prepared his scotch and then splashed just a dash of bourbon over ice cubes for herself.

She led him to the living room and gestured at the long white couch facing the almost room-wide window. "If I turn off the light, we can watch the river below. At night, it's rather a spectacular view really."

"Sounds good."

She snapped off the lights and sat next to him in the darkness. Below, the river looked like a dark ribbon winding between millions of city lights. Several boats, identifiable by their small navigation lights, worked their way across the dark water. Wisps of clouds scudded past a hazy moon hanging low in the night sky.

He tasted his drink. He was again acutely aware of his own excitement. Her close presence, the delicate scent of her perfume, had caused desire to flame up within him. He had almost forgotten how it felt: to want a woman, to know the intensity of that primal feeling.

"This is very pleasant," he said quietly.

"I like it," she replied. "Some nights I just sit here for hours. There's something absolutely fascinating about all those lights."

They sat in silence for a moment. Knapp tried to think of the right thing to say.

"Martha, I find you very attractive."

She turned to look at him, her face catching the light from the night sky. "All women like compliments."

"I mean it."

"Well, is this something new, or have I been missing some signals?"

He laughed. "Something new, I guess. You know how I am, I always get so damned wrapped up in things. I guess I just never really noticed you as a woman until tonight."

Martha nodded. "You certainly are single-minded sometimes, I'll have to admit that." She looked down at her glass. "Of course, you must know that it's common for women to find their boss attractive, if he's a nice boss, of course."

"Am I a nice boss, Martha?"

"I think you are," she said simply. "And I've found you attractive for a long time. It's nothing new with me."

"Why haven't you . . ."

"You're a married man. We work together. There was no purpose to it."

"But you know my marriage is . . . well . . . unhappy."

She nodded. "I know. I've felt very sorry for you, but there was nothing I could do—or can do," she added. "Just as there's nothing you can do about my situation."

"Just two lonely people."

"Something like that." Her voice was very low, with a hint of invitation.

Knapp realized his palms were perspiring. "Martha, when I was fifteen I took a girl to a movie. It was my first date. I planned it out very carefully. I thought I would start by putting my arm around her shoulders, and then, if that worked, I was going to try for the big prize, a kiss. I was deathly afraid she would push me away, but I was determined to try. A sort of go-for-broke thing, at least for a fifteen-year-old boy. It was all pretty scary, yet pretty exciting too."

"Being a teenager can be . . ."

Knapp put his drink down and gently pulled her toward him. Long-dead emotions seemed to explode into life as he kissed her. At first she didn't respond, then suddenly she returned the kiss with an ardor to match his own.

He held her tightly as their lips parted, his face buried in her hair.

"That girl," she whispered into his throat, "did she resist?"

"Damned if I can remember," he mumbled as he eagerly sought her mouth again.

*　　*　　*

Niles is a small city in Michigan just north of the Indiana border—a short drive from Chicago and about a half hour away from the campus of the University of Notre Dame. A combination of light industry, commerce, and farming, Niles is the typical middle-American town celebrated by country singers as the "home" to which they long to return. Plain and solid, nothing fancy about Niles, not a thing to call attention to it. It was not the sort of place that would ordinarily attract a man like Edward Teague, but he had driven into Niles, nevertheless.

Like other similar American towns, the main street was bordered on each side with shops and stores and a sprinkling of bars, a pleasant place. The window displays were new and bright but the buildings were old, although well kept and reassuring. People might come and go—they were mortal—but there was something very permanent about Niles.

Blend into your surroundings, his father had instructed him. Become part of where you are. The animals will come to you before they even sense you are there.

Teague had changed into faded work trousers and an equally worn work shirt. There was nothing about him that was different from any number of men who walked Niles's streets. Just another workman, normal in appearance, nothing about him to be remembered. A bit tall, but otherwise no different.

He tried one bar—it was a workingman's place and he had hoped to find the promise of action there—but as he sipped his beer the only quarry he saw was a middle-aged, overstuffed barmaid, who seemed to be concentrating on an equally overstuffed man in a bright sport shirt. She was not his type; she looked too hardened. Her eyes were the kind that showed only anger and never fear. He would not enjoy that.

He had become more wary since Indianapolis. It was not so much fear of arrest that prompted caution but the prospect that the pleasure of watching his victim at leisure might be denied him. And that seemed unfair; he put so much work and thought into his plans. He had decided to abandon prostitutes as targets, since they attracted the police and he did not need another Indianapolis, although he had been strangely stimulated by the thrill of danger.

He picked up his change from the bar and nodded in a friendly manner to the bartender, who returned a wave. Teague walked slowly down the main street, pretending to look in the windows but covertly watching the women who passed by. Several looked promising. He was about to follow a young girl when she was joined by several loud and swaggering teenage boys. She seemed annoyed and flounced away, unaware that the appearance of the pimply-faced youths had saved her life.

Patience. He could almost hear his father's whispered instructions. He could smell again the sweetness of the pine trees and feel the coolness of the autumn air. Patience, the voice whispered again.

She strode out of the drugstore door, her strong arms laden with packages. Her hair, coiled in plastic rings, was concealed beneath a colorful cloth. Her slacks clung suggestively to her wide hips and long legs. Young, beautiful, and newly married, she seemed in love with life— even without knowing that new life was already growing within her lush body. She hurried happily to her battered old car.

It whined impotently for a moment, but then the old engine finally came to life and she carefully pulled out into traffic.

Edward Teague had watched, and then he too hurried to his car. By the time he gained the street her car had disappeared, but he hoped he might follow and find her again. He had a hunter's sure instinct.

Tracking had always come easy for him. Although he preferred to stake out a likely area, he would track to find game if none came to him. He discovered he was capable of great concentration and could see trail signs that others missed.

The main street ended in a fork. One road continued toward the interstate highway and was so marked by a large sign. Teague reasoned that the girl's car did not look safe enough to drive the fast interstate, so he chose the other road. The traffic thinned and he kept a sharp eye as he passed every intersecting street.

A dirt road marked with several worn signposts advertising recreation lands attracted his attention. A cloud of dust caused by a receding car rose from its dry bed. Again he trusted to instinct. Carefully signaling for a left-hand turn, he patiently waited while a slow farm truck passed, then he wheeled into the dirt road and followed the dust cloud.

Teague realized it was a gamble. He had passed several paved roads where she could have turned. But he remembered that her ancient vehicle had been dust-covered and he knew she had driven a dirt road, although he had no assurance that this was the one.

He pressed down on the accelerator as his car rattled over the bumpy road. He did not wish to come up on the other car too fast, but he was anxious to get close enough to make an identification.

He had tracked the bear his father had shot. He remembered listening to his father crashing in the woods behind him as he hurried along, finding the telltale blood markings. He remembered his racing heart and the anticipation of danger, knowing full well that a wounded bear could become a raging predator rather than prey. He remembered the excitement of the chase and the blood pounding in his head.

She had noticed the car behind her. Barlett Road served as a trunk line to the next county seat, and although less traveled than the paved highway, it was a short cut for many people on their way to Algomac. So she was not alarmed by the car coming up behind her.

She wished she had remembered to stop at the library in town. Her husband had asked her to pick up a book and she had forgotten. She debated turning around and going back, but it was getting late and she wished to finish her hair before it was time to prepare dinner. She felt relaxed and happy and vaguely planned to interest her young husband in something more than a book. She abandoned the thought of returning to the library.

Slowing down to a crawl—she was careful to avoid the big rock that marked the entrance to their driveway—she turned and drove up the rutted pathway to their small frame home. She took no notice that the car behind her slowed as it drifted past or that the driver was watching her.

He recalled the thrill of triumph as he had come upon the dying bear. The animal sat in the midst of a clearing, its beady eyes watching him. The bear listed to one side, favoring its broken leg. He remembered its anguished groan that turned into a whimper of pain.

He continued driving after watching her pull into the driveway of the small house. His head pounded. Unless someone was home with her, it would be easy. His breathing was quick and shallow as his excitement grew. Even if someone was home, he was determined to do it anyway. He forced himself to drive until he was out of sight of the small house, then he found a place to turn around. He headed back very slowly, his mind afire with anticipation as he planned how he would gain entrance to her home.

The bear had tried to rise, to come at him. He remembered it clearly. The animal fell forward each time it tried to advance, stopped by its leg pain and weakness from blood loss. He raised his rifle and sighted, but was stopped by his father's shout. His father's rifle cracked and echoed as the bullet jolted the bear. He felt cheated that he had been denied the kill. He mentally promised himself that he would never hesitate again and give another hunter that pleasure—the pleasure he wanted for himself, the feeling of ultimate power; the power of destruction.

As he brought the car to a stop just in front of her place, he jerked the brake pedal to imitate motor trouble. He sat there a minute, leaning forward, as if vainly trying to start the car. Then he got out and walked around to the front of his car and raised the hood. He moved to the side so he could see her house, although it would look like he was inspecting the engine. He detected no movement inside. Her old car was the only vehicle parked at the place.

It was a desolate area. He guessed that the small frame home had once housed tenant labor for the large farms in the area. The nearest home was an ancient farmhouse a half mile up the road. It was perfect. Leaning against the car he realized he was having an erection. He pretended to work on the motor. Hoping that she was looking, he stood up and wiped his hands on his handkerchief. He looked up and down the deserted country road as if searching for a gas station or telephone booth. Finally, he left the car and walked across the road and proceeded up her driveway. His feet were silent as he walked along the grass next to the ruts.

There were no stairs to the front door, which looked as if it had not been used in years. He walked to the side door. The noise echoed back from within as he beat his knuckles against the wood frame of the rusting screen door.

At first he heard nothing. But nothing was better than a dog's bark. He was sure she was inside. Then he heard a door close somewhere and the sound of steps approaching. He waited, forcing himself to be calm.

She opened the lower door. Her hair was full now, she had removed the rollers and he could see it made her even more lovely. Her light blue eyes showed no apprehension, only curiosity.

"Yes?" She stood behind the closed screen door.

"I'm sorry to trouble you, miss," he said, smiling, "but I've developed some car trouble. I'm from Chicago and I notice you folks don't believe in telephone booths out here. I was wondering if you might be so kind as to call the local garage for me. In these times, I know you wouldn't expect folks to let you in their homes, but if you'd make the call for me, I would be ever so grateful."

She smiled widely. "It's different here in Niles. This isn't Chicago, we trust people around here." She unlatched the screen door and held it open for him. "Come in and make your own telephone call."

"Well, this certainly is different than Chicago! Thank you." He stepped by her, the rising excitement within him making it almost difficult to move. He could smell the fresh scent of soap. "Which way?"

"Come on, I'll show you." She bounded past him and he watched her buttocks and thighs move as she stepped up the few stairs into the kitchen.

He followed her, his eyes half-closed with pleasant anticipation.

"There," she pointed, "just above the table. There's several garages in Niles. We use Harry's. That's his number on the corkboard just above the telephone."

"You're sure I'm not disturbing anyone."

"No." She was about to add that she was alone but she noticed his eyes for the first time and thought better of telling him anything more.

"Well then, Harry's it is." He picked up the receiver. "This isn't one of those telephones where you tell the operator the number, is it?"

She laughed, relieved that he was making the call. "No, we're quite modern here. You just dial the number."

"That's good." He gripped the receiver tightly and snapped hard. The cord parted and the telephone fell to the linoleum with a loud crash.

"Why did you . . ." Her question faded and she turned to run for the side door, but he was on her before she could escape.

"Please don't." She was surprised at the calmness of her own voice. "Please!"

She struggled against him and felt his large hand roughly grip her breast. She tried to bite his arm but he jerked her head back by her hair. His hand kept digging and twisting into her breast and the pain made her cry out. She was aware of his rapid breathing and his almost feminine giggle as the pain seemed to spread through her entire body.

* * *

Teague felt pleasantly tired. It had been one of the best. He busied himself cleaning off all traces of blood from himself. It was getting late and he didn't want to encounter the woman's husband or family, although he found himself half tempted to wait and see their reaction when they found the severed head staring at them from the kitchen table. He decided to let well enough alone. He left the quiet house and walked to his car. He flipped down the hood and started the engine. He lit a cigarette and started his journey back to Chicago, tired but relaxed.

4

Russo sipped the tepid coffee from a paper cup. The liquid had picked up the chalky taste of its cardboard container, but he failed to notice; he was engrossed in the reports.

It had begun only because of a vague interest in the bizarre killing in Kokomo, Indiana, but after reading the details of the police report and the autopsy findings, Russo had sent around the country for recent reports of similar crimes. He had called Marie and told her he would be working late. She had invited him over for coffee when he was through, and they both understood the invitation was for more than coffee.

Although he would have preferred to be with her, his curiosity impelled him to follow out his lunch. Rosinski worked along with him, but only because he had nothing better to do and he thought he might learn something from the older detective.

Russo studied his partner for a moment. Joe Rosinski was in his early thirties. A young man, only five foot eight inches tall—short by police department standards—Rosinski was built like a fire hydrant: squat, hard, and made to last. His face was dominated by a square jaw, mashed nose, and Slavic cheekbones. His soft brown eyes, always friendly, revealed a quick intelligence. His hair, light brown and naturally curly, always flopped

down just over one eye. He was a good policeman and
Russo had come to like him very much.

Typed reports of murders together with some yellow
teletype follow-ups littered Russo's desk. As a gory tribute to the manic perversity of man they constituted a for-
midable pile of paper. Russo had spent the better part of
the day poring over the information, making lists with
notations as to the manner of death and details of the
autopsy findings.

"You know this stuff isn't even our job, don't you?"
Rosinski asked.

"Huh?" Russo's voice was distant and uninterested.

"I said this garbage," he gestured at the reports, "isn't
even in our ballpark, Lieutenant. We're not the FBI, you
know; we're what they call *local* police."

Russo paid no attention, his brow deeply furrowed.
"Did you check on Edward Teague, like I asked?"

"I already told you. He's a patient in the state hospital.
I talked to the records department. They've still got him.
He's safe."

"By phone?"

"Well, yes, by phone. Jesus, did you expect me to fly?
It's a hundred miles away."

Russo sat silently, staring out of the window, as if he
had not heard Rosinski's reply. He picked up his note
pad and studied it. "I think Teague is out," he said softly.
"And judging from the savage pathological pattern of
these murders I think he is systematically killing women.
I think he's out and back in business."

"Jesus, Tony, Teague doesn't hold a patent on being
nuts. There are a million loonies out there. It could be
any one of them or more; it doesn't mean Teague's committing these murders."

"Maybe not, but somebody is doing a perfect imitation, if it isn't him." Russo's face was troubled as he looked at his partner. "Besides, whoever it is, is spelling out the word *stalking* by using the first initial of the town where he selects his victims."

"Aw, come on!"

"I'm serious. I've gone over all these reports a dozen times. Each one is a report of a savage attack on a woman, right? Okay, I discarded all those where the killer is known—a boyfriend, husband, or pimp—that sort of thing. Then I took as a common denominator the sadistic way death was inflicted. That was Teague's old trademark. There was a sprinkling over on the West Coast and other places, but there's been a recent rash of such killings here in the Midwest. I took them in order of time and here's how I have it figured.

"In the first week of March they find a hooker named Vicky Drake in her apartment in St. Louis. She was beaten both before and after she died. There was nothing much left of her but jelly. That gives us our *S*."

"If you're right," Rosinski said.

Russo consulted his pad. "The last week in March Mildred S. Evans is killed. Her frozen body is found in a railroad car in Kansas City but she was killed in Toledo. She had an arrest record as a prostitute in Toledo. The medical examiner says she too was beaten after death. He describes the killer as being in a frenzy. That was a word they used in some of Teague's previous killings. And that gives us the letter *T*.

"About a week later, in April, a go-go dancer named Marilyn Rogers is stomped to death in a park in Akron. Almost every bone in her body had been fractured. The medical examiner there thought it was the work of a madman. That counts as our *A*."

Rosinski shook his head. "There were other murders around that time too."

"Yes," Russo agreed, "but not this kind. Like I said, I picked only the savage attacks upon women as the guide. In Louisville, Kentucky, in mid-April they find a hooker with her neck broken. That killed her, but someone kept on kicking her, caving in her ribs and breaking her arm. That's the kind of killing I'm talking about and that gives us our *L*.

"Of course, the girl in Kokomo is found nailed inside the barn in late April. She was tortured, then killed, right? Remember, that was the killing that started this whole thing off. It sounded just like my friend, and it spells out the letter *K*."

"I remember the autopsy report on her," Rosinski said. "Bad, man, real bad."

"Right. The only letter I'm not absolutely sure about is the *I*. They did have a prostitute murdered in Indianapolis along with a pair of vice squad cops. There was no identification of the killer except that he was big. Teague is big, but that description covers probably twenty percent of the males in this country, I suppose. So I'm not absolutely sure about the *I*.

"Now we get to the woman killed in Niles. That's a real Teague touch, leaving her head on the kitchen table. Same pattern—torture, death and continued punishment even after death. That's the *N*.

"So that's it, Rosinski. These murders are happening in a time progression, in roughly the same area of the country, and they are arranged to spell out the word *stalking*, although he hasn't selected the *G* victim yet."

Rosinski shook his head. "I think maybe you have some kind of fixation about this Teague guy, Lieutenant. Even screwballs don't go around spelling out their name in bodies. It's just a coincidence, if it's even that. Hell, you said you weren't sure about the killing in Indianapolis. If you're wrong about that one then your whole theory fails, if you see what I mean?"

Russo stared at his pad. "I realize that," he said, "but I have a real gut hunch about all this. Look, I practically had to crawl inside the guy's head the first time I collared him. He may be a psychopath, but he is not restricted by his illness. The doctors may be right and he may be insane, but he can think he's clever."

"Yeah, but if he's smart he wouldn't go around advertising by spelling out his name. That's not smart, no matter how you cut it."

"Edward Teague may be mad but he is a complete egotist. That was the key to catching him the first time. He believes he is invincible, at least when he has Knapp to defend him. This is just the sort of thing he would do—spelling out his name in murders—he would consider it a fine joke, a demonstration of his superiority."

"What's all this about Knapp?"

"Thomas Knapp defended Edward Teague after I arrested him. I'm not exactly wild about Knapp but I have to admit he did a good job." Russo leaned back in his chair, his expression thoughtful. "It was a close case at best. We had to connect Teague with all the assaults and killings. The surviving witnesses were so scared they couldn't positively identify Teague. I had a confession from Teague, but even I had to admit I tricked him into it. Like I said, the man is a supreme egotist. I kept pretending that he didn't have the ability to kill the victims.

He blew up and screamed at me that he'd done it, although I had not informed him of his constitutional rights at the time, so there was some question as to whether we could have used the confession.'' Russo paused. ''You know, I've always thought that Knapp might have had a better chance if he had tried to get him off by claiming we had the wrong man, but he went the insanity route instead.''

Russo stood up and stretched. ''Knapp changed the law on insanity with that case. The old rule was that a man was responsible for his acts if he knew the difference between right and wrong. Now, all you need to show is substantial disorder of thought or mood that significantly impairs judgment. Teague damn well knew the difference between right and wrong, but he had a psychotic hatred of women and an overwhelming desire to inflict pain and death upon them. The defense doctors at the trial said this was a substantial disorder of thought which impaired his judgment. Knapp convinced the jury that Teague was insane, and later, the State Supreme Court.'' He looked out the window. ''I don't know, maybe they're right, maybe Teague is insane, but he certainly knows what's happening and his reasoning is as sharp as a razor. Anyway, Knapp got him off by reason of insanity and they put Teague away in the state hospital.''

''And Teague appreciated what the lawyer did for him, eh?''

'' 'Appreciate' is sort of a weak word. He saw Knapp as some kind of protecting god. I guess he felt no harm could come to him if Knapp was looking out for him.'' Russo smiled wryly at the memory. ''The doctors tell me that he had a fixation about me too. Because I nailed him he thought I had some kind of super power. He thinks that he's a genius and I suppose if you think that way it stands to reason that only a person with some amazing super power could bring you down." Russo sighed. "Unfortunately, only Teague and myself know that to be true."

Rosinski took the pad and studied Russo's notes, shaking his head silently as he read. He looked up. "When I called the hospital I just asked if Edward Teague was still a patient there. I was passed along to a supervisor. We had a little spat about identification, but she finally told me that Teague was still a patient there. She said she checked it on the master roster they keep."

"A lot of loonies have walked away from those places before."

"Wouldn't they have made some kind of notation, if that had happened, I mean?"

Russo took back the pad and picked up the reports. He stacked them neatly in a desk drawer and then locked it. "You're asking me for a supposition. We aren't in the business of making suppositions. We deal only in facts. I'll take a run out to the state hospital and see for myself."

"That's a hundred miles. Hell, none of these killings are even our cases. Won't the skipper be sore?"

"I'll clear it with him. He should be interested. He remembers the Stalking Man."

Rosinski shook his head. "Christ, if you're right, I'd hate to be some broad living in a city starting with *G*."

Russo slipped into his suit coat. It was late and he remembered that Marie was waiting for him. "Well, that proves they're all wrong."

"What do you mean?"

"They say Polacks drop their *g*s, but, hell, you didn't.

You knew right off that *stalking* ended with a *g*.''

"I'm glad you're my boss so that I'm prevented from telling you to go screw yourself.''

"Screwing myself is not exactly what I planned for tonight. It's close; the verb is correct, but I have another object in mind.''

Rosinski laughed as they walked out of the homicide room together.

* * *

The Winkler case had caused a public furor. In the state legislature, members—who knew a good thing when they saw it—introduced a storm of bills, all aimed at closing the loopholes in the insanity laws.

Dr. Winkler, despite having killed his wife, had escaped all penalty. He was insane, said the criminal court jury; therefore, he escaped prison. He was sane, declared the doctors at the state civil hearing, and thus he avoided the confines of a mental institution. The public hue and cry forced the local medical association to examine his license to practice medicine. But it was privately admitted that they could do nothing, since he had legally committed no crime and had been declared to be legally competent. Thus, he also escaped any professional censure. It was as if Mrs. Winkler had passed away peacefully in her sleep.

It bothered Thomas Knapp.

The newspaper story about the girl in Kokomo bothered Knapp.

The newspaper story about the girl in Niles bothered Knapp.

His mind was haunted by dark questions. He dialed the

number of the State Center for Forensic Medicine and asked for Dr. Rose. The switchboard referred him to the doctor's secretary.

"Dr. Rose's office." Her voice was crisp and cold and indicated that she was all business.

"Dr. Rose, please."

"Dr. Rose is busy," she said, as if he should have known that without her having to tell him.

"My name is Knapp," he said. "Thomas Knapp, and I'd like to talk to the doctor."

"You are a patient?" It was more a statement than a question.

"No, even worse than that, I'm a lawyer. Dr. Rose testified on behalf of a client of mine and I have a few questions."

There was an icy silence. "Just a moment." He could sense her disapproval. The line went dead as she put him on hold.

He waited. He wondered if she was making a good faith attempt to locate the doctor or if she was just ignoring him.

He was beginning to lose patience when the familiar, slightly accented voice of Dr. Rose came on the line. "Mr. Knapp," he said irritably, "what is it that you want? I'm in the midst of a group therapy session."

"Doctor, I'll be brief. Is Edward Teague living in Niles or Kokomo, or anywhere in that general area?"

"Why do you ask?" Rose's voice was suddenly defensive.

"I don't know if you've noticed the stories or not, but a young girl was nailed inside a barn in Kokomo, and another was beheaded in Niles. Both women were beaten after death. You may remember, that was how the Stalking Man used to do it. I wondered if it might be possible that Edward Teague had become ill again.''

''I shouldn't even talk to you.'' The doctor was angry. ''I was right, you are not Edward's friend and you certainly aren't interested in his welfare. But to show you that you're wrong again, Edward lives nowhere near Niles or Kokomo. Just as before, you are inferring that he is a dangerous man, when he is not!''

The line went dead. The doctor had hung up.

Knapp replaced the receiver and leaned back in his chair. Perhaps he was being foolish. If society had decided to leave Edward Teague alone, so should he. He could visualize Teague's smiling face, his clear blue eyes, and the frightening madness that Knapp felt lurked behind them. It was no longer any of his business. Yet, did he still have some responsibility? He remembered the concern of the law student: What do you do if you feel your client has fooled the doctors?

Was there a continuing responsibility?

Which duty was greater? His duty to his client or to society?

Thomas Knapp was deeply troubled.

*   *   *

Dr. Rose sped along the country road. He drove mechanically, his mind busy with other things, disturbing things.

He turned into his long driveway and slowly passed between the narrow border of towering elm trees. It was Wednesday, his housekeeper's day off, and he would have to prepare his own dinner, and even this inconvenience failed to occupy his thoughts. He was satisfied to be home; it had been a disquieting day and he felt the need for quiet and solitude.

He parked his car in the attached garage—a structure he had ordered built as soon as they had moved into the renovated farmhouse as a protection for his beloved sports car. The house in the country had been her idea. He stepped into the kitchen and listened to the echo of his movements in the empty house.

Some men, he knew, equated divorce with death, fearing the void of loneliness, but he had welcomed it as a release from the prison of a neurotic wife and two eternally noisy children. He was still saddled with his two sons for several weeks every summer. He recognized that it was important to their egos to have contact with their father. Nevertheless, he found it distasteful. He planned to sever the connection as soon as conveniently possible.

Munching on a few crackers Dr. Rose prepared his nightly drink. At medical school he had been instructed to eat when consuming alcohol, as a hedge against liver disease, and he had faithfully followed that advice all his life. He allowed himself only one drink a night but he made a minor ritual of its preparation. Wednesday was martini night, and he stirred very gently as he measured out the gin and vermouth. He was as careful as a scientist working with explosives. He topped it off with a chilled olive and an ice cube.

He kicked off his shoes and walked into the soft carpeting of the dining room. The house was much too large for one man; but he liked the feeling of space, and his housekeeper was wise enough to do a good job caring for it and to stay out his way at the same time. He seldom had any contact with the woman and he preferred it that way. He padded across the long living room, looking at himself in the wall mirror. A vain man by nature, he liked the image in the glass: a small, lean man, a man with piercing eyes and a sure intelligence.

The den had always been his special place. No one was ever allowed here, not even Mrs. Williams, his housekeeper. It was a jumble of books and notes, all strewn about, covering the desk and leather sofa. His bookcases contained his lifeblood, tomes covering every aspect of the human mind, case histories of the most bizarre and interesting human behavior, a feast for the questing intellect. In the entire house it was the most comfortable place for him.

He savored a sip of the martini and then put the glass down on an uncovered spot on the desk. He removed his key ring from his pocket and inserted it into the lock on his old-fashioned steel file cabinet. The second drawer held his special secret file. Flipping through the entries, he stopped when he found the telephone number. Although he had a good memory for numbers, he jotted it down just to be sure. Then he relocked the file, returned to his drink, and sat in the high-back chair behind the desk. He sipped again, feeling the tension begin to slip away. This was his special world and he felt happy and secure. He picked up the telephone and dialed the long-distance number direct.

"Hello?" He instantly recognized her voice.

"Hello, Irene," he said pleasantly. "This is Dr. Rose. How have you been?"

"Dr. Rose?"

"Yes, my dear, just calling a few old friends to see how they are getting along."

"Oh. We're fine, Doctor. All of us are just fine."

The quickness of her reply seemed defensive. He supposed it was the surprise of his call, and realized that the sound of his voice was probably a memory bridge to her bitter past.

"How's your son?"

"Fine," she said. "We're all fine."

"Is Edward there?"

"Just a minute." He thought he detected just a hint of fear in the tone of her voice. He wondered if it might not be his imagination. Knapp's call had filled his mind with apprehension and concern over the welfare of his prize patient.

Prize patient—he was surprised that he thought of Edward Teague in that way, although he admitted to himself that he was extremely proud of his achievement. They had brought Teague to him, a mentally ruined man, a vulnerable human being who bore the brand of a woman-hating killer. But he had devoted intense work to the case and it had been well worth the effort. He had produced a healthy, well-balanced man who coped with his problems and now blended in society, a man who was capable and happy. It was as if Rose had raised a sunken wreck and turned it back into a beautiful sailing ship. Teague was indeed a prize patient.

"Hello," Teague answered the telephone.

"Edward, this is Carl Rose. How are you?"

"Just fine, Doctor," Teague answered. His voice sounded relaxed, even pleased.

"Irene says the family is good," Rose said. "How's the job going?"

"Couldn't be better. I'm making over eight dollars an hour. How about that?"

"Terrific. They must think highly of you."

"I guess they do. Anyway, I'm happy and they're

happy. I guess that's what counts, eh, Doc?''

"Sounds right, Edward.''

"Are you checking up on me?'' The words were spoken pleasantly without suspicion or resentment. "Because if you are, you have just wasted a long-distance telephone call. Everything's just swell.''

"How about Irene? Any problems there?''

Teague paused for a moment before replying. "Well, once in a while. You know how she is, she forgets her medicine or something gets on her nerves. She has her ups and downs, but she bounces back pretty quick. All in all, things have been working out pretty well.''

Rose concluded that the fear he thought he heard in Irene's voice was really just the manifestation of one of her minor emotional episodes and that he'd been mistaken. He was reassured. "Edward, how are you fixed for medicines? I notice I haven't renewed your prescriptions for some time.''

"I'm in good shape, Doc. I still have about a half bottle of those little green capsules. I take them when I get a little shaky. They calm me right down. And I have a good supply of everything else. Like I said, things are really perking along in great shape.''

"That's what I like to hear, Edward.''

"Say, what prompted you to call? Has somebody been asking about me?'' This time there was a restrained anxiety in the question.

"Nothing like that, Edward. I happened to have testified for a client of Mr. Knapp's the other day and he asked about you. I made a mental note to see how you were doing.''

"He asked about me?''

"Yes.''

"Did he say why?"

"No. It just came up in our conversation. The police officer in charge of the case was that policeman who arrested you."

"Jesus." The word was almost a whisper.

"Now, there is nothing to worry about, Edward. It was just a coincidence and Knapp brought your name up."

Again there was a pause before Teague spoke. "Did you tell him where I was?" Anxiety had become fear.

Dr. Rose laughed to reassure him. "Of course not, Edward. Your address, your new name and life are known only to me. As I told you before, you are completely safe and secure. Edward Teague has disappeared forever. You have nothing to worry about."

"But if he checks with the hospital?"

"There would be no reason for him to do that. But even if he did, I have taken great pains to see that no information about your new situation exists at the hospital. Of course, the record of your admission is there and you are carried on the books officially as an in-patient. Even the fact of your leave is not carried on the mail register. All details of your case are in my possession."

"Doctor, I know this sounds ungrateful, but are you sure?"

Rose saw nothing inappropriate about the concern. A mere oversight or clerical error might expose Teague's new life, and exposure could mean ruin and possible arrest by the authorities.

"Edward, please believe me, I have removed all references to your present situation from the hospital files. I keep them all here at my home under lock and key, and even then I have coded them. You have nothing to fear."

"But Knapp . . ."

"Edward, there you go again," Rose chuckled. "How many times have I told you, Thomas is just another attorney, he goes to court to represent people for money, that's all. He has no special interest in you. You don't want your old delusion to get a grip on you again, do you?"

"You mean about Knapp being like God?"

"But he isn't, Edward. He is just an ordinary man who passed through your life, that is all. Just the same as that detective, Russo. Just men. They have no special powers. You're completely secure."

"I know why Knapp asked about me."

"What do you mean?"

"He saw that story about the poor woman in Kokomo."

"What woman?"

"A while back the newspapers carried a story about some poor thing who had been beaten to death in Indiana. She was nailed to a barn wall, at least according to the newspaper. I suppose Knapp thought of me when he saw that story."

"Do you think you killed the woman in Kokomo?" Rose was suddenly tense, recalling that his patient could not remember whether he killed when he had first been brought to the state hospital.

"Hell, no," came the cheerful reply. "Don't worry, Carl, I haven't flipped my wig. I know what I do and what I don't do. My biggest sin is having a few too many beers on Friday night. That's about as wild as I get nowadays."

"I'm glad to hear that, Edward."

"If you say so, I'll even give up worrying about Knapp and Russo."

Dr. Rose chuckled. "That's a deal. I say so."

"Then it's done. Say, when are you going to come out and visit us? I think you'll be surprised at the way the kid has grown."

"I know I will. As usual, I've been working long hours at the hospital, Edward, but I do owe myself a little vacation time. Perhaps in a month or two I might drop by. I'll call and give you advance warning, of course."

"Don't worry about that. Drop everything and come as you are. We would all love to see you."

"Fine. I'll be in touch."

"I look forward to seeing you, Carl."

Dr. Rose hung up. He sat quietly and sipped the last of his drink, savoring the taste of the liquor as he savored the satisfaction of a job done. The human hulk he had salvaged was still sailing beautifully; Edward Teague was a model citizen, with a good family and a good job. Teague was consummate proof of Rose's skill; a living tribute, a true triumph.

*   *   *

The car radio played softly as they sped over the interstate highway, leaving the city and its traffic congestion far behind.

"You're brooding," she said, changing her position so that she faced him.

"Maybe." Russo's face, which had been somber, slowly loosened into a grin. "I still hate to admit that Rosinski was right. He predicted that the chief wouldn't be interested in old Edward Teague."

"Are you brooding because your boss wouldn't buy

your theory, or because your partner—younger but not nearly as smart—was right?''

''What difference does it make?''

''Oh, quite a difference. It might tell me just what kind of a man you really are.''

''For instance?''

Her eyes sparkled mischievously. ''Well, if you're brooding because your boss shot your pet idea down it may be because you are mad for power and depressed to find out that you aren't the godlike creature you thought you were.''

''Suppose it's just because I feel a small obligation to stop a killer?''

''Don't interrupt the doctor.''

''Sorry.''

She continued. ''Now, on the other hand, if you are brooding because the younger officer who works with you had the correct assessment of the situation in place of your rather blundering conception, it may mean that you are insecure and need a mother rather than a partner. Now which is it? Are you power mad or desperately insecure?''

''You forgot sexual frustration,'' Russo said.

She giggled and moved closer to him, her hand softly caressing his right thigh. ''Imagine that, the very first thing they taught us in psychiatry, and I forgot it. Of course, that's the answer, isn't it? You are sexually frustrated.'' Her hand slowly crept up his leg.

''And we'll be curled around a tree if you don't cut that out.''

''There are no trees nearby.'' Her voice was low and she moved her lips close to his ear as she spoke.

"Come on, Marie. I can't stand that, at least not when I'm driving."

"Okay," she said brightly. "I'll be good." She withdrew her hand but remained close to him. "That is, if you stop brooding and talk to me."

As usual, the contact with her had aroused him. No other woman he had ever known had been so provocative. He wondered if his fiery instincts had anything to do with age. A candle burns brightest, he reminded himself, just before it flutters out. But she was right, he was brooding about the whole situation. Maybe if he talked it out it would help. She always seemed so interested in what he was thinking.

"I don't mind the chief turning down my request to make this trip on city time, we are overloaded with the cases we already have, but what bothers me most is his attitude about the whole thing."

"What do you mean?"

Russo sighed. "Apathy isn't quite the word to describe it, but it comes close. Hell, Edward Teague may be loose and killing women right and left but the fact that he has been certified as insane seems to give him some sort of license. The chief is no fool. For my benefit, he speculated on just what might happen if we really went to work and caught Teague, if these killings are actually his work. He described what would probably happen. Teague would be arrested and found not guilty by reason of insanity again—that's practically guaranteed since he has already been declared legally insane—and afterwards he would be sent back to some state mental hospital where he would be able to talk himself into a trusty position, or even get leave, and go right back to his old habits. The problem with the chief's thinking is that he's right. That's exactly what would happen. Oh, maybe the publicity might be so strong that not even the nuttiest doctor would dare put Teague on the streets again, but even that isn't sure. The chief treated the whole matter as if Teague was just some sort of nuisance that society had to learn to live with.''

''Did he go along with your theory that the man is on the loose and spelling out his name in cities?''

Tony Russo laughed. ''Let's say that he had a few kind words about what overwork could do to an otherwise sound mind. He was kidding, but just beneath the surface I could sense that he was beginning to worry about me.''

''So you took your day off to run around on your own and drive up to the state hospital.''

''Yes, and because Rosinski declined the pleasure of my company, I asked you.''

''I was second choice?''

''I don't know if you've noticed, but that Polack has a really cute ass on him.''

''I see I have the whole world for a rival.''

''No, not the whole world, just women and male Polacks with nice asses.''

''That's comforting, Lieutenant, at least I can feel relaxed if you are around Polish men whose bottoms don't measure up to your exacting specifications.''

He didn't continue the banter and his face suddenly became serious. ''You know, Marie, it may be that I've built up just a screwball theory. Teague may be safely locked away and some other looney, or looneys, may be doing the killings and have no idea of spelling out *stalking* or any other word.''

''That's a possibility.''

''What do you honestly think?'' He looked over at her.

She studied his face for a moment before replying. "I can't give you an opinion on the facts, I really don't know all the facts, but I do know you and I know your reputation in the department. You aren't the type who lets his imagination run wild. I admire your mind and the way it works. So that's where I have to place my bet—on you. I don't know about Edward Teague, or very much about police work, or insanity, but I do know Tony Russo. I don't think you're ever very far off the mark."

He smiled. "I'm flattered."

"I didn't say it to flatter you. I don't know about this 'Stalking Man' business, but I do know you, at least I think I do. I believe in you, Tony."

The tires hummed on the concrete as they sped past the flat farmlands. He was silent for a few moments. "Hey, you want to know something?" His voice was a bit softer than usual.

"What's that?"

"It's been a long time since anyone has believed in me. I mean, like you just said."

Suddenly it was as if the interior of the car had become acutely sensitive. A deep awareness had been established between them, almost without warning. They both sensed it. She was almost afraid to speak, as if speech might somehow disturb the mood, but she felt she had to say something.

"What I said was true." Her words were spoken slowly and softly.

Russo was afraid that he might say or do something that would somehow destroy the sudden silent bond between them. He was surprised at his own reaction.

"Thanks, Marie."

Keeping his eyes on the road, Russo reached across

and took her hand. She moved closer to him and he was conscious of the soft press of her hip and the scent of her perfumed hair. Very gently, she laid her head on his shoulder.

He forgot their reason for being on the highway, he forgot everything. It was as if they were suspended in time and place, as if their trip was a pleasant dream that would last forever. He only knew that she was next to him.

The large highway marker came up and broke the dream. The next exit led to the state hospital. The dream fell away like smoke in a breeze. "We'll be there soon," he said, nodding at the sign.

She lifted her head and studied the sign as if it had some kind of special interest. It too had lifted her from her dream. "How far is the hospital?"

"About five miles north of the exit."

"How long do you expect to be there?"

He shrugged. "It depends. If they have let Teague go, I'll have to dig to get that fact out of them. That'll take a while. Of course, if Teague is still at the place, they'll just show him to me and it will only take a few minutes."

"And knock hell out of your theory."

"I'll say."

"So hope for a long session?"

He glanced over at her. "Long, short—it really doesn't matter to me."

"I'm the one who'll have to wait. It matters to me."

Russo tried to read her mood. "Remember, Marie, I told you that this might be a drag for you. I love having you along, but I think you were given fair warning, right?"

"I'm anxious, that's all."

"Anxious?"

"As soon as you finish with this hospital business I'm going to talk you into driving to a nice cozy motel where we can spend the rest of the day and night in delightful sin."

"As nice as that sounds and despite the fact it is my day off, I am still trying to do a job. Suggestions like yours don't help my concentration very much."

She touched his leg again. "I've some money, if that's the problem."

"That's not the problem." He started to laugh.

"What's so funny?"

"Just the idea of the thing, I guess. Hell, I haven't had a lady pay for the room in twenty years. You sure can boost an old man's ego."

Her eyebrows jutted up. "What was she like?"

"Who?"

"The lady who paid for the room."

He swung the car up the exit ramp. "I can't remember."

"Was she older than you?"

He waited until traffic cleared and then he turned right onto the two-lane highway leading to the state hospital. "As a matter of fact, she was older. She was, I think, an old crow of thirty-two or so, married, sexy, and very hot for my tender young body. At least that's the way I recall it."

"Did it bother you at the time, her paying for the room, I mean?"

He shook his head. "To tell you the truth, I thought it was very cool, like I was some kind of sex machine— available but expensive." He laughed. "Now you know what I would have become if I had been born a girl."

"Well, can we?"

"Can we what?"

"Stop at a motel on the way back?"

He sighed. "You have an apartment and I have an apartment. Why can't we just drive back to town and pick your place or mine?"

"It's not sexy."

"I think it is."

She laughed, characteristically throwing her head back and exposing the sensuous curve of her neck and throat. "You would think anyplace was sexy. I think stopping at a motel smacks of sin and sneaking around."

"And you like sin and sneaking around."

"With you. Yes."

"Okay, if it means that much to you. We'll find a little hot-pillow joint and fool around."

She squeezed his leg as she kissed his cheek.

"There it is," he said.

She looked up and saw the cluster of ancient redbrick buildings dotting the top of a hill in the distance. "My God, it looks like something out of Dickens!"

"Yeah, it's a very depressing place."

"I'll just keep my mind on what we'll be doing later."

"If they let me out."

"If they don't, I can probably pick up some young doctor."

"In that case, I'll get out even if I have to escape over the wall." He laughed and she grinned up at him. His concern about Edward Teague had been momentarily eased.

* * *

Dr. Rose snorted irritably as he worked the gearshift of his sports car, executing a skidding turn into the tree-lined drive leading to his home.

He had always resented police. They were small-minded men; like ferrets they were sniffing, suspicious creatures, forever interfering in his work. Russo was the worst, at least in Dr. Rose's mind. That square-faced detective always kept coming on, challenging and danger-ous. Rose resented having to be subjected to the man's relentless questions.

He braked the car, spraying white gravel from beneath its locked wheels. It was late and he knew that his house-keeper, Mrs. Williams, had gone. She lived in the village and usually left by the time he arrived home, leaving a warm supper in the oven and the large house spotlessly clean. It was an ideal arrangement for Dr. Rose. People got in the way of his work.

The car was tucked away in the garage. It was a low-slung, German-made model, racy and expensive. He rec-ognized the hidden meaning as a phallic symbol but wanted the car despite the obvious overtones. It was his private reward for attaining success. As a boy he'd al-ways wanted such a car, and now he had it.

The red light on the kitchen stove indicated that a meal was being kept heated, and the aroma filled the attractive kitchen. He was hungry, remembering he had forgotten to eat lunch. That damn cop had upset him so much that he had forgotten. He knew that part of his raging emo-tions was due to his falling blood sugar level, but that could be cured easily enough.

The nightly ritual of preparing his one drink was be-gun. He felt he deserved a strong one, tonight a Black Russian. He carefully measured out two shot glasses of vodka and one of thick, sugar-filled Mexican brandy. The sugar in the brandy would satisfy the needs of his system. Dr. Rose kicked off his shoes and padded through the house to his den.

He wiggled past a dangerously leaning column of books and sat down on the leather swivel chair, and began his ritual. He relaxed himself and fixed his eyes on a small flaw in the ceiling's paint, the spot he used for self-hypnosis. He concentrated on the spot, allowing his mind to go completely blank. Mentally he recited the now familiar litany to himself, a singsong of reassurance and relaxation. The same system he used on his patients for hypnosis. The spot began to take on a light of its own— he recognized the beginning of the familiar hallucination—and as he repeated the litany he felt his eyelids flutter and close. Quickly, he slipped into a deep trance, alone with only the sensation of his mind communicating to him, no other feelings or sensations. It should have been eerie, but somehow he always found it profoundly comforting. He told himself that when he came out of the trance he would be relaxed and refreshed, just as if he had had a full night's sleep. It always worked. It was the answer to his awesome ability to work long hours. For a few moments he allowed himself the peace of the trance sensation, then he reluctantly awakened himself.

He was always a bit surprised at how well it worked. Worry and anxiety had vanished and he was relaxed with a feeling of new energy. Taking another sip of his drink, he then got the card file he kept locked in the steel cabinet, and returned to the desk.

These were all his special patients, people whom he had restored to useful places in society. Technically most of them were still carried as inmates of the state hospital, but he had released them, keeping a watch to insure their continued mental health. Sadly, now and then, he would have to return one of his treasures, but most of them made it. He was proud of these men and women. But he also realized what a valuable tool his list might be to a blackmailer, so he had devised a code to protect them.

It was a simple code. Carolyn Pointer, the girl who had killed her parents, was a housewife in California now. Her code name—suitable for a pointer—was "Arrow." He had home addresses and telephone numbers on each card.

He flipped through to "Celery." The code name had come as an afterthought. They called Edward Teague the Stalking Man, so he had used the root word *stalk* as his inspiration for the code name "Celery."

Dr. Rose had removed from the hospital all reference to the new lives led by these patients. Only his small card file recorded their present whereabouts. He felt so relaxed from the hypnosis and the drink that he was reluctant to put the effort into telephoning. He debated eating dinner first but decided he would eat later.

He dialed the number.

He recognized Irene's voice.

"Hello, Irene. This is Carl Rose again."

"Dr. Rose?" Again he thought he sensed fear in her voice.

"Now, do you know any other Carl Roses, Irene?" He tried to make it sound lighthearted, but somehow he failed.

"Edward's not here," she said quickly.

"Maybe I wasn't calling Edward," he laughed. But there was no response at the other end of the line. "As a matter of fact, I did wish to speak to Edward. When will he be home?''

''Not for a few days.'' The answer came in clipped, anxious words.

''Is he all right?''

''Yes.'' The word had a tentative sound as if she wanted to say more.

''Is something wrong, Irene? Is there something about Edward that I should know?''

For a moment he wondered if she was still on the line, then she spoke, her voice barely audible. ''I think he's getting sick again.''

''Why do you say that?'' His voice reflected his defensive pride in his prize patient.

''Just a feeling I have,'' she said.

''Well, I'm sure you're wrong,'' he replied. ''He sounded just fine the other day when I called. Maybe you're the one having the problem, Irene. Did you ever think of that?''

She paused again before replying. ''I've been taking my medicine.''

''Well, sometimes medicines need changing. Have you been hearing the voices again, Irene?''

''No, nothing like that.''

''Well, tell me why you feel Edward might be getting sick again?'' The question was challenging, although he had not intended it to sound that way.

''I'm wrong,'' she said quickly. ''It's just that I've been very tired lately.''

''Please, Irene, tell me what you feel. Perhaps just talking it out for a few minutes will help.''

''No.'' She said the word listlessly. ''Nothing will help. Edward's gone on a trip. He said he wouldn't be home for a few days. It's a business trip, that's what he told me.''

"Maybe you think the trip isn't for business. Sometimes, Irene, we let suspicious thoughts creep into our minds. I'm sure Edward is . . .'' She quietly hung up the telephone.

He drained the last of his drink and thought about the telephone call. He would have to contact Edward. Irene sounded as if she were slipping back into a paranoid episode. It would be good to catch it in the bud if they could.

Rose played with the ice cubes, swishing them around in the glass as he mentally reviewed the day and the disturbing visit from Detective Lieutenant Russo. They would never let up. It angered him again when he thought of the single-mindedness of that policeman.

He remembered that he meant to pick up the cleaning he'd left in town. He fingered through his telephone book, then picked up the telephone to call and see if the cleaner was still open. There was no dial tone, no sound at all. He clicked the telephone buttons but nothing happened. The line was dead.

He slammed the receiver down in irritation. Country life had its advantages but the damn rural utilities were deplorable. He presumed that some farmer had backed his tractor over a trunk line and he would be without telephone service until the break was discovered.

Frustrated, Rose swore quietly to himself as he returned to the kitchen. Once again the delicious aroma awakened his appetite and he went to the cabinets over the sink for a dish. As he reached up for the dish he became aware that he was not alone.

A shiver of fear ran through him as he turned to face

the silent figure standing in the darkened dining room alcove.

"Who . . ."

A chuckle greeted his word. "You were trying to get in touch with me. I'd call that service." Edward Teague stepped into the kitchen, a friendly grin fixed on his handsome features.

"Edward, what does this mean?"

Teague laughed. "First things first. Why did you want to talk to me?" His right hand was concealed casually behind his back.

"I wanted to . . . to see how you were." Rose recovered from his spontaneous fright. There was no reason to suppose that Teague intended him harm, although he felt the skin-prickling sensation of danger nevertheless. Rose determined to be master of whatever developed. He had long ago learned that firmness was his best tool in handling patients.

"Edward, why didn't you knock? I would have let you in." He forced himself to speak slowly but firmly.

Teague shrugged. "I've been waiting for you, Carl. Sort of a surprise, you know? If I had just come up and knocked on the door it would have ruined the surprise, if you see what I mean?"

"It was rude, Edward. I know you didn't wish to be rude, but you should always knock before entering someone's house." Rose threw his shoulders back and stood very straight, trying to assume the authority he commanded in a hospital situation. "I am going to have dinner. Have you eaten?"

"I'm fine," Teague replied, amused at the doctor's discomfort.

"Then you won't mind if I go ahead?"

"Not at all."

Rose was determined to show no fear. He deliberately walked past Teague to get hot pads. The big man just watched him. Rose extracted the covered roasting pan from the hot oven. For an instant he was tempted to throw the steaming contents at Teague, but he still presumed that the man had come on a friendly visit, and if not, he felt he would be able to control him.

Dr. Rose placed the hot pan on top of the stove and removed the lid. A small roast of beef, garnished with baked potatoes, greeted his eyes. "Looks good, Edward. Are you sure you won't join me?"

"I'm sure."

Rose reached up to the wall rack containing the large carving knives. He felt a chill of fear as he saw that one of the knives was missing. Again he rationalized that perhaps his housekeeper had used the knife and had neglected to replace it, although he knew she was obsessively neat and that such an oversight was extremely unlikely.

He pretended not to notice and selected a short-bladed knife, carefully slicing the small roast. "What is this surprise business all about, Edward?" He asked the question in a casual way, as if he were really not particularly concerned about the answer. Teague had not changed his position near the dining room door.

"Eat first," he replied, "then we'll talk."

"As you wish." Rose placed the meat slices and one of the smaller potatoes on his plate, but all appetite had vanished. His mind raced, trying to think of a way to control his visitor, if indeed control was really needed. He assured himself that he had cured Edward Teague and he was only imagining danger.

Teague stepped aside to allow the doctor into the dining room. Rose turned on the light and set the plate on the place mat the housekeeper had laid on the shiny table. "Would you like something to drink, Edward?"

"A beer, if you've got it."

"I think I might have." He passed by Teague again and felt almost choking anxiety. He wondered how the man had entered the house and about the missing knife. He was irritated at himself for indulging his imagination.

There was some imported German beer at the rear of the refrigerator. Rose popped off the tops of two bottles and handed one to Teague as he returned to the dining room. Teague accepted the bottle with his left hand, his other hand remained behind his back.

"Sit down, Edward, please."

Teague shook his head. "I've been driving all day. It feels good to stand." His manner was still easy and relaxed.

Rose forced himself to eat, although he had no interest in the food.

"Why did you want to talk to me, Carl?" Teague asked, leaning casually against the door jamb and sipping at the beer. "I heard you on the telephone."

Rose studied him for a moment before answering. There seemed to be no threat in Teague's manner, just curiosity.

"I had a visitor today, your old friend, Detective Lieutenant Russo."

"He came to the hospital?"

Rose nodded.

"What did he want?"

Rose took a bite of the meat, trying to appear calm.

"He wanted to talk about you. In fact, he wanted to talk to you."

"So?"

"I told him the police have no further jurisdiction over your case, that it is a closed book."

"That's right," Teague agreed softly.

"However, Edward, there has been a rash of murders in the Midwest and Russo thought you might be the man committing them. It was about those killings that he wished to speak to you."

"Did he find out that I was released from the hospital?"

"At first I led him to believe you were still living there, but to show him his fears were foolish I made the point finally that you had been out for over a year on medical leave and you had not had even the slightest bit of trouble."

"Do you think that was wise?"

"Edward, you must realize what astounding progress you have made! You are one of my prime successes. You have conquered your problems, you have a fine family, and you lead a normal life. You are, my friend, a living tribute to the practice of modern psychiatry."

Teague's smile vanished. "Did you tell him where I live, or my new name?"

"Of course not. Do you really think I'd do a stupid thing like that? I know policemen, he would hound you and your family. Your very existence would be threatened. I protect my patients, Edward. You, above all others, should know that."

Concern clouded Teague's expression. "Perhaps I should contact Knapp?"

"Damn!" Rose exploded. "Look, Edward, you persist

in having some sort of fixation about that man. He is a lawyer. He defends people for money, nothing more. He is mortal and makes mistakes, just as other people do. I warned you at the hospital that you put too much confidence in his ability. He is not some kind of defending angel, in fact he is not even your friend.''

''You have no basis for that statement,'' Teague said petulantly.

Rose began to feel his confidence return, he was fast becoming master of this situation. ''You see, Edward, I have tried to protect you from many little worries when I can. I talked to your friend Knapp not over a week ago. When he found out you were released from the hospital he accused me of exceeding my authority. Your 'wonderful' lawyer thinks it is criminal that you are out in society. He is no friend to you, Edward. He is your enemy.''

His words seemed to be having an effect on Teague, so he continued. ''I know you believe he saved you from execution or life imprisonment, but that was never his intention. He wanted you locked away. I suppose he might have done a better job if he really believed in you, but all he did was arrange to substitute the hospital for jail. He was as determined as Detective Russo that you should be put away. They worked hand in hand.'' Rose felt it was a harmless lie, but persuasive. ''I hope you can now see just what he did.''

''But Knapp . . .''

Rose waved his hand to stop him. ''Please, Edward, you must realize you owe your freedom to only one man—me! If it had not been for me, my dear fellow, you would still be rotting away in the hospital. I am the only one who ever really believed in you.''

Teague's features deepened into a thoughtful frown. "You know, you might be right about Knapp at that," he said slowly. "He insisted that insanity was my only defense and ignored everything else. At the time I thought it was because he really cared. . . ." His voice trailed off for a moment. "Are you sure you're telling me the truth? I mean, that he was upset that I was out of the hospital?"

Rose held up both hands as if to proclaim his honesty. "When have I ever lied to you, Edward? Right from the first, I have told you nothing but the truth. That was part of my treatment, to have you see and recognize the truth, not only about yourself, but about the world. Truth was an extremely important part of your treatment."

"I suppose," Teague mumbled. He paused in thought for a moment. "What exactly did you tell Russo?"

"Now, Edward, you really mustn't concern yourself about these things. All this is my business. I will see that you are protected, but anxiety of this fashion can only be destructive to your mental health. You relax and let me take care of these matters."

Teague shrugged, as if in agreement, the half-smile again flickering across his features. "You have to understand how I feel, Doctor, my whole future depends on what happens now. It would be a greater worry if I didn't know what was happening, can you see that?"

Rose pursed his lips. "You might be right at that. The unknown can be the greatest fear of all. All right then, Edward, I'll tell you just what happened." Rose abandoned the rest of his dinner and pushed his plate away. He pulled a small cigar from the pack he carried in his shirt and lit it. Rose studied Teague as he puffed the cigar into life.

"Your friend, Russo, may be sick," Rose said.

"Oh, come on."

"No, I mean it. Sometimes an obsession can seize one's imagination and he can lose contact with reality, his basic judgments become distorted. I think this may be happening to your policeman friend."

"He's no friend of mine." Teague's voice was low and hostile.

"I know that, Edward, but you have become an obsession with him. I suppose your case was the biggest thing that man ever worked on. You know, he attained quite a reputation by tracking you down—as it were. Anyway, when a murder happens he apparently hopes you committed it and he can somehow relive those days of personal glory." Rose laughed. "He may end up in the hospital himself. I told him as much. He has built up quite a mad theory. He's convinced himself that you go about the countryside killing women in towns where the first initial of the city's name—when put together— would spell out the word *stalking*. Isn't that amazing?"

Teague's eyes narrowed. "He's on to it then."

"It's merely an obsession with him," Rose said, not understanding what Teague had said. "If he pushes it much further, Edward, I'm sure his superiors will see that he undergoes appropriate treatment."

"He is uncanny," Teague muttered. "It's like he knows what I'm thinking."

"Well, you certainly aren't running about spelling out *stalking* with dead bodies," Rose chuckled.

"But I am," Teague said softly, the half-smile again playing across his lips. "It's like a joke, you know. I'm doing it but they don't know it. I planned the whole thing. Eventually, I will spell out *stalking man* just the way Russo said I was doing."

"Edward, you are playing with me." Fear gripped Rose. "You can't be serious. You were never a killer, Edward, you know that."

"No, Doctor, you know that." Teague's smile remained fixed. "Or at least you convinced yourself. I'm smarter than you, Carl. Jesus! I fooled you easier than almost anyone I've ever known. I am the Stalking Man and I killed those women they tried me for, every single one of them. And I would have gotten away with it if it hadn't been for Russo. But they won't catch me this time, despite that damned cop." Teague removed his right hand from behind his back, and as Rose had feared, he held the large carving knife in a solid grip.

"Edward"—Rose fought to keep his voice calm—"I don't know what you plan, but please remember that I am your only protector. If anything happens to me, you will be alone. Russo and the rest of them will get you. Even Knapp is against you now." Rose stood up. "I am your only friend."

Teague nodded. "You know, you're probably right, Carl. You're a silly little man, but you're probably right. But even as my friend you would want me back in the hospital, right?"

"It is the only answer, Edward, believe me. We can get you straightened out again. We have new drugs. Everything will be fine, you will feel wonderful again."

"I feel wonderful now," Teague said, stepping around the table, coming toward Rose. "Hell, I feel like God Himself, I feel so good. They can only get at me through you, Carl. Only you know my new name and address. If I eliminate you they won't be able to find me. You told me yourself that you took all the information about me from the hospital files."

"Well, that isn't quite true," Rose said, moving backwards. "I left some information locked away. They'll get it if anything happens to me."

Teague laughed. "I think that's the first lie you've ever told me, Carl. You lie very badly, did you know that? It shows right away. No, Carl, I know you, you've got everything about your special patients hidden right in this house. That's your style. You never trusted the hospital staff, I remember that. You have it all right here. And of course, in your head. So you can see what I must do, can't you, Carl?"

Rose stopped his retreat, forcing his face to become stern. "Give me the knife, Edward," he commanded.

"That's what I've got in mind, Carl."

"You must hand me the knife, Edward. I am your only friend, your only protection. Hand it to me now!" Rose's voice snapped out the command as he stepped forward, his hand extended, palm up.

Teague chuckled as he slammed the long thin blade past the waiting hand, shoving it into the doctor's lower abdomen. Rose's eyes widened as he staggered back. Teague jerked the knife free. Blood welled from the doctor's wound. Rose ineffectively held his hands over it, his eyes fixed on the blood running between his fingers.

"Carl, you are the biggest pain in the ass I've ever known. Man, you think you are God Almighty, and that's a fact. This is something I've itched to do for a long time." Teague again slammed the knife into the doctor's stomach just above the red-stained hands, pulling it out as Rose fell to his knees.

"An asshole, that's what you are!" Teague's voice had risen to a scream. "I could never stand you or your pompous horseshit!" He drove the knife into the base of

Rose's neck, the long blade plunging down within the chest cavity. Rose tumbled sideways on the shag rug, his blood staining the carpet. He was conscious but his eyes stared straight ahead, unseeing, like an animal being slaughtered.

"I don't know how a dumb ass like you ever got through medical school!" He slammed the knife again into the body. Rose coughed and closed his eyes.

"Dumb ass! Dumb ass!" Teague screamed the words as he ripped with the knife, stabbing the now dead man again and again. At last he stopped.

He stood over the bloody body, panting from his exertions. Disdainfully he threw the blood-soaked knife at the corpse. "Dumb ass," he whispered.

Teague walked to the end of the table and retrieved his beer, gulping it down and emptying the bottle. "I'm going to clean myself up, Rose, and then I'm going to pour gasoline all through this fancy house of yours and burn every goddamn thing you have. If you have any records hidden away, dumb ass, they're going to go right along with you. I'm not going to be caught this time."

He looked down at the corpse and giggled. "You think that Russo will catch me again, don't you? Well, I've got news for you, dumb ass, I'm going to catch him this time. No more fucking around. He's the only one who can nail me, so I'm going to nail him first. And then I'll nail that motherfucking lawyer at the same time."

Teague laughed. "You know, you never frightened me. Oh, you tried, but I had you in my hip pocket from the beginning. That cop bothers me, I have to admit that, and Knapp, I worry about him too, but you never frightened me. Only Russo and Knapp have ever done that, but I'll take care of that soon enough."

He giggled again. "Of course, I'll have to finish spelling out the *G* in stalking. That ought to drive Russo right up the drapes. Then I'll get him." His eyes narrowed as if an idea had suddenly occured to him. "Maybe he's married or has a girlfriend. Jesus! Wouldn't that be sweet! I could get her first, you know, and then him. That would teach the bastard. Same with my good lawyer. I might as well have some fun while I'm doing this. Unless they're queer, there have got to be women in their lives."

He threw the beer bottle against the wall, creating an explosion of glass as it shattered. "And I'm just the boy to find them, because after the fire here they'll never find me."

* * *

The volunteer fire company answered the first alert, but by the time they arrived Dr. Rose's place was a mass of flames. Even the surrounding trees lost their leaves in the blaze.

Sheriff Soames arrived at the scene and thought he detected the smell of gasoline. He knew something had been used—the fire had gone up too quickly and had spread much too fast to be natural in origin. Later, he called the state police, who dispatched their arson squad the next day. The men on the arson squad discovered the burned remains of Dr. Rose. They also identified the chemical used to set the fire as gasoline. No effort had been made to conceal the arson. It was deliberate. They called in the homicide section even before the medical examiner discovered that Rose had been stabbed to death before he was burned.

Dr. Rose had been a controversial man, and the homicide detectives feared they faced a long investigation of many sources and many possible suspects. Few people had been fond of Carl Rose.

5

RUSSELL J. ANDERSON HAD BEEN IN AND OUT OF MENtal hospitals since the age of twelve. Now thirty-four, he was no longer the inmate of any institution. The diagnosis on the release papers was: schizophrenic (paranoid type) in remission. Russell Anderson used heavy doses of soothing drugs daily and he had been out of the hospital for over a year.

By choice, as well as circumstance, he led a lonely life as a hired farmhand. The work was hard but not mentally demanding. He felt no pressure, no mental stress. The rhythm of farm life suited him. His only recreation was his radio and his old guitar. He had no friends and he had long ago severed all ties with his relatives.

But he still heard the voices.

Russell Anderson had grown a long black beard and he lurched about on his polio-crippled left leg. The limp and his bulging, staring eyes marked him, and he was remembered by the few who saw him. In town it was general knowledge that Knute Van Pelt had hired a crazy man. They left him alone and he avoided all contact with the members of their small farming community.

Besides, it took all his energy to ignore the voices. He knew they were merely auditory hallucinations; the doctors had explained them and he knew they were just a trick of the mind. Yet the voices were always present, always whispering to him. The medicine and the hard work helped him to forget the awful urgings of the voices.

When Russell Anderson spoke—and that was as little as possible—his manner was blunt, even hostile. Farmer Van Pelt was used to him, but others found him rude, even frightening.

Fate provided Russell Anderson as a protection for Edward Teague.

Dr. Rose's charred remains had been very carefully examined. He had been stabbed to death and the blaze had been set as an obvious cover-up for the murder. That was the theory the police used as the basis for their investigation.

Several teams of state police detectives were assigned to the case. Rose had been less than popular with a number of people ranging from members of the state legislature to his staff and patients. The patients seemed the most probable source of suspects so the police began with them. A survey disclosed that Rose had received several death threats from patients. One patient was dead, three were still locked away in hospitals, but one was out. His name was Russell J. Anderson.

Anderson had been a patient of Rose's and had written a rambling letter to the governor telling of the doctor's alleged mistreatment and threatening to kill Rose unless official action was taken against the doctor. The only action was Anderson's transfer to another section of the hospital and to another doctor. Still, the letter remained a matter of record.

The large farm of Knute Van Pelt was located only eight miles away from the now ruins of Rose's former home.

It had been a bad day for Anderson even before the police came to talk to him. The voices had been particularly loud and Anderson was even more irritable than usual.

He was filling the tractor with gasoline from the farm's own gas pump when the police car drove up. This was a circumstance not lost on the visiting detectives—it meant that Anderson had easy access to all the gasoline needed to burn down a building.

Anderson's answers to the officer's questions were snarling and evasive. He soon tired of them and retreated to his home in the shed behind the Van Pelt house. But they followed. It soon became difficult for Anderson to distinguish between the imaginary voices and the real. He started shouting and when they would not go away he charged at them, his large labor-hardened fists swinging. The policemen had to use their blackjacks to protect themselves. Later that night, at the local sheriff's office where he had been locked up, Anderson's voices got the upper hand and he began to scream that he was Jesus and had punished Rose by condemning him to the fires of hell.

That was enough for the state police. They had their killer. There was no purpose in pursuing the matter further, and they felt it ironic that Rose had been destroyed by one of the crazies he had insisted on returning to society. They had no idea they had the wrong crazy.

Police work is routine for the most part and consists mostly of legwork, investigation that eats time and dulls the mind. If the Rose case had remained open, part of the routine would have entailed a check of his telephone calls. The police would have discovered his calls to Chicago, and in tracking them down, they would have stumbled across Edward Teague, the famous Stalking Man. They would have placed Teague under minute-by-minute surveillance.

But the police had their killer and so no such routine investigation was made.

Russell J. Anderson babbled away in his cell, carrying on intense conversations with his voices.

Edward Teague was home in Chicago, safe, satisfied, and ready to carry out his horrifying plan of revenge.

* * *

The last letter in *stalking* is, of course, *g*.

Edward Teague returned to his home. He had planned for this day and it had finally come. Teague did not know that the police had fixed upon Russell Anderson as Rose's killer, so he put his own escape plan into operation.

He had debated killing his wife and her sniveling son. However, such action was sure to pinpoint him, and despite her hysterical disposition he still felt an affection for her, so he dismissed that course of action from his mind. He did have alternative plans.

Edward Teague had worked hard long hours at premium pay to build a large bank account. He had saved over five thousand dollars. It had meant sacrifice, but he knew someday he might have to run. Money gave him the power to escape. Now that day had arrived.

Teague withdrew three thousand dollars from his account. The balance would be needed by his family. It meant a new life for him, another change of identity. He could never return to his family and the quiet Chicago suburb. It was a final severing, but he experienced little remorse. He had long ago grown tired of his mundane existence. He waited patiently while the teller had the withdrawal slip checked and approved. Then the money was counted out in one-hundred dollar bills.

Edward Teague was free: free to follow his own burning imperatives; free to wreak havoc; free to seek revenge. He walked from the bank and inhaled the crisp air as if he had been freed from a prison. He laughed, an expression of the emotion bubbling up within him, a feeling of new birth, new purpose.

Before he left he dropped two envelopes in the mail. One was to his employer telling of an immediate chance to better himself in another state. The other was to his wife, explaining how she could get the remaining money in the savings account. The letter also contained a threat of what might happen to her and her son if she was so unwise as to go to the police or to tell what she knew or suspected about his activities. He knew she feared him and he felt secure that the short letter would effectively seal her lips.

He continued to feel elated and free as he guided his car up the toll skyline drive, heading around the south end of Lake Michigan, heading into the state of Michigan. His destination was that state's "furniture city," the native city of Gerald Ford, Michigan's only president— the beautiful, quiet city of Grand Rapids.

Historic Grand Rapids was the home of several hundred thousand people, but its importance to Edward Teague was that its name began with the letter *G*.

* * *

Only a blackened stone chimney protruded from the charred rubble of what had once been a showplace home.

It resembled a black finger pointing heavenward as if protesting the injustice of some cloud-hidden god.

The state police had assigned Detective Masters to escort Lieutenant Russo around the murder scene. Dr. Rose had lived only a few miles from his hospital, so it had been another long drive up from the city for Russo. It was understood that Russo's presence was unofficial but it was a courtesy extended to a "visiting fireman." Masters was only months away from retirement. His arthritis rendered him stiff and sore and unfit for most police duties, so he was just putting in time at "make work" jobs. Therefore the hours spent with the visiting big city detective would not really be lost time anyway.

Russo kicked at the remains of a beam. "Jesus, there's nothing left but ashes," he remarked to Masters, who stood a few feet away watching him.

"Yeah," the older man replied. "The bastard used gasoline and it went up like the Fourth of July. The volunteer fire company couldn't even get close to the thing until it sizzled down, and by that time everything was gone." He paused for a moment, studying the wreckage. "Of course, it's lucky the stupid ass used gasoline. If he had used wood alcohol he might have got away with it. But that night, they tell me, you could even smell the stuff."

"No effort at concealment?"

The older man shook his head slowly. "I guess the voices he hears told him to use gasoline." He laughed. "That guy should get smarter voices the next time."

"You mean Anderson?"

"Sure. Or the Son of God, according to him. Looney bastard, and looks it too. Ever see him?"

Russo shook his head. "No."

"Big guy, hobbles around on a gimpy leg. He has a filthy-looking black beard and the biggest, wildest eyes you ever saw. His eyes are always rolling around, staring and angry. Spooky, you know what I mean?"

"He said he did this?" Russo nodded toward the ruins.

"Yeah, at least he did when they arrested him. He doesn't do anything much now but babble. But the officers got a statement out of him at the time. He said his voices commanded him to kill Rose and he did."

"What else do you have besides that?"

The older detective snorted. "A confession ain't bad."

Russo grinned. "I agree, but sometimes these looneys will say anything."

The other man nodded slowly. "I suppose, but this Anderson wrote a letter to the governor saying he was going to kill Dr. Rose."

"That was a couple of years ago."

"But he didn't get out of the booby hatch until last year," the other officer protested. "We think he was after Rose all that time, sort of working his way up to knocking him off, you know."

"He doesn't sound like the kind of nut who would plan things out. The ones who hear voices are usually explosive; they don't plan much, just act."

Masters laughed. "Maybe his voices were more intelligent. Who knows? Anyway, the guy only lived eight miles away from here, he had plenty of gasoline right on the farm where he worked, and nobody saw him on the night of the fire."

Russo looked up at the gathering clouds. "He more or less just hung out in his own room anyway, didn't he?"

"Yeah, he had a room back of the farmhouse, just a cubbyhole. It was as messy as he was."

"Did the farmer check on him that night?"

"No. Van Pelt is one of those old Bible-thumper types—early to bed, early to rise. Reads the Good Book and goes to bed, you know the type. I don't suppose they had much to talk about anyway. Van Pelt says Anderson never gave him any trouble. He stayed to himself, and I guess the farmer liked it that way too."

"Anyone see him around here the night of the fire?"

The other man shook his head.

"So, outside of his statement when he was arrested," Russo continued, "about all you have is an old threatening letter and access to this place and gasoline."

"Not a bad case," Masters said. "I've convicted a lot of people on one hell of a lot less."

Russo made no reply, but walked around the edge of the ruined house. The older man followed him, walking painfully.

"Do you know something we don't?" Masters asked. "I mean there must be something that would bring you up to this joint, besides curiosity."

"Well, I talked to Rose the day he was killed."

"By phone?"

Russo poked at a pile of charred wood. "No, in person. I drove up to the hospital. I talked to him about Edward Teague. Do you remember him?"

"Sure, the Stalking Man. Another looney."

"I found out Rose had released him and that Teague is out."

The other detective whistled. "Jesus, this Rose was quite a character. I think he hated courts and cops. It's just simple justice that one of his patients finally got him."

"I think you might have the wrong looney."

Masters scowled. "What makes you think that?" His manner was defensive.

"A hunch, nothing more. I think maybe Teague did this."

"Where is this Teague?"

Russo shrugged. "That's one of the tough ones. No one knows. Rose took all those records and kept them here. That's why I think Teague torched the joint and killed Rose. He didn't want anyone to find out where he was."

Masters lit a cigarette. He cupped his gnarled hands around the match to protect its flame from the wind. He inhaled deeply and the cigarette bobbled as he spoke with it held between his lips. "Did you tell my bosses about this guy Teague?"

Russo nodded. "I think they believe they have another crazy on their hands—me."

Masters pulled the cigarette from his mouth and spit away imaginary tobacco specks. "You collared this guy Teague, didn't you?"

"Yeah, but that was a couple of years ago."

Masters studied his cigarette for a moment. "I'll bet that hunch of yours didn't get much of a reception, right?"

Russo grinned. "They were polite, that's about all. As far as your people are concerned the case is all wrapped up."

"Funny thing about hunches," Masters said, almost to himself. "I've always believed in them, at least where veteran cops were concerned." He looked at Russo. "Before this arthritis tied me to a desk I used to be a pretty good detective. I always thought a hunch was something more than a guess, something maybe like an extrasensory perception. Your brain is like a computer, you know; it compiles a batch of information and then kicks it around and a printout pops out. Sometimes that's a definite idea and sometimes it's a hunch. Either way, it's the product of a complicated thinking machine.''

Russo looked at the older man with a new respect. ''I've never heard it put that way before but I agree with you. A cop gets to the point where he starts sensing things. It's hard to explain, but I suppose we get like doctors after a while, we diagnose our cases on the basis of a thousand past experiences. You know, that business about the computer and the hunch isn't bad.''

Masters smiled. ''I can't run anymore, but I still manage a thought now and then. Why do you think Teague did this? He must know that we can find him if we really get on it.''

Russo shoved his hands in his pockets. For the first time he felt at home with the older officer. Masters was a fellow detective, a man who understood. ''Teague is as crazy as Anderson, only in a different way. He hates women and gets a tremendous kick out of torturing and killing them. But in every other way he's normal. His thinking is sharp, he knows who he is and what he's doing. I don't know if he can help killing these women or not, but he has a superior mind and uses it very well. He almost got away with the other killings.''

Masters rubbed the small of his back. ''There would be no reason for Teague to move against this doctor. Hell, the guy was protecting him, wasn't he?''

''More or less, yes.''

The older man nodded. ''So Teague would be more interested in keeping this cookie alive and helpful, if you see what I mean?''

Russo shrugged. "I'd agree, except I've been on Rose's back about Teague and I have a hunch he called Teague to let him know I was nosing around. Teague is smart, he would know that the only way we could find him easily would be through Rose. Therefore, the murder and the fire. The fire wasn't to cover up the murder— hell, the smell of gasoline would almost guarantee an investigation—the fire was to burn any and all records pointing to Teague and his whereabouts."

Masters inhaled deeply on the cigarette, quietly digesting the other detective's statement. "Why were you on Rose's back?"

"There's been a rash of bizarre killings within a small area of the Midwest. Maybe you've read about some of them? One gal was crucified inside a barn, another had her head lopped off."

Masters nodded.

"Well, each was killed in a wild frenzy. Most were smashed into pulp. The other stuff, nailing a body to a wall or cutting off a head, was just for show. The way the women were killed bears the copyright of the Stalking Man." Russo paused. "I don't know if I should tell you the rest, you'll think I'm nuts too."

Masters smiled. "Anybody who becomes a cop has to be a little nuts to start with, so I'm ahead of you there."

"You may be right," Russo said. "It's an odd way to make a living when you think about it." Then he told him about the pattern of killings—whereby each succeeding murder location supplied a letter of the word *stalking*.

Masters studied Russo for a moment, considering what he had just been told. "Some of these murders are questionable, at least as far as the usual pattern of the Stalking

Man, right? Like the one in Indianapolis?''

"I admit it.''

"Still, if you're right, and he's spelling it out, then he should complete it pretty soon. I mean, he's scheduled to kill some woman in a city starting with the letter G, right?''

"That's what I think.''

Masters crushed out the cigarette beneath his heel. "And the brass don't agree with you?''

"I think they feel I have something personal against Teague. They keep reminding me that we have plenty of work without going looking for more. I suppose they think I'm letting this Teague bit work on me since I found out he was on the street.''

"Are you?'' Masters asked quietly.

Russo shrugged. "I don't think so, although I have to admit it's a possibility.''

"If you're right, the G killing will show up. Maybe then they'll listen to you.''

Russo smiled wryly. "I doubt it. Even if we nailed Teague and proved all my suppositions true, they would pop him right back into the same hospital that let him out.'' Russo stared at what was left of the house. "Teague is a clever man, and in his own way, charming. After things blew over and enough time had passed he'd probably just talk his way out again. Anyway, the top people in my department think it's a waste of time. They don't buy my theory. Even a G killing wouldn't make much difference. They'd need something more concrete than guesswork.''

Masters lit another cigarette, coughing as he inhaled. "You know, Russo, if you're right, there's another pretty good possibility.''

"What's that?"

"If this Teague is afraid of you, I mean if he did all this," Masters gestured at the ruins, "then he may fear you enough to come after you."

"I doubt it."

Masters let smoke flare from his nostrils. "Maybe, but just the same I've a hunch myself. If this looney actually thinks you are on his trail, he may try to take you out. I'd be careful if I were you."

Russo thought for a moment. "He is afraid of me— Rose told me that—but I don't think he would bother with me. Like I said, his madness is directed toward women, and while I have to admit I'm kind of cute, I don't think I'm his type."

Masters frowned, avoiding Russo's eyes. "You got a wife or girlfriend?" he asked quietly.

Russo's neck hair prickled as a ripple of fear touched him. "I'm divorced."

"Mind you, I'm just going along with your theory. You're probably all wet, and that would make me all wet too. But if you were right, this clown might come looking to punish you. In other words, if you were married he might go after your wife."

Russo thought of Marie, and he felt a revulsion at the thought that Teague might try to harm her. He looked over at the older man. "Like you say, we're probably both wrong, but I'll keep your hunch in mind. You never know in this business."

"A thrill a minute," Masters said. "Anything more you'd like to see out here, Lieutenant?"

"No."

"Want to stop for a beer before you start back for the city?"

Russo knew Marie was waiting for him and it would be a long drive. Still, Masters was one of a vanishing breed—detectives who had honed their senses to the point where they could penetrate the mind of the man they were after. There were few like him left. He felt he owed such a man at least one beer.

"Best offer I've had," Russo said. "Let's go."

They returned to the police car and roared down the driveway, leaving the lonely stone finger pointing at the darkening sky.

*   *   *

He spent the night in Holland, Michigan. He had registered at the small motel as Edward Viceroy, a name he fancied. It had a definite regal ring to it. He liked it when the room clerk called him Mr. Viceroy—a much better name than Teague, and not nearly as well known.

Holland was the site of Michigan's annual tulip festival, a springtime event when the small town attracted thousands who came to watch people in Dutch costumes and wooden shoes parade down the local streets. It was all over now and the streets were deserted, although the tulip motif was still evident in local advertising signs and billboards, reminders of the town's one big event of the year. Teague liked Holland, and in a bar next to the motel he had struck up a short acquaintance with a young blonde who laughed too loud and wore too much makeup. She would have been a perfect victim, but she was in the wrong city. He was determined to wait until he could fulfill his design, and that required that he execute his plan in Grand Rapids. So he had left the bar and gone to bed.

He had awakened refreshed and felt completely relaxed. For the first time while on the hunt he was not
fighting the clock. No longer did he have to account to
anyone for his time or his destination. There was no reason to rush, and that thought in itself soothed him. He
enjoyed a long shower with the water extra hot. Then,
using a towel to defog the mirror, he shaved.

For a while he lay naked on the bed half listening to
a local radio station, his mind at ease, his body relaxed.
It was pleasant. He forced himself to get up, and for a
few minutes he admired his body in the motel room's
long mirror. He flexed his muscles and felt particularly
proud of his large penis. As he admired himself he had
an erection. That made him laugh.

Teague dressed in casual slacks and a dark sport shirt.
He donned sunglasses and once again admired himself in
the mirror. He was tall, lean; and his blonde hair, he
knew, attracted women. And he meant to attract one before the day was done.

He left the motel and whipped his car along U.S. 196,
the interstate highway leading from Holland to Grand
Rapids. He enjoyed the sight of the rolling farmland. Although the day was partly cloudy, streaks of sunlight
painted themselves up and down the soft green ridges. It
was rich country and relaxing to drive through. He whistled in time with the music on the car radio.

The concrete ribbon that was the interstate highway
curved up around a long hill, and then suddenly the city
of Grand Rapids lay below, like a vista that might have
been painted by an artist interested in portraying Middle
America. Even from above and at a distance the city
looked inviting. Trains lay in rows on sidings, and smoke
drifted up from working factories. Beyond the trappings

of commerce and industry lay the thousands of rooftops that constituted the homes of the people of Grand Rapids.

The road twisted and plunged behind another hill and the vista was gone, like a picture suddenly covered. But it was enough for Teague. He felt excitement grow within him. This time it would be better than ever before. This time, in this delightful place, he would create his own masterpiece.

He had another erection just thinking about it.

* * *

The sun that dappled the farmlands of Grand Rapids danced in full beam upon the rippling waters of the river. They watched a barge passing below driven along by a large tugboat. The restaurant, called *The Crow's Nest*, was new, expensive, and sat atop the city's tallest building.

Thomas Knapp studied the ornate menu, aware that her eyes were on him. "What looks good?" he asked without looking up. He had noticed she had ignored the menu set in front of her.

"I'm not very hungry. Just a light salad for me, I think."

Their waitress—a tall, thin girl with a skin problem and a wide smile—hurried to their table. "Something from the bar, folks?" she asked pleasantly.

"Martha?"

She shook her head. "I won't be able to type this afternoon."

"Maybe your boss won't notice," he said as he looked up at the waitress. "One of your special rum fizzes for the lady and a bourbon and water for me." The girl dis-

appeared as if she had been jerked away by an invisible
rope.

"I'll be fuzzy all day. I'm not used to drinking very
much."

"Any and all errors are hereby forgiven in advance,
okay?"

She shook her head. "There's really no way I can get
around you, is there?"

"Do you want to?"

Martha Flowers looked away, her large dark eyes
watching the boats far below. "I'm worried."

"About what?"

She continued to look at the river. "About us. I'm in
the middle of a divorce. I'm vulnerable, I know that much
about my feelings. You have a bad marriage. You can't
help looking for something else or someone else. So suddenly we make some kind of magic chemistry together.
But this kind of affair is usually short and not sweet. It
hurts at the end."

He thought a moment before answering. Her mood had
caught him by surprise. "If you're feeling guilty about
the other night, Martha, don't. You mean more to me than
just . . ."

She held her hand up, stopping him. "Tom, please
don't. I don't need any assurance." She paused for a
moment, a wry smile playing across her full lips. "I've
seen it enough, God knows—the office affair." Her eyes
returned to the river. "Let's try to keep it in perspective.
I like you and I like my job. You're a married man. You
have a family. I can't afford to start dreaming dreams."

"Are you trying to say you want to stop, Martha?"

She looked at him. "Do you?"

He shook his head. "Only if this thing is becoming a burden to you. Is it?"

The waitress returned and put down their drinks. "Would you like to order now?" She obviously was under a management imperative to keep the customers moving along.

"Not at the moment." Knapp looked up to show his annoyance at being pushed, but even in that instant the girl had once again disappeared, busy now with the people at another table.

Knapp looked again at Martha. "This is no burden to me," he said softly. He drank, watching her toy with her own glass. "You make me happy. I recognize the dangers ahead just as you do. I don't know quite how to express my feelings about all this except to say I'm throwing my future up into the wind. I'll go where I'm blown. Maybe that's just an easy way out, but I'm letting fate play all the major hands from now on."

She looked down at her drink.

"Martha, we're the walking wounded right now. I doubt if either one of us wants to make a lifetime decision. I know I don't. This thing between you and me is, well, a dream in a way. I'm happy to let the dream go on for a while, if you do."

She studied the glass as intently as if she might somehow find an answer to her problem in the pineapple-studded ice. "I think a great deal of you," she said, her voice barely audible above the noise of the room. "Just as a boss and as a person you've meant a lot to me. I suppose I always did wonder what kind of a lover you might be." She looked up and smiled sheepishly. "Women are like that, you know.

"Tom, I know you'd never do anything to hurt me

intentionally. I know you well enough for that. But I don't want to be just another piece of office gossip. I don't want this to be reduced to a snickering, sordid joke. Do you see what I mean?''

''You're worried about your reputation. To be honest, I really hadn't thought how it might look. I'm so happy just to be with you, I forget things like that.''

She smiled. ''Well, Tom Knapp, I have no idea where you and I are going. Probably nowhere, but I'd hate to have one of your partners come sniffing around thinking that I went with the job. After all, I can type.''

''No more lunches then?''

She toyed with her drink, her eyes locked on his. The pineapple left a small yellow trace on her red lipstick. ''Maybe an occasional lunch, but I think we should be discreet. At least in the office we should pretend there's nothing between us.''

''But there is something between us,'' he said quietly.

She nodded. ''I know the circumstances are wrong, but you make me very happy. But, Tom, all I have right now is a world full of 'maybe.' Maybe something will come of this, maybe not. I think all this has to be our secret, for both of us, at least for now.''

He sighed. ''It'll be tough, Martha. I mean not touching you, being formal. It won't be easy.''

''For me too,'' she said.

The waitress popped up again. ''Ready now?'' She asked brightly, her pencil poised over her order pad.

''My sister here,'' he said, nodding at Martha, ''has been slow about these things since we were children.'' He pretended annoyance. ''Have you made up your mind?''

Martha Flowers began to giggle.

"You see," he said to the waitress, giving a small shrug to emphasize his point. "We'll have another drink, my dear, while my sister makes up her mind."

The waitress disappeared. "Is that discreet enough?" he whispered.

* * *

The interstate highway cut through the center of Grand Rapids, its concrete ribbons forming a long bridge over the shallow but wide Grand River, where the rapids had given the city its name. Dutch farmers had founded it as a small trading village, but its population had grown to several hundred thousand, who earned their daily bread from the dozens of industries that had sprouted up around the furniture factories.

Like all cities, Grand Rapids had obvious problems. The old section of town was dying; many of its ancient stores and houses were vacant and vandalized. But like fresh tree rings growing out from a rotting center, newer houses had blossomed beyond the core city and bright shopping centers dotted the pretty landscape like concrete-and-neon flowers.

Teague pulled off at a downtown exit and followed the curve until he found himself in the town's old center. It was dingy: Decay and ruin haunted it, second-hand shops dotted the roadway, hand-painted signs hung in the grimy windows of murky restaurants. Suspicious eyes staring out from black faces followed the path of his car.

Like Chicago's South Side, it was a place where a white face was unwelcome. But Edward Teague had other things on his mind. It was too early for the prostitutes to be on the street. He had heard that Grand Rapids cops were rough on prostitutes and their customers. It was known in Chicago that the Michigan city used police-women as decoys to put the lid on the passion of out-of-towners. Taking a prostitute was much too risky, at least in this city. He still remembered the close call in Indianapolis.

In a few minutes he had cruised past the seedy neighborhood and had climbed a gentle slope that brought him to a crest covered with more expensive and much newer ranch-style houses. Portable swimming pools dotted the backyards. There seemed to be a church on almost every corner.

He turned off the main highway and found a quiet side street. Slowly he followed the road as it circled back into a hilly, wooded area.

The expansive feelings of relaxation began to drift away as he felt the slight tenseness he always experienced upon stepping into the woods. He could remember just how it felt, that time so long ago. Sometimes they would park their car alongside the forest. He and his father would check their weapons. Perhaps his father would pause to give him a few words of advice, a tip on where he thought the game most plentiful, then they would begin. It was always a thrill to step off the hard surface of the road and onto the soft loam of the forest floor. He could remember the fragrance of the trees and the powerful weight of the weapon in his hands.

His attention was suddenly drawn to a pair of tawny legs, as a young woman bicycled quickly past him. He watched her trim buttocks working feverishly in his rear-view mirror. A health freak out for her morning exercise, he thought. He whistled softly to himself as he watched her disappear around a curve

With no sense of urgency he calmly sought a driveway. The drives here were spaced at long distances. He slid his car into the next one and backed out, turning back in the direction where he had last seen the young woman on her bicycle. He began to accelerate, remembering how the road had curved, planning the area where he would intercept her. Judging by her estimated speed he thought he would catch up with her just before the next cross street.

But by the time he had reached the stop sign at the cross street he had lost her.

Irritably he braked and skidded into a driveway, jerking the car back into the street and returning the way he had come. He now realized she had the turned into one of the driveways along the street. He glided slowly watching for the parked bicycle.

There was no bicycle to be seen, only the closed doors of the garages attached to the ornate houses. Somewhere along the route she had slipped into one of them. Somewhere her bicycle rested behind a closed garage door. He tried to recall if he saw an open garage door that was now closed, but he had not paid that kind of attention at the time. He cursed as he felt his irritation turn into anger. She had escaped. She was somewhere. Safe behind one of those doors. Tall, tawny, long-legged. She had been just right, but she had escaped him.

He remembered his father cursing when the long rifle shot had missed and the magnificent buck had slipped from the open meadow into the concealment of the forest. Usually his father displayed little emotion, yet on that

occasion his cheeks had reddened and he used foul lan-
guage, something he had always avoided in the boy's
presence before. Teague still vividly recalled it: the two
of them standing together in frustration, the sense of loss
growing with each moment. The buck would have made
an outstanding trophy, but he had escaped and was safely
away, bounding through the protection of the thick forest.
Teague remembered that he had been close to tears.

He covered the same territory again, hoping she would
show herself, but there was no sign of her anywhere.
Reluctantly, and with growing anger, he abandoned the
search.

Teague gunned the car and sped away from the empty
street. Suddenly he felt the need to be with people; a quiet
neighborhood would not do. He turned onto the main
road and drove until he spotted a small park. A pick-me-
up softball game was being played. Mixed teams of boys
and girls played a frenzied, shouting game of slow-pitch
softball.

He tried to concentrate on the softball game, using the
action of the young people to diminish his anger. He
knew he could not operate effectively if he let it consume
him. But even as he watched, he thought of her long legs,
and his hands became sweaty as he gripped the steering
wheel.

Anger had always been his most uncontrollable emotion. Now it raged up inside him and he could feel his
hands shake and hot tears begin to flush his eyes. He had
to do something to stop it. He backed out of the parking
space, feeling panic as he returned to the main highway.
He turned off the air-conditioner, rolled down the driver's
window, opened the vents, letting the warm wind blow

against his face as if it might somehow magically blow away his anguish. He paid little attention to where he was going, and finally the rage seemed to lift and he felt deeply fatigued, as if he had been engaged in a mighty struggle.

His throat was dry and he needed something to drink. Teague pulled into a tavern's nearly deserted parking lot. Inside, the place had the permanent aroma of stale beer, but it was dark, cool and peaceful. He picked a stool at the empty bar and ordered a beer.

They exchanged a few remarks about the pleasant weather; then the bartender left him alone. The salty beer tasted just right, cold and soothing, and he began to feel energy seep back into his body, like fuel slowly poured into an engine.

At the back of the bar several signs announced various civic and charity events. The local Catholic church advertised its weekly all-you-can-eat fish fry. The Rotary had a fund raiser going. A veterans' post had scheduled a carnival. He checked the dates. The carnival would still be in town.

"Where's that carnival?" he called to the bartender, who was reading a newspaper at the other end of the bar.

"Eh?"

"I said, where's that carnival?" Teague pointed to the sign.

"At Gallagher Field," the other man replied. "You can't miss it. It's about three miles down the road. You turn right at the Baptist church, go about a half mile, and there you are."

"Thanks." Teague emptied his glass.

"Won't be much going on down there now, though," the bartender said. "Most everything opens up right about supper time. Watch them booths if you go—I think they run them crooked.''

"Thanks, I'll watch out.'' Teague waved and left the bar. Bright sunshine had replaced the spotty clouds of early morning. He stretched happily. A carnival sounded made to order: plenty of people, and more important, plenty of girls.

6

As THEY APPROACHED THEY COULD SEE THE SMALL crowd of neighbors standing on the front lawn of the tiny frame house, their faces weirdly lit by the twirling red lights of the parked scout cars.

Rosinski pulled up behind one of the precinct cars, and he and Russo walked past the uniformed officer posted on the concrete slab front porch. Inside, they were greeted by Ned Beckman, a senior detective with the Seventeenth Precinct.

"How's it going, Tony?" Beckman's manner with his senior officer was informal, an attitude permitted by the fact that they had been classmates at the academy and friends since that beginning on the police force.

"Not bad, Ned. You?"

"Arthritis in the knees. Outside of that, still a young man. Want to see the lately departed?"

"Wouldn't miss it for the world."

The two homicide detectives followed Beckman past a thin woman who sat hunched up and sobbing in a worn chair in the tiny living room. In the kitchen a gray-haired, hawklike man stared at them as they passed. The old man was guarded by two young uniformed officers.

"In here," Beckman said, standing aside.

The bedroom was just large enough to accommodate a double bed. The bedside touched one wall and allowed only a narrow passage along the other wall. A man, extremely thin, lay face up in the narrow space between bed and wall. His sightless eyes were fixed on the ceiling. He was clad only in a pair of undershorts and white ankle socks. Two red wounds marred his thin chest. Looking like a pair of small lips, they were slightly swollen at the entry, and only a small amount of blood had spilled from them.

"Who is he?" Russo asked.

"A guy named Falls, Virgil Falls. He got in a shouting match in the kitchen with his father-in-law, and the old guy grabbed a kitchen knife, chased him in here, and finished him off."

"What was the beef about?"

"The old man, who lived with Virgil here and his daughter, kept leaving the basement light on. I suppose that was the straw that broke the camel's back. The wife says the two men hadn't been getting along. The old man kicked in part of the down payment for this house and he figured he had rights, I suppose. Anyway, the shit hit the fan tonight and Virgil and the basement light are both out now."

"Witnesses?"

Beckman shrugged. "Virgil's wife. She was hanging onto the old guy when he chased Virgil in here. I took a statement from her. Two kids, one six and the other eight. They heard the fight but didn't see anything. I have them staying next door with a neighbor."

"How about the neighbors?" Russo asked.

"I only talked to a couple. I guess everyone heard the two of them shouting at each other from time to time. That's about all though. I took their statements too."

"What's the old man say?"

"Same as everybody else. Except he says he was afraid of Virgil and what he might do, that's the only variation. He says Virgil has been threatening him about a number of things, including the basement light. Of course, it would take two Virgils to make one of that old gray wolf. Anyway, tonight they got into it again and Virgil ordered him out of the house. The old man claims that Virgil tried to get the knife first and that he beat him to the weapon. But he does admit chasing him into the bedroom. He said he thought Virgil might have had a gun back in there, so he stabbed him, he says, to save himself."

"Did he have a gun?"

"Virgil's wife says they have no firearms in the house. We gave it a good shakedown but we didn't find any gun."

"Good job, Ned," Russo said.

"Hell, no job at all," the other man replied. "Everything was laid out for me as I stepped in the door. Including Virgil." He laughed.

"Medical examiner on his way?"

"Yes."

"It's your collar, Ned. Bring everyone downtown and we'll have an assistant prosecutor take formal statements."

"What charge?"

Russo frowned. "It'll end up as second degree, but since there was no gun you might as well book him for first degree. Okay?"

"Suits me."

Russo turned to go.

"You want to talk to any of these people?" Beckman asked.

"No reason. You've got it all. I'll see you downtown, okay?"

Beckman nodded.

Rosinski followed Russo back out the way they had come.

"How come you didn't talk to the old man? That's the first time I ever saw you do that—I mean, not talk to a suspect," Rosinski said as they climbed into their unmarked car.

"Ned Beckman is a good detective. He'll have the case all wrapped up." Russo paused for a moment. "Beckman never had luck in the department, you know. Damn good cop, but he never had any powerful friends, nor was he lucky enough to hit on any big cases. He's as good as any man we have on homicide. Luck's a funny thing sometimes. Anyway, he's a good man and I trust his judgment."

Rosinski wheeled the car around and started back toward the city. "Imagine killing someone over a basement light."

"That's the usual kind of cause for murder, you should know that by now. People get on each other's nerves until some little thing explodes all their pent-up emotion. The light was just a symbol to both of them."

"I suppose."

"Methodical killers are as rare as a virgin in a whorehouse. That's why I suppose I'm running into so much opposition to my theory about Teague."

"How so?"

"All senior cops know that murder is usually a spur-of-the-moment thing with little or no thought behind it. So a nut like Teague who plans things just doesn't fit into that pattern. The brass tend to disregard anything that doesn't fit into established patterns. Sometimes I think it must be a rule written someplace.''

They rode in silence for a few minutes and then Rosinski spoke. ''I've been following the crime reports, there hasn't been a Teague-like killing in a *G* city yet. I suppose you noticed?''

''I noticed,'' Russo said. ''He has all the time in the world now. He's safe and he won't rush. Anyway, that's how I read him.''

''You really believe, don't you? I mean you are completely convinced.''

Russo nodded, looking at the storefronts as they raced by. ''Rosinski, is this your way of saying you think I'm nuts too?''

''No, Lieutenant. Of course I wouldn't tell you that, even if I thought it was true. I'm not that dumb.'' He smiled. ''But if I were in your shoes I would have some doubt. I mean, it would bother me that I could be all wet, especially about the spelling part. I might be on the alert, you know, but I could never be sure, at least not the way you're sure.''

''That's because you don't know Edward Teague. For some reason it's almost like I can read his thoughts. By the way, I know what a psychiatrist could do with that one, but it's true, nevertheless.''

''Maybe.''

''And after he spells out his name, he'll try something new. An old cop with the state police thinks he might come after me, or after any lady that meant anything to me.''

''Well, you say you can think for him, what do you think?''

Russo considered the question for a moment before

answering, and thought of Marie. "It's possible," he said in a low voice.

"Well, he's still got to do something about that *G* if you're right. After that is when you'd better start worrying."

"Right." But Russo had already started to worry.

* * *

The day had been an agony of waiting. He passed part of the time by driving around the Michigan countryside; the rest was spent in a downtown movie. The double feature bored him, but it helped him forget about time. He emerged into the beginning of night. Only the red lining on the high dark clouds recalled the lovely day that had died. Stars were becoming visible among the scattered cloud patches. It was a beautiful night.

He could hear the carnival before he saw it. The sound of loud and throbbing circus music blared from huge loudspeakers set overhead in the trees. He turned a corner and there it was, just as though he were a child again. The place was brilliantly lighted. A ferris wheel, its outer rim dotted with electric lights, turned gently in the night sky. The noise of the more violent rides and the screams of the people enjoying the thrills could be heard even over the blaring speaker music.

He parked his car in one of the rows in a vacant field and walked toward the carnival grounds. Dry dust soon covered his shoes. The smell of the earth blended with the aroma of cooking hot dogs, baking sugar candy, and a thousand other aromas. Other people also streamed in from the parking area. Mostly parents with young chil-

dren or young couples, all looking forward to an enjoyable evening.

Teague also anticipated an enjoyable evening.

It was a large carnival. As he walked along he noted
that the grounds had been divided into three parts. The
largest part was for the thrill rides. It was here that most
of the noise was generated. The second section—the midway—presented a collection of shoddy freak and girlie
shows, their barkers out front talking at the passing people, encouraging them to pay their money and come in
and see the wonders inside. The third part was devoted
to rows of game tents and a shooting gallery. The men
behind the counters of the game tents called to the people
passing by, urging them to try their luck. Each of the
tents was garnished with bunting and tinsel, and in the
garish floodlight they created a fairyland of color strung
on newly painted wooden poles.

Teague bought some popcorn and walked along with
the crowd. A woman's shriek made the back of his neck
tingle with anticipation. He smiled.

The ride that seemed to cause the most commotion was
the Silver Streak. It was a revolving metal cylinder which,
by means of a system of levers, drew in and propelled
out a number of small teacuplike vehicles. The riders
were pulled in and then snapped out with increasing velocity. The bravest clamped their hands on the safety bar
in front of them and rode it out, grimfaced. The others,
particularly the women, shrieked as they were snapped
out faster and faster. He stopped and watched the faces.
One young redhead clung desperately to her white-faced
boyfriend, her features a perfect mask of terror. Her eyes
seemed frozen open and her mouth was parted for a
scream, but it was obvious to onlookers that she could

not even marshall a sound. Teague watched her, conscious of his sudden desire. He turned away, afraid that others might see his face and read his thoughts.

He ambled over to the midway. For the price of fifty cents he could see such scientific wonders as two-headed children preserved in a bottle and a five-legged calf. Even more wondrous sights were hinted at. He passed the Wild Man show, an illusion he had read about. Teague stopped with a crowd of others in front of the Babylon Revue. On the bunting-covered stage several bored dancers surveyed the crowd in front of them. They were supposed to be exotic belly dancers from the East, but Teague knew they were only carny girls making a buck. One was so thin her rib cage was clearly visible. Another had such heavy legs that ripples of fat covered her thighs. They were dressed in imitation belly dancer costumes complete with see-through pantaloons and sequined brassieres. The barker, a small, evil-looking man, stalked up and down in front of the dancers, leering into his hand-held mike. A tall, gangly redheaded boy stood, awkward and embarrassed, at the fringe of the crowd. The barker picked him out, telling him that he was about to become a man, assuring him that by mere passage through the tent entrance he would no longer be a boy and that all the secrets of manhood awaited him. The kid blushed and the barker continued to taunt him.

Teague stepped away from the dance show and strolled along looking at the people. He headed up toward the game booths. At each booth he was greeted with calls to try his luck, to win something for the girl friend. He stopped for a few minutes and spent a few dollars at the shooting gallery. The rifles were small-bore and purposely untrue, but despite the built-in handicaps he scored well enough to win a large stuffed panda doll. At first he was going to decline the prize, but then he decided it might come in handy later.

He carried the cheap toy under his arm as he continued his stroll. There were no customers at the ring-toss. It was a common game at amusement parks. The customer bought three rings for a half-dollar. On raised blocks only a few tantalizing feet away were glittering watches and rings. All the customer had to do was throw the ring around one of the blocks so that it fell to the base and then claim the prize.

A young woman stood behind the counter, a cigarette dangling from her thin lips. She tried to look tough, but Teague was an excellent appraiser, and he knew immediately it was a facade. He guessed the girl had not been long with the carnival—her large eyes were still soft despite the heavy makeup she wore.

"How about it, Mister?" she called. "You look like you're lucky tonight—take the missus home a watch or a diamond ring. Three rings for half a dollah, you can't miss."

He walked over to her. "You sure about that last part?"

"Whad'ya mean?"

"About not missing?"

She started to frown and then she shrugged and laughed. "Hell yes, you can lose. That's the whole idea of this scam. We can't give no guarantees, if you see what I mean?"

"So I can't win then?"

Suddenly her eyes became wary. "I didn't say that. Sure you can win. Are you the law or something?"

"No, I'm not the law. You haven't been around carnivals much, have you?"

"As a matter of fact, I haven't. This is my uncle's booth. I'm just working it for the summer."

"Are you a college student?" he asked.

She laughed. "No. I got halfway through beauticians' school, that's as far as I ever went."

"You look like a college girl," he said.

"Thanks."

"Maybe I should take a crack at those rings."

"You look like a nice guy," she said quietly. "Save your money. The rings don't fit the little blocks. They look like they do, but they don't. Oh, I got a few under the counter that do, just in case some wise guy starts something. I show him how easy it is, you know what I mean?" She ground out the cigarette in the dirt at her feet. "Besides, even if you did win, those prizes are just junk. That diamond ring"—she nodded at the prize—"cost my uncle all of five cents. Keep your money, your family may need it."

He grinned. "Thanks for the tip. I don't have a family. I'm not married, at least not any more."

"Divorced?"

"Three years next October. Best thing I ever did." He laughed.

"Yeah, I'm divorced too, I know what you mean."

Teague grinned at the girl as if they had just discovered a close bond between them. "Look, I know you show people usually don't go out with the local folks, but I'd like to buy you a drink when you get off work. I mean, if that's okay? I wouldn't want you to get into trouble with your uncle."

She looked him up and down. "Well, ordinarily I

wouldn't take you up on that, but you seem like a nice guy. And don't worry about my uncle. Hell, he's back in South Bend with appendicitis. I'm running the booth until he gets well and joins up with the carnival.''

"When do you get off work?"

"What time is it now?" she asked.

"About half past ten."

She looked perplexed for a minute, then she shrugged. "Oh, what the hell, it's a bad night anyway. I might as well close up now for all the good I'm doing here. Give me a hand, will you?"

"Sure." He put the panda aside and helped her lower the wooden flap that fitted like a shutter over the front of the game booth. She switched off the lights and then attached a large lock. She checked her key ring and then snapped the lock shut. "I once locked my damned keys in there." She stuck the keys into the pocket of her jeans. "Okay, handsome," she said, "I'm all yours. Where shall we go?"

Teague took her to a bar, one far away from the carnival grounds. He did not want anyone from the carnival remembering him. She would be a stranger to the people in the bar, the same as himself. No one would remember either of them. It was a large place, crowded and noisy.

They danced together several times. The music was mostly country and western. He observed two things about her: first, she needed a bath; second, she needed a man. She kept rubbing her thigh between his legs, her wide eyes fixed provocatively on his, watching his reaction. He played her game. It was easy enough to do.

She practically dragged him out of the bar when he suggested they go for a ride.

The girl threw an arm around him as he started the car. "I like you," she giggled.

Before he had even cleared the parking lot he felt her hand at the top of his leg. She began to pull down his zipper. "Well, well, what do we have here?" she whispered as she slid her hand inside.

He had been watching for the place he had seen earlier. Suddenly he braked the car and swung into a deserted tree-lined lane. In the daytime he had noted that the rutted road led to a distant isolated clump of trees.

"Well, don't be in such a hurry, handsome." Her voice took on a velvet sensuous quality as she expertly fondled him.

She was getting hotter as he pulled into the concealment of the trees. The moonlight was bright but they were hidden from view.

"I'm glad you came along tonight," she said. "I've been so damned horny."

"You have no idea how I need you," he said, gripping her blouse.

"I can see that."

He ripped the blouse from her, the force pulling her up hard against him.

"Hey, goddamn you, don't tear my clothes! Listen, buster, if you're the kind that likes to play rough . . ."

He chopped his right hand hard into her mouth, jarring her head back. She slumped against the passenger door. "Oh, Jesus," she said evenly, "I've run into a fucking freak."

Teague saw her switchblade before she could use it. She snapped it open as she swung it from her pocket, aiming for his stomach, but he caught her wrist in time.

She began to squeal in rage as he twisted her arm until the knife fell to the floor of the car.

"Let me out of here, you melon-fucking son of a bitch!" She tried to pull away and kick open the car door, but he reached out and grabbed her hair, jerking her back violently. She screamed from the sudden pain.

"I thought you said you were horny," he whispered, half giggling. "First, I'm going to mess you up a bit, I like them bloody, and then you'll get all that fucking you were after. When I'm done, then I'm going to break every fucking bone in your whore's body."

She tried to bite him but he smashed her head against the steering wheel. It was too bad, she was not the kind to go limp with fear. She was one of the tough ones. He considered her a challenge.

He had never forgotten anything his father had taught him, every detail was carefully preserved. He remembered the first time he had helped his father dress a deer. It had been repulsive that first time, but later he became used to it. His father had hung the dead animal up by its hind legs, then he had taken his long knife and slashed a long steady line up the animal's stomach. The entrails had slid out. His father had used the knife to scrape the internal cavity of the animal clean. Later, he had taught him how to strip the hide from deer. He started with shallow even incisions, just enough to allow a good grip with the pliers. It was easy once the trick of it had been mastered. He had cleaned and skinned many deer and other animals on hunting excursions with his father. His father had said that all anyone needed was a sharp knife and a steady hand. He could remember those words as if his father were speaking to him now.

* * *

The ringing telephone penetrated his consciousness. He dreamed that Marie was still with him and he reached for her, forgetting that she had gone back to her own apartment. The empty place in bed startled him into opening his eyes. Light streamed in from the slits beneath the window shades. It was day, and he struggled to come awake. As the ringing persisted, Russo swung his legs over the side of the bed and found a cigarette. He fumbled for a match as he lifted the receiver.

"Yeah?"

"Hey, Lieutenant," Rosinski's excited voice blared in his ear, "guess what?"

"Jesus, what do you mean 'guess what'? You woke me up. This is our day off, isn't it?"

"Yeah, it's our day off, but you finally got your *G* and I thought you would want to know."

"What the hell are you talking about, Rosinski?"

"The morning television news, didn't you see it?"

"How the hell could I see it if you just woke me up?"

"Sorry about that, but I knew you'd want to know."

"Goddamn it, Rosinski, know what?"

"They've found the body of a woman who's been skinned alive. Her body was left in a carnival booth. Somebody opened the booth this morning and there she was, spread-eagled on the ring-toss game. The newscaster hinted that she had been cleaned—you know, degutted."

Russo was finally awake. "Where did this happen?"

"That's the reason I called. She got zapped in Grand Rapids. You finally got the *G* you've been waiting for." Rosinski paused. "And from the description of the kill it sure sounds like the sort of thing your friend Teague would do, if he's doing it.''

Russo inhaled a lungful of smoke and let it out slowly. ''He's doing it,'' he said quietly, ''and he's got to be stopped.''

''Are you going to talk to the chief about it?''

''I am,'' Russo said. ''Right now. I'll get dressed and get right down to headquarters, although I doubt that it'll do any good.''

''You want me to meet you there?'' Rosinski asked.

''Why? It's your day off.''

Rosinski chuckled. ''You've got me interested in this thing. I don't know if you're right or wrong about Teague, but I'd like to see the chief of detectives's face when you lay this Grand Rapids thing on him.'' His chuckle deepened into a laugh. ''You know, if things work out right, you may be demoted and end up working for me, you never know.''

''If you want to come with me, you're welcome.'' There was no amusement in Russo's voice. ''But I don't think that would be wise. The chief thinks I'm nuts and you might get tarred with the same brush, you know?''

''I'm not worried. Polacks never get very far in this department anyway. I'll meet you down there.''

''Give it to me again, about the girl?''

''There wasn't much to it, just a short item on the state news part of the morning TV. Christ, I can almost recite it word for word. It started out with the typical line about a grisly murder having been reported in Grand Rapids. A skinned body of a woman was found when they opened a game in a carnival up there—ring-toss—I remember that. They haven't identified her, but they think she was the game's operator. The newscaster said she had been skinned and dressed like a deer, so I presume he meant she had been degutted.''

"When did all this happen?"

"No mention of that, except it happened sometime last night, apparently. I figured it was bizarre enough to match your man's technique, and the city does start with a *G*, so I thought I'd give you a call.'' Rosinski paused. ''Of course, it could be somebody else, those carnivals attract weirdos.''

"It was Teague," Russo said. "I'll see you at head-quarters.''

*   *   *

Teague was awake. He had watched the same morning TV report seen by Rosinski. He had hoped for more coverage, but he supposed the death of a carnival worker, no matter how unique, did not rank high on the general news scale of importance. Still, it was enough; he had publicly signed the *G* and that was the important part.

He tried to go back to sleep. Although it had been a long and tiring night he was too excited by its memory to drift into sleep again. Taking her back to the booth was a stroke of genius. She would have been just a mutilated corpse otherwise, but stretching her out on her own game board gave it just the right touch to insure publicity.

It had all been so easy. One of the carnival roustabouts, on his way to the toilet, almost discovered him, but the laborer had been too drunk to notice the tall man with the large bundle wrapped in a tarpaulin. No one else had been stirring on the carnival grounds during the early morning hours. He had been careful: he had disposed of his gloves, tools and bloodstained clothing. Nothing could point to him. After he had completed dressing the body, he had buried the refuse and washed himself in a nearby stream. At the motel he had showered and double checked his car to make sure that no blood stained the interior. It was clean.

Edward Teague rolled over on his back and idly studied the motel ceiling. He felt completely satisfied and fulfilled. Everything had gone even better than he had hoped. He still intended to continue with his plan and eventually spell out the word *man*, but it was of secondary importance now. He would now make sure that no one suspected his intentions, and that meant killing Russo. He would punish him first, he had decided that. Just killing him would not be enough; the man had to be punished. Teague rolled over on his stomach and nestled his head into the softness of the pillow. And the lawyer too, he reminded himself, was an enemy. He would be killed, but like Russo he would be punished first. Dr. Rose had told the truth: Thomas Knapp didn't save him at all; the lawyer had actually seen to it that he be railroaded into a hospital for the insane. He was not insane; Rose had recognized that from the beginning. Knapp would have to be punished for the indignities he had forced Teague to suffer.

* * *

Like Russo and Teague, Thomas Knapp woke to find the sun streaming in his window. He liked the small guest room; it had become his "place" in the house, a sanctuary from his wife and a quiet haven for himself. The house had a strange empty sound to it. He always found it difficult to adjust when the children were away. Both of them were at summer camp. He missed them, but he was glad they were missing the tension in the household.

Divorce was the obvious answer, yet he knew she would get the children and Knapp couldn't live with that. It wasn't the separation—children adjusted much better to such things than adults. But he knew Helen would use them as tools against him. Although she loved them, in her own selfish, vindictive way she would make them suffer just to punish him. He was afraid they'd be emotionally damaged if they were left alone with her. At least with him around to bear the brunt of her anger and frustration there was some protection for them—at least he hoped the agony served some useful purpose. Even so, it was a hellish situation at best.

He was beginning to regret the affair with Martha, although it did offer him solace. He felt guilty. He didn't want to exploit her, aware that she was particularly vulnerable at this time in her life. A lady, newly separated, looking for affirmation that she was still worthwhile as a woman. Like shooting a bird in the water, it wasn't sporting. But there was no future for them, he knew that. The war with his wife would continue until the children became old enough to escape the tangle of their parents' lives. And that escape still lay years away. It was cruel to continue at the eventual expense of a nice lady like Martha Flowers.

Knapp sat up, dispirited. Lately he had found that his thoughts dwelled only on the joyless and drab prospects of his life. He knew he was mildly depressed, but he reasoned that it was a logical enough result of his situation.

Their life-style had become fixed. His wife spent most of her day—at least the part past noon—either lazing about the country club pool or taking tennis lessons. He knew by the bills that she was drinking heavily, but he knew it would be useless to discuss it with her. He continued to put in long hours, except that now Helen's everlasting fear of infidelity had finally come true. Instead of working, as he had for years, he was indeed seeing another woman. He wondered if he hadn't begun the affair out of spite.

Knapp showered and shaved quietly. He didn't want to wake his wife and give her another opportunity to create a scene. It was very late when he had come in the night before, and he knew she'd not been asleep. As he watched the river and talked with Martha, the evening had passed quickly. He was afraid Helen would be up and primed for battle, just as he now was afraid of waking her.

When he finally backed the Cadillac out of the garage and escaped what he called his home, he felt a sense of relief.

About the time Knapp was pulling onto the main highway, Edward Teague had packed up his car and was pulling away from the small motel. Both men were headed for the city.

* * *

The men in the department had tagged the chief of detectives ''Pig Eyes'' years before. The chief's eyes were peculiar—small, dark, and deeply set into his round, fleshy face, two tiny black agates staring out from their fat prison. If his eyes were not the windows to his soul, they were, perhaps, miniature peepholes. And now they were fixed on Russo.

"I think this is a lot of shit, Tony," he said after listening to the detective's theory again. "You've let this Teague business bend you out of whack, you know that?"

"I'm not nuts."

The chief had given up smoking, but he still perpetually held an unlit cigar clutched in his teeth—always an expensive brand—and this he chewed on during the day, causing his stomach a multitude of problems. Many thought this accounted for his continually sour disposition.

"Tony, not one of these murders has occurred in our jurisdiction. I'm not opposed to your letting the various law-enforcement agencies involved know about your Teague theory, although they'll think you've gone bananas. But that's up to you. But I can't let you devote any more time to this thing. Jesus, you guys in homicide have more work than a mosquito on a fat lady. I'd like to be able to let you go running around on this, but I can't. We just have too damn much work to do."

"Chief"—Russo's voice was calm, which surprised Rosinski who thought his partner might explode—"this is more than a theory. You should know me by now."

"Maybe so, but I have a department to run. We have enough business without your leaving town and setting up your own shop. The taxpayers of this city ain't paying you to protect the people of Grand Rapids, goddamn it, they are paying you to protect *them*!"

"If Teague is loose," Russo said calmly, "he's likely to come back here. He scored most of his kills here. This is his hunting ground and it's just natural that he'd come back."

"Bullshit! If that guy is on the loose, this is the last

place he'd come. Christ, everyone around here still remembers that case.''

''But he's older now and probably looks different. People might not even recognize him.''

The chief scowled in disgust, taking the soggy cigar from his mouth. He picked up a stained pair of scissors and snipped the soggy part into a wastepaper basket. Then he clamped the shortened cigar between his yellowed teeth. ''I'm sorry, Tony, I have too many problems without going outside my jurisdiction to look for more. Teague is probably a thousand miles away from here and never had any part in those murders. Jesus, a guy would have to be nuts to spell out his nickname in murders.''

Russo sighed. ''That's the point. Teague is insane.''

''Naw, it's just a coincidence. Hell, I'll bet I could pick out enough murders in the last month in different places to spell out *Tony Russo*, but I ain't about to arrest you. You see what I mean?''

Rosinski gathered his courage and spoke up. ''Uh, Chief, there's one more thing that Lieutenant Russo didn't mention. There's a possibility that Teague is headed here to go after him.''

''What?''

''It's just a hunch that one of the state cops had,'' Russo said. ''He thought Teague might come after me, maybe try to kill me or a girl friend.''

The chief snorted again. ''From what I hear about you, Russo, he'll have to knock off half the female population of the state, if that's the case. Sounds like a lot of crap to me.'' He paused. ''Last time I heard, you were divorced again anyway, right?''

Russo smiled slightly. ''Again yes. But I do have a girl friend.''

"Several," the chief said. "At least according to my sources."

"I don't think much of the idea either," Russo said. "I don't think Teague would come after me, but I can tell you he is killing women. Somebody has to do something."

"Like I said, you can let the other agencies know what you think, but don't be surprised if they laugh you out of the room."

Russo shrugged. "I'm thick-skinned. By the way, if you change your mind, let me know."

"Change my mind about what?"

"Letting me go after Teague."

The chief sighed. "I'll change my mind when a murder is committed within our jurisdiction and there is probable cause—probable cause like in court—that Edward Teague did it. Then I'll let you go to work."

"How about if I do something on my own time?" Russo asked.

"Christ, Tony, if you screw around with this thing much more you'll have every department in the country sore at us. Hell, they know their job, they don't need some outside cop telling them what to do."

"I won't be telling anybody what to do."

"Well, for the record, I'm not saying that you can't, but I'm not encouraging you either. I think it's a wild goose chase, frankly. If you want a hobby, why don't you take up checkers or chess or something that won't get this department into hot water?"

"I'll be careful. I won't step on any toes, Chief."

"See that you don't."

Russo and Rosinski stood up to leave.

"Rosinski," the chief said, his little eyes turning to the

young officer, "I wouldn't pay too much attention to this screwball, even if he is your boss. You keep your nose clean, you understand? You got a long career ahead of you, don't screw it up on some nutty deal like this."

"I'll be careful too," Rosinski said.

They left the chief's office. "Well," Rosinski said, "that went about the way you expected it to, didn't it?"

Russo nodded, his face grim.

"Don't you think that Teague might come after you?"

"No," Russo said, but he resolved to tell Marie that he wouldn't see her again until this Teague business was cleared up. It would be foolish to court danger.

As they left the headquarters building, Edward Teague was less than a hundred miles away, speeding along the interstate, headed for the city.

* * *

Teague began to feel the drain of fatigue as he approached the city. The lack of sleep rendered his mind incapable of formulating any specific plans. He pulled off the interstate and drove down the main street of Fordson, the sprawling suburb on the city's western border. The older part of that suburb was a jumble of specialty stores and restaurants. Shopping centers and rows of motels marked the newer area. He passed by the small, inexpensive motels, but he reasoned that the police might be watching them for prostitution. He needed to be lost among respectable people and so he pulled into the local Walther Inn.

It was a motor inn, four stories high. The rooms would number several hundred: just the place to get lost in for a while. He registered under Wilson, the name he had used in Chicago. The clerk took his Master Charge card and printed it onto his room bill, then returned the card to him. He listed his business as sales on the registration card and put down his correct Illinois license number. Even if someone were to check, which was not likely, they would find nothing suspicious about Mr. Wilson, the salesman from Chicago. His credit was good, and after all, that was all that mattered.

He drove his car around to the parking area near his room and carried his bags up to the second floor room. His room looked out on the roadway below, but it was quiet enough because the place was almost soundproof. Even the passing trucks made no more than a whisper as they whisked by below. For a while it would be a fine base for his preparations.

Teague lay down on the comfortable bed, intending only to rest for a moment. Several hours later he awoke and it was just past four. He felt irritated; he had not planned to fall asleep. Lifting himself from the bed he realized he had missed both breakfast and lunch and was hungry.

He changed from his wrinkled clothes and showered. Refreshed and dressed, Teague walked through the thickly carpeted hallway and downstairs to the restaurant. He bought a local newspaper from the container in the hallway. The restaurant was almost empty; only a few people occupied its many tables.

Once seated, Teague opened the newspaper. There was nothing about it on page one. He riffled through the pages until he found it. It was only a small one-column story in the second section of the newspaper. He felt slighted. Just the bare-boned facts were reported. The girl had been identified, they gave her age, and the story hinted at the grisly effect he had created at the ring-toss game, although they did not give the exact details. Probably the grotesque facts were omitted so the more delicate readers would be spared. But it was enough. He had spelled out *stalking*, if only they were smart enough to catch on. Only one man would be that smart, but Teague planned to eliminate him before he came after him.

He was in a better mood after having read the paper and tried to joke with the young spindly waitress, but she was disinterested and showed no response beyond a polite forced smile. Teague ordered a steak. He felt the need of substantial food, and it was a small reward to himself for a good night's work.

While he waited for his dinner, he left the table and went to a telephone booth. He looked the number up first, then dialed.

"Wolfson, Abner, Knapp and Fitch," the receptionist answered. "Can I help you?"

"I'd like to speak to Mr. Knapp, please."

There was a click. "Mr. Knapp's office," a new female voice inquired. Martha Flowers had answered the telephone.

"I'd like to speak to Mr. Knapp, please," he repeated.

"I'll see if he's in, sir. Who may I say is calling?"

Teague smiled. "Lieutenant Russo of the police."

"Just a minute, Lieutenant," she said, and then the line went dead as she put him on hold.

Teague wondered what she looked like. She was Knapp's private secretary. He wondered if there was anything between them. She might be the perfect way to get at Knapp.

A minute or two passed and Teague was just beginning to be annoyed when a familiar voice came on the line.

"This is Tom Knapp, Lieutenant. What can I do for you?"

Teague said nothing.

"Hello," Knapp repeated.

Teague still said nothing.

"Hello, Russo. Are you there?" Knapp's smooth voice betrayed a hint of irritation. "Oh crap," he said at last and hung up.

Teague hung up on his end. Dr. Rose was right. Knapp obviously knew Russo well. Teague needed no further proof. The fucking lawyer had railroaded him into the mental hospital. Now it was a matter of simple justice: The man had to be punished.

He returned to his table just as the girl was serving the salad.

* * *

Thomas Knapp snapped on the intercom. "Martha, apparently we were cut off. Would you please get me Lieutenant Russo, he's with the homicide bureau."

"Yes, Mr. Knapp." She sounded so formal that her voice had an icy edge to it. On the days when they both knew they'd be spending the evening together she became so professional that her responses were almost hostile. It would have been amusing except that he realized how important it was to her that she not be catalogued as an office plaything. He honored her wish by being equally as distant, and most likely anyone observing them closely would suspect that something was going on, if only because such pains were taken to conceal the possibility. There was no use, however, in explaining this to Martha; she was convinced hers was the right way.

He returned to the dry language of the trust document. Trusts were Wolfson's department; but he was on vacation, and old Mrs. Bronson had shuffled off her mortal coil despite his absence. The estate amounted to several million dollars; and although most of the work would be waiting for Wolfson when he got back, it was imperative that the firm take some fast action—or appear to do so— if they wished to keep the heirs happy and content with them as their legal representatives.

The intercom line buzzed and he picked up the receiver. "Yes?"

"I just called homicide and they said this is Lieutenant Russo's day off. Did you want me to get his home telephone number?"

Knapp chuckled. "They would never give that out, not even for you, Martha." He was going to drop the whole matter but he decided it might look rude. "Call them back and leave a message. Just say I'm returning his call."

"Yes sir."

Knapp returned to the trust document. The language was boring; but he would have to know every inch of it when he talked to the heirs, so he concentrated on each word. He completely forgot about the telephone call.

*   *   *

It was one of the ironies of his life that he, Harry Bartlett, who hated guns and the people who used them, was reduced to selling firearms to the very people he detested. He had floated from job to job, and now, to support his family, he was obliged to work in his father-in-law's sporting goods store. He was surrounded by what he considered implements of torture: curved ugly gaffs used to slash into the soft underjaw of some defenseless fish, barbed hooks, multi-pronged frog spears, and an array of other sharp and dangerous gadgets used by fishermen and hunters. The idea of sitting all day in a boat, dangling an impaled worm, hoping to snare a fish no longer than a few inches, seemed ridiculous to Harry Bartlett, yet he had studied such nonsense sufficiently to talk authoritatively on the subject with even the most avid fisherman.

He had even become a book expert on the racks of shotguns and rifles. They no longer carried pistols; the permit business entailed too much paperwork to justify the small profit to be made. Although he hated the men and women who hunted down and killed defenseless animals and birds, he had forced himself to become an authority on the velocity and striking-impact of these deadly weapons and the ammunition they expelled. It was hypocrisy of the highest order, he knew that, but his family had to eat. He had no choice.

He wondered if the customer idly surveying the rifles was a hunter. The man was tall—well over six feet—and lean; yet his face had a mild, friendly quality. His blonde hair had been nicely styled and it seemed to give him a gentle appearance. The customer's blue eyes moved from one weapon to another, but he seemed to view them more as pieces in a museum, and not with the almost sexual interest that Bartlett had seen in some other customers. The man looked peaceful, meditative, out of place in such violent surroundings.

Edward Teague was shopping.

"Can I help you, sir?" Bartlett inquired.

"Tell me, do you need a permit to buy one of those things?" He nodded at the rifles.

"No, the permit's just for pistols, and we don't sell pistols."

"Well, maybe you can help me. I'm not a hunter, but I'm looking for a gift for my father-in-law. He's a hunter, the kind that goes after deer, bear, or anything else that moves, that sort of thing."

"I understand," Bartlett said, delighted that his first impression had been confirmed.

"My wife thinks he might like a new gun. He hunts big game. What do you think might fill the bill? I don't want anything cheap, but on the other hand I don't want to mortgage the house either, if you see what I mean?"

"Of course. If he's a hunter, he'd know the value of the gun anyway. Big game, you say?"

"Yes."

Bartlett moved to the gun cabinet and unlocked it. "Here's a very nice weapon. It's a Remington automatic. One of the best guns made for its price, a very fine sporting rifle."

Teague hefted the gun, pretending that he knew nothing about weapons. "It seems to me I've heard him say something negative about automatic rifles, that they jam or something."

"Well, that can happen to all guns, of course. They have to be properly maintained. But automatics do have a tendency to jam on occasion. Perhaps something in a bolt action would be better."

"What about that one, the one with the telescopic sight on top?"

Bartlett replaced the Remington and picked up the rifle Teague indicated and handed it to him. "You have a good eye for guns, sir," he said. "This is a Winchester .30-06. The scope can be sold with the rifle or removed."

"Is this how you look through the thing?" Teague asked, sighting down the sporting goods store, aiming at the eye of a stuffed moosehead.

"Yes."

"Are those two intersecting lines supposed to be there, the ones I see in the telescope?"

Bartlett knew the man knew nothing about hunting. "That's where you aim those things, right where the lines—they are called cross hairs—meet."

Teague hefted the weapon in his large hands. "Will he have to adjust the telescope?"

"No. This rifle has been preset. The scope has been tested and corrected to fit perfectly. It is as accurate as they can make it."

Teague nodded. He would have no opportunity to test the weapon. Any number of things could have happened to the rifle after testing—just the handling in the store could have thrown off the sight's accuracy—yet it was the best he could hope for under the circumstances. "I suppose I really ought to get him a box of ammunition too—sort of symbolic, you know?"

Bartlett liked this customer. He obviously felt about hunters just as he did. "We have a variety of ammunition. Different charges and types—it depends on what you intend to use it for."

Teague frowned as if the statement presented a problem. "Mainly he hunts for bear. Deer too, but he is rather enthusiastic about going after bears. I don't understand it myself."

"I agree, sir," Bartlett smiled. "However, each of us is different. If he's hunting bear he'll want a magnum load, that's a bullet with extra power, gives more power to the shot, you see."

"I understand."

"Also, he would probably use a soft, hollow-point bullet. The nose of the bullet splits apart in the body of the target. It's a killing thing, but I suppose if you're going to shoot a bear, it's just good sense to make sure he doesn't turn around and start hunting you."

Teague smiled easily. "That does make a lot of sense. How many bullets to a box?"

"They come twenty or fifty to a box."

"Give me a box of twenty. Like I said, it's only symbolic. If he wants more he can buy more."

"Yes, sir." Bartlett laid the rifle on the counter and pulled out a box of ammunition. Then he began to figure the total.

"What's that wicked-looking knife over there?" Teague asked, knowing full well what it was.

"That's a skinning knife. It's Swedish steel, very good, very sharp."

"Mean-looking thing, isn't it?"

"Yes, it is," Bartlett agreed.

"Throw in one of those knives, and one of those leather doodads they stick them in."

"A scabbard?"

"Let me see it, okay?" Teague asked.

Bartlett handed the knife to him. The handle was wood, not plastic and Teague liked that. The long blade tapered to a spearlike end, its steel honed to a razor edge. "Well, that should take care of him in fine style," Teague said, returning the knife to the clerk. "I don't suppose you have gift boxes for these things by any chance?"

"No, I'm afraid not. Each one comes in its own box, though. I'm sure they'll make nice presents when they're wrapped.'' Bartlett added the price of the knife and scab-bard to the sales slip.

''Wrapping is the wife's department,'' Teague said, smiling.

''Anything else, sir?''

Teague thought for a moment. ''No, I think that takes care of it.''

''I'm sure your father-in-law will be very happy with these gifts.''

''I suppose he will,'' Teague replied.

Bartlett hurried away to box the rifle. Teague was happy. After having taken care of the carnival girl, he had buried his best skinning knife. The new one looked even better, and the rifle would provide an alternative if he couldn't get close enough to use the knife.

He looked around the sporting goods store. Trophies hung from each wall—animals, mounted fighting marlins and other game fish. Deer heads with flaring spiked antlers stared vacantly across the top of the store. It was traditional in sporting goods stores. He loved the places. He had loved it when his father had taken him to shop in the stores. They represented a world without women, and that in itself was a comforting feeling.

Bartlett returned with the packages. Teague paid in cash and carried his treasures to the car. He was now fully equipped for what he had to do. It was a satisfying feeling.

7

Rosinski's mouth felt dry and his head ached, but the hangover was minor compared to some of the others. Getting drunk was his answer to frustration. But he had made it to the job despite his protesting stomach and had been working. As Russo had requested, the call to Grand Rapids was made.

Russo was late. That in itself was unusual, and when he did appear he looked haggard. Rosinski wondered if the lieutenant was also finding solace in a bottle.

"You look a little peaked," Rosinski said in greeting. "Hang one on last night?"

Russo looked closely at his young partner. "No, as a matter of fact, I didn't, but I can see that you did. God, you look like they drained the blood out of you."

Rosinski grinned. "They might have. I don't remember much after eleven o'clock. But at least I have an excuse. How come you look like you didn't sleep?"

Russo yawned. "Best reason in the world: I didn't sleep."

"How come?"

Russo ignored the question. "You want some coffee? You look like you could use some."

"Stomach couldn't stand it," Rosinski replied. "I called Grand Rapids, by the way."

"What did they have to say?"

"Like the newspapers said, the girl was twenty-three, worked the ring-toss game for her uncle. He was in a South Bend hospital where his appendix had been removed, that's why she was alone. From what the cops could learn from the carnies, the girl was sort of a tramp and slept around a lot. She was into everything—booze, drugs—a real fallen sparrow."

"Christ, Rosinski, please spare me the poetry."

"One of the other game operators remembers seeing her close up, and he said some tall, blonde guy was helping her. He's not sure whether she left with him or not. There wasn't a trace of her after that until they forced open the ring-toss game."

"Why did they do that?" Russo asked.

"What?"

"Force open the game? They must have had some reason to do that."

"Oh yes, an X had been painted across the front of the thing in blood. They didn't know it was blood at the time, of course. A couple of dogs were sniffing around. The carny people got worried and popped the lock."

Rosinski's voice dropped to a near whisper. "It was even worse than the papers reported. The woman was beaten to death, plenty of fractures. She died of the beating apparently, anyway that's what their medical examiner thinks. Then she was degutted, just like I told you, the same as you would clean a deer. One incision down the abdomen and all the insides scraped out. Then she was skinned. The medical report said it was a good job. Again, it was done just the way hide is stripped from an animal, but only from the neck on down. They haven't found the skin or the guts so far."

"Jesus!"

"I haven't even come to the worst part yet. The guy propped her up on the ring-toss board, like a crucifixion, you know. Then he stuffed a cheap panda doll into the body cavity so that the head of the doll was looking out. Scared the shit out of the carny people who found her."

"There must have been plenty of fingerprints with all the blood around that game?"

Rosinski shook his head. "The guy used gloves. Besides, he didn't kill or skin her at the game. He did it somewhere else and delivered her, that's what they said. They found no tracks, except for some of drops of blood where he carried her from the car." Rosinski paused. "Well, does all that add up to your man Teague?"

There was no emotion in Russo's response. "That's him." He looked at Rosinski. "Did you tell the Grand Rapids police about my theory about Teague?"

"Yeah, but the guy I talked to didn't sound too impressed. He said he appreciated the tip and they'd check it out, but it was just a polite brush-off, at least that's the way it sounded to me."

Russo shook his head. "Damn it! I can't convince anyone."

Rosinski rubbed his aching temples. "Well, you've made one convert. I really didn't believe all this until he signed that *G*."

"It still could be just coincidence," Russo reminded him.

The young officer shook his head. "I don't think so now. I don't know if you've noticed or not, but each killing has been just a bit more bizarre than the last. I mean, he crucified one girl in a barn, then beheaded the next. God, that business of stuffing a panda doll inside a skinned corpse gives me the willies. It's Teague. And if it isn't him, then it has to be another real sicko—but as far as I'm concerned the pattern you figured out is there.''

Russo smiled wryly. ''Well, my first real disciple, maybe all isn't lost after all.''

''There's nothing much we can do about it though,'' Rosinski said, his voice reflecting the futility he felt.

''Maybe yes, maybe no,'' Russo replied as he glanced through his messages and mail. He stopped and looked at Rosinski. ''Did you call Tom Knapp yesterday?''

''I've never called him, at least not that I can ever remember.''

''Odd. Message here said he returned my call yesterday.''

''Knapp was Teague's lawyer, wasn't he?''

Russo frowned, lost in thought for a moment, then he replied, ''Yeah, he was. And I never made a call to him either. Strange, isn't it?''

''Maybe he's trying to sell you a ticket to the lawyer's ball.''

''I'll find out,'' Russo said. ''I'll call him later.''

* * *

Knapp was always punctual, Teague remembered that. Before the trial, the lawyer would always arrive at the jail right on the minute promised. A precise habit and helpful to someone wanting to track him down.

Knapp's law firm occupied offices in the Majestic Building, and this caused Teague some difficulty. There were two entrances; one on the east side on Garfield Street, and the other on the south side at Conner Avenue. At various locations inside the huge building multibanks of elevators waited to whisk customers up into the tower of the skyscraper.

Fortunately a coffee shop was located across the street from the Majestic Building at a corner where both entrances could be observed. Teague bought a morning newspaper and ordered breakfast at a table where he could see both entrances. There was no fear that Knapp might see and recognize him. When he had been sent away, Teague had worn glasses, was overweight and his hair was close-clipped. Now he was lean, his long blonde hair was styled gracefully, and the glasses had been replaced by contacts. Even Russo would have a tough time recognizing him now.

Edward Teague realized that the years might have also changed Knapp. He wondered if the tall attorney still had a full head of steel-gray hair or whether he might have changed in some way to make recognition difficult. It was a risk but there was no alternative.

Despite disapproving looks from the busy waitresses, he held his table as the morning rush began to descend on the Majestic Building. They came by the dozens—at first mostly young girls, the typists and secretaries who had come to open the offices; then a slightly older group—the management types—appeared; later, the well-dressed professionals arrived, most of them carrying briefcases as though they were some kind of badge of office. Teague's concentration became more intent as he divided his attention between the two entrances. He realized he could not be 100 percent effective, but he did his best. There was no assurance that Knapp would even come to the office. He might be away, or in court. Still, he knew that eventually Knapp would come to the office building. He was prepared to stake out his position for as long as necessary.

Then he saw him. He had not changed at all. Knapp crossed Conner Avenue and used that entrance. There was no mistaking the silver-gray hair or the long stride.

He remembered a morning, long ago, when a mist had lain in the woods. They had waited, his father and himself, by an old rotted tree. Patience, he said. It had been one of their first trips and he had doubted his father's wisdom. He had doubted until the big buck had emerged slowly out of the mist, its regal head held high and alert. He had experienced a shivering thrill of joy and triumph.

He was so pleased he almost laughed out loud. He left a big tip, picked up his newspaper, and nodded at a scowling waitress. It would be a long wait again in the evening; but at least he now knew which exit Knapp would probably use, and that was important to his plans.

Time passed slowly. Teague walked through the business section and the shops. It was the first time he had been back to his native city since they had sent him to the mental hospital. Like himself, the city too had changed. The Marple Department Store—the massive red-brick landmark—had been torn down and a gleaming stainless-steel skyscraper replaced it. Some of the shops which had formerly catered to the rich now displayed cheap merchandise, and some of the business places were vacant. The city had changed a great deal.

Teague walked along the downtown area noting the obvious contradiction: Part was growth and part was decay. But basically it was a dying city. It seemed that the improvements were out of place, like straightening the teeth of a terminal cancer patient—neither logical nor worth the effort.

He strolled through the shops, killing time. A dingy theater up the street announced its program began at noon. He waited until it opened and then sought the solace of its nearly empty dark cavern. It was a tawdry movie, but he barely saw the screen. It was time to formulate his plan of attack.

* * *

"Telephone for you, Lieutenant. Line eight."

"Russo," he said into the receiver.

"Tony, I have to see you." He recognized Marie's voice, and he was shocked that she was violating their rule which forbade her calling the bureau's office. He was afraid others would know her voice too.

"Look," he said, keeping his voice low, "we've been all over this. I won't see you again until this other business is cleared up."

"Tony, this whole thing is crazy, do you realize that? It may never be cleared up. Does that mean you and I are through? Is this your way of telling me?" She attempted to make her last statement sound light-hearted, but he read the real anxiety in her voice.

"We are not through," he said. "You know my reasons. Haven't we already been through that? It may never be cleared up. But until it is, my first concern is for your protection."

"If it's for my protection, then I should be entitled to some say in whether or not it's worth the risk."

"Not this time. This is serious." He was about to say her name but he checked himself. Other officers might be listening, and he had managed to keep their relationship secret so far, for the sake of her reputation. But now her life might depend on that secrecy.

She didn't reply for a moment. Finally she spoke, this time with an edge in her voice. "Harry Edwards has asked me out. If you aren't interested, I'll take him up on it."

Women, he thought ruefully to himself, they unerringly went for the jugular. Harry Edwards had an even worse reputation than he did, and well earned. A younger man with almost feminine eyelashes, Edwards was the reigning stud in the police department. He felt the pangs of jealousy. "Cut it out, for God's sake, you're being silly."

"I think we have a silly contest going, you and I," she said. "Tony, this is nonsense. If you can't even sneak over to my apartment without being seen, then you should have been a banker rather than a policeman." She paused. "I mean it, Tony, either you show up tonight, or I'll be out dancing with Harry Edwards tomorrow."

He doubted that she would, but he had enough experience with women to know that nothing was ever sure.

"I'll be there," he snapped irritably, knowing she would delight in her victory.

"For dinner?"

"No. I'll be over after dark, probably about ten."

She giggled in triumph. "It might be worth it, Tony," she laughed.

"I'll see you at ten," he growled, slamming down the receiver. "Goddamn it!" he snarled under his breath.

"What's that, Lieutenant?" Rosinski asked.

"Nothing!"

Rosinski's eyes were surprised.

"Sorry," Russo said, "I'm getting jumpy."

The other detective shrugged to show he understood. "Did you call Knapp?" he asked.

"I forgot. I'll do it now."

Russo dialed the number on the message slip and worked his way through the law firm's switchboard girl to Martha Flowers. Shortly thereafter Thomas Knapp came on the line.

"Hello, Lieutenant, how have you been?"

"Fine, Mr. Knapp. What can I do for you?"

"I was merely returning your call." The attorney sounded slightly puzzled.

"But I didn't call."

There was a pause at the other end. "That's odd, my girl distinctly received a message from someone who said he was Lieutenant Russo of homicide."

"That's strange," Russo said. "As I recall, we don't have any mutual customers at the moment."

Russo resented the cool voice of the lawyer. Knapp sounded so sure of himself. "Did you happen to see the article about the woman killed at the carnival in Grand Rapids?"

"Yes," Knapp replied.

"Well, I think your client, Edward Teague, killed her. How does that make you feel?"

"What proof do you have?" Knapp's voice was even, with no hint of challenge.

"To begin with, the Stalking Man is out of the hospital. Did you know that?"

"As a matter of fact, I did," Knapp replied. "Dr. Rose told me about his release at the time of the Winkler sanity hearing."

"There's been a trail of bodies across the Midwest in

the last few months, Counselor—murders committed in a frenzy of hate, all women.''

''That's unfortunate of course, but how does that affect Teague?''

''When you add up the first initial of each city, they spell out the word *stalking*—who do you think might be up to such a thing?''

There was a pause at the other end of the line. Finally, Knapp spoke; again his voice had the velvet quality of self-assurance. ''Obviously, you think Teague committed the murders. I would suggest that you arrest him before he does any more. That is, of course, if he actually did commit the homicides.''

''Why arrest him?'' Russo snarled. ''Just so you can go through your act and set him free again?''

''I have a job, just like you do, Russo.'' Knapp's words now carried the promise of anger. ''I do my job to the best of my ability. If the law allows people like Teague to go about free, complain to the state legislature, not to me. I act only within the limits of the law.''

''Bullshit!''

''Why don't you arrest him?''

Russo sighed. ''You really want to know the truth? Because no one believes me, that's why. You know Teague as well as I do, you know what he's like and what he can do.''

''I can't comment on that,'' Knapp said, his voice less sharp. ''Legal ethics forbid it.'' He paused. ''Russo, I have to admit privately that you may have a point, but I can't say anything for the record. A lawyer can't comment adversely on his client, not without his permission. You understand?''

''No, frankly, I don't. Jesus! I could use a little help

on this. Maybe if you talked to my bosses they might see the light.''

Again there was a pause. "All I am allowed to do is repeat that which is public record," Knapp said. "Edward Teague was adjudged to be insane. It is my belief that he killed the women he was charged with killing; that is why I chose the defense of insanity. I believed him then to be quite dangerous and insane under the law, and I convinced the jury of that position. I am not a doctor, Russo, I don't know what's happened to Teague since then. I can say, however that if he's as sick as he was when we tried the case it's entirely probable that he would do just exactly what you have described.''

"Well, I suppose that's something," Russo said. "I might call upon you, if I think it's needed. Right now, my credibility has a large gap when I talk to anybody about Teague.''

"I'll do what I can. Of course, you must understand that I'm limited by the canons of ethics which apply in these matters.''

"Knapp, can't you climb down off your high horse for a minute? You know, in a very real way, you're responsible for that looney being out on the street.''

"I'm not going to debate it with you, Russo. I doubt if either of us can persuade the other. If something comes up about Teague and I can help within the limits I described, I'll be glad to do so.''

Russo felt like yelling in frustration, but he controlled himself. The lawyer was probably right. Rules were rules. Cops had to obey their regulations, and he presumed lawyers had to toe their own particular lines. Besides, he realized no purpose would be served by arguing with the attorney.

"There's one more thing I think you should know," Russo said.

"What's that?"

"I talked to Rose the day he was killed. We had quite a hassle up at the state hospital over Teague. Needless to say, your name came up a few times."

"I suppose."

"Rose said Teague thought of you as his protector and that he, Rose, had gone to some lengths to persuade him that you were just an ordinary man. I had the feeling that Rose might have gone further than just that; he may have tried to poison Teague's mind against you. Rose was a jealous little bastard."

"You might be right," Knapp said, remembering his last conversation with the pompous psychiatrist. "But it's of no consequence."

"It might be," Russo continued. "That telephone call that was supposed to have been made by me might indicate that Teague is back in town."

"You mean, he may be the one who made it?"

"Maybe."

"Why?"

"God knows. He's insane and he may have been trying to connect you with me. He may have a grudge against you. I don't want to alarm you, but that's a possibility."

"I doubt it."

"Still, he's one of the few connections between you and me, and that telephone call might be his way of establishing some screwy theory of his, you never know."

Knapp's tone of quiet self-assurance returned. "Teague knows I saved his skin. I think it's more probable he'd want me around just in case he got into trouble again. I believe I'm safe enough."

"Maybe, but I'd be careful, if I were you." In his heart, Russo thought Knapp was responsible for Teague's release; but he knew the lawyer might actually be in danger, and that he himself might be the only person who could help. "Look, Knapp, I'm not trying to scare you, believe me, but if anything suspicious happens, give me a call, I might be of some assistance."

"I've managed to care for myself quite well, thanks." Knapp's reply was cool. "I thank you for your concern, but I think it's probably misplaced. Is there any other business between us?"

"No," Russo said.

"Nice talking to you, Lieutenant," Knapp said as he hung up.

If anything happens to him, the bastard deserves it, Russo thought to himself. But he felt a sense of inadequacy that he hadn't been able to persuade the lawyer of possible danger. He swore softly to himself.

The unexplained telephone call to the attorney would be typical of Teague. And if it was, then the Stalking Man was back in town—and busy.

* * *

One bus stop served three different bus lines according to the sign. The bus stop was directly across from the Conner Avenue entrance to the Majestic Building. Small knots of people formed clusters as they waited. As each bus stopped, those who wished that particular vehicle boarded and the rest continued to wait until their bus appeared. No one noticed the tall man who waited with them but never boarded any of the buses. Many passengers used the stop, and the blonde man blended with the rest of the waiting people. Other people read newspapers or were lost in thought, but his eyes remained fixed on the Majestic Building's revolving door.

Teague leaned against the building next to the bus stop, the afternoon newspaper tucked under his arm. He was the picture of the typical commuter on his way home. He watched the tide of workers flow from the Majestic Building. Since Knapp had gone in the Conner Avenue door, it was likely he would use it for his exit.

Animals follow habit patterns, his father had taught him. Learn the habit patterns. Learn their trails, their watering holes, their feeding grounds—the rest is easy.

Time was running out, the rush hour traffic was thinning out. Now Teague was one of only a few people waiting. Still he remained calm, practicing a hunter's patience.

His patience was rewarded as Thomas Knapp emerged from the building, engaged in an earnest conversation with a well-dressed stout man. Teague surmised that the other man was either an important client or a lawyer Knapp respected. He paid great attention to whatever the fat man was saying. They turned right and walked slowly up the street.

Teague paced them, but from across the street. He walked slowly so as to remain parallel with them. He ambled along casually, swinging his newspaper as he watched the two men. They crossed the street, trotting easily to catch the green light; then he took up a position about a hundred feet behind them.

The fat man waved a pudgy hand to Knapp and cut across Fairmount Street. Knapp kept going south up Ambler Boulevard, and Teague kept the hundred-foot distance between them, matching the tall lawyer's increased pace and stride. Knapp was in a hurry.

Even if the lawyer should suddenly turn around, Teague felt confident that his appearance had changed enough so that Knapp would never recognize him. He was elated that he'd found Knapp.

The lawyer turned into the Colonial Parking Garage. Teague passed by, keeping his pace brisk, walking past the door as though he had taken no notice. But he hurried to the corner and discovered there was only one entrance and exit from the parking garage: an opening onto narrow, one-way Calumet Street. He stopped at the corner and pretended to be looking for a ride, as if he expected someone to pick him up, but his eyes remained fastened on the garage exit. Mentally he estimated the time it might take Knapp to get to his car, start it, and drive to the street. Several cars came out the exit, but he could see the drivers clearly and none was the man he was waiting for.

Knapp's blue Cadillac rolled through the exit, pausing for a moment to allow another car to go by. Teague could see the lawyer's features quite clearly. He studied the Cadillac. He would know it again instantly. Just for good measure he noted the license number. Edward Teague had a remarkable memory for numbers and he did not need to write the number down; it was fixed in his mind.

Teague felt a warm flush of pleasure. Now he knew which exit Knapp used from his office building and he knew where he kept his car and what it looked like. Following him would be easy. Teague was relaxed and happy as he thought about dinner. Everything was going so very well.

* * *

Thomas Knapp drove to Martha Flowers's apartment. The food was good, the wine excellent, and he had an appreciative listener. It was a peaceful evening.

* * *

Edward Teague went for a long drive, cruising past the place where he had gone to high school, even past the place where he had experienced his first ultimate thrill—the site of his first killing. It excited him just to see the area again and remember the feelings and sensations of old. Eventually he tired of his old haunts and returned to his motel room. He ordered a smoked salmon dinner from room service and some imported beer. Like Knapp, he spent a tranquil evening, but he watched television and anticipated his plans for tomorrow.

* * *

Tony Russo worked late, catching up on the eternal paperwork that was the lot of every police officer. Later, he drove to a fast-food place and ordered the Monster—a triple-decker hamburger mounted by tomato, pickles, mustard, and ketchup. He spilled some of the ketchup on his tie and was angry at his own awkwardness.

Russo didn't know whether he should consider himself foolish or clever. If, in fact, Teague was following him, he was being clever. If not, he was a fool. Russo left the restaurant driving slowly and watching the traffic, which was light, behind him. He had a particular route in mind. It didn't appear that he was being followed, but he knew

Teague was smart, so he continued to carry out his plan.

The one-way street was short, only a few blocks long. An alley intersected it halfway to the end. He turned in, going the wrong way. There was no other traffic. He killed his lights as he carefully picked his way down the darkened street, his attention also on the rearview mirror. No other car turned. Maneuvering into the alleyway, he flipped on his lights and gunned the car through two more connecting alleys until he exited on busy Fullbright Street. No one could have pursued him without detection. Feeling relief, he hurried to Marie's apartment.

Again, Russo felt like an actor in a grade-B spy movie, although he had used the same technique a dozen times in real cases. He drove past her apartment house and parked two blocks away. Walking quickly, he stayed in the shadows, watching for anyone watching him. His coat was open and his pistol was within easy reach. The echo of his own footsteps was the only sound. Once inside the apartment house he pressed Marie's intercom buzzer and was admitted.

She answered the door dressed in a wraparound yellow robe. The nylon accentuated the fullness of her body. Her hair had been brushed but it still looked damp. The fresh smell of soap blossomed from her.

Fresh from her bath and without makeup, she looked even younger.

Russo stepped inside and closed the door. Without a word he gently pulled her to him. She did not resist at first as he brought his lips against her; then, as the kiss developed into deepening passion, she pushed him away.

She adjusted her robe. "Most gentlemen at least say 'hello' first, I believe."

Russo grinned. "Hello." He stepped toward her but she skipped away.

"My God, you haven't been spending the evening watching X-rated films, have you?"

"No, as a matter of fact, I spent an erotic evening going over my monthly investigation reports, topped off with a sloppy Monster hamburger for dinner. That's what really turns me on; one Monster, and I become a slavering sex maniac."

"So I see." She fluffed her hair. "Did the big bad wolf follow you over here?" Her voice was playful but he recognized the real taunt within the remark. It alarmed him that she was taking it all so lightly.

She sensed the change in him. "Tony, I think you're letting this thing get out of hand. Honestly, I do." She watched his face to see if her words were having any effect. "Can I get you a drink?"

"Whiskey and water, but I'll make it. How about you?"

She sat on the sofa, one long leg exposed. "A screwdriver, please. There's orange juice in the fridge."

He occupied himself in her small kitchen. "I can't find the orange juice—never mind—I found it." He prepared the drinks and returned.

Russo sat opposite and once again was dazzled by her. She was breathtakingly beautiful and he was very much in love with her. Also, he realized for the first time how afraid he was that he might lose her.

"Marie, I know how all this must sound to you, and maybe I'm going a little nuts, but until I'm sure that's what it is I don't want to do anything, not even the slightest thing, that might expose you to harm."

"I'm tired of hearing about your Stalking Man. You

talk about him as though he were some unstoppable evil spirit, something supernatural. He is a man. If you're right, Tony, he's a very sick man, nothing more. If he's committing all those murders he'll be caught. I'm sure that if he hasn't forgotten all about you, he'll stay as far from you as possible. You were the one who caught him in the first place. He can only fear you. That makes sense, doesn't it?''

He nodded. ''Ordinarily, it would, if you were dealing with a completely rational human being, but Teague isn't rational. He isn't an evil spirit either, although he comes pretty damn close. Picture this: Teague is a man of unusual strength and intellect. He was trained as a boy by his father to hunt. Hunting became the focal point of his life. He can shoot, ambush, track, do anything an expert hunter knows. And he has an uncanny knowledge of human psychology, especially female psychology. If you met him you would be instantly charmed. He's the kind of man who has a big, friendly smile, an open face, and honest blue eyes. But you would stand a better chance with a cobra. He developed a psychotic hatred of women, apparently because of his mother, although you really never know about those things, but that's what the doctors said at his trial.

''His hatred knows no bounds. He is totally without mercy where women are concerned. That's why he kills the way he does. Apparently he goes berserk after torturing them to death and continues to smash their dead bodies into bloody pulp. That's his trademark, the mangled body he leaves behind.''

''I know all that, Tony. You've told me all that before,'' she said petulantly. ''What I'm saying is that you have absolutely no proof he's even in this state, let alone coming after you. That's not even a guess, it's more like a small boy's nightmare." She paused. "What bothers me is that this preoccupation of yours is beginning to interfere with our private life."

"Marie, believe me, I know what I'm doing."

She looked away. "You're like no other man I've ever known, but I'm beginning to wonder about this secrecy kick of yours, Tony." She paused to light a cigarette. "When we first started going together you said you didn't want anyone in the department to know about us because you wanted to protect my reputation. Do you remember that?"

Russo nodded silently.

"You said you'd been such a woman-chaser that if my name were linked with yours I'd be branded as a scarlet woman. Well, that's meant meeting like two married people cheating on their spouses. Once in a while you pick me up at headquarters, but you're busy looking around as if a private detective were about to take a picture."

Her voice became more deliberate. "I've stood still for all that on the basis that you were really looking out for me. So we meet like two spies, I drive to a restaurant to see you, and if I'm lucky maybe we spend the night together. We sneak in here to my apartment, or we sneak in to your place. But the emphasis is on the word *sneak*. Now you've come up with a new wrinkle. Because of some Jack the Ripper you put away years ago I'm now supposed to get out of your life, to have no contact with you at all."

"Marie," he began, "please, it isn't like that at all."

"Oh no?" she snapped. "What about tonight? I drive home, fix my dinner, watch some television, take a bath, and spray myself with perfume. What for? So the midnight skulker can creep over here after the moon's gone down and knock off a quick piece of tail? Tony, that's no life for me. Can you understand that?''

Russo was miserable. He knew he was right, this was no time for taking risks. And yet he also knew that only he could comprehend the real situation, the real odds. Teague and he were wired to the same wavelength. Perhaps he was as mad as Teague in his own way, but he did understand the man. He tried to think of a way to convey this to Marie, to find a way to convince her of the possible danger.

''Edward Teague . . .'' he began.

''Oh, Christ,'' she said, ''here we go again, Tony—you and Mr. Edward Teague!'' Her eyes riveted on his, her face tense. ''You're a detective, give me one scintilla of proof that Teague's anywhere in this state, let alone this city.''

''Teague doesn't leave proof, I've told you that. He killed Dr. Rose, I'm convinced of that.''

She puffed irritably on her cigarette. ''Let's say, just for the sake of argument—since even the state police don't agree with you—that Teague did kill Rose. What in God's name makes you think he'd come back here, and especially what makes you think he'd risk getting anywhere near you: you, the only man who ever caught him?''

Russo felt defeated before he began. ''Instinct,'' he said. ''God, how I wish I could tell you that I saw him or that we found his fingerprints or anything concrete to get you to believe me, but I can't. I just know him. He is mad and he is coming here. The spelling out of the name was just to attract my attention, or at least something like that.''

Marie shook her head. "Tony, I have heard so many Russo stories in the department that they make you sound like something between Sherlock Holmes and a wizard; I'm programmed to believe what you say. But this time I think you've really let your compass get out of whack. I really do!"

"You mean that I'm obsessed with Edward Teague?"

She nodded. "Yes. This spelling idea is all yours. You've selected gruesome murders at appropriate cities. There have been other equally gruesome murders at other cities but you've discarded them because they would ruin your pet theory. Dr. Rose was killed by a lunatic who bore a grudge against him. The state police are confident they have the right man. The only one who thinks Teague is abroad and doing these terrible things is you. Don't you think you should give some credit to the men in the other police departments? They know what they are doing."

He sighed. "They're just like our department—undermanned and overworked. In the old days, even a screwball idea like mine would get a full ear. There would be people around to run it down, talk to a few people, test it out." He scowled. "Now, Teague would have to walk in with a prewritten confession to get noticed. It's damn near that bad, really."

She ground out her cigarette. "You're just making excuses."

"No, I'm not. I wish to God that I was. Look, Rosinski and I have a backlog of thirty homicide cases. Imagine that—two men to track down thirty killers. Just the two of us. We do it, you know, we give it a good shot; we question witnesses, we follow what leads we can, and we put in a lot of overtime, most of it for free, you know that.''

She nodded her head in reluctant agreement.

''It's that way all over. Hell, none of those other cops have the time or the inclination to try a complex tracking job in order to nail someone like Teague.'' He shook his head. ''You know, it's just like the chief said, even if we caught him, the likelihood is that he would be back in the hospital and would charm his way out as soon as things cooled off. I suppose that's reality and a lot of cops just face up to it. They feel it just isn't worth the effort.''

''Then why don't you follow that advice? Let it go, he'll make a mistake sometime. Someone will catch him, if he's the one. God didn't appoint you as a committee of one to nab Edward Teague. Leave it to someone else, start living your own life again.''

Russo looked at her. She was so beautiful. He could sense this was more than passing irritation. She resented the way he was treating her, and he couldn't make her realize it was for her own protection and that he was terrified for her safety. They were coming to a crossroads.

''Marie, I'd love to drop Teague, to forget him completely. But I know him; it's like I'm in his skin. He's in this city, I know it. Rose told me Teague sees me as his only threat. He will come. I know it and he'll try to hurt me. He does it through women, Marie. If he found out about you, you would be the target. He'd get at me through you. He'd get both his thrills and his revenge at the same time. That's why the secrecy.''

She sipped her drink again before replying. ''So how do you propose to handle this situation of yours?''

''Like I said, we'll cool it. I'll be able to duck over

here once in a while but we have to recognize the possibility that Teague may try to track me. He's good, but if we're careful, we can get together.''

''Just enough so you can have sex. Just enough to answer your basic biological urges, is that what you're saying, Tony?''

He shook his head. ''I'm not saying that at all. Marie, I love you. I don't want you exposed to any risk.''

''Tony, this isn't easy for me to say but we have to get something straight. I feel like a whore. We work together in the same building, but I can only see you in secret. Now you say even that's out.'' She lit another cigarette. ''Let's face it, this is absurd. I don't intend to go on living like this. It's up to you. Either we pursue a normal open relationship or I want out.''

''Marie, as soon as this Teague thing gets . . .''

She was on the verge of tears, but she was angry. ''Teague is just an excuse, and you know it. There's something else. I don't know what it is, but there's something else. When you get yourself together, Lieutenant Russo, maybe we can get back together, but until then I consider myself a free agent, and I intend to start enjoying life.''

''But Marie . . .''

''Can we go to a movie?''

''No, and you know why.''

''Can you take me dancing tonight, or even bowling?''

''Marie, this is serious. This isn't the school prom. Teague is . . .''

''I think you had better leave, Tony.'' She looked at him. She was about to lose control. ''I mean it.''

He stood up and put out his hands to her, but she drew away.

For a moment he looked at her, wanting more than anything in the world to agree, but he was convinced that to give in to her might well be the invitation to her death.

Slowly he got to his feet. "I'm in love with you, Marie," he said evenly. "I never thought I'd ever think of getting married again, but I want you so much. I don't want to leave you and yet I know what I'm doing. I'm not crazy and there is real danger. That's my only reason. I'm sorry."

Russo turned and walked toward the door.

Her sobbing stopped him. He rushed back and took her in his arms. "Please, baby, everything will be all right."

"I can't—" She tried to control her sobbing. "I can't let you go," she sobbed. "Damn you, you mean so much to me."

"I know, baby," he said softly as he buried his face in her hair. "I know. Everything will work out, you'll see."

Tony Russo prayed that he was right.

*   *   *

Teague cruised until a metered parking space became available and he pulled in. He could see the parking garage exit very clearly. Although he was almost a block away, he was close enough to recognize Knapp's blue Cadillac.

It was Wednesday. The day held no special significance for Teague, but it did for Knapp. Wednesday was the day of the ladies' tennis league cocktail party. Husbands were expected to attend. Knapp dreaded Wednesdays, but he faithfully joined his wife so that her status with her peers would not be diminished. It was the only time they went out together and he found it increasingly boring, but he knew a terrible penalty would be exacted if he failed to show up, so he made it a point always to leave the office on time on Wednesdays.

Teague had filled his gas tank, and he let the motor run so that he could enjoy the air conditioning and listen to the radio. The announcer predicted that a cold front would lift the warm, moist air from the area. This happy event would be marked by a line of thunderstorms. Teague paid attention, weather was always important to a hunter.

Knapp had left his office late the preceding evening, but Teague was taking no chances; he arrived well before the usual office closing time. There was joy in the anticipation, and the waiting itself could be exciting when on a hunt.

He settled back, his eyes fixed half dreamily on the garage exit. But he was jolted into action as the blue Cadillac emerged unexpectedly. Teague rammed his own car into gear and pulled out, just missing a passing pickup truck. He was dimly conscious that the other driver was yelling at him as he flashed by, but he gunned the engine and barely made the amber traffic light, closing quickly on the blue car. He wanted to get close enough to confirm the license number. The Cadillac turned at the next corner and Teague stepped on the accelerator.

He was close enough now and the license was Knapp's. He felt relieved and slowed down so that it wouldn't appear that he was following. The Cadillac swung down onto the interstate highway and Teague followed, knowing that his job would be much easier now—all exits were visible and Knapp couldn't escape him on the interstate. He kept well back, relaxed but watching.

Giant green signs marked the various exits and connecting roadways. Teague began to feel uneasy as they continued past a series of suburban towns. He thought he'd be tracking Knapp home, but now he wondered if the lawyer might be traveling north on a business or pleasure trip. That would ruin his plan.

But Teague smiled as he saw the blue car's turn signal blink as it approached the Chippewa Hills exit. He too eased into the right turn lane and followed Knapp up the ramp behind the two cars that separated them. Knapp turned right on Hemstead Road and proceeded west. Teague lay back and followed as they passed through the city of Chippewa Hills. To avoid being left behind, he was careful to catch the same green traffic lights as the Cadillac.

Teague again gave distance as they cleared the town and its lights. As they drove past the estates and the showplace houses, Teague reflected that Knapp had indeed succeeded and now lived among the very rich. It seemed to Teague that it was only fair that he punish Knapp for acquiring wealth from the blood of men like himself, men sent to insane asylums because of lawyers who failed to defend them properly.

Knapp turned through the stone gates of the Idaho Springs subdivision. Teague was concerned that the gate might be attended by a guard but was relieved to find the roadway open. He kept his distance but stayed close enough to keep Knapp's car in sight.

As they circled slowly through the curving streets, passing the manicured lawns and trimmed hedges, Teague began to feel a tingling tenseness.

The Cadillac slowed and pulled into the hedge-lined driveway of a large two-story brick-and-wood house. The front lawn and gardens were founded by a distinctive railroad tie fence. A pretty place, Teague thought, as he watched the automatic garage door open and Knapp drive in. Teague took in everything, including the racy small car parked in the garage. He guessed that the car belonged to Knapp's wife. The number over the front door was wrought iron and written in longhand—One Hundred Ninety-Four. The street was White Stag Lane.

Teague liked the street name; it was appropriate for a hunt. He turned around and passed Knapp's house again, fixing it forever in his mind. He was quite pleased with himself. He had tracked the animal to its lair.

Teague sped back to the city, delighted with the exciting anticipation of the hunt and the kill.

It would be good, he could sense it.

* * *

Rosinski shifted on his stool. He was still toying with his first drink, but Russo was motioning to the bartender for a third.

"Hitting that stuff pretty good tonight," the younger man said. "Things getting to you?"

Russo scowled. "I've always wanted to be a drunk, now I'm going to have my chance. This Teague business is just an excuse to realize a lifelong ambition."

"Sure," Rosinski said. "Say, how'd you like to stay with me for a couple of days? It would cut down on my love life, but other than that you'd be no bother. I have one of those sofa beds in my living room."

Russo smiled ruefully. "He won't come after me, at least not directly, and not yet. I'm not worried about that."

"What, then?"

"He'll come after my lady friend first. That bothers me a great deal."

"How can he know who she is? Hell, even I don't know."

"He'll stake me out. Really, that's his style. The man has a sure instinct and complete patience. He'll wait until I tip him off to who she is, then he'll come on."

Rosinski thought about that for a moment before speaking. "If he's such a big deal hunter, why don't you lay a trap for him?"

Russo looked at his partner.

"You know those hunting movies about Africa? The ones where they tie a sheep to the base of a tree and then climb up in the branches and wait until the lion comes after the sheep and then they kill it?"

"So?"

"So maybe we could figure out something like that. We could sort of stake out your girl—or any girl," he quickly added as he saw the alarm in Russo's eyes. "We could let him know where she was—he'd come after her—only we'd have you or me or some other cop concealed to take him as soon as he tried anything."

"Do you know what happens to that sheep they tie to the tree?" Russo asked.

"No, what?"

"The lion usually kills it before the hunters can bring him down."

"Well, we'd have to be faster than that, that's all."

Russo shook his head. "Damn it! No one seems to appreciate this guy except me. He is good, smart, and almost a genius. If he spotted the trap he'd turn it against us. No, we can't risk anyone else, too many girls have died already.''

"So? Are you just going to sit around until something happens?''

Russo took his third drink. ''Something like that. I might be able to think up something, but until I do all I can do is wait until Teague makes the first move.''

"Suppose nothing happens? Hell, he may be on his way to South America for all you know.''

"Something will happen,'' Russo said, feeling dread as he spoke the words. ''And if I know him we won't have long to wait.''

"You'd better stay at my place.''

Russo grinned. ''If I was cutting into your love life, how do I know you won't walk in your sleep? I think I prefer death to rape.''

"Too bad,'' Rosinski said. ''You'll never know what you've missed.''

* * *

Teague spent a restless night. The lawyer upset him. He understood the doctors. They told him he had confused Knapp with his father, constructing an unreal godlike creature, a protector. Even though he was now convinced that Rose was right and that Knapp had really acted against his best interests, his sleep was filled with disturbing dreams in which the lawyer's face appeared on his father's body. Although the dreams had awakened him several times, he still resolved to carry out the punishment despite his inner conflicts.

He parked within sight of the lighted stone gates of Idaho Springs. It was early, although traffic had gotten heavier on the dark road.

His father had always liked to get up before the sun, to dress and prepare in the dark. Then they would hurry to the hunting grounds to arrive before sunrise. It was the very best part of the day. Cool, quiet; and when the rays of the sun began to light up the dark sky it was like being at the birth of the world. He had always loved early morning. He associated it with excitement and the beginning of the chase.

A state police car passed him, but the officer had paid no attention. He was parked legally, and there was nothing suspicious to attract the officer's interest. The people of Idaho Springs began to emerge for the day, and Teague watched the stream of expensive cars as they passed through the stone gates and headed for the interstate and the city.

He felt awkward in a suit, but being well dressed was part of his role and essential to his plans.

It was just a few minutes after seven o'clock when the blue Cadillac drove through. Knapp too headed toward the city. Teague felt a rush. He savored the feeling as he put his car into gear and pulled out into the traffic. In a moment he swung his car through the gates and into the streets of Idaho Springs.

Helen Knapp lay sleeping. She had half heard her husband when he left, but she ignored the disturbance and slipped back into sleep. Her tennis lesson was at eleven and she had nothing to do before that. It was Thursday, and Armanda, her maid, only came in on Monday, Wednesday, and Friday, so there was no reason for her to get up.

The pounding on the door and the ringing of the bell at first seemed unreal to her, as if something very annoying was happening far away—something she hoped would stop. The dream faded into reality as she realized the noises were real and coming from her own house.

It took a moment for her to respond. She lay still, as if that alone might make the noise go away, but the racket persisted insistently.

She slid out of bed, noticing that she had a headache. Slipping into a dressing gown and slippers, she navigated the stairs very carefully.

"Hold on, for Christ's sake," she mumbled as she headed for the door off the kitchen. The pounding seemed to increase in frequency as well as intensity.

She looked out the kitchen window. A nice-looking blonde man, in a business suit, seemingly upset, looked back at her.

"What do you want?" she asked through the glass, shouting the words.

"Mrs. Knapp?" he asked. She could barely hear him.

"Yes."

"There's been an accident up the road." He gestured behind him. "Your husband asked me to let you know."

"What?"

"I say, there's been an accident."

Helen Knapp opened the kitchen door. "I'm sorry, I didn't hear you. What did you say?"

"There's nothing to worry about, Mrs. Knapp. Your husband has been in a minor traffic accident up the road.

His only injury is a bloody nose, but I'm afraid his Cadillac won't start.''

She looked puzzled.

"I happened to stop by the accident to see what I could do, and he asked me to come here and ask you to drive your other car over and pick him up. I can show you the way."

"Oh, Jesus! Isn't that just like him? Other people call the auto club, but not him." She stopped short. "I'm sorry, please come in. I'll throw on some clothes and be right with you."

"Sure," the man said, stepping into the kitchen. She liked his wide friendly smile. He was tall, blonde, and very attractive in a rugged way.

"Make yourself at home," she said. "I'll be right down." She hurried away, silently cursing her husband for ruining her morning. She trotted up the carpeted stairway. In the bedroom she hesitated. She had planned just to throw on slacks and a shirt; but she remembered her tennis date and speculated that by the time she had things straightened out it might be time for her lesson, so she decided to put on the tennis dress. There was another reason: She knew it was sexy and she hoped it might excite the handsome man downstairs.

She slipped out of her robe and nightgown and stood nude for a moment before her full-length mirror. The tennis was paying off, she noted that her stomach was almost flat.

Teague, out of her range of vision, admired her from the open bedroom door. Her buttocks were well formed and the full hips excited him.

The first time he had seen a deer, it was standing stock still in a ray of dappled sunlight, its shining coat reflect-

ing the glint of the sun. The animal was a sleek thing of beauty. He had leveled the sights of his rifle almost reluctantly. It was a reluctance he never again experienced after the thrill of seeing the animal fall.

"That's very nice," he said quietly.

She jumped as though she had been struck. She turned and faced him. "Get out!" she screamed. "Get the hell out of here!" She ran to the bed and grabbed her robe and held it in front of her.

"Eventually I will get out, Mrs. Knapp," he said evenly, his voice calm and reassuring. "First, please take a close look at me and see if you can recognize me."

"I'll call the police!" She moved awkwardly toward the telephone, trying to keep the robe in front of her.

He was on her before she could lift the receiver, grabbing the telephone away as he roughly backhanded her. She landed hard on the bed, her breath knocked out of her. He wound the telephone wire around his hand and pulled the entire apparatus away from its wall connection.

"Now, I'm going to repeat the question," he said. She lay completely nude now, her eyes wide with fright. "Take a good look at me. I'll give you a hint. I used to be a client of your husband's."

She was breathing rapidly and shallowly, her skin pale and ashen. She shook her head. "I don't know you." The words came out with a croaking sound.

"Oh, I'll bet you do." He smiled down at her and threw the telephone into a corner. "Of course, it's been a few years, but I was one of your husband's most important cases."

She tried to squirm off the bed, but he knelt next to

her and jammed her shoulders down. "Think, Mrs.
Knapp. Look at me and think."

Her eyes grew larger with fear.

*He remembered tracking the fox into a hollow. The
wounded animal had pulled its nose back exposing its
long curved teeth. The gesture was fierce and defiant, but
the animal's eyes gave it away; they were filled with fear.*

"Now, you aren't concentrating. Look at me. I'm thin-
ner now. My skin has cleared up and my hair style is
different. I don't wear glasses anymore, I have contacts.
That makes a big change, I suppose. Look!" He grabbed
her hair and jerked her trembling face close to his. "Now
you know me, eh?"

She said nothing. He threw her down violently.
"You're not trying, Mrs. Knapp!"

Helen Knapp's breath escaped in constricted sobs.

"Look at me, bitch!" The words hissed from between
his clenched teeth. "Look at me!"

Her eyes stared vacantly, she was too frightened to see
anything. Her flesh shook with uncontrollable tremors.

"My name is Teague, Edward J. Teague. Do you remember me?" Still no sign of recognition registered. He
grinned, his eyes flashing. "They used to call me the
Stalking Man."

She blinked vacantly for a moment and then she remembered. Her eyes widened in horror. A rumbling
sound from her stomach erupted into a full-blown scream
from her lips.

He hit her casually across the face to silence her.
"Now you remember." He sat back on the bed and
smiled at her. "My, how nice it is to be remembered."

Helen Knapp couldn't control herself and involuntarily wet the bed.

"Oh Jesus!" Teague cursed, jumping up. "You god-damned cow, you stink!" He reached over and slapped her, although the blow didn't carry much force. Actually, he was thrilled with this display of acute fright. He was becoming sexually aroused, as he always did with the ones who were truly terrified.

"Do you know what I did with the last woman I killed?" He grinned casually as if describing his latest golf match. "I fucked her. She didn't want to, you understand, but I gave her a great fuck. The best she ever had, I'm sure. Then I cleaned and skinned her. I did," he giggled. "I really did."

He moved to the other side of the bed. She did not move but her eyes followed him. "Now that last lady was just a warm-up for what I have planned for you, Mrs. Knapp. Just a warm-up." He sat next to her and gently began to massage the side of her buttock with his large hand. Then he drew back and slapped her.

"Don't . . . hurt . . . me." The words came out in gasps from Helen Knapp's lips. "My husband . . . helped . . . you," she managed to say.

"Bullshit!" Teague yelled, causing Helen Knapp to draw her body up defensively. "Your husband rail-roaded me. He helped me all right—right into the insane asylum." He paused, his face suddenly crafty. "Now I'm going to thank him for that."

Helen Knapp tried to inch away from him, but he laughed, grabbing her roughly by the ankle and pulling her back toward him. "Don't try to get away, bitch. It won't do you any good."

* * *

Wilma Oakes hated the job of chairperson. She hated the whole idea of the annual charity. thing. It was always the same—the same people did all the work, and the same people came—and the very few dollars raised probably did the poor little good. But socially it was one of the big status events of the country club, and chairing the committee carried a certain amount of prestige. She despised the whole thing; but her husband wanted to run for club office later in the year—he thought it would help his insurance business—so he had persuaded her to go after the job. She had a good reputation as an organizer and the job had really sought her.

But she loathed it. She would have to delegate responsibility to a bunch of witless women who would talk forever and do very little. It was her job to assign people to committee posts, trying to pick out women who were compatible and who might possibly put an hour or so into some kind of productive effort.

Last year Helen Knapp had served on the decoration committee and had shown a flair for imaginative use of cheap crepe paper and tinsel. Wilma Oakes decided to ask Helen to serve as head of the decoration committee. Everyone knew Helen Knapp. You had to see Helen early in the day or otherwise you were dealing with a quarrelsome drunk. Her husband and their family trouble were the high points of Helen's conversation, especially after a few drinks. It was interesting in the beginning—the business of Tom Knapp's suspected love life—but after constant repetition it had become tiresome. She hoped to see Helen early enough to avoid hearing more about the saga of the Knapp's marital difficulties.

Wilma Oakes drove past Edward Teague's car parked at the curb, not noticing it, and pulled into the driveway. She hopped out of her car and slammed the door. Walking to the side door she rang the bell. She didn't check to see if Helen's or Tom's car was in the closed garage. Wilma Oakes was not a nosy person.

* * *

Teague jumped up when he heard the car door slam, and the sound of the bell sounded like the tolling of a thousand sinister chimes as it echoed through the large empty house.

"Be quiet," he hissed at the frightened woman on the bed. He inched to the window and peeked down below. He couldn't see the side door, but a car was parked in front of the garage. The bell sounded again.

"Help me!" Her loud shriek seemed to fill the room, reverberating against the walls.

Helen Knapp was trying to scramble from the bed, her arms and legs flailing awkwardly.

"Help me!" The sound of her scream echoed throughout the house.

Teague moved like a panther. Taking two short smooth strides he leaped full out, diving over the bed and smashing his bulk into Helen Knapp's naked body. They fell to the floor together. Her eyes fluttered as he drove his thumbs into the base of her throat, cutting off her windpipe and stopping any possible sound. With all his strength he shook her several times, snapping her head back and forth. She went completely limp as her eyes closed.

Teague pushed himself up and raced to the window. A

middle-aged woman hurried around the car, got in on the driver's side, and backed the car quickly out of the drive-way.

Don't panic! How many times had he heard his father say that—don't panic! Panic causes the harm. Take several deep breaths, then coolly consider the situation. It was good advice, whether in the woods, where the advice had been given, or anywhere.

Teague turned from the window and stood quietly for a moment, inhaling deeply. There would be no time now; the woman could have heard the screams and might be on her way to the police. There was no time.

He picked up the telephone he had ripped from the wall and walked to the inert form of Helen Knapp. She was unconscious but he detected shallow breathing. He looped the telephone cord around her limp throat and pulled it taut, very taut, until the shallow breathing stopped. He half listened for the sound of sirens as he waited for her to die. There were no sounds.

After a few minutes he pulled her body up and threw it on the bed. He felt drained and defeated. She was dead but he had been cheated of his elaborate plan of revenge. He knew he had to move quickly. He tied her head to the bedpost with the cord, closed the bedroom door, and ran down the stairs.

He looked out the windows. There was no movement on the street, so he eased quietly out the kitchen door. It locked automatically behind him. He forced himself to stroll casually to his car. All his senses were tuned to their ultimate perception—but he saw and heard nothing out of the ordinary. He started his engine and rolled away from the curb carefully, obeying the twenty-five mile per hour speed limit. Slowly he drove through the winding streets until he reached the stone gates. His heart was pounding. The gates were his exit to freedom. There was no sign of the police yet. Turning left, he drove slowly away, still listening for sirens. There were none. He wondered if the woman had actually heard the screams. It would be too great a risk to return, although he reasoned that if the woman had called them, they would have responded more quickly.

Edward Teague felt cheated that he had been forced to kill Helen Knapp in such an unimaginative way. Knapp would never know it was his punishment. But Teague did feel elated that he had escaped. He still resolved to kill Thomas Knapp, but that could wait. He would punish Russo first. But this time he would make sure no one could interfere with his revenge or pleasure. He drove along, his spirits rising as he imagined the fulfillment of Russo's punishment.

8

WILMA OAKES DID HEAR THE SCREAMS. THE KNAPP house was air-conditioned and airtight, so the screams had been muted, hardly audible; but she had heard them nevertheless. Wilma Oakes concluded at the time that the Knapp's marital troubles had finally erupted into violence, and she wanted no role in such a messy situation. If Tom Knapp felt it was high time that he belted his mouthy wife, Wilma Oakes was one lady who wouldn't interfere. She went on about her business.

The stiffening body of Helen Knapp lay hung against the bedpost. Her husband came in late, being especially quiet in order to avoid her. He tiptoed past their closed bedroom door to the guest room that now constituted his permanent quarters. Thomas Knapp slept the balance of the night peacefully.

He was up early the next morning. Having no reason to look in on his wife, he quickly left for the city. Armanda, the maid, came in at nine o'clock. After fixing herself a cup of coffee she did the laundry in the basement. Then she attended to the rest of the house. It wasn't until eleven o'clock that she discovered the corpse, its face now grotesque and swollen.

The police were called. Chippewa Hills had never had a murder before, so they called in the state police for assistance. In the course of the investigation everyone was questioned: Thomas Knapp, the prominent attorney and husband of the deceased; the maid; the neighbors and friends; and, later in the day, Mrs. Wilma Oakes, who upon hearing the news came in and volunteered the account of her experience the previous day.

That night a meeting was held between the state police detective in charge, the local chief of police and the local prosecuting attorney. It was decided that at the moment they didn't have sufficient evidence against Thomas Knapp to recommend a warrant, but all three men were in agreement that he was the murderer. The exact time of death was in doubt. The problem was the Oakes woman's story. If it were true, then Knapp was already in the city and couldn't have been at the house at that time. Otherwise, it was the consensus that they needed only a few more items to make a good circumstantial case that the lawyer had strangled his wife. The stories about his infidelity—although the source was admittedly the late Mrs. Knapp—convinced the law enforcement men they were on the right trail.

Edward Teague passed a quiet night at a different motel. This time he used a false name, paid cash, and incorrectly jotted down his Illinois license plate on the registration card. He was taking precautions in case the woman at the Knapp house had spotted his car. She had not, but he had no way of knowing this and in his typical wary fashion was reducing the margin for error.

* * *

Two uniformed men standing in the hallway stepped aside as Russo stamped by them, his face set in slit-eyed anger. They wanted no part of a detective lieutenant in that kind of mood.

Russo stormed into the homicide section. Rosinski was waiting for him. Three other officers at the far end of the room were busy at telephones.

Russo slammed his body into the desk swivel chair with such force that Rosinski wondered why it didn't splinter apart. Russo said nothing. Rosinski was apprehensive about speaking to his partner. He tried to think of something that would prevent him from becoming the nearest target of the lieutenant's anger. "He turned you down again, right?" he asked, almost in a whisper.

"You know," Russo said, his voice low and strained, "why they let that senile old son-of-a-bitch run this outfit is life's greatest mystery. Jesus! He has a piece of cheese for a brain. He's a dumb bastard, Rosinski, do you understand me? Our chief of detectives is a senile, dumb bastard!"

Rosinski's heavy Slavic face split into a half grin. "He always speaks very well of you." He laughed tentatively, hoping that his joke wouldn't anger Russo.

Russo studied his young partner for a moment, his eyes expressionless. "He should speak well of me, that senile old bastard," he growled, "I'm one of the few honest-to-god detectives he has left."

"He didn't buy your theory that Teague killed Mrs. Knapp?"

Russo snorted. "Christ, he wouldn't even listen to it. Not our problem, that's what he said." Russo stood up and paced to the window. He looked down on the dingy street below. "I asked to be assigned to the Knapp case. You know, that's not out of line, not for a detective of my years and rank. Hell, a lot of times I've been loaned to small-town police departments in investigations." He shook his head. "We've got too much work now, he says. God, you'd think it's the only thing he knows how to say—we have too much work now. It's like arguing with a tape recorder. It just says the same thing over and over again, no matter how much you argue."

"Tape recorder or not," Rosinski said, "he's the boss."

"Yeah, he let me know that too."

"We got another case assigned while you were making war with the chief."

Russo shrugged and returned to the desk. This time he sat down slowly as if he were extremely tired. "It figures."

"They fire-bombed a family out on North Slocum Street."

"Who says?"

Rosinski sighed. "The arson squad. They found gasoline cans. A whole family went up, less one kid who was lucky enough to be sleeping out in an enclosed porch."

"How many dead?"

"Mother, father, three big kids—you know, sixteen and over—and one eleven-year-old."

Russo looked at his partner. "The arson people pretty sure about it?"

"Harris says there's no doubt. They're still running tests, but he says somebody splashed the whole rear of the house with gasoline, then threw bottles of the stuff in the windows and put a match to the whole thing. The people upstairs were cooked before they could get out of bed."

Russo nodded. "Harris is a good man. How many murders does that make for this year?"

Rosinski thought for a moment. "Well, they croaked that cab driver last night. He was four hundred and ninety-four. These six make it a nice round five hundred."

"How many are we ahead of last year's mark?"

"About fifty, give or take."

"Maybe we'll break our own record."

Rosinski shrugged. "Well, if our football and baseball teams can't do anything, at least our murderers will hold the city's banner high." He paused. Russo wasn't in the best mood to hear the news about the Knapp case, but he could think of no excuse to put off telling him. "By the way, I called the Chippewa Hills cops about the Knapp autopsy, like you asked."

"So?"

"Death by strangulation. She had been hit a few times in the face, had a few body bruises, but no broken bones. The job was done with a telephone cord. The telephone had been jerked right off the wall. The state police boys are pretty sure Knapp did it."

"Why?"

Rosinski pulled out his notes. "I knew you'd be interested," he said, indicating he had taken special pains. "It turns out Knapp and his wife were having big trouble for a number of years—country club gossip stuff. She was always getting tight and blabbing to the other ladies, who were probably getting tight too, that her old man was running around on her, and all the rest of that garbage that women complain about, late hours, that sort of thing."

"Go on."

"Anyway, it turns out that Thomas Knapp, attorney-at-law, has been lately fooling around with his secretary, a woman about his own age who's getting a divorce. So our brothers in the sticks figure he decided he couldn't afford a divorce and croaked her."

"What does Knapp say?"

"Nothing much. He retained an attorney immediately. He denies having anything to do with anything. He does admit to the affair, but that's about all."

"Any record that the cops were called out to answer any family trouble runs at the Knapps'? I mean, is there anything on the books to show that Knapp used to slap her around once in a while?"

Rosinski shook his head. "They didn't mention it. I think they would have. It would mean a lot to their case if they could show he was a violent man, given to temper, right?"

"You may become a detective yet."

Rosinski grimaced. "Thanks. Of course, that autopsy report blows your theory about Teague being the killer right out of the water."

Russo said nothing.

Rosinski continued. "Your man smashes his victims into jelly, right? I mean, he goes bananas and breaks bones, cuts off heads and all that kind of fun stuff, correct?"

"Usually."

"Usually, hell." Rosinski snorted. "That's his trademark. He hates women. This Knapp babe just got her wind cut off permanently, no broken bones, no bizarre torture—just a run-of-the-mill kind of killing—not like Teague at all."

"When did this fire on North Slocum happen?" Russo asked, ignoring Rosinski's remarks.

"This morning, just about dawn."

"Is Harris still at the site?"

Rosinski nodded. "Yeah. I asked him to wait for us."

"Come on, we'll hop out there and start working."

"You're not going to answer me about Teague, are you?" Rosinski persisted as he followed his partner from the room.

"Teague killed Mrs. Knapp," Russo said flatly. "Why she escaped being smashed up I don't know, but I know he killed her."

"Tell me, what evidence do you base that on?"

"The best, my gut hunch. I goddamn well know Teague did it."

"I think maybe the chief is right about you. You're getting a little kinky about Teague."

Russo walked down the hallway toward the elevators. "I'll tell you something else. Despite the chief, this department, or the goddamned United Nations, I am going to bring that looney in again. I'll prove that I'm right. You can count on it."

Rosinski winced. "That sounds like trouble. You know—going against direct orders."

"Rules," Russo growled, "were made for the weak."

Rosinski laughed. "I'll bet you don't know who said that."

"Who?"

"Napoleon, the Emperor of France."

"Good man."

Rosinski walked along behind Russo. "Maybe, but they put him away, which sort of waters down his advice, if you see what I mean?"

"I see."

They drove to the ruins of the house on North Slocum. It was just another job for the team of homicide detectives—a routine assignment—but it would provide Edward Teague with a means to reach his prey, Anthony Russo.

*   *   *

Teague sipped his cold coffee from its soggy container. It was the last vestige of his dinner—two hamburgers and a paper bag of french fries. He watched the evening news on the black-and-white television set. It was irritating—the picture slipped every few moments and then returned to normal. It was an old set, just as rundown as the motel itself.

The murder of Helen Knapp was given prime coverage, the camera playing on the expensive Knapp home while the broadcaster detailed the killing, making a point that Thomas Knapp, the well-known attorney, had been questioned twice during the day about his wife's death, thereby hinting strongly that the police suspected him without risking entanglement with libel laws.

Edward Teague giggled with pleasure. God had helped him. Although he had been denied the thrill of watching Helen Knapp die in agony, nevertheless his real objective—the punishment of Thomas Knapp—was being accomplished in a far better way than even he could have imagined. The lawyer would now get a taste of his own medicine, perhaps even end up in a mental hospital himself, confined behind locked doors, his life regulated even to the smallest detail. Teague was pleased.

He was about to shut off the set and savor his triumph

when the very next story concerned an arson bombing and the killing of six people. Teague paid little attention until the station ran a film clip of their interview with the officer in charge. Lieutenant Anthony Russo.

The sight of Russo's face instantly terrified Teague, as if the detective had somehow electronically appeared in the room ready to lock him up again. A shiver of fear trembled through him as he forced himself to realize he was merely watching a televised image. The feeling of fear lessened as Teague once again believed he was being sided by divine intervention. He had wanted to see Russo, to know what the cop looked like now in order to track him. Now he could watch his enemy in the safety of his motel room. He felt sure it was the hand of God. Russo had changed only slightly. He was still lean, tall, and powerfully built, although he appeared to be a bit more fleshy than Teague had remembered him. The wide shoulders and thick face were the same, although his black hair was now peppered with gray. Otherwise, Russo was the same, and even with the inferior television set Teague could see those hard eyes, knowing eyes—they had not changed. Teague feared the intelligence that lay behind those dark eyes.

Russo disappeared as the next item concerned itself with storm damage, but Teague still felt disoriented by the sight of the policeman. He snapped the set off and paced up and down in the small room to get control. He knew he had to fight the fear and plan an effective way to deal with Russo.

He remembered his father planning their trips. That was half the fun. He would spread out a county map on the kitchen table, and they would pore over it until they

*knew and memorized every obscure trail and road. His
father had instructed him that it was the only logical way
to hunt. Plan it first, he said. Just stepping into the woods
with a gun produced few results. Smart hunters knew exactly what they were going to do and how they were
going to do it.*

Teague sat on the edge of the bed for a moment and
then lay back, fixing his eyes on the ceiling. Slowly a
plan began to take shape in his mind. He played with
each possible consequence like a chess player calculating
every potential move and counter-move. He respected
Russo, and the plan had to be perfect.

*   *   *

The funeral home was quiet. Thomas Knapp sat alone in
the large viewing room. There was something eerie about
being alone with the waxlike body in the silk-lined coffin.
It was as if Helen had played a last vicious and tremendous joke on him by being murdered, letting the world
think he had killed her. It would have been her way, at
least it would have been her way during the past few
years. He knew, of course, that although she might have
contemplated suicide, there was no way she could have
physically strangled herself sitting on the side of the bed.
Someone else had killed her.

The children were with his sister and would be brought
over after dinner. The large room had been filled with
folding chairs for expected guests, but almost none had
appeared. The stigma of the murder plus the broad spec-
ulation that he had committed it had kept their friends
away. Only his own law partners had shown up, and then

only briefly and, for the most part, in obvious discomfort.

Knapp looked at the pitifully sparse floral displays surrounding the casket. He imagined the questions being asked by their friends and acquaintances. What does one send if the deceased has been murdered and the husband is apparently the murderer? Is there anything in the etiquette books about it? There isn't? Then we'd better ignore the whole thing.

He was feeling sorry for himself, he knew that. But self-pity, guilt, or remorse wouldn't help the situation. He had the children to think about. He had always heard that children handled death very well, but he wondered what the psychological effect might be when father was suspected of having killed mother.

And he wondered about his own future. The police knew about Martha Flowers. They knew about his stormy home life. It was a common enough story: the embattled husband with the waiting girlfriend, and murder was always so much more economical than a divorce settlement. He knew what they were thinking. Hell, he admitted to himself, if it were someone else, he would think that too.

Even if he was not arrested or convicted, the shadow would always remain over him. He was a lawyer, a man whose profession implied trust by necessity. But how many people would put their affairs into the hands of a man who they suspected was a killer? Not many, he knew that. His law partners were supportive now, but his membership in the firm would eventually prove a fatal liability. Soon—not too soon, otherwise it would look bad—he would be called in to have that little talk with the senior partner. There would be a cash settlement, and then he would be out on his own—a marred and marked man.

He listened to a fly buzz at one of the curtained windows, and felt a sense of revulsion that a fly would be in a funeral home. It somehow seemed obscene, this invasion. Damn the fly! He looked about for a newspaper or a magazine, or anything to use to kill the thing.

"Mr. Knapp."

The soft voice startled him and he spun around as if he'd been suddenly confronted. The icy blue eyes of Lieutenant Russo met his.

"I'm sorry about Mrs. Knapp," Russo said flatly, displaying no hint of emotion.

"Yes. Thank you," Knapp muttered.

"This must be very hard on you."

"Yes." Knapp heard the mechanical sound of his own voice. "These things always are." He sounded like a funeral director to himself.

A squat, brown-haired man, much younger than the detective, stood at his side. "This is Detective Rosinski, my partner," Russo said.

Rosinski muttered a condolence. Knapp nodded his appreciation.

"Can we talk to you in private for a minute, Mr. Knapp?"

"Good God! Does your department have something to do with this too?" Knapp was weary of answering police questions.

Russo's stonelike expression didn't change, although his eyes seemed to soften a bit. "This is quite unofficial. I think I might be able to help."

Knapp knew Russo's reputation, but he also knew the detective resented him. He was wary about an offer of help from such a questionable source. But anything was better than being alone with his thoughts.

"Come with me," Knapp said, leading them into a doorway near the foot of the casket into a small smoking room provided as a sanctuary for the immediate family.

The two detectives sat down opposite him as Knapp nervously lit a cigarette.

"They think you did it," Russo said bluntly.

"I know. The police out here in Chippewa Hills are somewhat more obvious than the big city variety."

Russo pursed his lips. "I don't think you did it."

"That happens to be true, but it is kind of you to say it." Knapp wondered in what direction the detective was going.

"Edward Teague killed your wife."

Knapp's head jerked up in surprise. "I had forgotten about him," he said softly. The attorney allowed his mind to sort out the detective's statement in the manner it was trained, as if it were a legal computer sorting out the impossible and cataloguing the probable. "Teague brutalized his victims," Knapp said slowly. "Smashed bones and that sort of thing." He dropped his voice as if the corpse in the next room could hear. "That didn't happen to Helen. The medical examiner says she was strangled. Slapped around some, then strangled. That doesn't quite fit in the Stalking Man's pattern, I'm afraid." He exhaled a stream of cigarette smoke. "Besides, Teague always thought of me as his savior, as I told you. I doubt he'd try to harm me."

Russo's smile was humorless. "Before I begin, let me say that some of my superiors think I've gone a little crazy about Teague. They think he's become an obsession with me."

"Has he?" Knapp asked, regretting the question as

soon as he spoke it. It was not the sort of thing to ask someone who might be trying to help.

"In a way I suppose he's become something like an obsession," Russo admitted. "He's out, I told you that."

"I originally found out from Dr. Rose, remember?"

Russo shook his head. "I forgot. You did tell me. And you remember my theory about Teague?"

"That he was spelling out *stalking* in bodies?"

"Yes. As part of trying to prove that, I talked to Dr. Rose, as I told you. He apparently laid it on Teague pretty heavy, the business that you really weren't special. I had the impression that Rose convinced Teague that you had not defended him properly and that he ended up in the hospital because you and I had cooked it up—sort of railroaded him."

"That's crazy!"

"There's a lot of that going around up at that hospital," Russo said dryly. "Anyway, that's what I got from Rose. I'm not saying it's true; I'm just telling you my impressions. But if it were true, that would give Teague an excellent reason to come after you, to punish you by killing your wife."

Knapp studied the detective, still not sure that the officer wasn't trying some elaborate trick. "I suppose it could be true," Knapp said, his voice almost inaudible. "Still, the manner of death, it differs so much from what we know about Edward Teague."

"Maybe not." Russo began to warm to his subject. "I've been thinking about it. Rosinski has reviewed the whole thing with the Chippewa Hills police. A woman came by your house that morning to try to get your wife to do some charity work. She said she thought she heard screams and presumed you were beating your wife, right?''

''That's what they tell me. You know, as long as we were married, I never struck Helen, not even once.''

''That's not the point,'' Russo said. ''If Teague was upstairs with your wife at that time he probably saw the woman. I understand she rang the bell before she heard the screams. He probably saw her drive off and thought she might go for help. In that case he would have killed your wife quickly and left. He would have been frightened off by that woman and he would not have had time for his usual work. You see, it could fit.''

Knapp shook his head. ''Maybe, but I really can't think now. I know that sounds bad, but I can't concentrate. So much has been happening.''

Russo nodded. ''The thing is, Teague may not be through with you.''

Fear gripped Thomas Knapp. He thought first of his children and then he thought of Martha Flowers.

''Look, Knapp, I may be as mad as Teague.'' Russo spoke quietly. ''That's always a risk, but if I'm right then we have a shark swimming in the pool. If I were you I'd get your children away from here, away from you, for a while. I know that's tough under the circumstances, but . . .''

Knapp sat quietly for a moment. ''It'll look bad, but it has to be done.'' He looked up at Russo. ''You may be quite insane but I can't take the chance that you are. I'll get my kids out of here, out of the state.'' His voice dropped almost to a whisper. ''My secretary will have to leave too.''

''And you,'' Russo said. ''It's you he's really after, if he's out there.''

"I can't leave or it'll look like something else altogether. But I'll be careful."

"You had better be more than careful. Teague, as you recall, is a clever man. I'd much rather have to fool around with a cobra in a dark room."

Knapp's face reflected his resolution. "I'll be careful, that's all I can do. If I run now, it would look like an admission of guilt, you know that."

Russo stood up. He scratched a pencil across a notepad, tore off the page, and handed it to Knapp. "This is my home telephone number and the office number—the direct bureau line. If you want me, give me a call."

"Are you assigned to this?" Knapp asked.

"Like I said," Russo smiled, "my people think I'm nuts. I'm not supposed to fool around with this case at all."

"I appreciate your help."

"We'll see if it's really any help at all." Russo nodded a good-bye to Knapp, who seemed lost in thought. Rosinski followed his partner out of the viewing room.

"You really expect Teague to go after Knapp?" Rosinski asked as they walked through the hallway of the funeral home.

"Maybe. Although he's probably tickled to death that the cops are looking at Knapp for the murder. He'd love it if the law got Knapp. On the other hand, if he thinks they aren't going to arrest him, he'll come after Knapp."

"What about you?"

Russo lit a cigarette on the steps of the funeral home, and studied the blue sky for a moment. "The way I figure it, Rosinski, I'm probably his next port of call."

"Maybe you better get out of town."

"You remember that idea of yours about setting a trap?"

"Like tying a sheep to a tree, you mean?"

"I like it. For a Polish person you're some great thinker."

"What are you going to do for a sheep?"

"I'm going to be the sheep," Russo said as he walked across the parking lot on the way to the car.

*   *   *

Teague made the telephone call from a booth, so there was no real risk they would trace the call even if they suspected who was making it. He was awaiting the third connection in a series of levels he had been passed through by police department telephone operators. His impatience grew with every passing second.

Finally he was greeted by a bored voice. "Homicide, Jenkins."

"I'd like to speak to Lieutenant Russo," Teague said evenly.

"Who's calling?" the voice inquired in a tone indicating that he could care less.

"I have some information he wants," Teague said. "Please let me talk to him."

"Name first, pal."

Teague had anticipated the officer's demand. "I don't want to give my name. I have some information on the person who set that fire on Slocum Street. I don't want to give my name because I'm afraid what might happen to me."

"We will assure you of complete protection," the

voice said, this time with a slight inflection of interest. "What's your name?"

"Damn it, I want to talk to Russo!"

"Can't do that, friend. Mainly because he ain't here. So you better give me your information. My name is Jenkins. I'm one of the homicide detectives."

"Russo's in charge."

"Yeah," Jenkins said with a sigh of tired resignation, "but we all work for the city. One detective is just like another. What's your information?"

"I want to talk to Russo."

"Look, I told you nice, he's not here." Jenkins was now irritated. "I don't think you have anything we'd be interested in anyway. I think you're a phony."

"There's no use trying to trick me into anything," Teague said coolly. "I want to talk to the man in charge. I know you cops, as soon as I tell what I know you arrest the man and I read my name in the newspapers. Then I'd have to leave town or face real trouble. I want to talk to someone of importance, someone who can give me some real assurance that my name will never be mentioned."

"Only the prosecuting attorney can do that. We're just cops, mister, not magicians. Hell, for all I know maybe you're the one who set the fire. How the hell do we know what you're going to say? Russo can't promise to keep your name out of things until he finds out what you've got. That is, if you have anything at all."

"That's all I want. I want to talk to Russo. When do you expect him?"

"Oh shit," the voice growled. "Hang on."

Again, Teague was tense as he waited. He breathed deeply and forced himself to remain calm.

Finally Jenkins came back on the line. "I'm not sure

when he's coming in. You'd better leave a number where he can call you.''

"Look, I'm not stupid,'' Teague said. "I'm a citizen trying to help the police and I'm trying to do it without bringing harm to my family or myself. I'm not going to be so dumb as to leave a telephone number. You tell me when he's coming in and I'll call him then.''

There was a pause before Jenkins spoke. "Well, maybe you're on the level. But I'm not sure when Lieutenant Russo is coming back. He may call in and he may not. He'll probably be here around four o'clock for checkout. You can try then.''

Teague hung up. He felt elated. Russo would be leaving the headquarters building sometime around four o'clock. He stepped out of the booth and quickly slid into his car. He had a few hours, but that would be more than enough time to set up the arrangements.

*　*　*

Normally Marie Coyle would never have worn the outfit to the office; it was too expensive just for work. It was a special dress chosen for its style and effect. The men in the record identification section had buzzed around her all day, so she knew the dress had been a good investment. Its material clung to her body, showing off her figure, but not too blatantly. The neckline was low, and she wore a silk scarf around her throat so that the ends of the scarf helped conceal the decolletage.

Her matching shoes had been almost as expensive as the dress. The wide-brimmed hat looked expensive but wasn't. It added just the right touch. She knew she looked good.

She kept her fancy shoes and hat in her locker during the day, and although she wore a plain low-heeled pump, the dress still worked its magic, much to her pleasure. Her intent was to smoke the elusive Tony Russo out of his den, and the outfit had been selected to accomplish that feat.

She had called several times during the day, but he was out. She took off a few minutes early so as not to miss him. Checking herself carefully in the cramped ladies' room after donning her hat and shoes, she headed for the detective squad rooms on the fourth floor.

A whistle followed her as she walked past the holdup bureau's doorway—a long and surprised whistle, full of true appreciation. She smiled to herself. A detective walking along in a rumpled open-necked shirt stopped and stared at her as though she were naked. She sensed that he hadn't moved but continued staring long after she'd gone by.

Homicide was the last major office in the long hallway. She turned into the open doorway. Many of the detectives were there, the day shift working to finish their paperwork before leaving for home and the afternoon detectives working out their schedules for the coming evening. She knew them all, at least by sight. They all came down to the record department at one time or another.

"Hey, look at this," one of them called. "Holy Jesus, Marie, I told you to wait in the car." It was Holman, the heavy-set, married man with ten children. He was bald, fat, and had acne. The other detectives laughed.

Tony Russo had his back to her but she saw him stiffen when Holman called her name.

"I'm here to collect someone," she said.

"How about me, Marie?" a tall cop with a wide grin

asked. "Hell, I'm almost divorced and have my car paid for. What more could a woman want?"

"I asked you not to come up here." Russo's voice was soft, but stern.

"You wouldn't return my calls, so this was the only way I could think of to talk to you."

The other detectives had stopped, and now waited, amused and expecting a confrontation.

Russo shook his head and then stood up. "I trust all you gentlemen know Miss Marie Coyle, the lady who works in the records department."

Evil grins spilled across some of the faces, other officers merely waved greetings.

Russo took his holstered pistol from his desk drawer and fixed it to his belt, then he slipped into his suit coat. "Let's get out of here." Again his voice was quiet but firm.

Rosinski grinned and walked over. "I've been wondering who's been beating my time with my partner. You may be prettier, Marie, but the boys say I've got a nice personality."

She laughed, brushing her hair back against the brim of her hat. "I've heard a lot about you, Rosinski. That's the only name I hear him call you. He never calls you by your first name, at least not around me."

"Me too. I don't think he knows it. It's Joseph, by the way—plain, but nice."

"I agree."

"Are you coming?" Russo stood by the door.

"Stay here, Marie," Detective Holman said. "You don't have to go with him. We'll protect you."

"Good-bye, fellows." She waved and brushed past Russo. He followed her down the hall. "You did everything but announce our engagement back there." There was no anger in his voice, which surprised her.

"I called you," she said. "Several times."

"I was out most of the afternoon, and when I returned I was waiting for an informant to call about that arson killing on Slocum."

"I believe you, Tony, but couldn't you have found a short minute to call me?"

"I was going to call you tonight," he said, almost petulantly.

"And maybe sneak over and knock off a piece, right?"

He sighed. "There's no need to do any more sneaking, at least not after your act back there. The whole department will know about us, it'll be the lead item on the gossip wire."

"And that displeases you?"

"Marie, I told you what they'll think."

"You mean they'll think that the dirty old man is sleeping with the nice young girl from records."

"Something like that."

"Well it's true. Let them think it."

"Damn it, don't you understand? Every two-bit Romeo in this department will now take a crack at you. Hell, they'll be buzzing around like flies."

She stopped. "You don't trust me, is that it?"

"No, nothing like that. It's just that I'm trying to protect . . ."

"Tony, are you jealous? Are you afraid someone might come along and take me away from you, is that it?"

He didn't reply for a moment. "You're beautiful. Any man in his right mind would want you, Marie. I don't think I'm jealous exactly, but I am worried about you."

She laughed, the anger gone. "You are jealous, you

really are. I hadn't even thought you might be. That's really been the whole reason for this entire business of sneaking around, you've been worried about stirring up some competition!''

He began to walk slowly as she followed. ''It may have been something like that in the beginning,'' he said. ''As far as the department goes, it doesn't matter now, but we still have Edward Teague to worry about.''

She grabbed his arm as they waited for the elevators. ''You know, Tony, most people run into trouble if they fail to communicate with each other. If I had known about your jealousy I could have put your mind at ease. If this Teague business is a masquerade for something else, please let me know. I'll try to understand.''

He shook his head. ''Damn, no one believes me. This is no joke. Edward Teague is real and I am really trying to protect you from him.''

She was silent as they got into the crowded elevator. Several of the older detectives greeted Russo. They all left the elevator at the ground floor.

''Did you drive?'' Russo asked.

''Yes, I parked in the Howard Street Garage.''

''Damn it, Marie, that's a dangerous place. There's no guards and anybody and his brother can just walk into the place. We've had a dozen robberies in that garage over the last few months. I told you. Don't you ever listen to anything I say?''

''I came down late this morning. All the surface lots were full, so I had to use the garage. Besides, it isn't dangerous at this hour. Everyone's leaving work and I'd guess that every other person is an armed policeman, so I'm perfectly safe.''

"God, even the armed cops aren't safe there. Now I'll have to walk you over there."

She looked up at him, her eyes narrowing slightly. "You don't have to do a thing."

He gripped her arm, his eyes fixed on hers. "I love you, Marie. You may think I'm nuts, but I'm not. Teague is out there somewhere and it's a good chance that he is looking for me or for someone I love. This is no time to run risks. Being seen with you is a risk. Not for me, understand, but for you. But I doubt that Teague would be anywhere around here now. He wouldn't know what shift I was working."

"He could be watching—God! you have me doing it now."

Russo laughed. "What could he be watching?"

"The police parking lot."

He nodded. "Yes, I suppose that might be true if he knew I parked there. It's only for senior officers, but there are no signs identifying it, so he'd have no way of knowing about it unless he hung around headquarters for a few days. But I think he'd be worried about being seen and recognized. It's possible but not probable."

He escorted her out of the south door of police headquarters. The Howard Street Garage was a half block away.

*   *   *

The parking garage was of the type constructed some years ago, three floors high and made of massive concrete. But it wasn't enclosed; each level was open to the elements, and the top level was no more than a flat roof with a concrete railing to prevent cars from toppling off.

A rented move-it-yourself panel truck had been backed up against the railing of the second level, the rear of the truck facing the police headquarters building. A blanket had been draped back of the forward seats, so that nothing could be seen of the interior of the truck if anyone was passing by.

The rear doors of the truck were open only slightly. Edward Teague sat with his back propped up against a box. He sat cross-legged with his elbows resting on his knees and watched the south exit of the headquarters building through his rifle's telescopic sight. He had a hunter's patience, even though he realized that Russo could use another exit from the building. He did know that the detective ended his work on the dayshift because of the information gained from his fake arson case telephone call. If this method failed, he was prepared to think up another way of stalking him.

His legs were stiff but he didn't notice. For the past fifteen minutes policemen and civilian workers had been pouring from the headquarters building. By using the rifle sight as a viewfinder, he could get a close-up view of the faces.

He wasn't afraid. The blanket obscured all view into the interior of the truck, and the door crack—even if noticed from the street—was too narrow and the inside too dark to allow anyone to see in.

Teague had planned it very carefully. The .30-06 shell was in the chamber ready to fire. The wind was almost nonexistent, so he wouldn't have to make allowance for any angle due to a cross breeze. The distance was just over a hundred yards, not a difficult shot with a telescopic sight. He watched the people as they passed before the cross hairs of his sight. He had also planned his escape.

The sound of the shot would bounce among the buildings and the location of the rifleman would be lost in the echoes. He would fire, pull the rear door of the truck shut, jerk down the blanket and spread it over the rifle, and then climb into the driver's seat. He would proceed down the ramp like any normal customer leaving the garage. He had the exact change in his pocket. He would pay the attendant whose booth was located on the side of the garage away from police headquarters and who would be completely unaware of the commotion, then he would leave the garage, drive down Howard Street to the expressway, and join in the stream of cars leaving the city as the rush hour was beginning.

It was a good plan, simple and easily carried out. He regretted that Russo would never know who had killed him. That robbed Teague of a great deal of satisfaction, but there was no other way.

He watched as the rush from headquarters dwindled. He could hear cars pulling away from adjoining parking spaces. Soon his truck would be one of the few cars left, and he'd have to move.

Suddenly Russo's face appeared in the scope's lens. He was just as Teague had remembered him, just as he had been on television—his face hard and expressionless.

Do not hurry your shot, his father had taught him— that was a sure way to miss. Calm yourself and force yourself to wait, to let your mind and body adjust, then aim carefully and squeeze the trigger as if you had all the time in the world. It was a matter of discipline. It had always worked.

Teague steadied the rifle, leaning forward until the tip of the barrel cleared the opening of the truck door by an inch. He used the door for an additional support. The cross hairs danced for a moment and then leveled on the center of Russo's face as the detective turned toward the garage. Teague took a deep breath and let a bit of air escape. The scope was steady now.

Then Teague noticed the girl.

Her face danced next to Russo's. She was a beauty with a soft oval face and light hair framed by a wide-brimmed hat. Teague didn't fire.

He watched them approach. She looked up at Russo. The look was unmistakable: she was in love with the lieutenant. Teague wondered if she might be his wife. He lowered the sight a bit. She had a full figure and good legs. Teague felt stirrings within himself. She held Russo's hand, clinging to his side. By the show of public affection Teague guessed that it was a love affair and not married. Married people were more restrained. He raised the sight and noticed that Russo seemed slightly annoyed by her attentions. Teague figured that Russo was a man who disliked open displays of affection.

Then Russo laughed at something she said. He looked down at her, and for a moment the hardness left his face and Teague knew this woman was very important to the detective. Teague put the rifle down and watched them approach without the aid of his telescopic sight.

They made a nice couple. The girl was much younger than Russo, but it was obvious they were in love, even to a man watching them approach without the aid of his telescopic sight. Teague was suddenly confused. In a few seconds Russo would disappear below and he would lose his chance at a shot. There was no assurance he would ever again have such a fine opportunity. But the girl made a difference. To shoot Russo would cause him only an instant of pain. True, it would take his life and it would stop him from pursuit, but it wasn't a fit punishment for what he had done to Edward Teague. To shoot the girl was far too quick, there'd be no great enjoyment in that. He would have to defer the shot for perhaps the chance of a greater punishment.

Teague laid the rifle down and moved closer to the door opening. He could see them crossing the street, coming toward the parking garage.

* * *

"Will you come over tonight?" Marie asked as the traffic light turned green.

"It's not a great idea."

"I'm lonesome."

Russo laughed. "You're always lonesome."

"Some men might like a girl who was always lonesome."

They stepped across the street. "Maybe some would, and maybe some might think she was sort of odd."

"Odd?"

"Oh, maybe an advanced case of nymphomania, something like that. Nuisance thing."

She looked up at him. "You regard nymphomania as a nuisance?"

He nodded. "Oh yes. The poor things are always trying to lure men up to their apartments in a frantic effort to quench their unslakable urges."

"You go to hell," she laughed. "I withdraw the invitation."

He opened the parking garage door for her and they walked past rows of cars on the first level. "I'll tell you what," he said. "I'll make an exception in your case. It would be cruel to allow a poor unsatisfied nymphomaniac to cry herself to sleep."

"How kind you are. Will you come for dinner?"

"No."

She led him to the stairway. "I'm parked on the second level. Is the reason you won't come to dinner because you won't come until after dark?"

"Something like that."

"You keep the same hours as Dracula, did you know that?"

"Yeah." He stepped ahead of her into the second level. Most of the cars were gone. His practiced eye scanned the others for a movement. He detected none. Her car was parked near the Clinton Street side. A rental panel truck, parked several spaces away, had a blanket hung back of the front seats. He guessed someone used it as motor home or the blanket had been rigged so that the interior couldn't be seen by thieves.

He walked her to her car.

"Come on," she said. "I'll give you a ride to your lot."

"Okay." He hopped in the passenger side.

She casually pulled up her skirt, exposing her shapely legs, and started the car.

She backed out and headed for the exit ramp.

Russo reached over and pulled down her skirt.

"Why did you do that?"

"The parking attendant should get only the correct change, nothing more."

"You're silly."

"Maybe," he said as they approached the little booth next to the exit leading to the street. There was no side-view mirror on Russo's side of the car so he couldn't see that the panel truck had followed them down the ramp, staying well back.

Marie paid the attendant and then turned into the street leading to the senior officers' parking lot. She pulled up to the lot entrance and reached across. "There's no use protecting my reputation anymore. Give me a kiss."

Russo leaned over and obeyed, enjoying the sensation. "I'll be over around ten," he said, hopping out of the car.

She sped away and he waved to the officer guarding the parking lot. Again he didn't see the panel truck speed by as it followed Marie's car. Russo was too busy thinking about Edward Teague.

Nor did Russo doubt that Marie was anything but safe as she hurried home.

Marie Coyle took no notice of the truck following behind. A taxi was between the two vehicles, so there was no reason to even see the truck. Her mind was occupied with other thoughts, thoughts about Tony Russo and the future—if any—they might have together.

She swung into the heavy traffic on Crocker Boulevard and then moved with the slow-moving river of vehicles until she approached Six Mile Road. She signaled for a left-hand turn. The panel truck, now several cars behind, also signaled for a left-hand turn. Both vehicles made it, although the truck had to accelerate to clear the intersection as the traffic light changed.

She thought about shopping first but decided against it. There was plenty of food in the apartment, and she wanted to be home in case he changed his mind and came over early. She knew it was unlikely, but she didn't want to take the chance of missing him. She dismissed and forgave him his preoccupation with his Stalking Man. She supposed that all policemen at some time or other went through such phases.

There was no parking lot for her apartment building. It was an older building, and at the time it was built such refinements hadn't been required by zoning ordinances. Sometimes finding a place to park was a minor annoyance, and sometimes it meant a long walk. But she was lucky. A blue car pulled out and provided an empty space almost in front of the entrance to her apartment building. She speeded up a bit, then swung her car into the opening before anyone else seized the treasure.

The panel truck had been following slowly behind her. Now she noticed it for the first time. The street was narrow and the approaching truck would make getting out from the driver's side of her car dangerous, so she slid across the seat and opened the passenger door.

Teague cursed as he saw her move to the other side of the car. He had planned to take her as she got out from the driver's side. It was a street lined with apartment buildings. She could be going into any one of them. He slowed down and a car behind him blew its horn.

Marie snapped the lock and slammed the door closed. She jumped slightly as a man in a car behind a panel truck blew his horn. City nerves, she thought to herself as she walked into the entrance. Like most of the apartment buildings on the street, hers now provided a lobby security guard. She nodded to him and he smiled a greeting.

The man in the car behind Teague now leaned on his horn. Under different circumstances Teague would have been enraged by the sound of the blatant horn, but he was preoccupied. He had lost the chance to grab Russo's girl. But he made note of the apartment—the Parkway—and the license number of her car. He started moving again, driving slowly down the street. At the next intersection the man in the following car pulled up alongside and shouted something. Teague paid no notice.

He drove around the block, this time at normal speed to avoid attention. He again noted the place where the girl had entered. He had to presume she lived there. If not, he'd find another way to get her, but if this was where she lived, he knew she had no chance of escaping him.

Find their dens, his father had instructed him about foxes. Just find their hole and wait. Foxes came and went on a regular schedule just like people. All you had to do was watch and wait. Eventually you would have a crack at the fox, no matter how clever or lucky the animal happened to be.

9

THOMAS KNAPP SAT ALONE IN THE QUIET HOUSE. THE funeral was over. The burial service had been simple and sparsely attended. Only the immediate family and a handful of friends had come to the cemetery. He felt the strangeness of the situation and so had they. Of course they all wondered if they were standing next to the man who had murdered the woman being lowered into the grave. He had walked alone from the grave site.

There was no post-funeral family get-together. He had merely driven home. The children were safe; far away in Connecticut with his other sister. His sister hadn't really believed his story about Edward Teague. He was wryly amused that she had almost condoned the idea that he had killed his wife, whom she had never liked. Loyal sisters were hard to come by. Other people had not been so kind, especially Helen's family.

But it was finally over. The whole morbid drama of the American way of death had been enacted and he was now left alone. Martha Flowers had protested, but she too had left town, to stay with relatives in California. She'd be safe from Teague—the Stalking Man would have no way of knowing about her. It was only Helen who had been so unlucky.

He poured some more brandy into his glass, wondering if it might not be beneficial to get drunk, to rage aloud in the silent house, to react in some human way to death. Drinking only made him sleepy, and somehow going to sleep hardly seemed a suitable escape for a tortured soul. His mind was working, there was just no drive, no ability to stay on a single thought for more than a few seconds.

The telephone rang. He ignored it. His was an unlisted telephone number, so he wasn't worried about crank calls, but he didn't want to listen to the excuses of some idiot who called to explain why he was ashamed to be seen in public with him. But the ringing was incessant, as if the person on the other end knew he was there and wouldn't give up until he answered.

The sun was going down, and only a red glow lit the gathering night clouds outside. Long evening shadows painted darkness into every bush and tree. He sat in the darkened house looking out the window, listening to the ring of the phone. Other people had his telephone number. The police had it. Suddenly he wondered if something might have happened. Perhaps they'd found the real killer. He felt a spark of hope. Something had to happen, otherwise he was facing the end of his career.

The ringing would not stop.

Knapp stood up, gulped down the last of the brandy, and walked to the telephone.

"Hello," he answered.

There was no response on the other end. "Hello," he repeated, this time with irritation.

"How does it feel?" a low voice asked.

"Who is this, please?"

A chuckle greeted his question. "Well, imagine that, you've forgotten all about me."

"Listen, I'm not up to playing games. Who the hell is this?"

The same chuckle answered him. "So you're human after all. Listen to you, you're ready to blow a blood vessel. I wonder how I ever got such a distorted picture of your ability to stay cool."

Knapp almost dropped the telephone.

"You remember me, big shot," the voice continued. "How does it feel, being at the other end of the stick? Think they'll convict you? Maybe you'll get a shitty lawyer and he'll put you away in a funny place where all the doors are locked. You should get so lucky."

"Teague?" Knapp could say the name. It came out as a soft whisper.

The chuckle developed into a high-pitched laugh. "Who else? Edward Teague at your service, you fuck. The same Edward Teague you salted away."

Knapp couldn't think. The explosion of fear he felt at hearing the voice was now giving way to rage.

"You're probably all alone tonight, you shit," Teague went on. "I know how people avoid you when they think you're a killer. Believe me, I know from personal experience. So I said to myself, Edward, you must call up nice Mr. Knapp and tell him you know how it feels. Talk to that prick and let him know he's sharing just a little of the pain you went through. I'm very good that way, you know, assisting people who need a little help."

"How did you get my telephone number?"

Teague laughed. "That's obvious. My God! How I overestimated you! I got your number when I was in your house. I have a trick memory for numbers, they just seem to stick somehow. I'll bet I'm the only person who calls you tonight. Everybody thinks you did it, you know." He giggled. "Of course, there are only two of us who know for sure that you didn't, but don't worry about it, your secret·is safe with me. I'll never tell." He laughed.

"Why did you do it?"

The laughter stopped. "Damn, how you fooled me. I thought you were the greatest thing since the wheel, did you know that? Like a fucking fool, I believed in you. You sent me to that hospital, no one else. Now you've paid for it. But I wanted you to know I did it. It wouldn't be any fun if you thought it was someone else."

"Why are you telling me this?"

"Why not? Who the hell would believe you anyway? They all think you chilled your old lady, at least that's what the newspapers hint at. Maybe they'll get you for it too, wouldn't that be beautiful? You'll be babbling about me and nobody'll believe you."

"You're sick, Edward, very sick."

"Up your ass! I'm not sick, you two-faced son of a bitch. I know what I'm doing. Hell, they had sick people at that hospital, people huddling in corners seeing things or talking to people who weren't there. They were sick, but I'm not sick. I know exactly what I'm doing all the time."

"You had better turn yourself in. I'll represent you. I'll get you off." Suddenly he was functioning again.

"What an offer! I'd be back in the rubber room and you'd be a big hero. No more of that shit for me. This time you'll be the one in the funny farm, not me."

"They already know it was you who killed my wife," Knapp lied.

Another chuckle was the response. "Clever bastard, aren't you? They don't even know I exist anymore. No, this time, my slimy friend, you'll be the one standing in front of the judge. Payment deferred, but payment nevertheless."

"Edward, I'm the only friend you have, the only person able to help you."

"Up your ass! Doesn't it make any difference that I killed your old lady? Jesus, talk about sickies!"

"We were being divorced," Knapp said quietly. "You didn't know that, did you?"

"You're just saying that, you fucker!"

"It's true, Teague," Knapp said softly. "You did me a favor. I wanted a quick divorce, but she was fighting me. That's why the police suspected me at first, you see. My late wife was a drunken bitch, Edward. She would have kept my children and most of my property. All this will blow over soon and I'll be just the same as I was. Only you have freed me from her. I really shouldn't be so ungallant as to thank you, but you really did me one hell of a favor."

"Liar!" Teague screamed. "You fucking liar, you're making all this up!"

Knapp felt the perspiration on his upper lip. "No. It's all true, every word, Edward. They can't convict me, I have an alibi—quite airtight—let me assure you of that. No, things couldn't be better for me. As a matter of fact, I was just sitting here drinking some brandy and celebrating. I didn't know it was really you that did it, but I thank you."

"I'll . . ." Teague almost strangled in his rage. "I'll get you, Knapp, you ugly fuck. I'll get you, so help me God!"

Knapp forced an easy laugh. "Don't be ridiculous, Teague, you're too hot now to get anybody. They'll have you back in that hospital in no time. Only this time I won't help you, Edward. This time I'll applaud as they lock you away forever."

"I'll . . . get . . . you!" The words were forced out in sheer rage, then the telephone connection was broken.

Knapp laid the telephone back in its cradle. His hands were shaking. He walked to the brandy bottle and poured an even stiffer shot. He went to the hall closet and got his wallet from his coat. He gulped the brandy as he picked through the business cards until he found the home telephone number of Lieutenant Anthony Russo.

* * *

Rosinski had been exceedingly careful driving home. Even loyalty among cops wouldn't help him if he slammed his car into another car—or worse, a pedestrian. He was loaded and he knew it.

Other men might call her a pig, but she was kind to him. A big, beefy waitress, she was full of life and she liked to drink almost as much as he did. The mixture of whiskey and beer meant a godawful head in the morning, but even with that knowledge it had seemed worth it as they drank and made love.

He had a difficult time trying to get his key into the lock. His own alcoholic ineptness made him smile. But it was still worth the price. He was content. Rosinski opened the door and flipped on the lights. Carefully, he extracted his pistol and belt holster and put them away in a dresser drawer. They called his small room an efficiency apartment: a fold-down bed and a nook for a kitchen. Still, it was home for him, and for one of nine Polish children, it was spacious compared to the crowded conditions of his youth.

Rosinski belched. "Nasty fellow," he said aloud in the empty apartment.

The telephone rang. He squinted to see the time on the wall clock, not thinking to look at his wristwatch. It was just three o'clock in the morning.

Damn the telephone, he thought to himself. His mind was a fog and he tried to muster up some control so that he wouldn't sound drunk when he answered.

"Hello," he said, although the word stretched out a bit long.

"Where in the hell have you been?" Russo's agitated voice inquired.

Rosinski's Slavic face broke into a wide grin. "It should make no difference to you, sir, or to the department for that matter, but I have been among evil companions. Sir, I confess to Almighty God and to you, sir, that Detective Second-Grade Joseph Rosinski was out getting laid this evening." He laughed. "I must point out, however, that this was on my own time."

There was a pause on the other end of the line. "Joe," Russo's voice was low but strong, "please sober up. We have work to do."

The room seemed to be spinning as Rosinski listened. "Oh, God, what now?"

"I'm at Knapp's house," Russo continued. "He's had a call from Teague."

"Good for him." The words slurred slightly as Rosinski spoke them, much to his embarrassment.

"Joe, straighten up. This is serious."

Rosinski shrugged. "I'm half looped," he said simply.

"Grab a cold shower. I have a job for you."

"Oh shit, I'm really loaded, you know that?"

"Loaded or not, this thing is breaking, Joe."

Rosinski cradled the receiver between his ear and

shoulder and sat down. He fished out a cigarette and lit up. "What's up?"

"Teague called Knapp to tell him that he killed Knapp's wife. He means business. I'm at Knapp's now, just in case he tries to come after him."

"Did you call the Chippewa Hills cops?"

"Do you think they'd believe this?"

"No."

"This is Knapp's address and telephone number. Take it down." Russo spoke the numbers carefully into the telephone. Rosinski jotted them down mechanically. "I'll be here," Russo added, "waiting for the son of a bitch."

"Do you want me to come out there?"

"No," Russo said. "I'll take care of this end. I want you to stake out Marie Coyle's place. There's a chance Teague might have seen me with her. Just a chance, but I don't want to risk anything, you understand?"

"Do you think you can trust me?" Rosinski taunted drunkenly. "She's a good-looking broad, and I'm younger than you, remember that."

"I remember." Russo's icy voice took on sudden authority. "Sober up, Rosinski. I mean it. You'll need all the edge you can get if I'm right about this."

"Edge, shit, I need sleep."

"Grab a quick shower and some coffee. Get something in your stomach. This is important, Rosinski."

"Why don't you call your girl friend and get her out of town for a while?"

There was a pause before Russo replied. "I tried that," he said quietly. "I can't seem to convince anyone about this guy. She won't go. And she insists on going to work in the morning."

"And you want me to run an escort service?"

"More than that. I want you to see that nothing happens to her at all, do you understand me?"

Rosinski nodded, inhaling on his cigarette. "I understand. It'll take me a while to get organized. Where does she live?"

Russo gave him the address. "She'll be leaving for work about a quarter after seven. She drives a green Chevrolet, about two years old. You can't miss it."

"Why don't I just pick her up and take her down?"

"She's touchy about the whole thing. Maybe she'll go with you, maybe not. I think she thinks I'm nuts."

"Well, that makes two of us. Okay, I'll play nursemaid for your girl friend. Want me to stick with her in the records department?"

"No, just get her down there safe. He won't try anything once she's in the building."

Rosinski yawned. "There's no way I can get out of this, right?"

"No."

"Crap. Okay, I'll deliver her safe and sound. I'll get over there early, about six thirty or so."

"Earlier."

"Jesus, have a heart."

"Get there at six, no later."

"It's three now."

"Then you have plenty of time."

"Not for a nap."

"This is no time for a nap, Rosinski. Get on the stick!"

The young detective nodded as if Russo could see him. "Okay, I'll be there," he sighed. "I'll call you if anything happens."

*   *   *

The telephone call to Knapp had upset him, and Edward Teague couldn't sleep. His mind churned with anger, and it was an emotion he couldn't afford. The doctors had convinced him that anger was destructive for him, and now it robbed him of any chance for sleep.

He had again shifted his base to a new motel, this time even more sleazy. The bed was hard and uncomfortable and gave off a musty odor. The walls were thin; he could hear a couple in the next unit arguing, their voices as clear as if they were in the room with him.

He switched on the television set. It was out of focus, and the fuzzy images of the old actors in the late movie irritated him. He snapped it off. His blood pounded in his temples. He was eager for action.

It had been like that years before, the first time his father had taken him up north. The other men in the cabin snored and the smells of the dying fire penetrated his nostrils. The air was cold. He found himself both stimulated and frightened. It was a new experience. The next day he would step out into the woods with these grown men and perhaps demonstrate that he too was a man— or worse, that he was not. He had lain awake all that night.

He walked to the window and pulled the drapes aside. The roadway was deserted; a streetlight shone down on the barren landscape. His rented panel truck was parked outside the motel unit. He had parked his own car in a shopping area parking lot near a twenty-four-hour grocery. It was safe. No one would notice the car, at least for a couple of days.

Teague glanced at his watch. It was just past three in

the morning. He estimated it would take an hour to drive to the girl's apartment. He planned to arrive there before six o'clock just in case she might be an early riser. He would take her when she came out. Then he would repay Russo—repay him in full.

Although his pulse continued to race, the lack of sleep began to have its effect. Soon he would shave and dress and then he would be ready, but now the minutes seemed to drag on forever.

* * *

Russo sat in Knapp's darkened living room, concealed behind the shadow of the wide draperies. He sat quietly, letting his eyes play over the empty street in front of the large house. He could hear only the sound of Knapp's soft breathing.

"He won't come," Knapp said in a near whisper.

"He might," Russo replied quietly. "You know, he wouldn't be out there at all if you hadn't done such a good job protecting his goddamned rights." Anger framed Russo's words.

"I don't make the laws, Russo, you know that. I do my job, just as you do yours, and we've had this argument before." Knapp paused and then continued, "You know, you could just as easily blame the doctors. They examined him, treated him, and made the decision that he was sane. They were the ones who let him go, not me."

"He was your client."

"How about yourself, Russo?" Knapp asked. "Did you ever consider that maybe you might be to blame? Perhaps if you had prepared a better case I might not have done so well, ever think about that?''

''I've thought about it,'' the detective replied. ''The case was perfect. Every fact was proven. It was your insanity defense that let that looney wiggle into the hands of those doctors. Doesn't that bother your conscience, just a little bit?''

''Can I smoke?''

Russo looked out at the empty street. ''Better not, at least not here. If he's out there he would spot the flare of the match and know we were waiting for him.''

''That makes sense,'' Knapp said.

Both men fell silent.

''Does this sort of thing bother you?'' Knapp asked after a few moments had passed.

''What?''

''Waiting around like this. You may have to kill a man.''

Russo laughed, but without humor. ''Or he may try to kill me. That bothers me much more.''

''But the other doesn't?''

''You mean killing another man?''

''Yes.''

Russo paused for a moment before replying. ''Do you know how many men I've killed?''

''No.''

''Zero—none. Most cops are the same. All that killing shit is on television. I have shot at a couple of men. And I once hit a burglar in the leg. That's the extent of my gory record.'' Russo turned from his vigil on the street and looked over at the lawyer. ''How about you, Counselor, any blood on your hands?''

''I was an intelligence officer in the army,'' Knapp replied. ''We were back of the line mostly. Once in a while we might catch some artillery fire but that was about all. I carried a carbine but I never fired it. I never had to.''

''Then we are really just a pair of virgins,'' Russo said as he stretched, ''waiting for one of the best non-virgins in the business.''

''I suppose.'' Knapp stood up in the darkness. ''Do you want a drink?''

''No,'' the detective replied. ''I notice you seem to have quite a capacity for that stuff.''

''Brandy,'' Knapp replied, ''is absorbed slowly by the blood. If you pace yourself you can drink brandy and stay nearly sober.''

''This is a good night to stay sober,'' Russo said.

The tall lawyer poured a few inches of brandy into his glass, measuring by the heft of the liquor. ''Or this could be a good night not to be sober.'' He returned to his chair. ''You know what this whole situation reminds me of?''

''What?''

''Do you remember that short story—'The Lady or the Tiger?' ''

''The name rings a bell.''

''Part of the story concerned a barbarian king who figured out a perfect method to try men accused of crimes. A defendant was pushed into an arena. At one end were two absolutely similar doors. Behind one was a ferocious, hungry tiger; behind the other door was a beautiful woman. In effect, the man tried himself. He had to choose one door to open. The doors were identical and the choice was his alone. The king believed guilt or innocence would be determined divinely by which door the man happened to choose. If he was truly innocent he would pick the door with the lady. All the people would cheer and the man would be given money and jewels and he would be married to the beautiful woman. Everyone would be happy and there would be one hell of a party.''

''So?''

''If he was guilty, he would choose the other door and the tiger would come out and tear him apart.''

''Does brandy always do this to you, Knapp?''

The lawyer shook his head. ''I'm trying to make a point. You seem to hold me responsible for Teague. But in almost every aspect of criminal law there are always two symbolic doors—one marked 'society's rights' and the other marked 'individual rights.' Basically, the legislature picks the door—the one they think will work best. They have no idea what might happen. In Germany they picked the door marked 'society's rights' and it was the wrong choice. A tiger named Hitler came out.''

Russo shook his head. ''I don't see the connection.''

''In this state the legislature—in drawing up the laws on insanity—picked the door marked 'individual rights.' '' The lawyer sipped his brandy. ''They too picked the wrong door, this time. They opened it and the tiger came out.''

''You mean Teague?''

''Yes, Teague and others like him.''

''Sounds like you're trying to salve your own conscience,'' Russo said.

''Everything is a choice really. Here the legislature had a real choice: Do you stick all the crazy people away and throw away the key? If you do that you have clearly picked the door marked 'society's rights,' but who knows who might get locked away? It might be a lawyer named Knapp or a cop named Russo. Sort of like what the Russians do. So there could be a tiger behind that door too, you understand?''

''I suppose.''

''Our lawmakers chose the other door. They figured they would protect you and me, and Teague. Only something went wrong. I'm not protected and you're not protected, and Teague is out killing people. They picked the wrong door.''

Russo sighed. ''You could be right.'' They sat in silence until Russo spoke again. ''Speaking of tigers, have you ever been tiger hunting?''

''That's not my bag. I've read about it though, all the unnerving business about waiting for the beast to strike. Hemingway stuff.''

Russo leaned back to ease a cramp in his back. He glanced at the luminous dial of his watch. It was after four o'clock. ''Staking out a tiger from what I've read is similar to staking out a criminal. It's a thing cops do for a living. Dull as hell usually, but you never know when the action might start. You might park across from a store that's been robbed and hope they'll try again, that sort of thing. Like waiting for a tiger in a way.''

''Tell me the truth, do you like that kind of thing, the danger, I mean?''

The detective shook his head. ''No. It scares you at first, but then you become a fatalist about the whole business. Usually, it's just a boring, distasteful job. I draw partners who eat onion sandwiches and have gas trouble.''

''Sounds dreadful.''

Russo spoke casually as he leaned forward slightly. ''I saw something move out there.''

''Where?''

"Down by that big tree, just at the driveway."

Both men were silent. A shadow moved by the tree and Russo silently drew his revolver from its holster.

The only sound in the empty house was the breathing of the two men.

"Oh shit!" Russo spat out the words. "It's only a dog."

A small dog trotted across the front lawn, its nose close to the ground, following some secret scent.

"Jesus," Knapp's voice was filled with relief.

Russo looked up at the sky. False dawn had begun. He sensed that Teague wouldn't come, and the tension flowed from his muscles and he felt almost crushing fatigue. "If our friend was out there," Russo said, "he would have made a move by now. I guess it would be safe to smoke now."

"I'll wait now. I've seen one too many movies about the man lighting the match in the dark."

"Suit yourself."

"What's your plan if he doesn't show up?" Knapp asked.

Russo leaned back in his chair and began to relax. He hadn't realized how tense he had been. "I'm going to stick with you for a while. If he's as angry as you said he was when he called he'll try something. I think you're his most probable target."

"Any other targets?"

"Just you and me." Russo stood up and stretched. "I have a girl, but I've seen to it that she's protected. I doubt that he'd know about her anyway. But with Teague you can't be too careful."

"You say she's protected?"

"My partner is watching out for her."

10

Rosinski HAD SHOWERED, FRIED SOME EGGS, AND brewed some strong coffee. Despite these ministrations, he knew he was still under the influence of alcohol, although his mind was beginning to clear. He drove carefully and slowly along the deserted streets, now and then passing another car. But otherwise the streets were empty.

His mouth was dry and still tasted like the bottom of a birdcage. He lit a cigarette, and he wasn't sure if that helped or made it worse. Above him the night clouds were beginning to catch the hint of dawn, but Rosinski was city bred and paid no notice to the sky; his was the world of concrete and streetlights.

He swung off the boulevard and drove down Marie Coyle's street, a narrow lane with cars jammed bumper to bumper along each curb. He watched for the Parkway Apartments, spotting them at mid-block. Some joker had illegally parked a panel truck in the loading zone in front of her apartment house. Rosinski wished he had a ticket book so he could slap a citation under the jerk's windshield wiper. He drove past and parked next to a fire hydrant. The apartment entrance was only a few cars back.

Rosinski sucked on the cigarette and twisted about in the seat to get comfortable. He adjusted the rearview mirror so that he could see the entrance to the apartments.

Russo said Marie would probably come out sometime before seven o'clock. He had about an hour to wait, so he settled back and thought about his muscular waitress, hoping his fantasies would help keep him awake.

*   *   *

Her car was parked exactly where she had left it the night before. Teague had parked right behind it in a loading zone. It was early, and he felt it was safe enough; no police car would bother giving out parking tickets at that hour in the morning. He raised the blanket and slipped into the interior of the truck.

He saw the plain sedan roll past about a half hour after he was in place. There was only one man, he could see that. The car passed him but parked beyond the building entrance next to a fire hydrant. The man stayed inside the car.

Teague knew it had to be a cop. Only a cop would park next to a fire hydrant. So the police had him figured. He looked out the rear window of the truck but saw no movement. Apparently the cop was alone. Teague's impulse was to run, to get away and try some other day, but time was running out. His money was going and so was his luck. He knew that today would be his last chance.

The sky was reddening. He remembered his father's old saying—red sky at night, sailor's delight, red sky in morning, sailor take warning. It meant they might be in for some rain later. For the first time he noticed the air was heavy and humid.

Teague sat on the truck's floor and made himself com-

fortable. Once again he made sure the rifle was loaded
and the safety off.

*The red sky stirred his memory. He recalled the after-
noon it had poured and they had been confined to the
cabin. But in the cool morning he had shot four rabbits.
His father had no luck, not even a shot. The rabbits had
been their dinner. He remembered how proud he felt, and
his joy in bettering his father in the primitive contest of
the hunt. It had been a long-savored pleasure, and now
the memory of it relaxed him.*

*   *   *

Marie Coyle awoke refreshed. She was a morning person
basically, and needed no time to pull herself together. She
quickly began her usual morning ritual: the hot shower,
the attention to her hair and her makeup, the breakfast of
toasted muffin and black coffee. She looked out her
kitchen window. The sky was a mellow orange and the
rising sun was brightening everything.

She dressed carefully, as she usually did, and she
thought of Tony Russo as she looked into the mirror.
Sometimes she wondered what she wanted out of life.
She was pretty, she knew that, and attractive to men. She
had a choice beyond policemen. Yet something in Russo
moved her like no other man she had ever met. He
seemed to her to be the embodiment of steely masculin-
ity, and yet he was a gentle lover, kind and not demanding, just the kind of a man she had often pictured as
perfect for herself.

Yesterday had been a crossroad in their relationship. It
was a risk, walking into his office like that. Now every-

one in the department would know about them, and he could no longer hide behind his flimsy excuse that he was protecting her reputation.

He was jealous of her. The thought delighted her. Every woman wanted her man to be jealous, not so much as to be a problem, but enough to be assured that he really cared.

She knew now that Lieutenant Anthony Russo cared very much about her, something she was not completely sure about before. She was happy.

Marie Coyle sang to herself as she prepared to go to work. It promised to be a lovely day.

* * *

Rosinski fought against the remorseless pressure of his need to sleep. He flipped on the police radio in the hope that the voice of the dispatcher might help keep him awake.

The radio squawked into life with the sound of sporadic static.

"Car 9-12, meet a man," the dispatcher intoned nasally. "Car 9-12, meet a man. 2217 North Bagley. Meet a man, 2217 North Bagley." That was the only call. The morning was always a quiet time. A man at 2217 North Bagley had called the police. It could be anything, Rosinski knew from experience, from a freshly discovered burglary to a drunk in someone's doorway. He felt reassured with this renewed contact with his world, the world of the police.

Life began to stir in the apartments and Rosinski was grateful for the activity. People began to emerge from their brick caves into the muted sunlight of the new day.

They blinked like moles and then hurried to their cars or buses. Traffic increased on the narrow street, and Rosinski began to feel more awake as the heavy fatigue began to lift. He lit another cigarette and continued his rearview mirror vigilance of the apartment doorway.

A heavy-hipped woman hurried by, her high heels clicking against the pavement of the sidewalk. Rosinski liked women with big hips. He wondered if it might be an inherited trait, a gift from his Polish ancestors, who like their women big, strong, and capable of helping in the fields. He watched her walk all the way to the corner.

He was so fascinated that he almost missed Marie Coyle.

She came out, pausing a moment to glance up at the sky. She was vibrant and fresh. Rosinski decided he would talk to her; it would be better if she knew he was guarding her, otherwise she might think he was Teague and panic. He climbed out of his car and walked toward her. She had not seen him so he called out to avoid startling her. "Good morning, Marie."

She looked up, her face a blank for a moment until she recognized him, and then a wide smile lit her face. "Well, good morning. This is a surprise."

"My boss decided you should have a little protection. I told him you should have some protection from me too, but he was too busy to bother about that."

"Oh," she grinned, "you look harmless enough, Joe."

"Looks aren't everything. But you're safe because I'm scared to death of Russo."

She laughed.

"Do you want to drive downtown and have me tag along behind, or would you like a chauffeur?"

''I really don't think this is necessary, Joe. I'm flattered but . . .''

The rifle slug hit Rosinski in the chest. He was thrown back like a broken doll, falling backward over a low iron railing and onto a small patch of grass in front of the apartment. He rolled over as if trying to regain his footing when the second shot rang out.

Marie Coyle's eyes widened in horror when she saw Rosinski's leg jerk violently as the second bullet hit him. The sound of the shots seemed to echo down the canyonlike street, and for a moment Marie Coyle's brain could not translate what her eyes were seeing.

She started toward him when a force jarred her just back of her ear. She was unconscious before she hit the pavement.

Rosinski lay twisted on the ground. He was conscious but he couldn't move. He could feel nothing, no pain, no sensation. His head was jammed into a position from which he could see the tall man with the rifle come up behind Marie. There was nothing he could do; he tried to cry out but could not, nor could he move to get his gun. He was experiencing short blackouts, so that the world looked like a badly-run silent movie, with little spaces of black between the action.

Rosinski recognized the man from his pictures. Teague brought the rifle butt up against the girl's head, not hard, but with enough force to knock her out. It was sharp and quick, the blow of an expert.

Holding the rifle in one hand Teague grasped the back of the girl's dress and dragged her to the rear of a panel truck. Rosinski felt an overwhelming wave of nausea sweep over him as he fought to stay conscious. Things went black again for a moment, and then he could see.

He presumed Teague had loaded the girl into the truck as he watched it swing out of the loading zone and into traffic.

Rosinski saw a face looking down at him. The face seemed distorted, like a reflection in an amusement park mirror.

"Help me," Rosinski whispered, surprised at the effort it took to speak.

The face wavered for a moment and then reappeared.

"I'll call an ambulance," the face said.

"I am a police officer," Rosinski said, now becoming aware of the growing and extreme pain, a pain that seemed to be everywhere. "Help me to my car, the green one over at the curb with the door open, I have to use the radio."

"Jesus, mister, you're hurt pretty bad, I don't think you should be moved."

Rosinski was conscious of other faces staring down at him—some just curious, others concerned.

"A woman's been kidnapped. I have to use the radio," he said. They all disappeared for a moment, and Rosinski realized when they reappeared that he had lost consciousness for a second or two. The pain was getting worse.

"Hurry," he said. "Pull me by my shoulders. Just get me over to that car."

He felt timid hands take hold of his suit jacket. He clenched his teeth to stop from screaming. When the faces reappeared, he found himself propped up against the car. It took him a moment to recognize the car door a few inches from his face. The pain was growing and his breathing was sporadic, as if he had run a long distance.

"Under the dash," he said to the now familiar face,

"radio. Push red lever down and give me the hand microphone." He could feel the vibration of his car's motor.

Again he lost consciousness, although he didn't know it until he discovered the microphone in his hand. He depressed the activating trigger and identified himself slowly, giving the special police emergency code, clearing the air for an important message. As he talked he felt as short of breath as if he were climbing a mountain. It required such great effort that he felt he wanted to just slip away, but he forced himself to give the bare essentials of what had happened, the location, the description of the panel truck and its direction. He told the mute crackling radio that Edward Teague had seized Marie Coyle and that he had positively identified the Stalking Man. Almost as an afterthought he asked them to notify Lieutenant Anthony Russo. To his surprise Rosinski remembered the phone number that Russo had given him. He was very proud that he could retain that little scrap of information and said so aloud to the little thing he held in his hand.

The pain was gone now and so was the nausea. He felt quite comfortable although the faces now only appeared occasionally. He mentioned as an afterthought that he was wounded, although that seemed somehow unimportant.

"Thanks," Rosinski said, handing the microphone back to the face, now even more distorted and blurred. The radio was crackling some sort of words and he tried to concentrate on what was being said, but it was impossible.

The face melted away and the feeling of being on the side of a steep mountain passed. For a moment only a floating sensation remained, and then nothing.

"Hey, mister," the man said to Rosinski as the detective's head slumped against the car seat. "Hold on, help is coming now. They got it on your radio, do you hear that? They're sending an ambulance over here now. Just hang on."

A young woman pushed her way through the knot of people gathered around the car. "I'm a nurse," she said, brushing the man aside. She glanced at the blood-soaked chest and the blood-filled trouser leg. She grasped Rosinski's wrist for a moment, then placed her fingertips against the side of his neck. She stood up slowly.

"There's a nurse here already, mister," the man said to Rosinski. "They'll have you fixed up in no time."

"It's no use talking to him," the nurse said gently to the man kneeling next to Rosinski. "He's dead."

The man's head jerked up at her, his face almost angry. Then his eyes seemed to fill with tears and he looked away quickly.

"Did you know him?" the nurse asked.

The man stood up. "No," he said quietly. As they stood next to the car, a distant siren cut faintly above the morning traffic noise.

* * *

Everything was working. Edward Teague drove until he reached the ramp to the southbound expressway. He planned to switch from the expressway to the interstate highway and then proceed to his motel. It would be a glorious day.

The girl, still unconscious, lay quietly in the rear of the truck. He hoped the blow to her head hadn't done excessive damage. It was not his intent that she die quickly.

Food had always been one of the high points of the hunting trips with his father. Sometimes they ate steak for breakfast or had a plate stacked high with bacon strips and fried eggs. But it was the satisfaction of the large dinners—especially after a successful hunt—that he remembered best of all: the smell of frying onions, the spicy aromas from mounds of steaming food, a mouth-watering reward for their long hours in the woods.

Teague realized he was hungry. He liked shooting the big blonde cop. There had been no sexual thrill in the kill, but there had been a feeling of triumph very much like the thrill of a good clean hunting shot, a feeling of intense satisfaction. He supposed the hunger was a conditioned response and that his stomach was demanding a reward for a good hunt. But he had no time for food.

He merged with the heavy traffic that was moving very quickly toward the city. The junction with the interstate was almost a mile away, so he began to maneuver through the moving lanes of traffic to reach the inside lane. It was difficult; the cars were bumper to bumper, and drivers pretended not to see his turn signals.

Teague noticed a police car moving along on the service drive, the street above, which bordered the concrete expressway ditch. The police car rolled along slowly, the officers keeping an eye on the traffic below. Teague was driving within the lawful speed, so he had no worries, but he watched the scout car as he passed by below. After he passed he tried to find the police car in his rearview mirror, but it wasn't there. He glanced up. The scout car was speeding along the service drive, keeping pace with him. He was momentarily concerned but presumed the officers had spotted someone speeding. An entrance ramp in the expressway was coming up.

Instinctively, he swung out into the center lanes, moving between cars, to avoid the police car when it came down the ramp, if it did.

A number of cars waited in the ramp, waiting their turn to mesh with the moving line of traffic. The police car sped down the ramp just as Teague passed it. He saw the car whip out onto the slanted grass area and around the waiting cars. The police flipped on their revolving red light and he heard the scream of their siren.

There was one exit ramp before the interchange junction. He could see the flashing red light behind him as the cars began to slow down and their drivers very reluctantly began to make room for the approaching police car.

Teague was conscious of a squeal of brakes as he wheeled his truck in front of a taxi. He realized that the police car might be after him, and if that was true he was trapped on the subsurface expressway. He had to escape to the streets above. And if the police were chasing someone else, it would mean only a few minutes lost in his overall plan. He forced his way through the traffic and gained the inner lane just as the exit ramp came up. He threw his gearshift into high and roared up the deserted ramp.

The next sound he heard was the crashing of metal behind him, and as he looked up into his rearview mirror he saw the squad car hit another car. Like a frantic bug it was now backing up, trying to find a way through the steel wall of stopped cars that formed a barrier to the exit ramp.

Rage and frustration exploded within Edward Teague.

Somehow the police had a description of his rented truck. How it happened didn't matter, it was now a fact. He had escaped momentarily, but he knew all the city police would be looking for him now.

He sped along the service drive and then swung into an alley. He was in the center city now and near the area where he had been raised. He knew every street and—more important—every alley. He turned into another alley and bumped along the rutted concrete for several blocks, exiting into a rundown residential street. He came up behind a crawling car filled with four black women. He was forced to stay behind them as they inched along, looking for an address or a parking space. He blew his horn. The middle-aged women looked back at him, their black faces filled with indignation.

They slowed down as a lesson to the short-tempered white man. Teague picked up the rifle from the seat next to him and held it up to the view of the women seated in the back of the car. Suddenly their car shot ahead, its tires screeching. He swore as they disappeared down the street, and then he turned off at the next intersection.

Teague tried to force himself to relax so that he could plan his next move. The drive back to the motel was possible only on well-traveled major streets. The police would patrol those streets and capture was certain. The old abandoned warehouse section, an area slated for demolition, was just a few miles away, and it seemed the only alternative for what he had in mind.

He could work his way to the warehouse section by using alleyways, thereby having to cross main streets only occasionally. He had driven by the decaying warehouses on his tour when he had returned to his home city. Even the railroad yards were abandoned, and the whole section was scheduled for leveling and rebuilding. At the edge of the area, two supertowers were being constructed that would overlook the river. The towers would be among the highest buildings in the Midwest and even now soared far above the city. He saw the towers in the distance as he crossed Almont Street.

The alley he had planned to use was blocked by a garbage truck, so he turned down another residential street. He almost hit a newspaper boy who swung his bicycle into the truck's path but swerved back just in time, although the boy did fall in avoiding a collision.

In his rearview mirror Teague saw the boy crawl from the tangle of his bicycle, apparently unhurt. He could hear the boy's reed-thin voice screaming insults.

Teague turned and glanced at the unconscious girl in the back. He would have even more problems if she came to while he was driving. He stepped on the accelerator, and the truck shot past the rows of parked cars as he rocketed down the street.

He was the hunted now. It was a new experience and panic gripped him. He had to escape. He had to get away. He tried to call up the image of his father, to recall some axiom of the hunt that might help him now, but his mind would not work and panic obliterated his memory. All he had left was instinct, the wild-eyed instinct of a hunted animal.

A car ahead pulled slowly from the curb. Teague hit the horn and the driver panicked and stopped dead. There wasn't enough room to clear; the truck ripped into the front of the car and tore off half a fender as it roared by.

The truck still ran well enough, although now there

was a wobble noticeable in the steering wheel. Teague presumed that one of his tires had been knocked out of line. He had planned to change cars anyway, since the police knew about the truck; now such an exchange became imperative.

Teague stopped for a signal light at the intersection of Field Street. He looked around for a likely car. He planned to force a driver out with the rifle and kill him if he resisted.

He looked again at the girl. She lay still but she whimpered softly. She would soon revive.

The police car spotted him at the same moment he saw it. The red light flashed on and the siren wailed.

Teague spun the wheel and ripped through the traffic, roaring down the vacant left-turn lane of Field Street. The police car was behind him now, only a block back. He almost overturned the truck as he spun left into Central Boulevard, the city's main street, and the police car made a racing turn behind him.

Cars ahead of him began to pull over as he sped through an intersection, running a red light and barely missing a giant semitrailer truck. They were racing into the city's main business section. Masses of work-bound people were alighting from buses and cars and hurrying across busy streets.

The people parted and ran as the police siren warned them of the speeding truck approaching. Another police car joined in the chase, its siren blending with the other. Teague had the accelerator down to the floorboard and the steering wheel was almost shaking out of his hands.

Three blocks ahead the river marked the end of Central Boulevard. He could see police cars converging at that point. He braked and swung the truck into Cardwell

Street, a one-way avenue clogged with incoming traffic. He jumped the curb and ran the panel truck down the sidewalk. Pedestrians jumped into the street or into doorways to escape him. One old lady, too slow to get out of the way, was hit and sent cartwheeling into the air.

One of the police cars followed, but at a much slower pace.

Teague turned into Adams and found both ends of the street blocked by squad cars.

Gunning his engine, Teague shot across the concrete street and roared over a grassy traffic island, bouncing down into the far lane. The entrance to the towers lay dead ahead. A uniformed security guard, watching him come, tried to stop the panel truck as it approached the narrow entrance for construction traffic. The guard tried to jump out of the way, but his lack of success was recorded by the loud metallic clang sent resounding through the truck. Teague kept the accelerator down as the truck hit an earthen ridge, and the truck actually flew a few feet in the air before crashing back on its tires. Men in white hard hats watched the spectacle as the panel truck raced for the base of the highest tower.

The two towers rose up like giant steel fingers. The main tower was the more complete of the two, and a temporary outside elevator shaft rose from its base like a popped blood vessel all the way to the highest point of the structure.

Teague heard the sounds of pursuing sirens as the police cars entered the construction site. He braked next to the empty elevator, and he hopped into the back of the truck, throwing open the rear doors. Taking up the rifle he fired one shot through the windshield of an approaching squad car. It spun sideways, throwing up a spray of dirt as the officers scrambled out the far side of the car.

The girl was reviving. He grabbed her by her hair.

"Get up, bitch!" he screamed in her ear. Her eyes fluttered open and immediately gave way to fright.

He jerked her roughly from the panel truck by her hair. She screamed at the pain. A shot fired by one of the policeman sang by Teague. He pulled the girl in front of him and held her there, his hand twisted securely in her hair, using her as a shield. More police cars came bouncing into the construction area.

He menaced a nearby construction worker with the rifle and the man froze, afraid to move. Teague forced the girl into the open cage of the elevator and found a well-worn set of controls with a foot pedal. He pushed the foot pedal and jammed the rifle into the handle turning it. The elevator rose very rapidly through the air, shooting past the floors, climbing high into the sky. Below, it seemed as if armies of police were swarming into the site, their faces turned skyward, watching as he climbed toward the top of the tower.

They were rising fast and were almost to the top when the elevator stopped with a sudden jolt, knocking the girl down and pulling Teague down on top of her. They had shut off the power below. The elevator was even with the forty-fifth floor. That level was open; it had a floor but no walls. At the far side a tarpaulin had been stretched across to protect the workers from the winds. But it was too early for the construction men to be aloft. The wind rattled the canvas tarpaulin. Teague stood up and forced the girl to climb out of the elevator to the flat surface of the deserted forty-fifth floor.

The view below was dizzying. The police and workers were mere specks below. The girl was whimpering.

Teague pulled her away from the edge. He needed time, time to force himself to relax, time to force himself to think.

*   *   *

Russo fought frantically through the sea of city-bound traffic. His unmarked car had a siren, but its scream helped very little in clearing the way ahead. Knapp sat next to him, obviously frightened at Russo's recklessness.

The police radio detailed the search for Teague's panel truck. The thought that Teague had Marie Coyle made Russo physically sick, and he had to fight down nausea as he raced for the city. Furious that Rosinski hadn't stopped Teague, Russo had no idea that his partner was dead and that, at the moment, his body was en route to the county morgue.

The radio carried the squad car report of the contact with the panel truck and the beginning of the chase. Then the truck was lost again. Despair and foreboding propelled Russo to risk even faster speed and more daring driving. Knapp braced himself for the collision he considered inevitable.

Russo's radio crackled into life to report that the truck had once again been found and was being pursued. Ahead of them Russo and Knapp could see the rising silhouette of the new towers as they neared the core city. The traffic was heavier, and Russo had several near-misses as he whipped the car in and out of lanes.

An impersonal voice laconically reported the pursuit as police cars joined the chase through the morning rush hour crowds in the downtown section. Teague's truck had hit a woman and an ambulance was called.

The report that the truck had smashed its way into the towers construction site and that shots had been exchanged jarred both Russo and Knapp, as they neared the skeletonlike towers.

Russo stopped breathing as he heard the dispatcher order all units not to fire because Teague had the girl with him. The radio reported that Teague and the girl were in an elevator rising up on the outside of the giant main tower.

Russo jammed the accelerator down and raced the car up the wrong way on an entrance ramp. He roared down Adams Street and within minutes brought the car to a squealing stop at what seemed to be a sea of police cars in the fenced-in construction site at the base of the towers.

Policemen crouched close by their cars or stared up from behind other cover. Russo looked up and felt a wave of dizziness. He looked down quickly. Knapp followed him as he strode between the cars heading for the base of the tower.

A stout policeman in a uniform shirt with a gold braid hat seemed to be directing things from beneath the roof of an open shed. He had several radios and walkie-talkies set up on a metal folding table in front of him. Several construction officials, dressed in shirts and ties but with white hard hats on their heads, stood by the senior policeman.

Russo grabbed the cop and half spun him around. "What's the situation?" he demanded, his voice tense.

Captain Flynn's eyes flashed annoyance and then softened. "Hello, Tony. I'm glad you're here."

"Teague has my girl," Russo said urgently. "Where is he?"

"I know about it, Tony," the officer said. "You try to

calm down now. This will probably take quite a while."

"Where is he?" Russo's face twisted as he almost screamed the question.

The cop was impassive. "He's almost to the top of the main tower. He's on the forty-fifth floor. The girl's with him. Step out and take a look. You'll see the elevator cage way up the shaft. That's where he is."

Russo stepped outside the shed and his eyes followed the elevator shaft up higher and higher. The elevator cage was so high that it looked like a toy.

"We shut off the power in the elevator," Flynn said as Russo stepped back into the shed. "So he's not going anywhere for a while."

Before Russo could speak, Flynn continued, "Here's how it looks. He's got a high-powered rifle and the girl up on the forty-fifth floor of the main tower. The work shift hadn't started, so no one else is up in that building. That's the only elevator, the inside ones haven't been installed yet. There's a staircase, but it's only built as far as the forty-second floor. From that point on there are ladders running up the empty stairwells. He can hold off anyone coming up the ladder route."

Flynn relit the stub of a cigar and then continued. "The second tower isn't as far along as the main one, it only has flooring as far as the forty-first floor. Above that, it's just a skeletal steel structure. They have a similar elevator, but after the forty-first floor it's out in the open and would make an easy target.

"I've sent for department marksmen. I'll send some of them up the main tower and the rest up the second, at least as far as the forty-first floor. They'll have some cover from there. But there's a hell of a wind blowing, so I'm not too optimistic about any accurate shooting."

"What about Marie, Captain?"

"We'll do our best, Tony. But he's sitting up there with the whole city to pick from if he decides to start shooting. I'll do everything I can, but we do have priorities." His voice trailed off.

"Christ," Russo spoke softly.

"Of course," Flynn said, "he may be out of ammunition."

Russo shook his head. "He wouldn't fire now, there's no purpose in it. He'll wait and pick off your men as they come up that other tower."

The captain frowned. "He'd have to be damn good. That wind up there's a bastard."

"He's a crack rifle shot. He's as good, if not better, than anybody we have to send up against him. Besides, he'll have the advantage of watching them come up. If they try to get into a firing position, he'll pick them off like clay pigeons."

"Shit!" Flynn took the cigar from his mouth and spit.

"What about helicopters?" Russo asked. "We could land a couple of men on top and let them work their way down."

Flynn shook his head. "Can't set one down up there, or even get close. They've got two big cranes on the top floor. There's no place to land. The wind's high and these guys"—he nodded at the construction people—"don't think a chopper can work its way in there without hitting the cranes. Besides, your man could probably shoot a chopper down if he's as good as you say he is."

"He's good," Russo said. "Look, I have to get up there."

"We'll wait him out," Flynn said. "We'll try the snipers, but until then we'll wait."

"We can't wait," Russo said. "Teague's into torture. He'll hurt her, that's what turns him on. We have to do something now and damn quick."

As if to underscore his words, a hint of windblown scream drifted down from the tower.

"Is there a way I can get up there without climbing all the way up the main tower?" Russo asked the construction men.

"No way," the older of the two said.

The other man, somewhat younger, spoke slowly. "There's one possible way. I don't know if it would actually work, but we have a large crane on the fortieth floor of the second tower. Your gunman can't see it because it's under the last section of flooring on the forty-first floor. We sort of 'walk' the crane up as we floor each section in. We use it to bring up materials. You can use the elevator to get to the fortieth floor; it's out of sight at that point too. A crane operator could swing the arm over to the main tower. I know it reaches that far because last week some idiot smashed the steel panel in the main tower with the tip of the thing. So it's long enough to make it. You could put a man in a bucket and then swing the bucket across to the main tower." He stopped for a moment. "As your man swung over there between the buildings he wouldn't have any protection, so you'd have to have a piece of sheet steel over the bucket to protect him from gunfire." He took off his hard hat and scratched his matted hair. "From the fortieth floor it wouldn't be such a long climb up those damn ladders. I don't know how you would get up the last ladder. But if everything worked out you could at least get to the floor below, for whatever help that might be."

"Set it up. I'll go," Russo said.

Captain Flynn shook his head. "You know better than that, Tony. First, you're getting a little old to be swinging around buildings, but mainly it's because that's your girl up there. I'd trust you with the assignment if you weren't emotionally involved, but whoever goes up will need an absolutely cool head."

"Harry, that's Teague up there—and nobody knows him like I do. I can almost think for him. I know him better than I know my own brother. I have to go. I know it's not good policy to let a cop who's got a personal stake go into a situation like this, but this is one that can't be handled by the book. Honest to God, I'm the only man who stands a chance of taking him. Otherwise, Marie might just as well be dead right now."

Harry Flynn thought about it, his face masklike, his eyes searching. "I know your reputation, Russo. If you really think you can handle it, then you can take a shot at it."

"I can handle it."

"How many people can travel in that bucket?" Knapp asked, speaking for the first time.

The construction man looked at him. "Two, no more. We can rig a larger bucket but it would take too long. The bucket that's on the rig now can only handle two men."

Flynn brightened. "Good, we can send a sniper up with you, Tony. He might get into a position to waste the bastard."

"I'd better go," Knapp said quietly.

"Who the hell are you?" the police captain asked.

"Knapp, Thomas Knapp," Russo said. "He was Teague's lawyer."

"Didn't I just read . . ." Flynn started to speak.

"Teague killed Knapp's wife," Russo interrupted. "Despite that, it might be a good idea if Knapp went along. He used to have a lot of influence over Teague. Maybe if we can get close enough he can talk him into giving up Marie."

"Goddammit, this is police business. I'm not about to ship a fucking lawyer to some lunatic who's in a position to shoot up half this goddamn town. He can have counsel when he comes down. Jesus! Even the Supreme Court wouldn't go that far."

"Harry, it might work. Look, the whole idea is to get Marie out safely."

The captain paused before speaking. His voice was low. "There's even more at stake here. That bastard could start sniping at everyone in the downtown district. If he starts to open up it'll be like that sniper years ago in that Texas tower. He could kill a hundred people. I said we have to do all that's reasonable to protect the girl, Tony, but I'll have to contain him if he starts to open up. Do you understand? We'll have to hit him with everything we have, no matter what happens to the girl."

"I know, but having Knapp along could help. It's worth a try. You can always send up your snipers after we get across."

"Okay, get going."

"Wait a minute." The man in the hard hat spoke up. "I can't expose any of the workmen to danger. The risk to the company's too great. If you want someone to operate that crane, you'd better find a cop who can do it."

Russo felt his face flush with anger.

"Take it easy," the other construction man said. "He's just doing his job. I'm the head foreman for the general contractor. I can run a crane better than anybody in the business. And I'm an executive, no union contract will be broken if I get shot.''

''Don't be a fool,'' the other man protested. ''You could get yourself killed.''

''You're an architect, and I'm a hard hat. Christ, during the war I was building airfields while the Japs were trying to shoot my nuts off. Let's go.''

The man led Russo and Knapp around the east side of the construction site. Other workmen sat in groups, like spectators at an air show, all looking up at the dark and lifeless main tower, waiting for something to happen.

* * *

Teague had worked out a regular schedule to check on the activity beneath. He reasoned they could attack him only from below or from the skeletal structure of the other tower. And there was always the possibility of a helicopter attack. So he checked the empty stairwell and the other tower from time to time to make sure no riflemen were scaling toward him and he'd be able to hear any helicopters. He was safe. There were no tall buildings near enough to provide a good range even for an excellent marksman. And the wind made even the idea of such a long-range shot impossible. Besides, he knew they wouldn't attack, at least not while he had the girl.

There were only a dozen or so shells left, but they'd have no way of knowing how much ammunition he had. He guessed they'd have to assume he was well stocked with bullets.

Although the stairs weren't built yet, the steel railings were in place. Teague tied Marie Coyle spread-eagled to the top railing. If riflemen came up from below they'd see her, and that sight would stop any attempts to gain his level. It was a good position.

The girl watched his every move. Blood had caked beneath her nose where he'd hit her, and the side of her face was swollen. Occasionally, he'd stop by and hurt her—not much, not yet, just enough to make her scream, and enough so that the scream was heard by the people below. He was sure that by now one of those people would have to be Lieutenant Anthony Russo.

And it was Russo he wanted. Eventually, Russo would come up to get him. And that would be the finishing stroke for the plan he'd formed, a plan he considered an inspiration. The thought of it sent a shiver of delight through him. He walked to the edge but held on to a beam for support as he looked down. The wind whipped his trouser legs and he knew without the support of the beam a gust might send him sailing down. He was careful not to overexpose himself so that a marksman below might be tempted. So far the police hadn't fired a shot when he had looked down at them, but caution always paid off.

His father had disliked wind, he said it complicated aim and made shots untrue. But Teague, even as a boy, liked the wind. He liked the way it sounded through the trees and the dry brush, and if it wasn't too cold he liked the feeling of it blowing over his skin. The wind was free, and he wanted to be free, like the wind, and to rise above the chains of earth and fly on forever. He closed his eyes and enjoyed the sensation again.

* * *

Knapp regretted his offer to help almost as soon as the wire cage elevator rose beyond the first floor. He was terrified of heights, a fear forgotten in the general excitement, but remembered now. The lawyer shut his eyes and clutched the steel rail of the elevator as the cage shot upward.

As they ascended, the strong wind shook the elevator and Knapp tried to think of other things, like the girl trapped above, or Teague, the man who had killed his wife; but as the panic seized him he couldn't think. Knapp opened his eyes when the elevator stopped with a jolt. It was a mistake to look down. The city and river lay beneath them, the height awesome. Knapp shuddered as a wave of dizziness swept over him.

"This is it," the construction man said, flipping open the door of the cage and leading the way across the rough tiled floor. "Be careful, we've left holes for conduits and plumbing, you could fall all the way down if you stepped in one." He laughed, as though the statement were somehow amusing.

Knapp felt the grip of the wind as he followed the other two men across the open floor of the skyscraper. He watched where he walked as if rattlesnakes occupied the floor. Straggling along behind the others, he gasped at the gaping holes.

It was a standard crane, its powerful motor located behind the operator's cab and its long steel arm thrust out into the space between the two buildings. A steel cable dangled from the end of the arm. Across from them the floor of the main tower was also open. The distance between the buildings wasn't much, but to Knapp it looked as though the main tower were a mile away.

"They've put a piece of sheet steel across the bucket

down on ground level,'' the construction man said. ''I'll haul it up here, then you two can climb aboard and I'll swing you across. It'll be a helluva job climbing up those ladders when you get to them. And your man may have pulled his ladder up with him.''

''We'll just have to find that out for ourselves,'' Russo replied. ''Let's get going.''

The construction man stepped up into the cab of the crane and pumped the choke a few times before the engine roared into life.

The man knew his machine. As the winch whined into operation, the steel cable whirled around the revolving drum while the bucket began its ascent. Russo walked to the edge of the building, wrapped his arm around a beam and looked up. He had lost his perspective and couldn't estimate which floor Teague was on. But as he squinted upward, the outline of a man's head popped over the edge of one of the main tower's upper levels. Teague had been attracted by the noise of the crane. Now he would know they were coming.

Russo judged that not even an Olympic pistol champion could make an accurate shot at such a small target at that distance, particularly in the swirling uncertain wind, so he fought against the temptation to try it. He drew back so that Teague wouldn't see him and returned to Knapp who stood near the crane, his face ashen.

''He heard the noise,'' Russo shouted over the roar of the machine and wind. ''I saw him looking out.''

Knapp merely nodded. Russo wondered if it was a mistake to have brought him up.

''Are you okay, Knapp?''

The lawyer's expression was grim as his eyes met Russo's. ''I'm fine,'' he said in a low voice.

Looking like a large steel teacup, the bucket appeared, wide at the top and narrow at the bottom. A square piece of sheet steel had been laid over its top.

The construction foreman manipulated the levers in the cab and expertly swung the bucket in, gently setting it down on the rough flooring. "I'll help you pull that steel to one side, it's heavy as hell."

Although it was only an inch or so thick, to the three men struggling with the steel covering it seemed to weigh a ton.

"Don't let it slip off the top or we'll all get hernias trying to lift it back on," the hard hat said. "After you get in, between the three of us we should be able to slide it back over you."

Russo's unexpected physical grace surprised Knapp. The detective hopped up like a gymnast, balancing on the lip of the bucket for a moment before climbing into the space left by the steel lid. Knapp needed help climbing in. With great difficulty they managed to wiggle the steel sheet over them, shutting out the light. The two men were pressed together, their legs jammed into the narrow bottom. The bucket smelled of concrete dust and metal. Knapp's heart raced as he heard the crane's motor rise as the construction man put it back into gear, gently lifting it from the floor.

Although they were already in the dark, Knapp closed his eyes tightly as he felt the bucket swing and heard the wind. He realized they were hanging over the yawning canyon formed by the two towers, swinging free in air, and nausea swept over him.

Even before the crane set them down, they knew the bucket had entered the main tower by the change in the sound of the wind. Russo and Knapp shoved hard against the heavy steel lid and it slammed to the floor below with an echoing crash. Russo lifted himself up and swung one leg over the lip of the bucket; then he helped Knapp up.

Knapp almost sank back into the protection of the bucket when he realized it had been placed only a few feet from the edge. Nevertheless, he awkwardly climbed out and dropped to the floor, moving quickly away from the edge and the drop below.

The wind was overwhelmingly powerful, and Knapp thought he might pass out.

"Let's go," Russo said.

Gingerly, he followed the detective across the floor. The main tower construction was further along; the concrete casings for the electrical wiring were in and plumbing pipes had been installed. At the fortieth level the stairways were in. They began to climb upward, Russo running, Knapp following.

Thomas Knapp noticed that Russo had drawn his pistol, apparently on guard against the possibility that Teague might descend and ambush them.

As they climbed, the lawyer almost forgot his fear of heights when he realized the real danger was only a few floors above them. Edward Teague, psychopath, whose only joy was killing, was waiting for them, armed and ready.

*　*　*

Teague had watched the crane deliver the bucket to the floors below. There was a steel shield across its mouth as a protection against his rifle fire, but how were they to know that he had no intention of firing? He wanted them to come, and he hoped it was Russo in the bucket.

It would be typical of the detective to be first, especially considering whom Teague held as prisoner.

The girl's terrified eyes followed him as he made the rounds of his guard posts. There were no snipers coming up; that was a good sign. Of course, whoever came across in the bucket was on his way up. Teague had noticed that the stairwells had steps only up until the last few floors below him, and that ladders then were laid into the holes where the stairs would be built.

He had tested the ladder leading to his floor. It was made of heavy, sturdy wood, wide and safe, solid and substantial.

He could have hauled it up and been as safe as if he had pulled up the drawbridge to a castle; but he had other plans, and it would be important that Russo, if he came, have access to his floor.

Teague walked back to the girl.

"How do you like the view up here, you bitch?" he said, raising his voice against the wind.

She looked away from him.

She reminded him of his mother; but then, they all reminded him of his mother.

"Lots of people pay money to come up to a place like this and look at the view. Hell, you're getting it for free." He took her broken nose between his fingers and twisted. The piercing scream thrilled him. He hoped they heard it below. "Fun, huh?" He laughed as he walked away from her. Fresh blood cascaded from her nose.

Teague felt the wind whip about him and it was exhilarating, like being at the top of the world. But there was no time to luxuriate. It was time to begin the preparations to receive his visitor.

*   *   *

Knapp wondered if he would have the courage to continue. He remembered how difficult the obstacle course in the army had been for him. He hated having to climb up thick ropes and scale high walls. Those heights had frightened him, and now as he scaled the ladder behind Russo he felt that numbing fear again. He tried to keep his eyes up, to concentrate on the sight of Russo's feet so that he would not look down between the rungs of the ladder. Each rung was a challenge, and Russo moved much faster than he.

They were nearing Teague's floor. Thomas Knapp's legs ached and his breath came in tortured gasps. Below he could hear the noise of the crane again. They would be sending reinforcements across; and although he wondered if they would really be of any practical help, still he found solace in the thought that others were coming to join them.

Russo had reached the forty-fourth floor as Knapp made it to the forty-third. Knapp, who was out of sight because of the angle of the ladder, heard Russo shout up to Teague.

"Come down, Teague!" Russo's voice was almost carried away by the howl of the wind.

"Why don't you come up, Russo? Your girlfriend's up here. I'm sure she'd love to see you."

"Teague, you're a sick man. Surrender and I promise no harm will come to you."

"Sick, Russo? The doctors don't think so, why should

you? Come on up. You can bring your gun. I'm not really worried.''

"Throw down your rifle," Russo commanded, "then I'll come up."

"Why? Are you afraid I'll shoot you if you poke your head up?"

"Throw the gun down."

Knapp listened but stopped climbing. He was ready to assist if called on, but some instinct seemed to warn him to stay out of sight.

"Throw your gun down, Teague, and then I'll come up," Russo repeated.

"Just a minute, I have to do something first." Teague's words seemed distant.

Knapp could see Russo now as he began to move up a few rungs on the ladder. The detective had his pistol aimed at the hole above him.

Knapp quickly climbed the ladder to the forty-fourth floor, and then moved toward the next ladder to join Russo.

The detective looked down and motioned him to get away, to stay out of sight.

Knapp stepped well back from the hole separating the floors.

"Teague, I've just about had it. Let Marie go and come down.''

"You come up. I'm almost ready."

"Throw down your gun."

"I'll make you a deal." Teague's voice was high and excited. "I'll leave the rifle right by the hole. You can run up and get it, okay?"

"Throw it down!" Russo yelled, appalled by the manic quality in Teague's voice.

"Here's the rifle!"

Knapp couldn't see the gun from his position, but it was obvious that Russo did.

"If I come up, you'll just snatch it back and shoot me," Russo called.

"No I won't, and that's a promise." Teague's voice sounded as though he were far from the ladder. "But you'll have to come up and see if it's true."

Knapp watched Russo as he slowly began to ascend the ladder, his gun still aimed at the hole above him. Russo's one-handed climb was awkward and slow.

Nearing the top, Russo laid his stomach against the ladder, reached up, and knocked the rifle down. It clattered to the floor. Knapp was tempted to run forward and pick it up, but again felt that Teague shouldn't know he was there.

Russo climbed through the hole.

11

TEAGUE WAS READY. HE HAD UNTIED THE GIRL AND released her from the railing, but he had tied the end of a rope securely to her ankle, holding it like a leash. Tying knots was another woodsman's skill his father had taught him.

He looped the rope around one of the steel beam supports. He was confident he had enough strength to do the job, but he was concerned that he might be knocked off balance by the wind. His revenge was too perfect to be ruined by some freak of nature.

Only semiconscious now, the girl sat on the floor near the edge, her head resting against Teague's knee.

As Russo came through the hole, his pistol swung toward Teague.

He let Russo see her before he kicked her off the edge. The rope jerked taut in his hands as she fell and was caught up.

"If you shoot me, I'll drop the rope and your precious girlfriend will fall forty-five stories. She'll be just jelly, Russo, nothing but jelly." Teague giggled.

Russo said nothing as he climbed up.

"And if you try to jump me, the same thing will happen." Teague smiled. "She'll drop like a rock and they'll need a blotter to pick her up." He laughed. "I have her down there swinging by one ankle, just hanging out in space tied up by one little ankle. I wonder what she's thinking about, don't you? Maybe she thinks you'll save her. Women are like that, Russo, they always think you can do more things than you really can.''

"Pull her up," Russo said, taking a step forward.

"If you come near me, I'll drop her."

"If you do, I'll kill you."

"Maybe, maybe not. Anyway, while I have her you have no choice but to do what I tell you."

"Teague, it's me you want. Don't hurt her. Hell, she doesn't even know you. She has no part in this."

"Of course not, but what sweeter punishment could I inflict upon you?" Teague's manic giggle rose and joined the whine of the increasing wind.

*   *   *

The girl hurtled down past Knapp and then snapped back as if she were on a rubber line. Now she swung to and fro, twisting in the wind, her skirt bunched up at her waist, a rope from above tied to one ankle. Her other leg lay off at an angle, making her look like a broken puppet. Knapp wondered if she was dead. Her eyes were closed as if in peaceful sleep and there was blood on her face. The wind swung her in close to the edge and then pulled her away.

Knapp's fear prevented him from going near the edge. He was paralyzed by the thought that an errant breeze could pull him off and sail him out into the void below. Fighting against it, he worked his way over to the edge. He heard voices from above, but he was concentrating on the girl's body that swung in and out like a ball on a string.

Trembling, he tried to force himself to reach out for her. If she had been conscious she might have been able to reach for him, but she wasn't. As he reached out, the wind knocked him to the floor and he made the mistake of looking down.

Like a land crab he scurried back from the edge. Knapp lay flat but his eyes didn't leave the body of the girl swinging in the wind. Once again he forced himself to approach the edge, but this time he crawled on his stomach. He tried again to reach out for her, but now he was too low to make contact.

He would have to stand up. For a moment he froze, unable to move; and then slowly, tentatively, he got to his feet. The wind swirled and the girl swung in close. He grabbed part of her skirt. For a moment he teetered on the edge as her limp body threatened to pull him off; but he leaned back, calling on a strength born of terror, using all his energy to hold onto the skirt. He clutched at her like a madman, circling her waist, trying to pull her in, trying desperately to pull against the restraint of the rope.

"I have her!" he screamed at the top of his lungs, hoping somehow that the rope above would be loosened and that he and the girl would be released from the peril of the edge and the abyss below.

* * *

Russo saw the expression on Teague's face change. Something was wrong with the rope. Suddenly Teague seemed to be pulling frantically against it.

From below, like a scream from a tortured soul, Russo heard Knapp's call. He leaped forward as Teague struggled, but he was afraid to shoot, afraid that the rope and Marie might disappear forever. He brought the gun butt up like a club and caught Teague under the jaw, and as Teague fell he reached for the rope. To his horror, the rope escaped his grasp, slithering like a snake from around the beam, and then falling away into space.

"I have her! I have her!" Knapp's shaky voice was as welcome as the voice of God.

Teague lay unconscious at Russo's feet. For a moment the detective was tempted—strongly tempted—to kick him over the side, but he couldn't bring himself to kill. Training and discipline won out over temptation.

Rolling Teague over face first, he handcuffed Teague's wrists behind his back.

Russo stood up. His hands were shaking and he realized that his clothes were soaked through with sweat.

"I have him," he shouted down to Knapp.

Russo stood quietly for a moment, trying to control the shaking. He was surprised at his own reaction.

He turned as he heard someone coming up the ladder. Knapp was climbing up very carefully. "Two policemen just came up," Knapp said, raising his voice to be heard above the wind. "They're taking your girl friend down. I think she's okay. She's got a broken nose and maybe a broken ankle, but I think that's all."

Russo started toward the stairwell.

"Are you just going to leave him there?" Knapp asked, nodding at Teague.

Russo stopped.

Teague was coming around. His eyes blinked open, and for a moment it was obvious that he didn't know where he was.

"Hello, Teague," Knapp said.

"I killed that bitch, didn't I?" Teague grinned, looking past Knapp at Russo. "She's a jelly pancake somewhere down there, Russo," he snarled.

"No, you didn't kill the girl," Knapp said. "I grabbed her while you were dangling her. She's safe."

Teague's face clouded over. "Well, at least I killed that bitch of yours, that's something. Somebody paid for what you all did to me."

"I already told you, we were having family trouble. You did me a favor, I suppose." The lawyer looked down at him. "Did you really kill all those women? Did you really spell out the word *stalking* like Russo thinks you did?"

Teague, now fully recovered, laughed. "Yeah, though most of you people were too thick to even know it was happening. Sure I killed them." He looked up at Knapp. "You and your fucking hospitals. I'm going back there again, but I'll get out. It's easy for someone who's smart. Besides, I don't belong there, I'm as sane as you are."

"I feel responsible for you, Edward," Knapp said, helping him to his feet.

"You should. It was you who put me in the hospital in the first place."

"Yes," Knapp said quietly. "And you got out."

"We'll take him down with us," Russo said, stepping forward.

"No, you go ahead," Knapp said.

"We'll take him with us," Russo repeated.

"Edward, I want you to think about all those women," Knapp said, taking hold of Teague's manacled wrists. "I want you to think about them all the way down."

Before Russo could even shout a protest, the lawyer ran Teague toward the edge. Abruptly Knapp halted, but

Teague was going too fast to stop. He tried, seesawed for a moment, then screamed wildly as he toppled forward. He screamed all the way down.

The two men stood silently for a moment.

"It was like shooting a mad dog; it had to be done." Knapp's words were barely audible. "I was responsible for his release once. I could not bear that cross again."

The wind whined through the empty building.

"You can arrest me," Knapp said.

"For what?" Russo asked, his face expressionless.

"For murder, of course."

"Teague got up and jumped," Russo said. "I saw it myself."

Knapp shook his head. "People in the downtown buildings have been watching. They saw what happened."

"You tried to stop him," Russo said. "That's what I saw and that's what they'll believe they saw."

"That makes you an accomplice."

Russo's rugged face showed the strain. "It was a suicide. You tried to stop him. There was no crime so there was no accomplice. You're a lawyer, you should know that." He reached over and gently patted Knapp on the shoulder. "Come on, I want to check on Marie."

Knapp followed Russo as far as the ladder, then stopped. Russo looked up. "What's the matter?"

"I can't go down. I'm afraid of heights."

"But you must have had to hang over the side of the building to pull in Marie."

"Yes, but that was different. I had no choice. But I'm afraid I just can't do this. I'm sorry."

Russo's haggard face slowly broke into a grin.

"Damn it, man, for what you've done for me, I'll carry you down on my back."

Knapp shook his head. "No, just send an officer back. If someone can sort of help me down those ladders I can make it to the stairs."

"What about the crane? That didn't bother you."

"Sure it did," Knapp said as if admitting a sin. "When I reach the stairs I shall walk the rest of the way down."

"The elevator'll be working by then."

"It's on the outside. I'll walk, thanks just the same."

Russo's sudden laughter sounded eerie as it echoed through the empty building and was carried away on the wind.

* * *

The wedding was put off until her face healed following the plastic surgery to repair her nose. She was just as beautiful as before, although her eyes had lost some of their sparkle, and maybe forever. She was on crutches; the ankle would take much longer to heal. Anthony Russo was proud to become Marie's husband.

Thomas Knapp was a hero. According to Lieutenant Russo, Teague had confessed to killing Mrs. Knapp just before his bizarre suicide. The newspapers had a real story. Here was a noble lawyer who had saved Marie Coyle and, in spite of the fact that Teague had killed his wife, still tried to prevent Teague's suicide. And since all these feats were performed despite an overwhelming fear of heights, Knapp had gone from a man suspected of murder to a veritable monument to courage. A living legend.

But he left it all behind.

He had taken an extended vacation by himself, leaving his children with his sister. Martha Flowers returned to her old job, but even she didn't hear from the attorney as several months passed. Knapp lived a quiet life on a Caribbean island, doing some fishing, but mostly spending his days walking the beaches.

He returned one morning, walking into his office unannounced as though nothing had happened and it was the beginning of just another routine business day.

The sight of him so startled Martha Flowers that she was speechless.

"Good morning, Martha," he said, as he walked past her. Her instincts were to rush to him, to hold him and sob out the worry that had consumed her, but she didn't.

She sat at her desk and waited.

Knapp buzzed the intercom and she came into his office.

"Close the door, please."

She closed the door.

"Please sit down, Martha."

She sat in her accustomed chair, close to the desk where she could take dictation.

"I've been thinking about some things, at some length and some depth."

She nodded.

"How do the kids say it?—I've been trying to get my head together, do you understand?"

She nodded again.

"I suppose many men and women go through these personal crises. I don't know how they handle their situations, but I had to have time away, to think and sort things out. Can you understand that?"

"Yes."

"I suppose the psychiatrists might characterize it as an identity crisis. But anyway, it's over. I've made up my mind as to who I am, what I am, and why I'm here. I could be wrong, but at least I think I have my answers."

She waited.

"I've decided to talk to the other partners. I'm through with criminal trial work. If that's agreeable to them, I'll stay with the firm, otherwise I'll leave. I want no more Edward Teagues on my conscience."

"You didn't . . ."

He held up his hand. "The other thing I've discovered is that I've been married to this profession. I spend entirely too much time at the law. I've neglected my children. I may have been quite responsible for . . . for Helen's attitude, like it or not. I can't change the past, of course, but I can alter the future."

She looked puzzled.

"What's the status of your divorce?"

"It became final last week."

He began pacing, then suddenly he stopped and turned. "Tell me honestly, Martha, what do you feel for me?"

She felt her face flush. "I love you," she said quietly.

He nodded, then continued pacing. "That's good. I love you too. I thought as soon as a decent interval had elapsed you and I might be married. Does that meet with your approval?"

"That's a proposal?" she asked, smiling slightly.

"Yes."

"Any conditions?"

His eyebrows arched in surprise. "None."

"Then I shall accept." Her eyes were laughing. "Is there anything you'd like me to sign?"

He began to smile and then laughed with her. "No, this is a verbal contract—equally as binding, under the circumstances, as anything in writing, let me assure you."

Turn the page for a look at

The Judgment—
The latest electrifying novel from
William J. Coughlin,
now available in hardcover from
St. Martin's Press . . .

"CHARLEY, IT'S SUE. CAN I COME OVER?"

"Are you in trouble?"

"No. Nothing like that. I just need to talk. I know it's late."

"Never too late to see you. Come on over."

"I'm really sorry to be a nuisance." Her voice had a sad, keening tone, the kind of sound she got after a few drinks.

"I can pick you up," I said.

"No. I'm a block away, calling from a pay phone. I'll be right there."

I put on some coffee while I waited.

When she arrived, we kissed. I could smell the gin, but she wasn't drunk. She held me in a long embrace before letting go. I thought I felt her tremble.

She took the coffee I poured and sat down. "I feel like a fool, Charley, barging in at this hour."

"You're not. Bad case, eh?"

"In a way yes, but in a way no."

"Do you want to talk about it?"

She sipped the coffee and smiled weakly. "I suppose that's apparent, isn't it?"

"Tell me about it."

"A little boy," she said slowly. "There was identification on him. His name was Lee Higgins, a kid from

Hub City. Eight years old. He didn't come home from school. His parents had called the Hub City police and they had taken a report, but that sort of thing happens often—kids stay at friends' and forget the time, so no one except the parents really got excited.''

"How was he killed?"

"Asphyxiation. The medical examiner thinks he may have been suffocated with a pillow. There were no marks or bruises. The blood work won't be back until tomorrow but the doctor thinks he may have been sedated. There was no sign of a struggle. Just a dead boy, a beautiful boy. He looked like a sleeping angel.''

"Raped?"

"Apparently not. There were no signs of sexual abuse. He was a small little boy. No anal penetration. Nothing to suggest oral contact, although it's possible.''

"No murder is gentle, but this one sounds relatively shock free. How come it shook you up so?"

She shook her head. "I don't know, honestly. I think it was that he was so beautiful and so young. The parents, of course, were in shock, but they described him as a perfect little kid.''

"How did they find him? I would have thought the snow would have covered him up.''

"A motorist saw him on the side of the road. Whoever dumped him must have done so just minutes before. The motorist stopped and walked all around the body. Other people stopped to see what happened. Tire tracks, foot prints, everything is pretty much screwed up, although we'll get some.''

"There are a lot of crazies out there, Sue.''

She nodded. "This one especially.''

"Why do you say that?"

"The medical examiner says whoever murdered the boy washed the body and the clothes afterwards, then redressed the dead child. He was wrapped in plastic wrap, the kind you buy at any grocery store."

"I suppose the killer was counting on the snow to cover up what he had done."

"Not really. The body was set out there on the roadside as if the killer wanted him found."

"Well, don't worry, Sue. The sick ones usually are the first caught."

"Sometimes." The word was just a whisper.

"You'll get this guy, whoever he is."

She stood up. "Hold me, Charley?"

"Sure."

We ended up in bed, but not for sex. She fell asleep almost instantly, her arms wrapped tightly about me. Her breathing, at first troubled, became even.

It was the first time since I'd known her that a case had affected her so deeply. I wondered if she was upset because her cop instinct told her this was the beginning of something, and not the end.

She had given me something to think about, too. The name Higgins and Hub City had clicked in my memory. A couple of years ago I'd handled a routine matter for a couple in Hub City named Higgins. Frank Higgins and his wife, Betty. Lying in bed, I remembered it had been a real estate closing; they were buying a big old place right in Hub City. They had kids, of course, enough to make the purchase of an eight-room house reasonably practical. I suspected, and feared, that one of those kids was named Lee.

* * *

I hadn't been asleep long when the telephone rang. I'd listened one last time to the all-news station at the top of the hour just to reassure myself that nothing had happened, no plastic-wrapped package had been found by the side of the road; they didn't even rerun the feature on Kerry County's vigil. I'd say the call must have come about ten-thirty, certainly not much later. The funny thing was, I never looked at my watch, just reacted sort of zombielike, sleep fogged.

"Charley, it's Sue. There's . . ."

I waited for her to finish the sentence, fearing, knowing just how it would end.

"There's been another murder. This one was closer to us here in town, at our end of Copper Creek Road."

"Everything else the same?"

"That's what I'm going to find out." She hesitated. "Charley, I was wondering . . . Look, I know I woke you up."

"That's all right."

"I know we've been sort of on the outs because of this investigation, but Charley, could you go out to the crime scene with me? I know it's a lot to ask. I remember how you reacted before, but I'm scared to death I'm going to lose it again. What I need badly is some support out there, the kind you could give."

She sounded desperate, already near tears.

"Where are you now?"

"I'm downstairs in my car."

"Okay," I said. "I just have to get dressed. I'll be there in a couple of minutes."

I hung up and stood there for a moment, blinking in the dark. What else could I say to her? What else could I do? Whatever else she was, she was a friend in that

peculiarly complicated way in which love and sex get
mixed into the equation and confuse things so. But a
friend nevertheless. I couldn't have said no to her, but
later, knowing the price I would pay, I wished to God
that I had.

All right, it may have taken me three minutes, although
I'm sure it was less than five from the time I hung up
the telephone to the time I slid in beside her in the front
seat of the Chevy Caprice. I gave her a hug. She seemed
to need that.

"Thanks, Charley. I knew I could count on you."

She started the car, put the emergency light on the
dashboard and activated it.

"This stuff is terrible to drive in," she said. "We've
already lost one car tonight."

"How was that?"

"We almost got him. We came so close. This time we
had a plan. Every patrol car we had was out on the road,
the Hub City cars, too."

"I know. I heard about it beforehand."

"Oh?"—suddenly cautious—"who from?"

"Stash Olesky."

"Well," she said uncertainly, "it was his idea, so I
guess he can talk about it if he wanted to. The point is,
it almost worked."

She went on to tell how Steve Majeski had been patrolling Copper Creek Road out as far as Beulah, with
his dome lights flashing. Back and forth, for about four
hours, he drove, there in the snow. He had slowed after-
work traffic on the road considerably in the beginning,
but three hours later there was really very little traffic
anyway. Once home, people were kept in by the snow.
And after all, Copper Creek Road went as far as the edge

of the county, and not many lived out that way. It wasn't a direct route to anyplace.

That was probably why they'd assigned it to Majeski, in his mid-twenties and the youngest man on the Kerry County police force. More important, he'd had a little less than a year in a patrol car, so they tucked him off in a corner of the grid they'd drawn around Hub City. One thing about Copper Creek Road, however: It's damned tricky to drive it even in good weather. There aren't many straight stretches on it. Winding along the creek bed, it runs from Pickeral Point, meets Beulah Road out in the country someplace, then gets lost way up in the north-western reaches of the country.

This was the road, in any case, that Officer Steve Majeski was patrolling that night. He'd been fighting the snow for four hours and was bored and close to exhaustion. He rounded a bend, and just beyond his high beams, he saw a car's lights come on. A second later those lights began to move, swing out, disappear; Majeski had the presence of mind to punch his odometer to mark the location, then went after the vehicle, whatever it was, with his siren going full blast. In decent road conditions, he would have caught up with it without difficulty, but in the snow, it was an unequal pursuit. The Caprice, with its big engine, was just too much car for the road. In his eagerness to overtake the car ahead, he kept his foot heavy on the gas, too heavy, and the Chevy slowed back and forth in the snow at every curve, while the one ahead went around each bend like it was on rails. Majeski realized he was chasing some sort of four-wheel-drive vehicle. Still, he managed to keep it in sight. As he would emerge perilously from one curve, whipping the steering wheel left and right, he would see his quarry disappearing around the next. So it went until he hit the straightaway leading to the junction with Beulah Road. Majeski picked up speed and saw that the general shape of the car ahead conformed to that of a so-called off-road vehicle, but he couldn't get close enough to read the license plate. He tried a little too hard to do that and still had his foot on the accelerator as the junction loomed up ahead. The off-roader made the turn onto Beulah Road, but Majeski's patrol car did not.

The Caprice made two complete revolutions in the middle of the intersection, then ended up in a ditch by the side of the road. It was in deep, snow up to his hubcaps. Majeski hadn't a chance in the world of getting it out. Because he'd had his hands full during the chase, he hadn't radioed in. He did that at last, giving his position and asking for help, telling what had happened, and describing how the off-roader somehow slipped through. Taking the reading from the odometer in his own patrol car, he was able to guide his rescuer back to the approximate place where the pursuit began. After a bit of searching, they found the body of a young boy, sheathed in plastic, half covered in snow.

By the time Sue finished telling the story, we were on Copper Creek Road and close to the crime scene. She had it only in fragments she'd heard from the radio dispatcher, then direct from Officer Majeski before she headed out to my place. But it seemed to do her good to tell it to me. She was less distraught and more professional in manner, apparently ready to meet what lay ahead. I only hoped that I was, too.

There was a cop stationed in the road to direct traffic around the line of patrol cars on the right. He stopped us with his flashlight, then walked up when he recognized the county plate on our car.

When he stuck his head in the window, I recognized him, more or less, but couldn't come up with his name.

"Yeah, hi, Sue. Just pull in behind my car there."

She nodded and mumbled a few words I didn't catch.

"We kept a clean scene for you this time," he said. "I guess we're learning the hard way."

A swirl of snow swept into the car before she could get the window up. She guided her car into the spot to which she'd been directed, then cut the motor and killed the lights.

"Stay close to me, Charley, unless I tell you different," she said, now the complete professional.

"Fair enough," I agreed.

I followed in her footsteps, shuffling through the soft snow. There was a wet hard pack beneath it. All told, I thought about three inches had fallen. The temperature had dropped steadily, and it had to be well down in the twenties. I was glad I'd worn my snow boots and remembered my new gloves.

Emergency lights running off the generators of two of the patrol cars were pointed at a mound in the snow beyond the yellow tape. There was a slight glint on the plastic and an indication of flesh color beneath it where the face would be. If they left the corpse undisturbed, it would be only a matter of minutes until it was invisible beneath the snow. There was just one set of footprints leading up to the mound.

"All right," said Sue, "who was it just had to take a look? Who tracked up there to the body?"

"It was me." The cop's name was Bert Bossey. I knew him from a trial a year ago, a tough, no-nonsense police officer. He stepped forward to face her. "We were the first on the scene. Steve Majeski found the body; because I was senior officer, I took charge."

"Did that mean you had to mess things up like that?"

"For Christ's sake, Sue, I had to see if the kid was dead."

"You satisfied that he is?"

"Yeah, I cut into the plastic, felt for a pulse and didn't get any, then I tried for a heartbeat. Nothing."

All the cops were edgy because they were tired. They'd been out a long time, and the effort they'd put in patrolling the roads had gone for nothing. And the proof of that was before them right there under the lights.

"Larry?" she called out. "Are you here?"

Larry Antonovich came forward, a camera in hand. Sue took him over to one side. The two detectives held a hurried conference in whispers. One or two of the cops, those who recognized me, looked at me curiously, all but asking out loud what I was doing there.

As they talked on, flashing lights down the road caught my eye. The cops saw it, too, but barely glanced up. It was all part of the routine. It was moving along from the direction we had come at a speed so deliberate that the flashing lights in the rack on the roof seemed altogether unnecessary. It looked like an ambulance, but it turned out to be the county coroner's van from Pickeral Point. Identification was emblazoned in big letters on the side.

They pulled up on the highway just opposite the yellow tape, and there they waited, motor running. The window came down on the passenger's side.

"How long?" came the call from inside.

"Not long," Sue called back.

The window rolled back up. The snow had slacked off,

nearly stopped. Sue took a deep breath, led Antonovich to the tape, and ducked under, approaching the body from one side. Did she intend that I should accompany her? She must have remembered me at the last moment, for she looked back and made a quick gesture that told me to stay where I was. Antonovich ducked under. I noticed that in addition to the camera, he had something that looked like a screen under his arm, about a foot-and-a-half square.

He began taking pictures, circling the mound, getting it from every angle. Sue produced a carpenter's tape from her coat pocket and called over one of the cops, telling him to measure from the edge of the road. She took it to the mound and noted the figure in a notebook, all business but not a glance at the small window left uncovered by the snow. When Antonovich had finished that round of picture taking, she carefully scooped the snow from the plastic wrap and placed it on the screen, yet doing it in such a way that her eyes never seemed to leave her hands. She stepped away and sifted the snow through the screen. Nothing stuck; it was all snow and nothing more. Antonovich took more pictures. Then Sue beckoned in the direction of the county coroner's van, and the two inside got out, opened up the back, and pulled out a stretcher.

They weren't so careful once they'd stepped inside the perimeter. Sue warned them away from the direct route and made them take the circular way that she and Larry Antonovich had taken. In any case, the body was shifted onto the stretcher and moved in less than a minute. Somehow she managed to be looking the other way through it all. More pictures of the spot where the body had lain, then they both went to work sifting through the snow beneath the resting place and all around it—again, nothing, nothing but snow. Finished, they left a marker, and returned the long way around.

"Steve Majeski?" Sue called. "I need to get a statement from you."

She produced a small, hand-held tape recorder from that voluminous coat pocket and talked him through the chase from this point to Beulah Road, a good three miles, and she wanted all the details.

Sue was doing pretty well through this ordeal she had dreaded. She recovered well after a bad start by admitting her error to the cops assembled at the scene. Whatever help she supposed I might provide was unneeded.

How was I doing? Not quite so well.

Standing by myself, off to one side, I had looked on, not so much with interest but with fascination. Every time Sue turned away from that mound nearly covered by snow, I found myself staring at it. I wasn't even sure of the contents of that plastic-wrapped package. I hadn't heard whether it was a boy or a girl inside, only that it was a child. Another child, the fourth in this monstrous chain of killings. It had to be a kind of monster responsible, didn't it? There was such a confusion of purpose evident: the care taken with the bodies, clothes washed, the plastic shroud to protect each one from the snow. Yes, the snow. What did that mean? Clearly, it meant a great deal to the murderer. What was the snow symbolizing? Purity? Theirs, not his? How could you get into such a mind to even begin to guess what went on there?

I thought I'd distanced myself pretty well from the county coroner's team as they returned with the small body on the stretcher. Yet as they came, the cops seemed to drift away, leaving me alone, the only one within calling distance when they cleared the yellow tape.

Me? I was staring in spite of myself.

"Hey buddy, want to give us a hand here? Come on over and open the door to the van."

I couldn't say no. I couldn't say, Get one of those cops to help you—they've seen more death than I have, more than I ever want to. No, I couldn't say that, so I nodded and went to help.

It was a boy. Dark haired and darker skinned than was usual in this county of Slavs, Scandinavians, and Celtics. His features suggested he might have a bit of Indian blood. Though his eyes were shut, his mouth was stern. He looked angry. I'll bet he'd put up a fight.

I walked away. My vision was blurred. Hell, who am I kidding? I was half blind from the tears that wouldn't stop. I wiped at them, then more sobs came and more tears. So I just kept walking, trying to get away. I heard the county coroner's van turn around in the road and start on its trip back. Finally, I was surprised when I heard Sue's voice calling me back, not so much that she called but that her voice was so distant. I turned around and saw that I was a good city block away.

"Charley," she called. "Where are you? Charley!"

She must have lost me in the darkness. I cleared my throat and yelled back as loudly as I was able, "I'm here. I'm coming, I'm coming."

On the drive back to Pickeral Point, neither Sue nor Larry Antonovich said a word about my disappearance. Not much was said at all. But I had a question.

"Who was the boy?"

"We don't know yet," said Sue.

"No missing child reported? What did Hub City have to say?"

"Nothing there. We just don't know."

"Strange."

Yes, it was strange. Could the boy have been picked off the streets of Detroit? Port Huron? Mount Clemens? Wherever he had come from, he had parents who missed him, lost him, who were frantic to find him. The dead boy in plastic wrap on the stretcher looked like he was about the same age as the first three victims. He couldn't have been a runaway, not likely at that age.

When we came to Pickeral Point, Sue headed for Kerry County Police Headquarters. Larry Antonovich was to be dropped off there. He had been driving up and down Beulah Road with one of the two cars assigned to that stretch. The idea was to have one detective rolling and Sue back at headquarters to coordinate things. He was young, from Detroit, and had gone to Wayne State.

"Wouldn't it be nice," he said to Sue, "if we had a crime-scene squad like a big grown-up police department?"

"Not likely," said Sue, "with all the budget cuts."

"I hope these pictures I took come out. You think there was enough light out there?"

"You'd know that better than I would, Larry. I'm no photographer."

He was quiet for a moment. "They'll be okay, I guess."

She pulled up in the lot, which was nearly empty by now, well after midnight. Antonovich got out, taking his camera equipment with him.

"I'll leave the film with a note before I go. If George

Bester gets right on it, the roll should be printed by mid-morning."

"Do that. I'll be back by eleven. We'll go to the location on Copper Creek Road then."

"I don't envy you."

Sue drove out of the parking lot and turned in the direction of my place. She turned to me.

"Charley, I was wondering . . ."

I knew that approach, and I thought I knew what her request would be.

"Sure, Sue, you can stay with me tonight."

"You really know me inside and out, don't you?"

"Let's just say I know you pretty well by now."

We drove in silence for a block or two.

"I got off on the wrong foot with the cops, didn't I? Of course Bossey was right. He had to make sure the kid was dead."

"But you handled it right from then on."

"There's a few things different about this one, you know."

"Well, for one thing," I said, "no report of a missing child. You don't know who the kid is."

"Right, but finding him on Copper Creek Road is sort of odd—miles from Hub City. The location was a lot closer to town, this town, than any of the others. And there was something else, too."

"Oh? What's that?"

"Larry said it looked like the kid's clothes were dirty—not filthy or anything, just like he'd been out in the snow—his hands, too, the way kids get dirty playing anyplace. I didn't see it myself. I made it a point not to look at the body."

"Yeah, I noticed."

She sighed. "Well, I got through it."

"Whatever works, Sue. You did fine."

"At least we know now what kind of car the killer has."

"Four-wheel drive."

"Dark color, black or maybe brown. I wonder how many of those there are in the county."

"Not an infinite number. It's a place to start."

"Oh, yes."

My apartment building loomed ahead. Emotionally, rather than physically, I was exhausted. Perhaps, in a way, I felt even worse than I had that night on Clarion Road when little Catherine Quigley was found. But I felt different. I had no wish to talk with Bob Williams about what it all meant, nor certainly with Sue Gillis. My problems with the higher power remained unsolved.

Something struck me just then. "Larry said something when you dropped him off. He said he didn't envy you. What did he mean?"

"I have to go to the autopsy tomorrow morning," she said, turning into my driveway. "It's customary for an officer to be present. Since I'm heading the investigation now, it's up to me."

It wasn't until later, when we were in bed and I was close to sleep that she asked me to go with her to the autopsy.

"I don't believe I was much help to you out there tonight," I responded.

"Yes you were. Just having you there meant everything to me."

* * *

About what happened during the next three days, I don't have much to say. That's partly because I feel a certain guilt, even shame, about it all. After all, I'd gone years without a drink, and though I never lost sight of the fact that I was a recovering alcoholic, I had built up confidence that I could go years more without a drink. I thought I had the problem under control.

I didn't.

At Jimmy Doyle's I had three straight shots of bar Scotch, but they weren't enough to erase those images from the autopsy from my mind. The two old geezers at the end of the bar watched me rather carefully; they seemed to know something was seriously wrong. When I called for a fourth shot, the bartender refused to serve me. I didn't make a fuss; I couldn't; he was right to cut me off. I paid up, remembering to tip him just to show there were no hard feelings, went out to my car, and vomited in the gutter. What a pretty picture.

That didn't stop me, didn't even slow me down. I got into the car and drove in that slow, extra-careful way that drunks do. Not directly home, but to a liquor store on the way. If I was going to do this, then I was going to do it right. I bought a half gallon bottle of Johnnie Walker Red, my old brand of preference, assuring myself that the reason I'd thrown up was that I'd drunk bad Scotch. That never happened when I drank Johnnie Walker. Then, as an afterthought, since I was obliged to keep office hours the next day, I bought a bottle of vodka. At some unspecified time later today, I would switch to vodka, and no one would know tomorrow that I'd been drinking. Sure.

Returning to my apartment, I made a vow not to answer the telephone—it was sure to be Sue, and I had no wish to speak to her—and settled down for some serious drinking. I can't say that I didn't enjoy it. The rich, golden liquid hit my tongue like so much nectar, yet there was enough bite to it to let me know that this was the real stuff, the right stuff. Oh yes, I remembered it well.

I started out drinking it on ice, more civilized that way and settled in a living room chair with the television set switched on. I can't say that I was watching it. But the changing flow of images on the screen gave me something on which to concentrate my vision, and the voices occupied some part of my mind. I heard, I saw, though I didn't really listen or watch. I was in my old drinking mode, running on automatic pilot. The idea was not to think and not to remember. And for a while it was working pretty well. I eventually decided it wasn't really necessary to put ice in the glass. No ice, more Scotch. Then I passed out, unconscious, a dreamless sleep.

The telephone woke me. Sue, of course, and the thought of her annoyed me, no, more than that, it made me angry. Or perhaps it was simply the persistent ringing that made me angry. In any case, I decided to do something about it. I slipped off the chair and crawled over to the telephone. Reaching up, I pulled the receiver off its cradle. Then I went into the next room and collapsed on the bed.

Some time later, Sue was at my door, banging, kicking, and yelling about Thanksgiving. She said she knew I was there because my car was in the parking lot. There were some other things, too, that I didn't quite understand or don't remember. I do recall, though, that I wished she wouldn't make such a racket because it was a holiday— that much I knew, at least—and all the neighbors, such as they were, would be around to hear her. I couldn't call the cops because she was the cops.

How long did she continue? Not long, probably, but she had succeeded in bringing me to some degree of wakefulness. I got up, relieved myself in the bathroom, and sat down in the living room again and finished off the half-full glass of Scotch I'd left. There was a football game on television, Dallas and some other team. Dazed, I tried to give some attention to the progress of the game. Failing that, I could at least find out the score, or what team Dallas was playing. But no, even that proved too much. After another drink, a short one this time, I stumbled back to the bedroom.

Bad dreams. Maybe it was the violence of the football game, or maybe I failed to drink enough to obliterate those images I'd tried to escape earlier. Whatever the cause, along with sleep came something like a movie montage of all the worst I had known and seen in these past weeks. There were monster football players pulling apart children. There was a hanging man, eviscerated, trying to talk without a tongue. There were angels in the snow—Catherine Quigley and Richard Fauret—rising, trailing their plastic shrouds. There were other horrors, too, which were, I guess, just the product of my alcoholic state, fantasies unconnected to memories.

They seemed to last a long time, but how could I tell? It was enough to wake me in a sweat about half sober. It was dark out. I threw off my clothes and took a shower and realized I was hungry, a good sign. Wrapped in my bathrobe, I had a cheese sandwich and a glass of orange juice, a strange combination, but the orange juice tasted good. And so, when I'd finished, I kept on drinking orange juice with vodka. There went the rest of the evening and a good deal of the next day.

I'm not going to prolong this account because the truth

is, I don't remember much of the rest of it. I do know that sometime during the day on Saturday I drank the last of the Johnnie Walker Red and, having also finished up the vodka, went out and bought some more. I managed to eat something each day and kept drinking orange juice with the new bottle of vodka, because I'd made up my mind that no matter what condition I was in, I had to get into the office on Monday. During the weekend I must also have replaced the telephone receiver, because later on the calls started again, though I didn't answer them. I was doing a pretty good imitation of Ray Milland in *The Lost Weekend*.

Late Sunday afternoon or early evening, I was dozing in the living room chair in front of the television. Another football game, this one from the West Coast, was rocketing to a finish. There was a knock on the door, followed by another one, followed by another and another. This couldn't be Sue. Whoever this was at the door wasn't interested in making a fuss; he intended to break it down. He beat it. He kicked it. But he didn't say a word.

I struggled out of the chair and made it to the door.

"Who is it?" I yelled, trying to sound gruff. "Who's there?" Actually, I was kind of frightened, knowing how incapable I was at that moment.

"Bob Williams. And you'd better open this door while it's still in one piece."

He was the last guy in the world I wanted to see. My best friend? My AA sponsor? Forget it. When he saw me in the condition I was in, he'd be my worst enemy. I couldn't deal with him. I didn't want to try.

"Go away, Bob. I'll see you tomorrow."

He let fly a great kick right around the lock. I saw it give. A couple more like that, and it would fly open. I could put on the chain, but the damage would still be done. And so I surrendered, unlocking the door, opening it, and I saw him poised to deliver the next threatened kick. A couple of doors were open down the hall. My so-called neighbors peeked out at us. They didn't know me, and I didn't know them.

Bob rushed in, perhaps fearing I might change my mind and close the door again. He pulled it shut behind him, and then he looked me up and down.

"Just what I suspected," he said, his face filled with concern.

I didn't answer. At various times in the last few days I knew I'd been in worse condition than I was then. There was no point in telling him that.

He swept past me, picked up the glass of vodka with its faint orange coloration, and headed for the kitchen. Without a pause, he dumped its contents down the drain of the kitchen sink.

"Hey," I said, "who gave you permission?"

"You did, when you joined the program. Or have you forgotten? I'm your sponsor. Remember?"

He turned and looked at the table with its array of bottles, then he shook his head in disbelief.

"Did you drink all that?"

"It was a long weekend."

"You ever hear of alcohol poisoning?"

He grabbed the quarter-full bottle of vodka and the supplementary fifth of Johnnie Walker Red, just about half full. "Go on," he said. "Take a shower. You smell bad. Shave, if you can manage it. If you've got an electric razor, it might be safer."

Arms folded, feet planted wide, I stared at him, trying to decide whether to tell him to go to hell and get out of my kitchen. But in the end, I turned around, went into the bathroom, and did as I was told. On my way, I heard the gurgle from the bottles as he emptied them down the drain.

* * *

I started through the pile of call slips Mrs. Fenton had left me, wadding up two from Sue and filing them in the basket. I came across one that made me curious. Bud Billings had called a little before noon from county police headquarters. I dialed the number, and he picked up immediately.

"I guess you've heard by now, Charley."

"Heard what?"

I still had my mind on the Conroy business. Nothing would have been made public on that yet. Besides, Bud wouldn't have called me about Conroy, no matter what the news.

"The Evans kid was shot dead."

"What? Sam Evans? Who did it, his father?" I wouldn't put it past that nut case.

"No, Delbert was confirmed clear over on the other side of the county. It happened right on the Evans place around ten o'clock. The kid's mother was looking out the window at the time and saw him go down like he'd been knocked over with a baseball bat. It wasn't any baseball bat knocked him down."

"What did?"

"It looks like it was a 30-30 fired from quite some distance away. There's a grove of trees about five hundred yards from where the kid was hit. They figure it came from there. I'll tell you, it was a great shot at that distance, and it went right through his heart. Mrs. Evans didn't hear it, but from five hundred yards away, and with her inside the house, she wouldn't have, not necessarily.''

"Where'd you get all this information?" I asked. "You weren't there, were you?"

"Oh, no, they've still got me pushing papers here at headquarters because of the false arrest suit.''

"So they know where you were at ten o'clock this morning."

"Yeah, thank God," he said. "It was Sue Gillis who called it in. They're tying it to the other murders. They sent her and Antonovich out to the crime scene.''

"How does that figure? I don't quite see the connection to the murders."

"I hate to say it, but they're examining the possibility that maybe one of the fathers of the children was so convinced that Sam Evans did it, he decided to play judge and jury. Sue's out talking to Catherine Quigley's father now."

Jesus. Weren't four murders of innocent children in one small county enough for anyone to bear? Now there was the possibility that a vigilante was out there, a father deranged and destroyed by grief seeking revenge. If someone murdered my daughter Lisa, would I do the same? I had never taken the life of another human being, but under similar circumstances, would I be able to kill?

"I thought I would call you and let you know. Evans was your client, after all. Oh, and by the way, it's working out fine for me with John Dibble. You were right. He's behind me all the way. I don't know how the kid's death is going to change things, though.''

Billings and I said our good-byes and hung up. Stunned by what I'd just learned, I sat nearly immobile, staring out into the middle distance. Swinging my chair around to face the river, I knew I needed to do some thinking. Some very serious thinking . . .

THE JUDGMENT
BY WILLIAM J. COUGHLIN—
Look for it
at your local
bookstore!

THE LAWYER—CHARLEY SLOAN:

His sobriety and his career hang in the balance.

HIS EX-LOVER—ROBIN HARWELL:

When her sensuous daughter is accused of murdering her millionaire husband, she begs him to take the case. But is that the real reason she wants him back in her life?

THE CASE THAT COULD SAVE THEM...
OR SHATTER THEM ALL:

High-stakes and high-profile, the dramatic trial draws them passionately together, even as it threatens to tear a city apart.

SHADOW OF A DOUBT

THE NATIONAL BESTSELLER BY

WILLIAM J. COUGHLIN

"A GREAT READ!"—Scott Turow

SHADOW OF A DOUBT

William J. Coughlin

_____ 92745-2 $5.99 U.S./$6.99 Can.

Elizabeth Daren is in dire straits. With evidence missing and key witnesses changing their stories, the battle for her dead husband's fortune is turning ugly. Someone is out to get her, and only Jake Martin, one of the country's shrewdest, most battle-hardened lawyers, can save her. If he can trust her.

IN THE PRESENCE OF ENEMIES

WILLIAM COUGHLIN

Judge Paul Murray fought his way up from his working-class Irish roots to the Federal bench. Tough and honest, dedicated to the law, he relishes sitting on the headline-grabbing case before him. The outcome is worth billions, the tactics cutthroat, and suddenly, with the threatened exposure of a ruinous secret, everything Paul cares about is on the line—his marriage, his career, his reputation. Now, faced with choices he never thought he'd have to make, he must confront what truly lies at the heart of justice...

WILLIAM J. COUGHLIN

National bestselling author of In the Presence of Enemies

The Heart of Justice

"Satisfying and right on target...among Coughlin's best."
—Detroit News